Moses Thursten Runnels, Dartmouth College

Memorial Sketches and History of the Class of 1853, Dartmouth College

Moses Thursten Runnels, Dartmouth College

Memorial Sketches and History of the Class of 1853, Dartmouth College

ISBN/EAN: 9783337096182

Printed in Europe, USA, Canada, Australia, Japan

Cover: Foto ©Andreas Hilbeck / pixelio.de

More available books at **www.hansebooks.com**

Memorial Sketches

and

History

of the

Class of 1853,

Dartmouth College.

by

MOSES T. RUNNELS,

Class Secretary.

"We thank thee, Father! let thy grace
Our narrowing circle still embrace,
Thy mercy shed its heavenly store,
Thy peace be with us evermore!"

O. W. HOLMES.

NEWPORT, N. H.:
BARTON & WHEELER,
1895.

TO THE PRECIOUS MEMORIES OF THE

TWENTY-NINE

WHO HAVE PASSED ON BEFORE US, AND

TO THE CHARITABLE REGARD OF THE

THIRTY-FOUR

MEMBERS OF

THE CLASS OF 1853,

WHO

"A LITTLE LONGER WAIT,"

THIS VOLUME IS AFFECTIONATELY INSCRIBED

BY THEIR BROTHER CLASS-MATE

AND SECRETARY,

THE AUTHOR.

INTRODUCTION.

This little book, though chiefly designed for distribution among survivors of the Class and the relatives of its deceased members, is yet commended to the Alumni and friends of the College with the hope that no discredit may have been cast upon the name of our beloved Alma Mater, in its latter pages at least, as showing how widely and favorably her influence has been diffused.

In one point of view the present volume is simply a second edition of the smaller Memorial printed in 1864 ; and the record of those brothers who had passed from earth at or before that time—but whose memory we wish still to perpetuate—is not, in many cases, essentially different.

The ancestral notes prefixed to these sketches constitute a new feature in the work, and are more or less full accordingly as material for the same was furnished to the Class Secretary.

The figures with dashes, "1 ——," "2——," etc., stand as abbreviated expressions which are common to all the biographies, and are used to save space and avoid the monotony of repetition, being fully explained below. The compiler determined not to disfigure the personal or family sketches with such abbreviations as "unm.," "s. p." (sine prole) or "no child." If numbers "3 —— " or "4 —— " are wanting in any sketch, the facts respecting family relations, are sufficiently made known.

The non-graduates of the Class are with us still, as they used to be upon the recitation seats ; not in a separate portion of the volume, and with no peculiar designation except the "N. G." after each name.

It must be borne in mind that the attachments formed by some of us with brothers who were with us but comparatively a short time, at the first or middle of our course, were very strong and have proved life-long. Some of these brothers, though graduates of other Colleges, have yet shown a loyalty to our Class quite as ardent as some others who graduated with us. They have been among the most constant and ready to supply the Secretary with material for the Class records. It would therefore have proved unjust and discourteous to such, if their "sketches" had been withheld or essentially curtailed.

In the case of all living members of the Class, the Secretary has embodied or "dove-tailed" the facts and items of the former Memorial upon those which subsequently came to hand, so as to make one continuous life-history. Inasmuch as a MS. copy of his completed sketch was sent to every class-mate for his approval and modification (nearly all being promptly returned), and as the corrections and suggestions thus made were in every case heeded, to the last particular, it is confidently believed that a commendable degree of accuracy has been attained, and that no one can reasonably complain in reference either to the facts themselves on their mode of presentation.

In conclusion, the Secretary needs only to add that had it not been for the very liberal pecuniary aid proffered him by a noble class-mate, who stipulates that no clue shall be given to his name, the now issued volume could never have been attempted. To him, therefore, our special thanks should be rendered; while the Secretary feels that to all his class-mates and their friends who have furnished the desired facts and information; to the printers and artists who have made the book, in its material aspects, what it is; and above all to the Infinite Preserver and Guide of our lives and destinies, the sincere gratitude of all our hearts is justly due.

Newport, N. H., Jan. 1, 1895.

EXPLANATIONS.

An asterisk (*) following a name indicates, as usual, the death of the individual. "N. G." also following a name, shows that the individual did not graduate with us; and was a member of the Class for only a portion of the under-graduate course.

Following every name is a designation of the town and state where was the home residence of each individual on the College catalogues while connected with Dartmouth.

"1 —— " introduces place and date of birth, with parents' names and ancestral notes. Supply, in place of dash: "He "was born at."

"2 —— " introduces place of preparatory studies, before entering Dartmouth College. Supply in place of dash: "He "fitted for College at."

"3 —— " introduces marriage (first). Supply in place of dash: "He married."

"4 —— " introduces the Christian names of children, in the order of their birth. Supply in place of dash: "His children "were."

The following are the more common abbreviations employed:

"N. G."—non-graduate.	"b."—born.
"m."—married.	"d."—died.
"dau."—daughter.	"grad."—graduated.
"Acad."—Academy.	"D. C."—Dartmouth College, especially in parenthesis.

In explanation of the "Pedigrees," the small index figures represent the generations, in order; the person whose pedigree is given having the largest or latest number. For example, "Levi[5]" (Robinson), his father being "Charles[4]," his grandfather "Joseph[3]," etc., back to "Levi[1]," his earliest known ancestor in this country.

The following is established as the uniform order of the sketches :

After "1 ——— " are the birth, parentage and pedigree, (so far as known) of each class-mate ; with such genealogical or ancestral notes, as have been supplied.

After "2 ——— " are the places of preparatory study, and usually the names of instructors with whom each member of the Class fitted for College.

After "3 ——— " comes the first marriage record, with subsequent marriages, if any ; and such information respecting the parents and ancestors of our wives as were furnished to the Secretary.

After "4 ——— " come the full Christian names of the children, in order, with birth dates and places of birth, and usually with dates and notices of their deaths, if in early life. These children are introduced by the Roman numerals, I., II., etc.

Next is given the connected narrative of each life, from leaving Dartmouth to the present. Notices of published works ; and, in some cases, places of residence or professional labor are introduced by Arabic numerals in parenthesis. More extended obituary notices are often added, of those who have died, with places of burial, etc. Quotations are given from letters or other writings of the subjects themselves, or from others respecting them, as the case may be.

. At the conclusion of most sketches of those whose children have arrived at maturity—having passed their educational careers or become settled in life—the children's names reappear under the same Roman numerals as before. The grandchildren, whose names and birth dates have been furnished, are also introduced by Arabic numerals in parenthesis.

The sketches, of course, vary in length or fulness. Where much was not given, much cannot reasonably be required.

CONTENTS.

LIST OF ILLUSTRATIONS.

Note. — The frontispiece and seven other views of Dartmouth buildings and surroundings were printed by Messrs. Barton & Wheeler, the printers of the book, from plates kindly loaned by Prof. Charles F. Emerson, Dean of the College Faculty at Hanover. Most of the portraits are the so called "Half Tones;" those of Allen, Dickson, Hulbert, Morrison, Reed, Waterhouse, Whitcomb and Young were printed by the "Republican Press Association," Concord, N. H., which company also made most of the plates from original photographs. The steel plates of McDuffee and Runnels were executed some years ago by F. T. Stuart for town histories and were printed by J. H. Daniels & Son of Boston, Mass. The "Group" of '93 was printed, as well as originally taken, by H. H. H. Langill, of Hanover. Of the other portraits, Palmer's was supplied from Lippincott's, in Philadelphia, Pa., through the kindness of Gen. John Eaton, LL. D. ; and the other five, Chase, Fairbanks, Hayward, Lamson and Parker, were furnished by themselves from various artists in different parts of the country.

JUSTIN ALLEN, M. D.

MEMORIAL SKETCHES

OF THE

CLASS OF 1853,

DARTMOUTH COLLEGE.

ALLEN, JUSTIN, N. G.,
HAMILTON, MASS.

1 —— Hamilton, Mass., Sept. 29, 1826; the son of Ezekiel and Sally (Roberts) Allen.

2 —— Williston Seminary, East Hampton, Mass., 1845-6 and '48; Rockingham Academy, Hampton Falls, N. H., 1847, and Hampton Academy, N. H., 1847 and '49-'50.

He left Dartmouth our Sophomore spring, 1851; graduated A. B., at Brown University 1852; studied medicine 1853-4, with his brother, D. S. Allen, M. D., (Berkshire Medical Institute, 1846), interspersed with teaching; attended lectures at the Berkshire Medical Institute, Pittsfield, Mass., 1854, and at the Tremont Medical School, Boston, 1855; graduated M. D., from the medical department of Harvard University, 1856.

Removed to Topsfield, Mass., in June, 1857, and has continued there in the practice of medicine, uninterruptedly, for the period of thirty-seven years.

It was reported of him, in 1864, that he was having "a good run of practice, is popular with the "people, and enjoys the respect of his professional "brethren."

In 1878 was commanding a practice of about $2,000 per annum. Had also held the office of superintending school committee in Topsfield.

From 1862 to 1892, the inhabitants, not only of Topsfield, but of the adjoining parish of East Boxford, were depending upon him, almost exclusively, for their physician; while his practice also extended into Middleton, Ipswich and other towns.

He spent a week at the "Centennial Exposition," at Philadelphia, in 1876; but, aside from this and a few hurried trips, of not over two days each, he had, in 1879, been on the ground nearly every day for twenty-two years, and every day visiting the sick.

He had relinquished the more laborious duties of his profession in 1893, and had made vacation tours through the provinces to head of navigation, on the Saguenay river, and, in the opposite direction, to the Natural Bridge in Va., also, in the autumn of the same year, took another western trip, of a month's duration, a week of which was devoted to the "Columbian Exposition."

His grandfathers, both paternal and maternal, did honorable service, one or the other of them, in the campaigns of Bunker Hill, Rhode Island, Long Island, Saratoga and other fields in the Revolutionary War.

He has probably enjoyed life as much as many who have had more leisure to devote to occupations other than their stated business.

BABCOCK, HENRY HOMES, *, N. G.,
THETFORD, VT.

1 —— Thetford, Vt., Dec. 19, 1832; the son of Rev. Elisha G. and Eliza (Hibbard) Babcock, his father being for seventeen and one-half years pastor of the Congregational church in Thetford.

2 —— Thetford Academy, under Hiram Orcutt (D. C., 1842).

3 —— Mary Porter Lincoln Keyes, a native of Putney, Vt., at Somerville, Mass., July 30, 1861.

4 —— I. MABEL, b. May 30, 1862.

II. ROLLIN KEYES, b. Aug. 20, 1863.

During our Sophomore winter, 1850–1, not succeeding to his mind in a school at New Braintree, Mass., he determined to leave College, and engaged himself to Dr. J. J. Fales, of East Boston, to attend an apothecary's store, and receive instruction in medicine. Passed six months with Fred. Brown, apothecary, corner of Washington and State Sts., Boston, but returning to Thetford in ill health, relinquished the idea of being a physician.

In Nov., 1852, he turned his attention once more to the business of teaching; was principal of a grammar school in Dedham, Mass., till Apr., 1854; a similar work in Newton, Mass., till Aug., 1859; then obtained the situation of principal of the High School in Somerville, Mass., which he retained till 1867; his salary in his chosen profession having gradually increased from $420 per annum, in 1852, to $1500, in 1863. Having removed, with high recommendations, to Chicago, Ill., he there opened, at 218 Wabash Ave., Sept. 18, 1867, a school for both sexes, called the "Chicago Academy." This school was moved, 1868–9, to No. 11 18th St., being highly prospered, with "Primary," "Intermediate" and "Collegiate" departments. In its "Twelfth Annual Announcement," 1878–9, Mrs. B. is noticed as one of his assistants; and a peculiarity of the Institution is said to be, that "no public examina-"tions or exhibitions are held, in any department, "but parents and guardians are cordially invited "to visit the class-rooms, at all times, to observe "the regular work of the school." He remained principal and proprietor of this Academy till his decease, Nov. 7, 1881, in the 49th year of his age. He was also Professor of Botany in the Chicago College of Pharmacy, and Director of the Botanical Garden, in which office he achieved a wide and merited distinction.

He was a leading member of the Illinois State Microscopical Society; was long identified with the "Chicago Academy of Natural Sciences" and its president at his death. Was regarded as one of the best botanists in the country. He was one of the founders of the Union Swedenborgian Church, of Chicago, and president also of that organization at the time of his departure.

Especially was he a highly esteemed member of the "Chicago Literary Club," his name standing upon their "Scheme of Exercises," as the leader appointed to conduct a conversation on "Our Native Flora", at a meeting to be held May 8, 1882. This Club published a memorial at his death, for its reccords, his family and the Chicago papers, from which the following extract is taken ("Chicago Tribune" Nov. 11): "In all positions he did his work well. "In manner, he was kind and dignified; in spirit, "noble; in character, pure; in conduct, just; in "scholarship, eminent; and in devotion to duty, "unswerving."

BLAISDELL, ALFRED OSGOOD,

HANOVER, N. H.

1 —— Lebanon, N. H., March 13, 1833. His father was Hon. Daniel Blaisdell, (D. C., 1827), for forty years treasurer of the College; his mother, before marriage, Charlotte Osgood, of Haverhill, N. H. His grandparents were Hon. Elijah and Mary (Fogg) Blaisdell of Pittsfield, N. H. His ancestors came from England and settled in Salisbury, Mass., about the year 1640.

2 —— Hanover, under the care of Prof. Stephen Chase and Edward Webster, Esq., (D. C. 1848).

3 —— Mary Estabrook Martin, daughter of Hon. Wheeler Martin of Providence, R. I., Dec. 31, 1860, at P., by Rev. Dr. Caldwell. Her family is traced from England to Swansea, Mass., in 1690.

4 —— I. RALPH, b. August 23, 1864, at Hanover, N. H.

II. EDITH, b. Feb. 24, 1874, at Brooklyn, N. Y.

Pursued his scientific studies, under Prof. Ira Young at Hanover, for two years after graduation;

and secured a practical preparation, for his profession as an engineer, in the Amoskeag Machine Shop, Manchester, N. H., from July, 1855, till April, 1857, and, thenceforward, in the Providence Machine Co.'s works, Providence, R. I., till June, 1858. Was employed by Wm. T. Nicholson, and the Hope Brothers (manufacturers of engraving machinery) in Providence, till April, 1861.

One month of the following summer, in the shop of E. & T. Fairbanks, St. Johnsbury, Vt., and, returning to Providence with the revival of business, in Dec., 1861, took charge of Nicholson's shop till June, 1862, and was for six months, mechanical draftsman for the Providence Tool Co., designing machinery for gun-making, till December of the same year.

He then went to New York City and obtained employment in the office of A. C. Stimers, where the fleet of monitors were designed, and in May 1863, engaged himself as draftsman at Secor's Foundry and Shipyard, Jersey City, N. J. (residing in New York), and worked on drawings of various monitors and other vessels for the U. S. government, then being built or repaired in that yard, till July, 1865. He next sought a more intimate acquaintance with "the dear old Uncle Sam," who proved a kind employer, for about ten years longer, in the Brooklyn Navy Yard. On the slacking of government works in 1875, he found a variety of employments on gas works, sugar houses, and the New York and Brooklyn Bridge, till August, 1880, when the chief engineer of the U. S. Navy

Yard at Brooklyn, Mr. Loring, offered him a desirable situation, made vacant by the death of its former incumbent; placing him "in charge of the "Drawing Room, in the department of Steam Engi-"neering." This berth and the same work at mechanical drawing is still (1894) supplied to him by the same kind "Uncle Samuel."

His residence, for 26 years, has been at 268 Clermont Ave., Brooklyn, N. Y.; his church home, the Clinton Ave. Congregational church, of which he has lately been elected one of the deacons.

His religious work, however, has, for many years, been largely for the benefit of the poor children in Mission Sunday Schools, mostly between the ages of four and twelve. As early as 1873, he was reported at our class meeting as having developed a remarkable talent for interesting the young people of these mission schools; his blackboard delineations being hardly less sought after than his spoken addresses.

He had also enlisted the sympathy of the Hanover Christian ladies, prior to 1878, in these objects of his care, numbering about one hundred; to whom he still devotes much of his time with unabated zeal.

Brother Blaisdell was the Secretary of our Class from 1853 to 1863; entered the first records in the "Class Book", and gave a rich account of our first post-graduate Class meeting, in 1856. His son,

I. RALPH (1894) resides in Springfield, Ill., and is Auditor of the St. Louis, Chicago and St. Paul R. R. Was married, Oct. 11, 1888, to Miss Lilian

LaDow, of Mechanicsville, N. Y. Children:

  (1) Jerome, b. Dec. 14, 1890.

  (2) Eunice Osgood, b. June 3, 1893.

II. Edith is now at home, pursuing the study of music, especially of the organ.

BLOOD, CHARLES SULLIVAN, *, n. g.,
St. Louis, Mo.

1 —— St. Louis, Mo., April 1, 1832, son of Sullivan and Sophia (Hall) Blood. His father was a native of Windsor, Vt., and d., suddenly, at St. Louis, Nov. 27, 1875, in his 81st year. His grandfather, Sewall Blood, was b. in Mass., May 24, 1765.

2 —— St. Louis, at the high school of Edward Wyman.

3 —— Endora M. Ware, of St. Louis, March 31, 1859.

4 —— I. Nellie Ware, b. Jan. 30, 1860.

    II. Harry Sullivan, b. Feb. 9, 1864, both in St. Louis.

On leaving our ranks in 1851, he became a book-keeper in the banking business at St. Louis; and, from 1857, was two years in the commission business for himself. This not proving remunerative, owing to the condition of the country, he closed it up, in 1860, and returned to his former pursuit.

In military life, was "Corporal of Co. A., 7th "Reg., Enrolled Missouri Militia," and served a short time in the Civil War.

In 1864, was notary public and general bookkeeper in the "Boatsman's Saving Institution", and followed the same business till about two months before his death. Was taken very suddenly with hemorrhage of the lungs, which terminated in rapid consumption. A council of physicians was held soon after the first attack; and, when informed by his mother, that he could not survive but a few weeks or months at farthest, he received the intelligence with perfect composure, only regretting to leave those behind whom he so dearly loved. The consolations of religion were imparted to him, during his sickness, by Rev. Dr. Elliott, his wife's pastor, and the Sabbath before his death the sacrament of the Lord's Supper was administered to him, with his nearest friends.

"He died a happy man, and with faith and hope "in a far better world to come", June 16, 1867, aged 35.

His funeral was largely attended, and he sleeps in the family burying-ground, called Belle Fountain Cemetery, about six miles north of the city. A headstone of white marble, and a monument in the center of the lot, bear his name and dates of birth and death.

He had a policy of insurance on his life for $5,000, which was paid to his widow, to whom he had given full instructions in reference to his earthly affairs. They talked them over and over again, with the utmost calmness on his part, while she scarcely left his bedside, day or night, proving herself a most devoted wife.

He suffered but very little pain during his illness,

and was conscious to the last moment.

His widow has since married, 2d, H. W. Warmington, and was residing, with his two children, in Virginia City, Montana Territory, in 1878; though the older child, I. NELLIE W., had been attending school in St. Louis for two years, 1875-77.

BROWN, JONATHAN C., *,.

CANDIA, N. H.

1 —— Candia, N. H., Jan. 19, 1827; being the son of Jonathan and Sally (Fitts) Brown.

2 —— Atkinson, N. H., Academy, under E. H. Greeley (D. C., 1845); at the Blanchard Academy, Pembroke, N. H., under Jonathan Tenney (D. C., 1843); and at Andover, Mass., for about one year.

Taught the Academy in Fitchburg, Mass., for one year after graduating; then the High School in South Weymouth, Mass., one term; next the Academy at Deerfield, Mass., during the year 1855.

In Jan., 1856, he removed to Cincinnati, O.; was one of a business firm in a book-store, and at the same time studied law. Overwork and hard study soon began to wear upon his health, and he was prostrated by a brain fever, from which he never fully recovered. In 1858, the disease had assumed the form of insanity, and he was for a short time a patient at the Insane Retreat in Dayton, O., from which, with temporary relief, he returned to the home of his childhood in March, 1859. His malady

increasing during the year and five months he remained at home, his friends were obliged to take
him, Aug. 4, 1860, to the asylum at Concord, where
he resided, under the medical treatment of Dr. J. P.
Bancroft (D. C., 1841) and others, till his death,
Aug. 18, 1881, "of chronic mania and phthisis",
aged 54 years and 7 months.

Through the period of his health and usefulness,
he was accustomed to write articles for newspapers,
and deliver lectures from time to time.

Dr. Bancroft said (Feb. 8, 1864): "I have no
"doubt that the case is confirmed and entirely in-
"curable. The form of his insanity is this: His
"mind is wholly possessed with certain delusions.
"He believes that his mind is, and has been from
"boyhood, taken possession of and controlled by
"other minds, by some process of animal magnet-
"ism, and thus diverted from his own control and
"legitimate use, and made to subserve the will of
"those who control him. This belief irritates and
"sours his moral feelings toward most persons,
"especially his relatives and those who have the
"charge of him here."

Dr. Bancroft's latest testimony respecting our
afflicted class-mate (Aug. 4, 1878) was "that there
"is no change in Mr. Brown's mental condition. He
"is somewhat demented, but still has not lapsed
"into complete dementia. His mind is filled with
"delusions, more or less active. He talks but little,
"and that almost entirely to himself. Always
"returns the salutation of 'Good morning!' but
"enters into no conversation. Physically he is

"quite well and strong."

McDuffee, also, at our meeting, the same year, reported an interview with him to the effect that his case seemed utterly hopeless; that the nature of his vagary appeared to be that he was a super-human being, and that his plans were thwarted by evil spirits. Others could draw from him; hence he would not talk with his friends.

The "silver lining" to this dark cloud seems to have been that his brothers were very successful in business, that they liberally supported him in his retirement, and had him furnished with all admissible comforts to the last.

BROWN, MOSES DAKEN,

CARMEL, ME.

1 —— Appleton, Me., May 22, 1828.

2 —— East Corinth, Me., under the instruction of D. S. True, afterwards of Davenport, Ia.

3 —— Henrietta White, of Pittsburg, Pa., eldest daughter of D. M. White, former editor of the "Pittsburg Gazette", Oct. 8, 1857. She died prior to Sept., 1878.

4 —— I. ELLA M., b. Sept. 18, 1858.
     II. WALTER MEREDITH.
     III. HARRY SIMPSON.

Both the two last died in infancy.

He was principal of an academy at Randolph, Vt., in 1854-5, during which time he also read law, as far as possible, in the office of Hon. J. P. Kidder of Randolph.

In Nov., 1855, removed to Chicago, Ill., and in January following was admitted to the practice of his profession. Was there located, in 1864; was visited by Cahoon in 1866, and had his office at 194 Clark Street, in 1878. He spoke of his first three or four years of professional life in Chicago as a "struggle between life and death, with pover-"ty, grim and hungry, staring him in the face." After that the tide of battle turned, and his profession, adhered to with commendable industry and energy, became both pleasant and lucrative.

His standing was represented by two eminent lawyers of Chicago, in 1864, as remarkably good, and his prospects flattering. "He seems to enjoy "a high degree of success in the winning of his "cases." In the "List of Addresses", published by a committee of the Dartmouth Alumni in 1892, his location is given as "69 Dearborn Street, Chicago, Ill."; but repeated efforts on the part of the Class Secretary have failed to secure any response from him since 1864. Of his parentage we have only learned that his mother's Christian name was Deborah.

BURNET, CLARENCE LINDEN, *,

TICONDEROGA, N. Y.

1 ——Ticonderoga, N. Y., Aug. 17, 1831. He was the son of Hon. Jonathan (D. C., 1824) and Augusta (Russell) Burnet.

His father died at Ticonderoga, Feb. 6, 1868, aged 68, and his mother was still living there, in 1878. His grandfather was Jonathan Burnet, Sen., of Bethel, Vt., and his paternal grandmother, Abigail Parish.

2 —— Ticonderoga, for the most part, under his father, and partly at Waterford, N. Y., with the Rev. E. F. Edwards.

3 —— Mrs. Helen (Brown) Hunt, by Bishop Littlejohn, of the Long Island diocese, July 1, 1875.

4 —— I. HELEN, b. July 12, 1876.
II. CLARENCE LINDEN, JR., b. Aug. 12, 1878.

He taught a classical school at Staten Island, N. Y., for one year after graduating; also six months at Berkshire, N. Y.; and for a year and three months was Principal of an academy at Warwick, N. Y.

Studied law in New York City until 1857, when he entered the Law School at Albany, and there graduated in Feb., 1858.

The first of March following he commenced the practice of law at 11 Wall Street, New York, where he continued till Jan. 7, 1862. On that day was ordered to report for duty on board the U. S.

gunboat " Kennebec", as paymaster; for in a moment of enthusiasm, he had determined to see something of "this accursed rebellion" with his own eyes, and to "do something to put down treason." Nothing else presented itself but this position in the navy; and, having previously had a taste of salt water, he left desk, brief and profession, as above.

In Dec., 1863, was off Mobile, Ala., and in Feb., 1864, had witnessed the encouragement implied in the fact that when he went out "the government "had no foothold in the Gulf, west of the Tortugas, "except Ship Island; while in two years, only "Mobile and Galveston remained to be occupied."

Was transferred to the U. S. receiving ship "North Carolina", May, 1864, at the Brooklyn Navy Yard, N. Y., and was there remaining on duty Aug. 22, following.

In Sept., 1868, was again at his law office, 15 Nassau Street, having just returned from an extended tour through the great west and the Rocky Mountains. While living in New York, was the superintendent of the "Trinity Church" Sunday School, and afterwards of a Mission Sunday School in that city.

In the autumn of 1872 had lost his leg by acute necrosis, amputation above the knee being necessary.

Office had been changed to 213 Montague Street, Brooklyn, prior to Dec. 15, 1873, and during the fall election of 1878, when he was unanimously chosen for the third year, Alderman of the First

Ward in Brooklyn, he was visited by the first symptoms of a nerve disease which obliged him, in the following April, to resign his office as Alderman, give up business, and retire to Ticonderoga, where he continued with his family till Jan., 1880.

Then, on the advice of his physician to seek a warmer climate, he again removed to Cambridge, Dorchester Co., Md., and there remained a year and a half, with flattering prospects at first, but with no permanent relief.

His wife also being a constant sufferer from the climate, they sold their place in Maryland, and "went into the north woods" (state of New York), where he was so much improved that he came back to Brooklyn and again began work, Nov. 1, 1881, "not with the old vigor, but finding it a decidedly "better thing than enforced idleness."

The next winter he received an invitation to the Dartmouth dinner in New York, with a request that he speak on that occasion; but was hardly well enough to go over.

"As a proof of his popularity, he was nominated "for Surrogate in Brooklyn, in the spring of 1882, "and would easily have been elected, but was com- "pelled by poor health to decline the offer." [Classmate Blaisdell's letter of May, 1883].

His lamented death occurred at Ticonderoga, May 5, 1883, in his 52d year. In the midst of much physical suffering, he had kept cheerfully about his work; had made money, made friends, lived liberally, and given liberally to others who needed it, especially to an aged mother and infirm sister.

Better than all, he found from what he suffered (as he writes in 1879), "now, at my 48th year, "that there is very little in this brief life, at the "best; and that were it not for the hopes of the life "to come, it were better to have never been born."

His widow is now (1894) the wife of Rev. James Davis, of Beatrice, Neb.

I. HELEN is a student at Brownwell Hall, Omaha, Neb.

II. CLARENCE L. is with his mother at Beatrice.

BURTON, HORATIO NELSON, *,

WASHINGTON, VT.

1 —— Washington, Vt., Dec. 17, 1826. His parents were Stephen and Judith (Nelson) Burton; his pedigree in the paternal line, Horatio Nelson[4], (Stephen[3], Jacob[2], Israel[1]).

2 —— Kimball Union Academy, Meriden, N. H., from 1845 to 1849, under C. S. Richards (D. C., 1835).

3 —— Amelia Newell, at her former residence, Burke, Vt., May 18, 1858; the daughter of Hon. Charles Newell, a judge in the Caledonia Co. courts for many years.

4 —— I. CHARLOTTE ELIZABETH, b. April 10, 1860.

II. STEPHEN E., b. Nov. 8, 1862.

III. CHARLES NEWELL, b. March 20, 1866. Studied theology two years at the Theological

Institute of Conn., East Windsor Hill, meanwhile teaching in the academy at that place; completed his third year at Andover, Mass.

Was approbated to preach by the Essex Association, at Lynn, Mass., in 1856.

Did Home Missionary service at Concord, Vt., eight months, 1856-7; also at Burke; and preached three months of 1857 at St. Johnsbury.

His pastorates are tabulated as follows:

(1) Ordained as Pastor of the Cong. Church in Newbury, Vt., Dec. 31, 1857; dismissed March 17, 1869. (2) Settled over the Cong. Church in Sandusky, Ohio, Sept., 1869, till April, 1876; when (3) he became pastor of the Plymouth Cong. Church, Kalamazoo, Mich., and there continued four years. (4) Was pastor of the Cong. Church in Sycamore, Ill., from 1882 to 1885, three years; (5) of the Cong. Church, Union City, Mich., from 1885 to 1888, three years; and (6) finally, having returned to Vermont, was acting pastor at Lyndon and Kirby from January, 1888, to April, 1890, two and one-fourth years, residing at Mrs. B's. old home, in East Burke. His pastorate at Kalamazoo seemed to "move on the most prosperously and "happily" of all his ministerial engagements. Dr. Homer O. Hitchcock (D. C., 1851), was one of his leading members, and he retired to the woods of Northern Michigan, each summer, "to play Indian "with his boys." After this, for the recruiting of health he was on a farm, with his brother, at Grand View, Jackson Co., Mo., 17 miles from Kansas City, nearly two years.

In May, 1890, at East Burke, he met with a severe accident, being thrown from a carriage with great violence, while returning from a benevolent errand for one of his former parishioners, a mile or two distant. This mostly incapacitated him for preaching. In August following the family homestead at East Burke was finally sold, and he again removed to the west, to be chiefly with his sons at Minneapolis, Minn.; though from April to November, '92, he was again at Grand View, Mo., with his wife and daughter, who were his very useful and efficient aids in managing the business of his stock farm. His health still failing, they hastened back to Minneapolis, Nov. 10, and a council of physicians decided that "softening of the brain" had been insidiously developed. He lingered in growing feebleness, though not with extreme pain, and his last hours were singularly tranquil. "It "was the beautiful morning of Communion Sab-"bath, March 5, 1893, at half-past 5, the hour he "was accustomed to arise, when in health, to begin "his Sabbath's labors. It seemed as if the morning "stars sang and the heavens rejoiced to welcome "him. After he was at rest, there was an expres-"sion of peace and joy in his face, we had not seen "for months. How could we but feel that the "clouds had all lifted, and he had received the " 'well done, good and faithful servant,' and 'had "entered into the joy of his Lord.' "

[Mrs. Burton's letter.]

His age was 66 years and 3 months. His funeral services were conducted by his brother-in-law,

Dr. E. P. Goodwin of Chicago, at his late residence, No. 1010 21st ave., on the Tuesday following.

The "Minneapolis Journal" said: "He was an "earnest Christian worker, strong in his beliefs, "yet gifted with that respect for the opinions of "others, that he could lend his aid to all; devoted "to the laws of God and his country, and never "afraid to declare his position in politics or church, "when once he had carefully decided the best step "to take."

The "Union City Register" added to the above:

"Dr. Burton, while pastor of the Cong. Church "in this city, endeared himself to our people per- "haps as no other pastor has ever done before. "About a year and a half ago, Gen. Daniel Dustin, "in speaking of him, as an old class-mate, said to "us, 'he is one of God's noblemen; and if anyone "gets a seat near the Great White Throne, that "man will be Dr. Burton.' "

In his own letter to our class meeting from Kalamazoo, Aug. 20, 1878, he says: "And so tell "the boys my life has rolled on like the volume of "a sweet song, more sweet, more loud from the be- "ginning to the end. * * One thing more, the "greatest, the grandest, and best of all, the life of "God within the soul has been as some *celestial* "*melody* telephoned daily to my heart from the "better land, where the King dwelleth in His glory. "Amid all the surging seas and howling storms of "popular and scientific skepticism, I have heard in "sweeter and sweeter accents, the voice of him who

"hushed and walked the waves, saying 'It is I, be
"not afraid.' I want especially, and above all else
"to bear my testimony, to my class-mates who may
"be present, to an unfaltering, growing faith in
"that Book which demands all virtues that ever
"blessed society, or adorned human character, and
"which utterly proscribes all vices that have ever
"disgraced and debased mankind, and which above
"all, points us to the one propitiation for the remis-
"sion of sins that are past."

While at Newbury, he was scribe of the "Orange
Association." The degree of S. T. D. was conferred
upon him by Old Dartmouth in 1865. He was on
the Examining Committee at Dartmouth College,
November, 1867; and a delegate to the National
Congregational Council, at New Haven, Conn., in
1874.

Publications:

(1) Discourse preached at the Semi-Centennial
Anniversary of the "Vermont Domestic Missionary
Society," at St. Johnsbury, June 17, 1868; pub-
lished in "Home Missionary" the next October.

(2) Article of 13 pp., "The Blessed Hope of
"the Church according to Christ and His Apos-
"tles," in "Way Marks in the Wilderness" (Vol.
8, No. 4, Oct., 1870).

(3) Memorial of Dea. Freeman Keyes, of Newbury, Vt., 1872. Has written many articles for
periodicals, usually without signature. The publication of his sermons and discourses, though often
sought, has almost always been declined.

I. Charlotte Elizabeth was a superior classical scholar, especially in Greek, and has been a successful teacher; now residing with her mother and brothers in Minneapolis.

II. STEPHEN E. has been in the employ of the "Guaranty Loan Co. of the Northwest" for several years.

III. CHARLES N. has graduated as a physician; was first in Burke, and is now (1892-4 in) Minneapolis, "in a fair practice of medicine."

CAHOON, GEORGE WILLIAM, *,

LYNDON, VT.

1 —— Lyndon, Vt., Dec. 15, 1831. His great-grandfather, Daniel Cahoon, was an original grantee of Lyndon in 1788; his grandfather, William, one of the earliest settlers, and the most prominent man in town for many years; was also Lieut.-Gov. of Vermont, 1820-21, and Representative in Congress from 1829 till his death, in 1833. His father, Hon. George Clinton Cahoon, was born in 1798; educated at the Vermont University, Burlington; a successful lawyer in Lyndon, and there died in 1879, aged 81. His mother was Mary Ripley Baylies, the daughter of Hon. Nicholas Baylies, of Montpelier (D. C., 1794), who was the son of Dea. Nicholas, of Uxbridge, Mass., and married Mary, daughter of Rev. Prof. Sylvanus Ripley, of Hanover, (D. C., 1771). Her mother was Abigail, daughter of Pres. Eleazer Wheelock. Hence he was the great-great-grandson of the founder and first president of Dartmouth College;

his pedigree being: George W.[5] (Cahoon), Mary[4] (Baylies), Mary[3] (Ripley), Abigail[2] (Wheelock), Eleazer[1].

2 —— Lyndon Academy, under Alexander Miller; also at St. Johnsbury Academy, under J. K. Colby.

3 —— Charlotte D. Cahoon, Jan. 23, 1856, at her residence in Portland, Me. She was the daughter of Mayor Cahoon of Portland, attended the Young Ladies' School at Hanover, and died July 11, 1868, after a protracted illness.

He was married, second, to Mary Lydia Bellows, of Lancaster, N. H., Sept. 9, 1869, who died Feb., 1881, at Lyndon, of gastric fever, after an illness of nine weeks.

Was married, third, to Mrs. Sarah E. Russell (Pearson before marriage), of Newburyport, Mass., who had been a widow for three or four years, and returned to Newburyport a year or two after her second husband's (Cahoon's) death.

4 —— I. James William, born Dec. 22, 1856.

II. George Clinton, born Aug. 3, 1858.

III. Mary Elizabeth, born Aug. 26, 1862.

IV. Charlotte Deming (second wife), born Nov. 16, 1870.

V. Grace Wilson, born Feb. 19, 1872.

He studied law with his father at Lyndon, from graduation till the June term, Caledonia Co. Court, 1855, when admitted as attorney-at-law on the second Tuesday in July.

Was in practice with his father at Lyndon for several years, "George C. & George W. Cahoon."

Early in his practice was appointed notary public, and afterwards admitted to practice in Supreme Court, and Court of Chancery. In the winter of 1859 was admitted Attorney and Counsellor of the U. S. Court at Washington, on motion of Hon. Jacob Collamer, M. C. Elected State's Attorney of Caledonia County in September, 1860, and served in that capacity two years. He was very favorably noticed in the "Vermont Union," 1867, as a successful lawyer, both in the business of collecting and in managing and winning his cases at the courts. His business connection, May 8, 1885, (as per card in "Vermont Union") was "Cahoon "& Hoffman, Lawyers and General Insurance "agents, Lyndon and Lyndonville. One of the firm "will be at office in Fletcher's block, Lyndonville, "every day." In February, 1889, however, he had a similar office by himself at Lyndonville.

He was first attacked with la grippe, early in 1891. Spent a few weeks in Newburyport, and "returned not much improved. His trouble then "developed into Bright's disease, and as some "thought, softening of the brain." He was quite cheerful; fully expecting to recover, when last seen by Chase, June 19, "little realizing that the 13th of "the next month (July, 1891) was to be his last "day on earth." His age was 59 years and 7 months; and it was "a singular coincidence, that "the death of the only male descendant in Lyndon "of the family which first settled in town should "occur so soon after its centennial celebration," (July 4 and 5.)

His funeral was largely attended on the Wednesday following his death, with an eloquent and comforting address from his pastor, the Rev. J. C. Bodwell.

"As a lawyer he was well read; unusually famil-
"iar with the Vermont statutes and decisions; and
"his strongest point was in the preparation of his
"cases. Was in a constant practice for thirty-one
"years, his name appearing on the docket as often
"as that of any other attorney, and at one time
"with more cases than the name of any other law-
"yer at the bar. A large degree of his success
"was due to his persistent push. He never tired,
"and was never humiliated or discouraged by de-
"feat, but was always ready to try it again. Mr.
"Cahoon was a public spirited man, always ready
"to contribute, according to his means, to town
"improvements, and to any worthy enterprise. In
"his business he earned a good fortune, but believed
"in the principle of enjoying it as he went along.
"He was of the wrong material to make a miser of.
"He was a man of generous impulses and kindly
"feelings; very indulgent in his family, and court-
"eous in his bearing among men. He will be much
"missed in Lyndon."
[From Class-mate Chase's tributes, "Vermont
Union."]

I. JAMES W. graduated at the U. S. Naval School, Annapolis, Md., 1878; married Mary Bellows Perkins, of Portland, Me.; was stationed as ensign at Newport, R. I., 1885, having previously returned from a three years' cruise to South

America and Africa, including a station for some 'time at Montevideo. He has since been an electrician in Boston, with residence in Lynn, Mass.

II. GEORGE C. first learned the printers' trade of Chase in Lyndon, but studied law and was admitted to the bar in 1882. Was settled in Carthage, Dakota; had married, and there d. Dec. 25, 1888, aged 30 years, 4 months, leaving a dau. five months old. His son's widow and her little child were kindly cared for by our class-mate.

III. MARY E. m. Edward H. Hoffman, Esq., the law partner of her father, about 1881. Her two oldest children were (1) Helen (Hoffman), and (2) Lottie; to which family group three other little girls and one boy have since been added (1894).

IV. CHARLOTTE D. and

V. GRACE W., were educated in the graded school and "Institute" and follow teaching as their profession, with good positions in Minnesota.

CARTER, NATHAN FRANKLIN,

HENNIKER, N. H.

1 —— Henniker, Jan. 6, 1830, being the son of Nathan and Margery (Wadsworth) Carter. His grandfather was Samuel Carter, of Hillsboro, N. H. His father settled at Henniker in 1819. He is of the fifth generation on his mother's side, from the Rev. Aaron Hutchinson, earliest pastor in Woodstock, Vt., who preached there and at Hartland and Pomfret alternately.

2 —— Meriden, N. H., 1846-8, under C. S. Richards (D. C. 1835).

3 —— Hattie Frances Weeks, at Exeter, N. H., by Rev. Nathan Lasell, of Amesbury, Mass., March 12, 1860. She was a dau. of Major Nathaniel and Harriet Byram (Gilman) Weeks, of Exeter; there b. July 15, 1833, and d. in Concord, Oct. 8, 1890, aged 57 years and 3 months.

He was m., second, at Exeter, by Rev. Swift Byington, to Mrs. Harriet Louisa Gale, dau. of Nathaniel, and Mary Elizabeth (Lovering) Jewell, Oct. 12, 1892. She was b. in Exeter, Jan. 9, 1842, and was the widow of Dea. Joseph Wakefield Gale, at the time of her second marriage to Mr. Carter. The coincidences may be noted that he saw both the Mrs. Carters for the first time at the same place, on the same evening; that the parents of both lived not far from each other on the same street in Exeter, and that the last was afterwards his pupil for four years.

He was principal of the Highland Lake Institute, East Andover, N. H., from Aug., 1853, to Nov., 1854; of the High School, Concord, N. H., three months, 1854-5, and of the High School, Exeter, N. H., from April, 1855, to Feb. 26, 1864, a period of nine consecutive years. Meanwhile he had been approbated to preach by the Piscataqua Association, April 20, 1859, for four years; May 15, 1863, for four years more, and July 16, 1867, for four years more. In May, 1864, he connected himself with the middle class, Bangor (Me.) Theological Seminary, and was there graduated July, 1865.

Besides temporarily supplying various other pulpits, he was stated supply at Pembroke, N. H., one year, Aug., 1865, to Aug., 1866, and at North Yarmouth, Me., from May, 1867, till April 1, 1869, where he was also ordained an Evangelist, Dec. 19, 1867. Was pastor at Orfordville, N. H., from Aug. 1, 1869, till Sept. 1, 1874. Installed at Bellows Falls, Vt., Oct. 28, 1874; dismissed Oct. 28, 1879. Acting pastor of the Cong. Church, Quechee, Vt., June 1, 1879, till Feb. 18, 1880, when he was installed pastor; and dismissed Sept. 22, 1887. Owing to the failing health of his wife, an accepted call to South Deerfield, Mass., was rescinded for lack of suitable house accommodations, and he took up his residence at Concord, N. H., Oct. 1, 1887, finally purchasing a pleasant home at 51 Rumford street.

He has continued his Sabbath labors, supplying at Wilmot, N. H., July 29, 1888, till 1890; at East Andover and Andover, N. H., Nov., 1890, till April 15, 1891; at East Concord, July 1, till Oct. 1, 1891, and at Campton, N. H., from April, 1892, till Nov., 1893.

His ministerial labors, in each of his earlier fields, were attended with powerful revivals, about forty uniting with his church at North Yarmouth, on the 1st of Jan., 1868, 84 while at Orfordville, 70 at Bellows Falls, and about 40 at Quechee. He was superintending school com. of Andover in 1854; one of the editors of the "N. H. Journal of Edu-"cation," 1858 to 1861, and acting local editor of the "Exeter News-Letter," 1859-60. Was councillor and vice-president of the N. H. State Teachers' Association, and president of the Young Men's Christian Association at Exeter. In 1864 had contributed upwards of 600 articles, mostly short, to some 30 different newspapers, magazines and one hymn book, the most extended being a valuable religious series of 107 "Bible Pictures" in the "Congregational Journal" of N. H. During his leisure time, for several years, was employed upon "The Native Ministry of New Hampshire," which appeared by installments in the "N. H. Statesman" in 1883, and is now ready to be issued, more completely, in book form. "The Ride for "Life," and other occasional poems, appeared about the same time. "Names of the Master" is another series of poems, upwards of 200 in number, now ready for the press. "Social Life,—Responsibility of "Church Members," an essay before the Merrimack Co. Conference, published by request in the "N. "H. Journal" of Dec. 9, 1892. "The History of "Pembroke, N. H.," which he has succeeded in bringing out, after several failures on the part of others, is this year (1894) being published. Besides these literary "Children" of his, he patented in 1878 an improved "Rotary Library Reference "Table," a vade mecum for professional men, especially ministers. He has been the highly esteemed and efficient secretary of the "Central N. "H. Congregational Club" since its organization, and of the "N. H. Prisoners' Aid Association" since 1891, also a member of the "N. H. Historical "Society" since 1890.

His mottoes seem to have been to "fill life with "hard work," and "be helpful to as many a weary "pilgrim as possible on the way to Heaven."
(For his class poem see Records of Class Meetings.)

CHASE, CHARLES MONROE,
LYNDON, VT.

1 —— Lyndon, Nov. 6, 1829; his father being Gen. Epaphras B. Chase, and his mother, before marriage, Louisa Baldwin, of Bradford, Vt.

2 —— The Caledonia Co. Grammar School, Lyndon, under Alexander Miller, at St. Johnsbury, Vt., and finally at Meriden, N. H., under Cyrus S. Richards, A. M.

3 —— Lizzie M. Wells, of Sycamore, Ill., June 15, 1864, by Rev. J. Alden (D. C. 1852).

4 —— I. EVERETT BALDWIN, b. Dec. 26, 1865.

II. MARY LOUISE, b. Oct. 16, 1867; d. April 26, 1872, of malignant canker-rash, aged four and a half years.

III. FREDERICK CHARLES, b. Aug. 26, 1870; d. April 30, 1872, of canker-rash, followed by lung fever, aged 1 year and 8 months.

IV. JOHN BRYANT, b. Sept. 24, 1872.

V. GEORGE AUGUSTUS, b. March 5, 1875.

VI. JENNIE WELLS, b. Feb. 17, 1879.

VII. NELLIE LOUISE, b. May 17, 1881; all in Lyndon.

From the fall of 1853 till the spring of 1856 (except the summer of 1854, which he spent in Madison, Wis.,) he was in Cincinnati, Ohio, teach-

C. M. CHASE, at 63.

ing music in the city, and at Farmer's College and the Ohio Female College, five miles out. Also read law with President Allen of Farmer's College, and passed one summer with his uncle, Alphonso Wood, A. M. (D. C. 1834), studying botany. Next removed to Sycamore, Ill., still teaching music and reading law. In 1857 was admitted to the bar, and in 1858 entered into partnership with Jacob A. Simons, Esq. (Simons & Chase), continuing till 1862. Was police magistrate in Sycamore from 1858 to 1862; edited the "De Kalb Co. Sentinel" during the year 1858; was the leader of a band at Sycamore for several years, and took the same into the 13th Illinois Infantry, enlisting for three years, but was discharged after three months' service, under Gen. Fremont's order reducing the number of bands in that department. Was Kansas correspondent of the "Sycamore True Republican "and Sentinel" during the summer and fall of 1863. On the morning of the Lawrence massacre he and Adj.-Gen. E. Russell were approaching Lawrence from the south, over the road taken by the guerillas in their flight from the burning city. Nothing but "tall running" (for a place of obscurity) avoided contact with that bloodthirsty gang. During his residence at Leavenworth he was employed by Gov. Tom Carney as city editor of the "Leavenworth Daily Times;" had charge of the City Musical Association, embracing most of its prominent singers; taught music in the churches; had charge of the largest choir in the city, and was for a time teacher in Leavenworth College. In

June, 1864, returning to Lyndon on a visit, he prolonged his stay till Feb. 10, 1865, when he issued, as editor and publisher, the first number of the "Vermont Union," a weekly newspaper which he has continued at Lyndon for nearly 30 years without interruption. Was reported at class meeting in 1878 to have made journalism in connection with the "Union" quite profitable, pecuniarily. The "Union," it is claimed, was the first paper in the U. S. which adopted the practice of giving localities, within the scope of its circulation, special heads of their own, or of grouping all items concerning a town or a village under its own name. Apparently a trifling invention in the make-up of a country paper, it proved important, was soon copied, and is now the universal custom throughout the country.

The address of Mr. Chase before the "Vermont "Editors' and Publishers' Association" at Burlington, June 4, 1873, on the "Local Paper and How "to Make It," was well received and published in the "Daily Free Press and Times" of June 5.

Was Democratic candidate for Representative to Congress, from the Second Vermont District, in 1866, and again by a second regular nomination in 1868; also delegate to the Democratic National Convention, at St. Louis, Mo., in 1876. He was one of the judges at a brass band tournament at Owl's Head, Lake Memphremagog, in the fall of 1878, at which five bands contested for prizes. Was admitted to the Caledonia County bar in 1866; was for a time notary public, and 20 years justice of the peace.

He is a liberal supporter of the Cong. Church and Society at Lyndon, and in 1869 began to labor for the establishment of a first-class graded school, to take the place of the old Lyndon Academy, established in 1831. As the result, a new school building was erected, at a cost of $13,000; and, with the assistance of class-mate Cahoon, the old school district was enlarged and incorporated. For 14 years he was president of the school board of six members.

For many years has been in the habit of making annual trips to distant states, and by his correspondence has given the "Union" something more than a local reputation.

(1) A long series of racy and interesting letters were written from the Philadelphia Exposition of 1876.

(2) "The Editor's Run in New Mexico and Col-"orado" was a trip made in October, November and December, 1881; making 28 letters and 63 newspaper columns of 25 inches each.

(3) "Out on a Fly" was a series of North Carolina letters, April and May, 1884; making 16 letters and filling 32 columns.

(4) "Drifting in the Sunny South" was in Florida, Feb. to May, 1885; 24 letters, 54 columns.

(5) "Out West Again" was in New Mexico, Feb. to May, 1886; 18 letters, 33 columns.

(6) "A Southern Raid" was through Florida again, Feb. to May, 1887; 29 letters, 65 columns.

(7) "California" was on the Pacific coast, Feb.

to June, 1888; 30 letters, 67 columns.

(8) "Cape Cod," Aug., 1890; 9 columns.

(9) "Iowa," Sept., 1890; 5 columns.

(10) "Off for Kansas," Sept., 1891; 9 letters, 15 columns.

(11) "Reminiscences" was a series of 28 articles which appeared in the "Union" regularly every week, from Dec. 16, 1892, to June 30, 1893; varying from one to nine columns each. They embraced a refreshing mixture of serious and racy descriptions of Lyndon people, places and customs, from the earliest to the present time.

"The Editor's Run" was published in book form in 1882, making a vol. of 240 pages. Out of some 26 different press notices of this book, which have met your secretary's eye, he would select the three or four following, to give his class-mates some idea of Bro. Chase's success in this department of his newspaper work:

[Newport (N H.) Argus.]

"Interesting and valuable."

[Davenport (Ia.) Democrat.]

"The book contains more real valuable informa-
"tion regarding Colorado, New Mexico and Santa
"Fe, the oldest city on the continent, than any
"book of western travel we have seen."

[Springfield (Mass.) Republican.]

"His book shows a habit of shrewd observation,
"a perception of humor and an ability to get the
"news and facts, and write them out in a free and
"easy way, which has brought success to the
" 'Union' as a local paper."

" 'The Editor's Run' is by C. M. Chase, the able
"and witty editor of the 'Vermont Union,' one of
"the best papers of the Green Mountain State.
"Mr. Chase is a man of sense and observation, as
"well as of original wit, and he has a faculty of
"getting at all the material facts, and setting them
"forth clearly, simply and entertainingly."

In his busy life our class-mate has not forgotten
his old love for music, but has found time to compose and publish a goodly number of church tunes,
which have appeared in several different singing
books since 1855. Among his last publications
was the "Vermont Union Polka," dedicated to the
Vermont editors.

"It is bright, vivacious and sparkling, with tak-
"ing bits of melody, which will make it a favorite,
"and is lively enough to set the editors of the
"Green Mountain State on a dance to the cornet."

"Many of our townsmen will remember Mr.
"Chase as a gentleman of rare musical attain-
"ments, as well as of agreeable social qualities.
"We take pleasure in recommending this last
"musical production of his to those who want a
"really good thing."

CROSBY, ALPHEUS BENNING, *,

HANOVER, N. H.

1 —— Gilmanton, N. H., Feb. 22, 1832. He was the son of Prof. Dixi Crosby, M. D., of Dart. College, and Mary Jane, dau. of Stephen Moody, Esq., of Gilmanton. His father was b. Feb. 8, 1800, in Sandwich, N. H., and d. at Hanover Sept. 26, 1873, in his 74th year. His mother was b. Dec. 18, 1807, and m. July 2, 1827. His pedigree runs: Alpheus Benning[8], (Dixi[7], Asa[6], Josiah[5], Josiah[4], Josiah[3], Simon[2], Simon[1]). His grandfather, Asa, was a distinguished physician, and father of physicians, in Sandwich and Gilmanton. The three ancestral Josiahs were b. in Billerica, Mass.; the second Simon was b. June, 1637, in Cambridge, Mass., and Simon, 1st, the immigrant, arrived with his wife, Ann, in 1635, at the age of 26, and settled in Cambridge.

2 —— Hanover, under Asa Weeks, M. A. (D. C., 1846).

3 —— Mildred Glassell Smith, in Baltimore, Md., at St. Paul's Church, July 26, 1862. She was b. Nov. 7, 1840, at Spring Hill, near Mobile, Ala., the dau. of Dr. William Robert Smith, afterwards of Galveston, Texas. She d. in Galveston, Feb. 3, 1882, aged 41 years, and 3 months.

4 —— I. MAYRANT MOODY, b. Dec. 27, 1863; d. Dec. 23, 1867, aged 4 years. "Extinctus amabitur "idem."

II. MILDRED MORTON, b. June 2, 1865, in Hanover.

III. Dixi, b. July 25, 1869, in Hanover.

IV. William Pierce, b. June 14, 1874, in New York.

Studied medicine at the Dart. Medical School, 1853-4; passed one year (1855) as assistant surgeon in the Marine Hospital, Chelsea, Mass.; graduated M. D., at Hanover, in 1856.

Practiced medicine in Hanover five years, till May 1, 1861, when he entered the service of the government, as surgeon of the 1st Regiment of N. H. Volunteers. Aug. 12, promoted to brigade surgeon, and assigned as division surgeon to Gen. Charles P. Stone's staff. Afterwards served as "Medical Director" in departments of Gens. Sedgewick, Casey and Peck, successively. Officiated at the battle of Ball's Bluff, during the seven days' fight before Richmond, Va., June, 1862, and through all the principal engagements of the army of the Potomac, up to the second battle of Bull Run.

Resigned his commission July 16, 1862; resumed practice in Hanover; re-appointed by the Secretary of War in September following, but declined, and in 1863 was appointed "Associate Professor of Surgery" in Dart. College, delivering lectures on military surgery. In 1870, on the resignation of his father, was chosen "Professor of Surgery," and so continued till his death. Was also professor of surgery in the Vermont Medical College, Burlington, from 1865 onwards; the same chair in the University of Michigan at Ann Arbor, 1869-72, and in the Long Island College Hospital, Brooklyn, N. Y. Also delivered a course of medical lectures at Bowdoin College, Maine, in 1869. He was professor of anatomy at Bellevue Hospital Medical College, New York, in 1873, and declined invitations to chairs in medicine from the "University of New York," and from the "Jefferson College" in Philadelphia, Pa.

He suffered from dissection poison and had a long and severe illness after the death of his little boy, winter of 1867-8. Was hence advised by his medical friends to seek a warmer climate, and accordingly opened an office in New York, which continued to be his winter residence through life.

His first published medical pamphlets were: (1) "Foreign Bodies in the Knee Joint, with Seven "Cases of Removal." (2) "A Successful Case of "Ovariotomy." Also in the Boston Medical Journal two papers: (1) "Diabetes," and (2) "A "Month in a Volunteer Camp."

The following is a completed list of his articles, published in the transactions of the N. H. Medical Society, and in the N. H. Medical Journal: (1) "Abscesses" (a series), 1863. (2) "Commemora-"tive Address on Prof. David Conant." (3) "Gun-"shot Injuries of the Knee Joint, requiring Am-"putation." (4) "The Significance of Pain." (5) "Septicæmia," 1868. (6) "Commemorative Ad-"dress on Dr. R. D. Muzzy," 1869. (7) "The "Early Medical History of New Hampshire." (8) "A Contribution to the Medical History of New "Hampshire," 1870; same in pamphlet form.

There were also published his "Eulogy on Pres. "N. Lord, D. D.," delivered at Dartmouth commencement, 1872, and his "Valedictory Address" in the medical department of the University of Michigan, 1872.

He was honored with membership in many medical associations, and was president of the "N. H. "Medical Society" in 1877. He d. of acute diabetes at Hanover, Aug. 9, 1877, aged 45 years, 6 mos., partly as the result of over-work, and the taking of extra doses of quinine to ward off disease.

From Prof. Parker's funeral address, the "In "Memoriam" of his life-long friend, J. Whitney Barston, M. D. (D. C. 1846), before the N. H. Medical Society, in 1878, and from other sources the following items are gathered:

"With an exuberance of animal spirits, he had "also a natural balance of caution. He was ardent, "but not hasty; self-reliant and fearless, but never "precipitate." At the age of 15 he began to assist his father in the administration of chloroform; and had become his constant and sympathetic associate, so that he "gravitated by a sort of natural law into "his father's profession, as he did, later, into his "father's place." Many of us remember that cold November morning of our sophomore year, when Prof. Chase swooned and fell heavily forward upon his desk; and with what promptness and presence of mind Crosby sprang to his rescue, ordered the movements of the rest of us, and soon restored him to consciousness.

"It is no small encomium for any man, when the "place where he has grown up, and in which he "has spent both his earlier and his riper years, has

"no recollection of him other than what is to his
"praise." Let this be added to the "noble record
"of his army services," that to him "belongs the
"credit of having originated and erected the first
"complete military hospital on the modern pavilion
"plan, that was built during the War of the Re-
"bellion."

From the time of his appointment as adjunct
professor of surgery in Dart. College, autumn of
1862 "his honors literally outran his years. The
"number of his appointments to professional chairs
"in different institutions, is something beyond pre-
"cedent in the history of any young American
"practitioner."

For, what other young medical man of our time,
at the age of 38, ever enjoyed the distinction of
holding professorships in five or six prominent
medical schools at once, and of declining, when
scarcely in his 40th year, two other like positions?
As a lecturer he was "master of his subject, clear
"and definite in his demonstrations, direct and in-
"cisive in his manner, apt in illustration, brim full
"of good humor and pointed anecdote, and fluent,
"even to prodigality, in his words, so that his
"power over students was immense, and his class-
"room was crowded."

In the 21 years of his practice he operated more
times than any other surgeon of his age in New
England, and performed, without exception, every
capital operation known in surgery. His last two
years in New York were years of remarkable industry and incessant toil. Two of his popular

lectures in the Cooper Institute, winter of 1876-7, on "The Foot" and "The Hand" were marvels of wit and common sense; were fully reported in the daily press, and were read and admired throughout the land. His "anatomical analysis of the violin "playing of Ole Bull," with whom he enjoyed an intimate acquaintance, was also an able and ingenious paper. His last lengthy address was by special invitation, at a meeting of the White Mountain Medical Society, at Lancaster, N. H., on "Recent Improvements in Surgery," which effort, with the discussions following the wide range of his subject, kept him on his feet for five consecutive hours.

A few days later he drove to Chelsea, Vt., and performed two operations, one of which occupied nearly three hours and was finished by candle light. Yet he delivered the opening lecture of his medical course Aug. 2; made his last professional visit, and enjoyed his last hour of communion with nature, Aug. 5, and the next day lectured to his class for the last time. In 48 hours more he was insensible; "and the next morning, rallying for the "effort to bid the last farewell to those he loved "best on earth, he breathed away his precious life "into the hands of that God whom he served and "trusted to the end."

It was Dr. Peaslee's verdict (D. C. 1836), himself so soon to follow, that "his brain had been "over-taxed for years, and had been but irregular-"ly repaired by a sufficient amount of sleep. He "rose early, but retired late. * * He was at a

"critical age between the sixth and seventh sep-
"tennium, yet he consented to assume one extra
"task after another, and these he always fulfilled
"conscientiously and nobly, but neglected the only
"means of escape from the danger of overwork.
"He recognized his mistake only when it was too
"late."

He was acknowledged to be one of the most
brilliant "post prandial" orators in the country.
His effort at the last Dartmouth commencement,
before his death, will never be forgotten, and he
was under appointment to speak to a toast at the
Bennington, Vt., celebration in the August following.

We, his class-mates, are well prepared to sub-
scribe to the sentiment so beautifully expressed by
Prof. Parker (D. C. 1841), that "in all his widen-
"ing range of work, and of social activities, his
"large heart seemed as incapable of being over-
"loaded with friendship, as it was inexhaustible in
"its overflowing friendliness."

His children have resided in Hanover since the
death of their mother. The oldest, (II) Mildred
M., keeping house for her brothers, of whom (III)
Dixi, studied medicine in the Dartmouth Medical
College, graduating in 1890, and (IV) William P.
is at present (1894) a student in the same institution.

DEARBORN, PITT FRANCIS, *, N. G.,

EFFINGHAM, N. H.

1 —— Effingham, May 11, 1832. His father, Josiah Dearborn, was b. Sept. 25, 1790, and d. March 31, 1873, aged 82 years, 6 months. Pedigree: Pitt Francis[4], Josiah[3], Asahel[2], Josiah[1]. His great-grandfather, Josiah[1], came from North Hampton, N. H., to Effingham, in 1760. His mother, before marriage, was Belinda Knight Quarles, of Ossipee (Belinda K.[4], Samuel[3], Jonathan[2], Francis[1]). She was b. Feb. 25, 1811, and d. Oct. 6, 1853, aged 42 years, 7 months, the very autumn after he *would* have graduated. His earliest maternal ancestor, Francis Quarles, emigrated from England and settled in Hamilton, Mass. His grandfather, Asahel Dearborn, m. Elizabeth Drake, as his grandmother, the dau. of William Drake. The wife of his grandfather, Samuel Quarles, who was also his grandmother, was Abigail, the dau. of Enoch and Anna (Eastman) Knight.

Samuel Q. Dearborn, of Effingham, kindly furnishes these genealogical notes, and is pleased to know that his brother is remembered by us (1878).

2 —— North Parsonsfield (Me.) Academy; at Effingham Academy (under the instruction of Mr. Walsh), and finally at Kennebunk, Me.

We vividly recall his manly form, and dignified but courteous bearing, during our Freshman year. Sitting beside Crosby, in the recitation room, he was his rival in scholarship, as he might have

proved in usefulness and fame.   He ranked among
the very first of the class; but the growing pallor
of his countenance, the last few months of the year,
betokened his early departure from us.

We give his subsequent record precisely as it
stood in the "Class Memorial" of 1864:

"Having left us in poor health, at the close of
"Freshman year, he was advised by his physician
"to journey south, but did not start till about the
"1st of January, 1851, his mother accompanying
"him as far as New York City.   Thence he pur-
"sued his journey alone, feeble as he was, to Sa-
"vannah, Ga., where he remained for some time,
"and then proceeding to Jacksonville, Fla., he re-
"sided in the family of Mr. A. Parsons.   With Mr.
"Parsons' family he moved some fifty miles back
"into the country, and soon after arriving at their
"destination, he was brought under peculiar cir-
"cumstances of distress and discomfort to his feeble
"body, to cast his soul unconditionally upon the
"mercy of God.   From this time forth he had con-
"stant peace in believing in Christ, and consolation
"in the promises of the Holy Scriptures.   But his
"health not improving, he returned to his father's
"in Effingham in April, and in July of the same
"year (1851) was present with us at commence-
"ment, settled for his room in Lang Hall, which he
"had hired but not occupied during the year, and
"took his leave of class-mates, never more to meet
"them on earth, but hoping to meet them where
"sickness, pain, sorrow and parting are unknown.
"At home again, after the fatigues of this journey

CALIFORNIA

Rev. Jos. M. Dickson, D. D.

"to Hanover, he continued gradually to lose
"strength, with increasing suffering, all of which
"he bore without a murmur, until Dec. 30, 1851,
"when he expired (in his 20th year) calmly and
"happily, strong in the faith and in the hope of the
"gospel. His disease was consumption of the
"lungs. He was buried in the garden, near his
"father's residence, a spot of his own selection, and
"a marble slab over his grave bears this inscription:

" 'Friends of my youth, let sorrow cease,
 " 'Hope whispers—we shall meet again,
 " 'Restored to safety, love and peace.' "

DICKSON, JAMES MILLIGAN,

RYGATE, VT.

1 —— Rygate, Feb. 6, 1831; the son of Robert
and Janet Dickson, both from Scotland, the former
from Paisley, when 12 years old, with his father,
Robert Dixon, who purchased and occupied the
farm in Rygate, that is still in the family, in the
fourth generation. Robert Dickson (2d) lived to
the age of 72, was a public spirited man, for years
town trustee, also for many years an elder in the
Reformed Presbyterian Church at Rygate. Mrs.
Dickson came later from Belfrou, a suburb of
Glasgow; a widow at 18—Mrs. Carmichael—her
maiden name Lenny. She was a woman of great
refinement, and unusually versed in the Scriptures.

2 —— Peacham Academy, under William Brad-
ley, John Paul and A. Rix, in view of Dartmouth;
first three years at Geneva Hall College, Ohio

(now Geneva College, at Beaver Falls, Pa.); returning east, entered senior class at Dartmouth on examination, and graduated with us. Has always prized his early western experience.

3 —— Agnes Annot M. Nelson, of Rygate, Vt., April 7, 1858. "Was permitted to enjoy his happy "home but a short time," as she d. Feb. 23, 1859. Was married (2d) to Helen Alrina West of Dorset, Vt. (previously of Brooklyn, N. Y.), Sept. 30, 1863.

4 —— I. Nelson James, b. Feb. 21, 1859, in Brooklyn, N. Y.

II. William Millard, b. Dec. 19, 1866, in Newark, N. J.; d. Jan. 1, 1867.

III. Clarence Haines, b. Aug. 31, 1869, in Newark.

IV. Margarella May, b. April 29, 1874, at Montgomery, N. Y.

Was offered at graduation the Greek Professorship at Geneva Hall College, but chose otherwise. Was associate principal of a classical school on Staten Island, N. Y., from Sept., 1853, till the spring of '54; then for six months teacher of languages and mathematics in the Haverstraw Mountain Institute, Haverstraw, N. Y. Three years a student at the Union Theological Seminary, New York City, teaching an hour or two daily in a young ladies' school; graduated in the spring of 1857; a few weeks later was licensed to preach by the New York Presbytery of the Reformed Presbyterian Church. Spent the summer chiefly in rest and recreation, first at the home of an aged clergyman (Rev. Dr. Christie) at Lebanon, N. J., and afterwards at his own home in Vermont, preaching occasionally; Nov. 18 was ordained and installed pastor of the "Church of the Covenanters," Brooklyn, N. Y. After burying his wife, as above, at Rygate, "in the little village on the hill, re-"turned to pursue his work alone and desolate," but with marked success, till April, 1862, when, much against the expressed will of his people, he resigned his charge; spent the summer at his Vermont home again, where he was urged to accept a call (as he has been twice since); returned to New York in the fall and was almost at once called to the Sixth Presbyterian Church, Newark, N. J., where he was installed March 11, 1863. His work here was not limited to this immediate church, but as Secretary of the Essex Co. Bible Society he had a more extensive field, and on leaving was made an honorary member of the American Bible Society; finding himself at length overworked, he resigned all in Oct., 1869, to accept a call to the Goodwill Presbyterian Church, Montgomery, N. Y., where he was installed Nov. 1. A revival of religion soon began, which gave an impetus to work through thirteen and a half exceedingly happy years. The old house of worship, built in 1765, was enlarged and remodeled in 1871, and the membership of the church more than doubled. As president of the Orange Co. Sunday School Association, and as the conductor of Temperance Councils in connection with the M. E. camp meetings in Wesley Grove, which was within the bounds

of his parish, his influence became general throughout the county.

In the spring of 1883 resigned all again to accept a call to the 34th Street Reformed Church,
New York City, with his residence at 450 West
34th street, where he labored successfully till the
spring of 1889, when he resigned to accept a call
to the Pilgrim Congregational Church, Providence, R. I., where he was installed March 6, with
the learned Dr. Thomas Laurie as pastor emeritus—
the two becoming and continuing the most devoted
friends. Now just as this goes to press Dr. Dickson accepts a call to, and is installed pastor of the
East New York Reformed Church, Brooklyn, N.
Y., the installation taking place July 2, 1894. He
says: "I have always worked to the extent of my
"physical ability, and have endeavored to keep in
"step with the times, in sympathy with the age."
From an editorial sketch of Dr. Dickson in the
Treasury (New York) of May, 1889, we quote the
following, which may account for his manifest ig-
noring of denominational lines: "He is thorough-
"ly orthodox in his theology, but broad, almost
"latitudinarian in his views of church government.
"When he came to New York our attention was
"called to him as a remarkable preacher and as we
"have once and again listened to him, we have ap-
"proved the judgment expressed." In writing to
us he once said: "Yes, I have been in several de-
"nominations, and I hardly think the difference
"between them, in view of practical results, worth
"the turn of one's hand. Have in every case had

"a choice of fields in making a change, and have
"invariably taken the one that seemed the most
"urgent in its demands. I have never aspired to
"the high places of the earth. Faithfulness is
"what God requires. To him I have committed
"my life." Our records show Brother Dickson on
the examining committee of the Union Theological
Seminary, New York, in May, 1868. He received
the degree of A. M. from Alma Mater in 1878, and
that of D. D. from Drury College, Mo., June 11,
1884.

He has written considerably for the press. Several sermons have appeared in pamphlet form, and
in 1880 he prepared the "Goodwill Memorial," a
history of the original Presbyterian Church at
Montgomery, N. Y., which was substantially the
early history of the town.

Brother Dickson's present address is

53 Vermont ave.,

Brooklyn, N. Y.

He writes: "My church here celebrated its
"fiftieth anniversary some three years ago; yet,
"with the recent growth of the city in this direc-
"tion, it is in membership and spirit new. I was
"unanimously called to it, notwithstanding many
"applicants. Have been most heartily welcomed,
"and never felt more in the spirit of work than
"now. I began my ministry in Brooklyn, and, if
"the Lord designs I shall end it here, I shall not
"object. The day on which I announced my in-
"tention to resign my charge in Providence, I
"welcomed to the church 38 new members; and in

"the morning I preached my farewell sermon, I
"baptized seven children. If the Spirit thus works
"here, I shall be satisfied. Let me express my sin-
"cere regard for all the living members of the class
"and my sympathies for the friends of the depart-
"ed. May the good Lord bless and keep us all for
"time and eternity."

His oldest child, I. NELSON JAMES, left mother-
less when three days old, was not physically strong
enough to pursue studies, or he would have been,
in all probability, in the ministry. After serving
as a clerk, first with Shepard, Norwell & Co.,
Boston, Mass., and afterwards with Ballene, Moore
& Emery, Kansas City, Mo., he found out-door
life a necessity and located at North Yakima,
Washington; m. Miss Lita Conrad; has two children, (1) James G., and (2) Warren Graham.

II. CLARENCE HAINES, after fitting for college,
turned to business, and is with James McGovern
& Co., stock and bond brokers, 6 Wall St., New
York, with his home at Ridgewood, N. J. Married
Miss Florence H. Muns, of Brooklyn, N. Y.; one
child, (1) James Donald.

III. MARGARILLA MAY has just completed her
first year (1894) as a student in the Woman's College, connected with Brown University, Providence, R. I.

All three are members of the church and have
good promise of success in life.

EMERSON, JOHN DOLBEER,

CANDIA, N. H.

1 —— Candia, May 29, 1828; son of Hon. Abraham and Abigail (Dolbeer) Emerson. His pedigree is John D.[5], Abraham[4], Moses[3], Samuel[2], Michael[1]; Michael[1] being a settler in Haverhill, Mass., in 1652, and his daughter being the renowned Mrs. Dustan, who killed the Indians.

Abigail Dolbeer, his mother, was the dau. of John Dolbeer, of Candia; b. Oct. 23, 1802.

2 —— Pembroke (N. H.) Academy, under Jonathan Tenney, 1847-8; where, also, most of the time, assistant teacher.

3 —— Sarah Jane Dudley, of Candia, June 2, 1859, at the residence of her father, by Rev. John Fullonton, D. D. She was the only daughter of Dea. Samuel Dudley; grad. at Thetford Academy, Vt., in 1854, and taught four years in the academies at Pittsfield and New Hampton, N. H. She combined rare excellencies of mind and heart, with efficiency in every department of life, and a highly cultivated literary taste, all of which made her, in more than one sense, "an help meet" for a minister of the gospel. A lover of hospitality, ready for every good word and work, her Christian life of remarkable devotedness, sincerity, and honesty in thought and act, was followed by a death singularly peaceful and triumphant, at Haverhill, Sept. 15, 1862. Her disease was consumption of the blood.

He was m., second, to Mrs. Elizabeth F. Bell, at her residence in Chelsea, Mass., by Rev. A. H.

Plumb, Nov. 25, 1863. She was b. at Chester, N. H., March 29, 1835, only dau. of Dea. Nathaniel French Emerson. (Elizabeth F.[5], Nathaniel F.[4], John [3], Samuel [2], Michael [1]). Was, at her marriage to Mr. Emerson, the widow of Dr. Charles Bell, who d. at Concord, N. H., Feb. 29, 1856. She d. at Biddeford, Me., July 28, 1869, aged 34 years, 4 months.

He was m., third, to Lelia Florence Kendall, at Biddeford, by Rev. A. S. Ladd, Aug. 19, 1873. She was b. in Biddeford, Feb. 2, 1850, the only dau. of Nathan Otis and Susan (Lowe) Kendall. Her grandfather was Dea. Nathan Kendall, of Alfred, Me., who m. Lydia Emerson of Parsonsfield. Her maternal grandfather was Capt. Joseph Lowe, and her great-grandfather, Capt. John Lowe, both seamen.

4 —— I. EDWARDS DUDLEY, b. May 30, 1862, at Haverhill.

II. LUCY CHARLES (BELL), (2d wife's dau.), b. March 14, 1856, at Chester, N. H.

III. STEPHEN GOODHUE (2d wife), b. Oct. 19, 1864, at Haverhill.

IV. SARAH DELLE, b. May 31, 1867, at Haverhill; d. at Biddeford, Me., May 19, 1869, aged 1 year, 11 months and 19 days.

V. LIZZIE, b. July 5; d. Aug. 9, 1869, aged 1 month, 4 days, in Biddeford.

VI. WINNIFRED (3d wife), b. Sept. 24, 1874, in Biddeford.

VII. RALPH OTIS, b. March 3, 1876, in Biddeford.

VIII. Leon Lowe, b. Feb. 13, 1878, in Underhill, Vt.; d. at Underhill, July 13, 1882, aged 4 years and 5 months.

IX. Alfreda, b. March 3, 1881, in Underhill.

X. Margaret Hill, b. Dec. 8, 1883, at Kennebunkport.

XI. John Robie, b. Nov. 18, 1886, at Kennebunkport.

XII. Evelyn, b. April 17, 1893, at Biddeford.

He became principal of the Pembroke Academy, May, 1853, and remained there two years. Entered Andover Theological Seminary, Sept., 1855; was approbated to preach by the Andover Association, in the autumn of 1857, and spent six weeks, in the spring of 1858, as a Home Missionary at West Newbury, Vt. Was graduated from Andover, August, 1858, and ordained and installed over the Congregational Church at Haverhill, N. H., Oct. 1, of the same year, Pres. N. Lord, of Dart. College, preaching the sermon.

Dismissed from Haverhill in November, 1867, after a nine years' pastorate, and commenced his labors at Biddeford, Me., Jan. 1, 1868, where he was installed as pastor over the Second Cong. Church the March following, Prof. John R. Herrick, of Bangor, preaching the sermon. Closed his labors at Biddeford, April 1, 1876; began work at Underhill and Jericho Corners, Vt., second Sabbath of November, 1876, and was dismissed from Biddeford, Feb. 1877.

In 1883 his field was changed from Vermont again to Maine, at Kennebunkport, where he remained five years. Was engaged at Red Beach and Robbinston, Me., for six months in 1891. June 1, 1893, had purchased a home for his family at 155 Hill St., Biddeford, supplying pulpits, "as "eager as ever for the work of preaching the "gospel."

Jan. 1, 1894, again in Vermont, he was holding a commission from the "Vermont Domestic Mis-"sionary Society," and laboring in Weston and Simonsville. Is now (Since April 1, 1894) pastor of the Cong. Church in Peru, Vt. "My health "is splendid and am happy in my work."

His pastorates in Haverhill and Biddeford were highly prospered; and during the latter there were additions to his church on every communion but two. Is enabled to look upon the starting of twelve young men for the ministry, in Haverhill and Biddeford, largely by their pastor's influence, as being, under God, his great work.

He was on the examining committee at Dart. College, in company with Waterhouse, in July, 1864; and again in November, 1867.

Held the office of school superintendent and agent, on a board of three, in Biddeford, 1871-74.

Was scribe of the "York Association" seven years; presided over the York County Conference three years; was also on the first committee to advise about a classical school in Maine, and on the Board of Trust from its institution in 1873 till 1877.

The following is a list of his publications:

(1) "Christian Character of the Apostle John," Cong. Journal, 1854.

(2) "Report of Examination at K. U. Academy," Meriden, 1863.

(3) Ditto, "at Tilden Female Seminary," West Lebanon, 1864.

(4) "Comfort from Contrast;" discourse, commemorative of Charles McQuesten, at Wentworth, N. H. (2d Timo., 4:8), July, 1864.

(5) "Discourse in memory of Corp. Jerome B. "Carr" (Matt., 14:10), North Haverhill, Mar. 19, 1865.

(6) "Pastoral Letter," (Exodus 34:24, l. c.); in N. H. Minutes, 1865.

(7) History of the Second Cong. Church, Biddeford, Me., Congregational Quarterly, April, 1869.

(8) Sermon, "Memorial of the Pilgrims," 1620-1870 (Prov. 14:6), by request of parishioners, Dec., 1870.

(9) Sermon, "Mercantile Gambling" (Isa. 5:18); by the business men of Saco and Biddeford, Sept. 17, 1871.

(10) "Thanksgiving Sermon" (Psalm 103:2), in Biddeford Union and Journal, Nov. 30, 1871.

(11) "Address at Fifth Annual Convention" of the Maine S. S. Association, 1873.

(12) Articles in the "Maine Journal of Education;" "Tact," "Originality," "Methods," etc., 1873.

(13) "Christ Our Sanctification" (1st Cor. 1:30), at the request of Hon. D. McDonald and wife of

Toronto, C. W. (16 pp.), September 24, 1874.

(14) "Thanksgiving Sermon" (Acts 28:15), at Baptist Church, by request (16 pp.), Nov. 26, 1874. .

(15) "The Second Advent" (John, 14:18), in a Biddeford paper, 1875.

(16) "Report of Superintending School Com. of Biddeford (10 pp.), 1875.

(17) "Sermon," from Eph. 4:5, on "Christian "Union," and "Church Union," 1875.

(18) "Sermon," in the Maine Minutes (Luke, 7:22), 1875.

(19) "History of the York Co. Conference" (pamphlet), 1876.

(20) "Female Ornament" (1st Peter, 3:4); funeral of Miss Nellie J. Holmes (16 pp.), Sept. 13, 1877.

(21) "Faith and Things;" a funeral sermon (Heb. 11:1), 1879.

(22) Address at the 60th anniversary of Pembroke Academy, 1879.

(23) "Teaching and Voting," "New Hampton "Educator," Fairfax, Vt., 1880.

(24) "The Living Temple" (Psalm, 1:3), "The "Church Union," 1880.

(25) "The Three Worthies;" a funeral sermon (Rev. 2:10), 1880.

(26) Two School Reports, town of Jericho, Vt., 1880-81.

(27) "The Mother;" an affectionate tribute to his own (in part), 1881.

(28) "Twelve Men of Ephesus;" a sermon, 1889.

(29) "Earnest of our Inheritance;" sermon, 1890.

(30) "Ask, Seek, Knock;" a sermon, 1891.

He also published extended "Memorials" of his two wives, and of Theodosia G. Emerson, Charles Henry Griffin, and Mrs. John L. Rix. The abstracts of 20 of his sermons appeared in the daily papers of Biddeford, and 20 of his articles in the "Congregationalist" and "Church Union."

I. EDWARDS D., was baptized over his mother's casket; grad. at Phillip's Exeter Academy, and at D. C., 1884. Is now settled in business at Buffalo, N. Y., being an elder in the Presbyterian Church, and Superintendent of the S. S. Was m. to Mary Louise Underhill, of Buffalo, June 30, 1892.

Child (1) Josephine Dudley, b. April 16, 1893; not quite a day older than her little "aunt," XII.

III. STEPHEN G., grad. D. C., 1887, and at the Oberlin, O., Theological Seminary, 1890. Was m. to Florence Grafton Stone, of Kennebunkport (a graduate of Mt. Holyoke Seminary, 1890), Sept. 18, 1890, by Dr. A. H. Plumb, of Boston Highlands (see father's 2d marriage). The same day started for his field in Oakland, Cali. Has been blessed in his labors in California, and is now (1894) pastor of the Cong. Church at Moreno, Cali. Child (1) Muriel Dana, b. Sept. 8, 1891, at Oakland, Cali.; (2) Adelle, b. May 5, 1894.

His children, VI to XI, are now receiving their education in the schools, of different grades, at Biddeford.

FAIRBANKS, HENRY,

St. Johnsbury, Vt.

1 —— St. Johnsbury, May 6, 1830. His father was Hon. Thaddeus Fairbanks, of the well-known firm "E. & T. Fairbanks & Co.," and the original inventor of the Fairbanks' scales. Born at Brimfield, Mass., Jan. 17, 1796; d. at St. Johnsbury, Vt., April 12, 1886.

He stands in the eighth generation from Jonathan Fairbanke, of Old Sowerby, England, who settled in Dedham, Mass., 1636. Pedigree: Henry[8], (Thaddeus[7], Joseph[6], Ebenezer[5], Eleasur[4], Eliesur[3], George[2], Jonathan[1]).

His mother was Lucy Peck Barker, b. St. Johnsbury, Vt., April 29, 1798; d. Dec. 29, 1866.

2 —— St. Johnsbury Academy, under the instruction of James K. Colby, A. M.

3 —— Annie S. Noyes, at her father's residence in Hanover, April 30, 1862. She was b. June 14, 1845, the dau. of Prof. Daniel J. Noyes, D. D. (D. C., 1832), her grandparents being Daniel and Nancy (Weare) Noyes, of Springfield, N. H. Her religious character was finely developed, her life as a Christian useful; her death, occasioned by a fever patiently endured from Aug. 18, peaceful and triumphant; occurring Sept. 11, 1872, at the age of 27.

He was m., second, to Ruthy B. Page, of Newport, Vt., May 5, 1874; daughter of Phinehas and Jacintha B. Page.

4 —— I. Arthur, b. Nov. 13, 1864, at Hanover.

Henry Fairbanks.

II. ROBERT, b. Nov. 19, 1866, at Hanover.

III. LUCY, b. Oct. 15, 1868.

IV. CHARLOTTE, b. Dec. 11, 1871.

V. ALBERT THADDEUS (2d wife), b. July 3, 1876; d. of typhoid fever, Dec. 16, 1891, aged 15 years, 5 months. "Mature, accomplished, "remarkably sincere, absolutely true."

VI. MARION, b. April 27, 1881.

VII. DOROTHY, b. March 9, 1887.

VIII. RUTH COMFORT, b. May 28, 1892; d. Sept. 17, 1893, of cholera infantum, aged one year and four months. The last six were all born in St. Johnsbury.

He was a student at the Andover Theological Seminary from the fall of 1853, till March, 1856, when he sailed for Europe, in company with S. H. Taylor, LL. D. (D. C., 1832).

Resumed his study, and grad. at Andover in the summer of 1857, having been licensed to preach by the Andover Association Feb. 12, 1856. One year later (Feb. 17) he was ordained as an evangelist at St. Johnsbury, with H. A. Hazen (D. C., 1854).

For nearly three years, after leaving the Seminary, was engaged in the service of the "Vermont "Domestic Missionary Society," superintending their itinerant department, and laboring in nearly all the destitute missionary parishes of the state, especially at Burke and Barnet.

Was appointed Appleton Professor of Natural Philosophy in Dartmouth College, July 29, 1859, and the year following (Aug. 24) commenced his labors there, which were continued five years. In 1865 received the appointment of "Professor of "Natural History," which he had resigned prior to September, 1868, when he had again taken up his residence in St. Johnsbury. His cabinet of the "Birds of New England" was donated to our Alma Mater. Was elected a member of the corporation (Trustees) of Dart. College, in 1870; which institution also conferred upon him the degree of "Ph. D." in 1880. After leaving Dartmouth, he was preaching, as supplies were needed, and engaged in the evangelistic work, as Chairman of the State Committee of the Y. M. C. A., and later, and until now, as President of the Vermont Domestic Missionary Society. In 1869 had issued a patent for a scale for weighing grain, and has since been perfecting various other inventions, for fifteen or more of which he has received letters patent. Is Secretary of the corporation of "E. & T. Fairbanks "& Co.," and an officer in two other business corporations. Is President of the Trustees of St. Johnsbury Academy. Is a corporate member of the American Board of Commissioners for Foreign Missions; a uniform attendant upon its annual meetings, east and west, and an essential aid to its counsels by the contributions of his pen in the various religious journals. The most ornate and commodious building for the St. Johnsbury Y. M. C. A., as his gift, is one of the evidences of the interest which he takes in the moral and social welfare of his native town, as are his various donations to the Academy. From the former edition of our "Class Memorial," we quote the following notice of his tour abroad in 1856:

"He went through France, almost directly, to "Malta and Egypt, thence to Palestine (tarrying "at Jerusalem) and Constantinople. He then "visited Greece, where he was taken sick, and owes "perhaps his life, under Providence, to the skill of "the good Dr. King. In Italy, crossed from Brun- "dusium, and visited Naples, Rome, Florence, "Pisa, Genoa, Milan and Venice. In Switzerland "climbed Mt. Blanc, with 'perfect weather,' and re- "turned through the Rhine valley and parts of "Belgium, France, England and Scotland."

He visited Europe a third time, with his family, in 1891, enjoying again its scenery and its art galleries, and attending the International Congregational Council in London, as a delegate representing the National Council of the United States.

He has published:

(1) "In Christian Remembrance;" a beautiful tribute to the memory of the former Mrs. Fairbanks, in a circular form; 1872.

(2) "The Crucifixion Day;" a Sunday School concert exercise, pamphlet, 12 pp.; 1873.

(3) "The Cross;" a Sunday School concert exercise, 8 pp.

(4) "An Easter Service" for the South Cong. Church, St. Johnsbury, ·as Superintendent of its Sunday School, 14 pp.; 1882.

(5). "Easter Lilies," which also appeared in a newspaper; 1883.

(6) "Appointing Foreign Missionaries, the Con-"gregational Method," pamphlet, 16 pp.; Sept., 1887.

(7) "Prudential Conditions of Missionary Ap-"pointment;" pamphlet, 8 vo., 11 pp., 1893.

Also, previously:

(8) "The Problem of the Evangelization of "Vermont" (charts and maps); 1886.

(9) "The Needs of the Rural Districts;" an address delivered before the Boston Conference of the Evangelical Alliance, Dec. 4, 1889.

(10) Memorial of Thaddeus Fairbanks, his father, for "Men of Vermont."

I. ARTHUR was tutor at Dartmouth as soon as graduated (1886); was at Union and Yale Theological Seminaries two years, and in Germany one year, receiving the degree of Ph. D.; was tutor in Greek one year, and Assistant Professor one year at Dartmouth.

In 1892, was appointed Lecturer in the Yale Divinity School, Conn.

He m., May 2, 1889, Bessie Leland Moody, a grand-daughter of President Lord; has one dau., (1) Mary Lord Fairbanks, b. Mar. 25, 1890.

II. ROBERT went from college (1888), into business with "Fairbanks & Co.;" had spent the year previously to June, 1893, in Australia and New Zealand, and is still in their business in New York. Married Miss Camilla Van Klack, of New York, Jan. 1, 1890; and has one daughter, (1) Beatrice Helen Fairbanks, b. April 27, 1894.

III. LUCY had graduated at Smith College

(1891), and was a member of Mr. Moody's Bible Institution, Chicago, Ill., in 1893.

IV. CHARLOTTE was graduated at Smith College, class of 1894.

The two youngest children are now at school in St. Johnsbury.

FARNSWORTH, JONATHAN BREWER,

WOODSTOCK, VT.

1 —— South Woodstock, April 20, 1826, being the son of Capt. Jonathan Brewer and Sarah (Slayton) Farnsworth. His grandfather, Jonathan, came from Massachusetts in 1775; took up a farm in South Woodstock, returned for the winter, and finally brought his bride, Susannah Brewer, also from Mass., in 1790.

2 —— Ludlow, Vt., under Brownell, Smith and Knowlton, and finished the preparatory course at South Woodstock, under John Ward (D. C., 1847).

3 —— Maria Augusta Hatch, June 23, 1859, the dau. of Henry and Emily (White) Hatch of Woodstock. Josiah Hatch, the father of Henry, rem. from Alstead, N. H., to Bethel, Vt., about 1815. Henry, after marriage, rem. from Bethel to Woodstock, in 1832. The father of Emily White was Ebenezer, who settled in Braintree, Vt., from Braintree, Mass.

4 —— I. GEORGE HENRY, b. April 21, 1860, in Detroit, Mich.

II. JAMES SLAYTON, b. July 15, 1866.

III. WALTER KELLOGG, b. Nov. 17, 1870.

IV. ARTHUR WHITE, b. Nov. 16, 1873; the three last in Windsor, Vt.

He resided in Washington, D. C., one year after leaving college, 1853-4; employed as teacher of Greek and Latin in the Rittenhouse Academy. Was in Woodstock from 1854 till 1857, most of the time studying law, and was there admitted to practice, Dec., 1856. In Feb., 1857, removed to Detroit, Mich., where he practiced his profession till July, 1862, part of the time by himself, afterwards in partnership with his old preceptor, John Ward, Esq.

Leaving Detroit, at the last date mentioned, he resumed his business in Chicago, Ill., and there resided till Jan. 25, 1864, when he returned to New England, and soon after located in Windsor, Vt., as successor in the law business of his late classmate, William W. Howard, Esq.

This has been his principal home till the present (1894), occupying a retired and beautiful residence in the west part of the village. Was reported at our 25th anniversary in 1878, as still in practice at Windsor, with some insurance business and some farming, "driving a good horse and tak-"ing life easily." He has, however, lived temporarily in other places, partly for the sake of his boys, and on the 23d of May, 1887, was found by the class secretary occupying, as owner, the broad acres of one of the best farms of the Williams River valley, in Chester, Vt.; the farm having been purchased by his sister's husband upon the condition that he would move there and hold the farm during the life of his brother-in-law. His sons were there engaged in practical farming with himself. A large and valuable barn, which he built in 1881, had been crushed by the heavy snows of the previous winter. When, thus, the rebuilding of this barn became necessary, his brother-in-law desired his occupancy to cease, and having his millions with which to push his purposes, and manifesting his intention to use them, the occupant peaceably surrendered.

The Secretary has since enjoyed two or three exceedingly pleasant visits with him and his amiable lady, at the Windsor home.

Our class-mate is highly respected there. He united with the Congregational Church of Windsor, in June, 1869, and represented the town in the Vermont Legislature two terms, annual and bi-ennial, 1869 and 1870-71.

His professional business has not been, as a general thing, of the sensational kind, though he has been in some important cases, and as a rule, on the winning side. A divorce case was among these, "Edminster vs. Edminster," where both sides applied for bills, and his client won after a long and very sharp contest.

In criminal business he has been for the defence in some noted cases, as "State vs. John Vaughan," for arson, who was acquitted; and "State vs. Lull" (Warden of state's prison) for assault on a convict. Lull was at first convicted, but after going to the Supreme Court he was let off.

Mr. Farnsworth has been called upon for occasional speeches at home and public gatherings. His last and most acceptable effort in that line was on "Columbus Day," Oct. 20, 1892. His address was desired for publication, but not submitted.

I. GEORGE H. is a veterinary surgeon in Rutland, Vt., having an extended patronage over the adjoining country, and very successful. He was m. to Jessie Kelley, of Rutland, Dec. 5, 1886.

II. JAMES S. is residing in Springfield, Mass., as Secretary and business manager of a private institute, or Retreat for Invalids.

III. WALTER K. was clerk in a store at Rutland; has now (1894) gone quite extensively into poultry raising on an Otter Creek farm.

IV. ARTHUR W. was clerk in a broker's office at Rutland, but now resides in Barton, Vt. (1894), as railroad station agent, telegraph operator, etc. These two youngest sons were boarding with their oldest brother (I) while in Rutland.

GOODWIN, ANDREW JACKSON, *, N. G.,
SOUTH BERWICK, ME.

1 —— South Berwick, Nov. 15, 1831.

2 —— Berwick Academy, under the instruction of Aurin M. Payson, A. M. (D. C. 1840), afterwards Principal of the Boys' High School, at Portsmouth, N. H.

In August, 1850, having studied one year in advance with Mr. Payson, he entered the sophomore class of Dart. College; remained with us four weeks, was taken sick with typhoid fever, returned home and was confined for three weeks. He was then considered out of danger. On Sunday, Oct. 27, was visited by his friend, Horatio N. Twombly (D. C., 1854); had a long talk with him and seemed very cheerful. The next morning, Oct. 28, in attempting to rise from his bed, he ruptured a blood vessel and expired in a few minutes, aged 18 years, 11 months and 18 days. His remains lie in the "Old Parish" cemetery at South Berwick, in which also were buried Rev. Jonathan Wise, the first settled minister of the town, Rev. Mr. Moore, Rev. John Thompson, and others of distinction. The sad intelligence of his death—the first to occur in our ranks—was received by his class-mates, Oct. 30, when they passed the following resolutions:

"*Resolved*, That we, members of the sophomore "class of Dart. College, hear, with the deepest sen-"sibility, of the sudden death of our class-mate, "Mr. Andrew J. Goodwin, of South Berwick, Me.

"*Resolved*, That as a testimony of our respect "for our much esteemed friend, we will bear the "usual badge of mourning for thirty days.

"*Resolved*, That this event of Divine Provi-"dence, which has severed at a blow the endearing "ties of kindness, of friendship and love, calls forth "our strongest sympathy for his bereaved friends, "and especially for his deeply afflicted parents.

"*Resolved*, That in giving utterance to the feel-"ings of our own hearts we are confident that it

"will meet response from all who intimately knew
"him; that he was exemplary in all those virtues
"which ornament life, which exalt and refine the
"human character.

"*Resolved*, That his elevated principle of action,
"his frankness, his integrity, evinced in eagerly
"pursuing the sentiments he uttered, his 'good will
" 'towards men,' his pure and benevolent ambition,
"united with habits of unwearied application, not
"only merited our esteem and confidence during
"the brief period of our companionship, but
"brought us *all* to honor and love him.

"*Resolved*, That, as we pay this last sad tribute
"to our departed friend, while we mingle our griefs
"with those who mourn this great bereavement, we
"would not forget that God is wise and omniscient
"and be admonished by this dispensation of His
"will; and thus

" 'So live that we shall die never,
" 'So die that we may live ever.' "

HAYWARD, SILVANUS,

GILSUM, N. H.

1 —— Gilsum, Dec. 3, 1828. He was the son
of Dea. Amherst, and Sarah (Fish) Hayward, in
the sixth generation from Jonathan, of Mendon,
Mass. But his earliest known ancestor, in the
direct line in this country, was William Hayward,
of Dedham, Mass. Pedigree as follows: Silvanus[8], (Amherst[7], Silvanus[6], Peter[5], William[4],

Silvanus Hayward.

Jonathan³, William², William¹). His mother, Sarah Fish, was grand-daughter of the Rev. Elisha Fish, of Upton, Mass., and was first cousin to W. C. Bryant, the poet; and, in one of her lines of descent, goes back to the famous John Alden.

2 —— Gilsum, under the tuition of the Rev. James Tisdale.

3 —— Harriot Elvira Eaton, of Middleboro, Mass., Nov. 23, 1853, by Rev. Lorenzo Tandy. She was b. April 6, 1829, in Middleboro, the dau. of Ziba, and Jedidah (Washburn) Eaton; Ziba⁶, (Nathan⁵, Barnabas⁴, Samuel³, Francis², Francis¹); Francis¹ Eaton being of the "May-"flower." She d. March 2, 1890, at Globe Village, Mass., in her 61st year. He was m., second, to Miss Lucy Anna Keays, of Berwick, Me., at South Berwick, Dec. 17, 1891. She was a niece both of Gov. Ichabod Goodwin and of Rev. Daniel R. Goodwin, D. D., Provost of the University of Pennsylvania.

The "York Courant" represents her to have been "one of the most estimable and popular ladies in "his old parish; descended from one of the oldest "families in Maine, residing on an estate which has "been handed down through seven generations," and is still in her possession.

4 —— I. ARTHUR JAMESON, b. Sept. 14, 1854, in Francestown, N. H.; d. Sept. 12, 1855, aged one year, less two days, at Middleboro, Mass.

II. BELL, b. July 1, 1856, in Francestown.

III. GRACE, b. Aug. 27, 1858, at Pembroke, N. H.

IV. Paul, b. Oct. 16, 1863, in Dunbarton, N. H.; d. in South Berwick, Me., Aug. 28, 1873, aged 9 years and 10 months.

V. John Stark, b. Nov. 28, 1866, in South Berwick, and there d. Aug. 18, 1873, aged 6 years and 8 months.

He was Principal of the academy at Francestown, N. H., from graduation till July, 1856; a similar situation at McIndoe's Falls (Barnet), Vt., till May, 1858. Next taught the academy at Pembroke, N. H., for one year; was teacher at the Kimball Union Academy, Meriden, N. H., during the summer and fall terms of 1859, and the spring term of 1860; and in April, 1860, removed to New Ipswich, N. H., to assist E. T. Quimby (D. C., 1851), in the Appleton Academy. Had been studying for the ministry, in private and without assistance, especially during the previous winter, while out of employment in Meriden, and was approbated as a preacher by the Hollis Association at Amherst, N. H., in May, 1860; after which he supplied the pulpit of the Second Cong. Church in N. I., till Jan., 1861, when the two churches were united. His labors as teacher there closed with the summer of 1861. In Sept. of the same year he accepted a call to the First Cong. Church in Dunbarton, N. H., and was ordained and installed Oct. 9, 1861, our old instructor, Prof. S. G. Brown, D. D., of Dart. College, preaching the sermon from 2d Cor. 4:16-18.

Was dismissed from Dunbarton April 8, 1866—though in the face of an increased salary, on the part of his people there—and installed at South Berwick, Me., in May, 1866. Dismissed from South Berwick April 12, 1873, on account of impaired health and for needed rest; and accepted the professorship of mathematics in the Fisk University, Nashville, Tenn., where he remained two years, from Nov., 1873.

Returning to his native town, in Nov., 1875, he was pastor of the Cong. Church there four years; meanwhile writing and publishing the "History of "Gilsum," and residing in Keene one year while reading his proof.

From Jan. 1, 1881, to the present, has been the highly esteemed and successful pastor of the "Evangelical Free Church" in Globe Village, Southbridge, Mass., where also he has served ten years as Chairman of the Board of Education for the town.

He held the office of County Commissioner for common schools, in Merrimack Co., N. H., during the years 1864-65. Was on the Examining Committee at Dartmouth, July, 1865, and once afterwards; also at the Bangor Theological Seminary, in July, 1867, and at Andover Seminary on a similar errand.

His name also appears in the August No. of the "Hartford Sem. Record" (1894), as one of the three years' Examining Committee at the Seminary; he being a member of the "Pastoral Union.'

His first publication was (1) a sermon, "Liberty— "of God," by invitation of his people at Dunbarton, 1863.

To this have been added the following:

(2) "Creeds, as a test of Fellowship among "Christians." Cong. Quarterly, Oct., 1866.

(3) Address at dedication of Masonic Lodge, Lyman, Me., 1872.

(4) Address at Centennial Celebration of the Cong. Church in Gilsum, Oct. 28, 1872; pamphlet with appendix, 63 pp., 1873.

(5) Paper on the National Cong. Council at Oberlin, O., at the General Conference of Maine, 1873.

(6) "The History of Gilsum, N. H.," printed by J. B. Clarke & Co., of Manchester, one of the most elaborate and complete town histories in the country, pp. 468, 1881.

(7) "A Pointed Sermon on Current Events" (Isa. 26:9) ; Southbridge paper, 1883.

(8) Obituary sketch of our class-mate McDuffee, admirably written in the ornate "History of Straf-"ford County, N. H.," 1883.

(9) "Temperance in its Relation to the Family, "the Church and the State"; a sermon from Matt. 3:10; twice repeated and then published by request in the "Southbridge Herald," April 21, 1887; also as a broadside.

(10) "The History of Rochester, N. H.," by Franklin McDuffee, Esq., edited, revised and in part written by himself, pp. 688; 2 vols., 1892.

(11) A poetical "Memorial Address," entitled "Freedom," before the Malcolm Ammidown Post, No. 168, G. A. R., at town hall, Southbridge, May 30, 1892, pamphlet, 26 pp.

(12) "The King's Daughter;" a sermon preached by request, June 4, 1893, and expensively printed. Text: Psalm 45:15; pp. 18.

Besides the above, there were printed in the "Southbridge Journal," by request:

(13) A sermon from Jer. 51:27, before the G. A. R. Post of that place, about the year 1889. Also in the same paper, (14) a sermon on Marriage, preached June 28, 1891, from Genesis 2:18; entitled by the editor, "A Pastor's Tribute to Woman "and Advice to Young Men."

(15) His address before the graduating class of the Woodstock, Ct., Academy, June 15, 1894, has been fully published in the "Putnam Patriot."

(16) Sermon, "The Signs of the Times" (Matt. 16:3); preached July 15 and 22, 1894; pamphlet, 34 pp.

"The Schools of Misertown," a satirical poem, and also his Dart. poem of 1870, were delivered in various places.

His poems at the anniversary of the Literary Societies, Dart. Commencement, 1870 (just alluded to), and at the Alumni Dinner, Com., 1893, were not printed; but a poem read at an anniversary dinner of Andover Theological Seminary, and another (one of his best) on the occasion of the Class Secretary's silver wedding (1886) were both published.

For his poems at our 25th and 40th class anniversaries, see reports of those meetings.

His dau., (II) BELL, his only surviving child, makes it her home with her father; received a diploma for reading the "Chautauqua Course," in the first class,—the "Pioneers."

III. GRACE fitted for college at the K. U. Acad., Meriden, finishing her course there in 1877, and graduated from Smith College, Northampton, Mass., in 1885.

We take the following from the Springfield (Mass.) High School "Recorder" of March, 1891:

"We learn, with the deepest sorrow, of the death "of Miss Grace Hayward, a former teacher of the "High School. * * She first taught at the "Hitchcock Free High School, at Brimfield, and "afterwards came to Springfield. Here she soon "became known in the educational circles for her "ability as a teacher; and it is only right to say "that there was not a scholar in the school who "did not admire and esteem her. But after teaching "two years with the greatest success, she was "obliged to resign on account of poor health. She "went to Colorado, hoping the change of climate "would prove beneficial, but after staying six "months returned home much weaker. After a "year of suffering, she died of consumption, at her "home," Feb. 23, 1891, in her thirty-third year.

HOLLENBUSH, CALVIN GROSS, *,

NEW BERLIN, PA.

1 —— Freeburg, Snyder Co., Pa., Aug. 24, 1830. His parents' names were originally, John H., and Sarah (Gross) Hilbish; his grandparents, Peter and Susannah (Schell) Hilbish, his patronymic being changed to Hollenbush in his early childhood.

2 —— Tuscarora Acad., Juniata Co., Pa., under David Wilson; entering Dart. College, Feb., 1851.

This sketch will be mostly a reprint from the former "Class Memorial." He commenced the study of medicine in the office of his brother, at Freeburg, Sept., 1853, and continued for one year, when he went to Philadelphia to attend medical lectures, at the same time entering Prof. Gilbert's office, as a private pupil. Grad. from the Penn. Medical College, in March, 1856. The first of April following, Dr. Hollenbush entered Blockley Hospital, as assistant physician, being one of six elected out of twelve or fifteen applicants. In Nov. of the same year he was examined before the Army Board in St. Louis, Mo., for the position of surgeon, there being 22 candidates, of whom two passed a satisfactory examination, himself and Dr. Taylor of Philadelphia. Was ordered to California in March, 1857, and sent to a post in the extreme north of the state,—Fort Crook, Shasta County. Here, remaining three years, he contracted laryngeal phthisis, and in May, 1860, returned home on sick-leave. Consulted Dr. Horace Greene of New York City, and in October following repaired to Magnolia, Fla., for the winter. In March, 1861, sick-leave having expired, he reported health better and able to go to the assistance of another surgeon. Accordingly ordered to Fort Pickens, Fla., at that time garrisoned by 70 men, all told. Quoting from his letter: "We are in "constant fear of an attack from the enemy. Three "times, since I came here, have I been roused up, "between midnight and morning, by the hurried "beating of the 'long roll', and the cry 'To arms!' "But it turned out, each time, to be a false alarm. "We have more cannon than men, and now every "man has charge of a piece loaded with 'grape' and "ready to touch off. I shall, during the fight, "throw aside my profession, and take charge of the "case-mate guns."

In May, 1861, after the reinforcement of Fort Pickens, he was ordered to Governor's Island, N. Y., where he remained till the first of August; his health still feeble, and his disease upon him, though permitting him to walk or ride out.

On that day (Aug. 1) he started from New York to go to his old home at Freeburg. Arrived at his brother's house, the same evening, and there breathed his last, on Tuesday, Aug. 6, 1861, at the age of nearly 31 years.

His mind was sound till the last moment. His mortal remains are now reposing beside those of his parents, in the old church yard at Freeburg.

From the time of his uniting with the church at

Hanover, our senior year, he was known to his room-mate (now the Class Secretary) and to all his friends, both in college and afterwards, as a humble, devoted and remarkably conscientious Christian. While residing in Philadelphia he was a worthy member of the Rev. Dr. Boardman's church, and active in the Sunday School enterprise; and, to the last, none of his friends had ever a doubt as to the sincerity of his piety, and the consistency of his life. His eminent medical career—though brief—his unflinching patriotism, and his perseverance to the end, while baffled by the discouragements of disease, are worthy of notice. Yet, while he expressed himself, in his last hours, as ready and willing to die, he also regretted that he had not chosen the ministry for his profession, thinking that he thus might have been more useful in the cause of Christ, and have served *Him* more faithfully.

His sister, Sarah S., it may be remembered, was present at our graduation, 41 years ago. She afterwards married George Merrill, and now resides in "Abilene, Dickinson Co., Kansas."

Her youngest son is a worthy and promising young man, but greatly needing a little aid just now, for the completing of his education. If any of our class-brotherhood, who are blessed with abundant means should feel moved to confer with Mrs. Merrill very soon (address as above), with a view to assisting this nephew of our beloved *classmate*, we should, in a pleasing and effective manner, be doing honor to *his memory*.

HOWARD, WILLIAM WALLACE, *,

JAMAICA, VT.

1 —— Jamaica, Dec. 31, 1827. His parents were Nahum and Sophia (Howard) Howard; being, before marriage, only distantly, if at all, related.

2 —— Townshend, Vt., under Moses Lyford, A. M., and at Thetford, Vt., under Hiram Orcutt.

3 —— Mary A. B. Pollard, of Plymouth, Vt., Aug. 3, 1853, by the Rev. Thomas Baldwin. She was b. April 13, 1830, in Plymouth. Her father was Amos Boynton Pollard, and her mother's maiden name, Mary Ann Brown.

4 —— I. CLARA POLLARD, b. June 11, 1854, at Plymouth.

II. FRANK, b. Jan. 30, 1856, at Plymouth.

III. ERNEST, b. March 20, 1860, at Windsor, Vt.

IV. MARY ANN, b. March 5, 1864, at Windsor.

He taught the West Randolph (Vt.) Academy two terms, 1853 and '54; also the fall term of 1854 in Black River Acad. at Ludlow, Vt., as assistant.

Commenced the study of Law in the winter of 1854 and '55, in the office of Converse & Barrett, Woodstock, Vt., and was admitted to the bar, at the Dec. term of court, 1856.

Commenced the practice of his profession Feb., 1857, in partnership with ex-Gov. Coolidge, at Windsor, Vt., and continued thus about two years, when the partnership was dissolved; though it may be added that the warmest friendship existed between them, as long as Mr. Howard lived; so much so, that they each had a key to the other's office.

Continuing in practice by himself, in Windsor, he was elected, on the 1st of Jan., 1858, treasurer of the Windsor Savings Bank, which office, as also that of First Selectman for the town, he held at the time of his death. Besides these, he had holden various offices in the Cong. church and society, the corporation, the town and other societies.

His health remained excellent, until the evening of Jan. 1, 1864, when he was taken with chills. The disease soon settled on the brain, and he continued to fail until half-past one of the morning of Jan. 6,—not probably at all realizing his situation; but having previously given his friends great reason for the assurance that for him to die was gain. His age was 36 years and 6 days.

The "Aurora of the Valley," a paper published in Windsor, contained the following notices:

"It is with sadness that we record the sudden "death of William W. Howard, Esq., of Windsor; "a man of moral worth and esteem, and who had "been growing into a good professional business, "as a lawyer. He was attacked with congestion "of the brain on Friday night, and expired last "Tuesday night, Jan. 5, 1864. During the seven "years of his residence here, he has maintained the "character of an upright, laborious and Christian "lawyer. We have occasion to know that he "possessed the respect and confidence of the leading

"members of the bar, and was regarded as a rising
"man in his profession. We are glad to bear tes-
"timony to the integrity which controlled his busi-
"ness transactions. He was far above that lax
"standard of morality, which obtains, we will not
"say in his profession, but too generally, in all
"business relations. He had connected himself
"with the general interests of our village; had ren-
"dered important service in directing our village
"schools, and did much to promote the best inter-
"ests of the community. He was an active mem-
"ber of the Cong. church and society—having
"first made profession of his faith in Christ at
"West Randolph, in 1853—and, by his consistent
"life and efforts, rendered valuable aid in strength-
"ening the religious interests of the town. His
"premature death in the full maturity of his powers
"and of his usefulness, is felt to be a public ca-
"lamity."

His mortal remains were interred in the cemetery of Windsor village, near the Cong. house of
worship.

Mrs. Howard was residing at Adrian, Mich., in
Dec., 1878, and in her letter of that date, acknowledged her gratitude to the class for their interest in her family and, "thanks to the Secretary
for expressing it."

I. Clara P., the oldest "child," of our class,
had graduated from the Adrian High School,
June, 1876, and had been, for two years, a clerk in
the Adrian post-office.

II. Frank was completing his law studies in

CALIFORNIA

REV. C. B. HULBERT, D. D.

Adrian, expecting to be admitted to the bar in about six months (Jan., 1879). He had twice made the journey from southwestern Texas on horseback; first, at the age of 16, alone, to Carthage, Mo.; the last time (1878) extending his trip to Bismarck, Dakota.

III. ERNEST, having served two years' apprenticeship in a printing office, had just entered the Preparatory Department of Oberlin (Ohio) College with the ministry in view.

IV. MARY A., then in the Adrian High School, was a fine musician, and designing to fit herself for a music teacher.

Later intelligence from the family, though solicited, has not been received.

HULBERT, CALVIN BUTLER,

EAST SHELDON, VT.

1 —— East Sheldon, Oct. 18, 1827. His pedigree, so far as established, is Calvin B.[4], Chauncey[3], Samuel[2], Elisha[1]; the last named his great-grandfather, having resided in Canaan, Conn. His mother was Charlotte, dau. of Joseph Munsell, of Swanton, Vt.

2 —— Bakersfield, Vt., under the instruction of Jacob S. Spaulding, LL. D.; also at Thetford, Vt., under Prin. Hiram Orcutt, LL. D.

3 —— Mary Elizabeth Woodward, at her residence, Sandwich Centre, N. H., Aug. 28, 1854, by Rev. J. W. Guernsey, pastor of the M. E. church.

Her father was Rev. Henry Woodward (D. C., 1815), missionary in Ceylon, and his father, Prof. Bezaleel Woodward, who was connected with Dart. College, as tutor, 1770-78, and Professor of Mathematics and Natural Philosophy, 1782-1804. Her grandmother (wife of Prof. B. W.) was Mary, dau. of President Wheelock. She was born Sept. 21, 1833, in Batticotta, Ceylon, India. Her mother's maiden name (afterwards Mrs. Henry Woodward) was Clarissa Emerson, dau. of Capt. John Emerson, of Chester, N. H., and sister of Rev. John Emerson, of the Sandwich Islands Mission. She was brought up by her aunt and foster mother, Betsey Emerson, the wife of Hon. Daniel Hoit, of Sandwich Center, where they were m. as above.

4 —— I. MARY ELIZABETH, b. Oct. 16, 1855, in Sheldon, Vt.

II. HENRY WOODWARD, b. Jan. 26, 1858, in Sheldon.

III. ELLA GERTRUDE, b. March 25, 1861, in New Haven, Vt.

IV. HOMER BEZALEEL, b. Jan. 26, 1863, in New Haven.

V. ARCHER BUTLER, b. Jan. 26, 1873, in Bennington, Vt.

VI. ANNE WHEELOCK, b. July 23, 1877, in Middlebury, Vt.

It will be noticed that his three boys were born on the same day of the same month—"a stroke of "ministerial economy," as he supposes, "to save "birthday celebrations."

After graduating, he had charge of the Swanton (Vt.) Acad. for one year; and in August, 1854, accepted an offer of the Franklin Co. Grammar School, at St. Albans, Vt., in which he remained two years.

Entered Andover Theological Seminary Oct., 1856, and graduated thence in 1859. Was licensed to preach by the Derry (N. H.) Association, Feb. 1, 1859. Ordained and settled over the Cong. Church at New Haven, Vt., Oct. 20, 1859, "an ex-"cellent parish, and pleasantly situated in every "respect," where his labors were signally blessed, 170 uniting with the church by profession in 10 years. His labors here closed with the year 1869, and Jan. 19, 1870, he was installed over the Belleville Avenue Cong. Church, Newark, N. J., Rev. Ray Palmer, D. D., being moderator of the council, and Rev. J. E. Rankin, D. D., preaching the sermon. He continued in this field two years and four months—years of great service to himself—when he was recalled to Vermont and installed pastor of the Second Cong. Church in Bennington, May 1, 1872. Having some years been a trustee of Middlebury College, he was next called to the Presidency, and inaugurated July 21, 1875, his pastorate in Bennington finally closing the first Sabbath of September in the same year. Resigning the office of President at Middlebury, in 1880, he supplied the First Cong. Church in Dover, N. H., during the pastor's absence. Was acting pastor of the Cong. Church in Lyndonville, Vt., from 1881 till 1887, and, after temporary residences in

Hartford, Conn., and New York City, succeeded his son-in-law, the Rev. E. E. Rogers, at East Hardwick, Vt., for two years and four months, till April, 1890, when he removed to Zanesville, Ohio. In the spring of 1891 he took his son Henry's place, while in Europe, as teacher of English Literature, in Marietta College, Ohio. In Sept., 1891, he began, with improved voice, to supply the pulpit of the Madison Presbyterian Church, at Adams Mills, town of Cass, Ohio, a niece of the Hon. Lewis Cass being one of its leading supporters. Was there installed its following June, and still continues (1894).

He was honored with the degree of S. T. D. from Dart. College in 1876.

Dr. Hulbert is blessed with an iron constitution, and with the single exception of impaired voice for awhile, has enjoyed, with Mrs. H., most excellent health. He has given many lectures and addresses, largely in Vermont, and in other states, which have been well received.

Among his numerous publications the Secretary finds the following, noted in the class book:

Inaugural address at Middlebury, 1875.

"God not Altogether like Ourselves" (Ps., 50:21); Baccalaureate sermon, 1876.

"The Academy; Demands for It, and the Con-"ditions of its Success;" an address delivered at the reunion and anniversary of Barre (Vt.) Acad., June, 1877; pamphlet, 29 pp.

"The Sword Sheathed, or the Service of the "Sanctuary, the Defence of the State;" a discourse at Windsor, Vt., July 8, 1877, at the 100th anniversary of the adoption of the name and constitution of the State, in volume of centennial addresses.

"What is Involved in a Preparation for College;" address before the societies of Kimball Union Acad., June 19, 1878; pamphlet, 20 pp.

"Christ, the Harmony of the Doctrines," and "The Unity of the Race;" bac. sermons, at Middlebury College for 1877 and '78, published by the liberality of L. M. Bates, of New York, 1879; pamphlet, 46 pp.

One of his lectures, "The Distinctive Idea in "Education," which has had a large sale, was published by J. B. Alden, New York City.

Besides the above, Bro. H. has written often for the "Vermont Chronicle," "The Religious "Herald," "The Interior," etc. His most important contributions have appeared in the "Homi-"letic Review." One article was published in the "New Englander and Yale Review" (Jan., 1892), "Abolitionists and Prohibitionists, or Moral Re-"form Embarrassed by Ultraism."

He modestly desires the Secretary to suppress from this sketch the titles of twelve other published productions, mostly sermons, and all able ones, which are also found on the class records; while all his articles, including sermons not here enumerated, number at least 77 in different periodicals and newspapers, two as leading editorials in the "New York Observer" and "The Interior," and one of his latest being in the Hartford, Ct., "Re-

"ligious Herald," of Aug. 30, 1894, on "The "Nature and Power of Faith in Christian Experi- "ence."

I. MARY E. entered Wellesley College, and afterwards pursued elective studies in Smith. Was m. to Rev. Edwin E. Rogers, who graduated at Middlebury College (class 1878) and Union Theological Seminary, New York City, 1881. Preached at Hammonton, N. J., New York City (Allen St. Pres. Church), East Hardwick, Vt., Covenant Chapel, New York City, and was installed pastor of the Putnam Pres. Church, Zanesville, Ohio, Nov., 1889. Two weeks before leaving New York City for Zanesville their only child, Olive Rogers, (born Nov. 1, 1886) fell from a fifth story window and was instantly killed. This sad bereavement was one of the occasions that induced Bro. H. to remove to Zanesville.

II. HENRY W. grad. from Middlebury College 1879. Spent a year in England, and under direction of the Bureau of Education at Washington, prepared a pamphlet on "Rural Schools in England." Taught a year at Mechanicsville, N. Y.; was instructor a year in Middlebury College; entered Union Theological Seminary, New York City, and graduated 1885; spent three years as instructor in the Protestant Syrian College at Beirut, Syria; in 1888 was elected Professor of Political Science and History in Marrietta College, Ohio, where he still teaches. For the present year (1894-5) he is granted leave of absence to teach in the chair of Church History in Lane Theological Seminary.

March 31, 1891, he m. Lily L. Pinnio, Newark, N. J. It was during his wedding tour in Europe that his father occupied his place in the College. Children: (1) Winnifred, b. July 4, 1892; (2) Chauncey Pinnio, b. Jan. 21, 1894.

III. ELLA GERTRUDE, grad. St. Johnsbury Academy 1882, and from Smith College 1886; taught two years in Wheaton College, Wheaton, Ill.; was at the head of the ladies' department in Mr. Moody's Bible Institute in Chicago, Ill., one year, and then in similar service at his school in Northfield, Mass., till her marriage to Rev. Edgar B. Wylie, May 7, 1891, who is now installed pastor of the Cong. Church at Summerdale, Ill. Mr. W. was born in Rochester, N. H., and a grad. of Wheaton College and at the Chicago Cong. Theological Seminary. Child: (1) Margaret Wylie, b. Feb. 26, 1892.

IV. HOMER BEZALEEL, grad. Dartmouth College, 1884. Was two years in the Union Theological Seminary, New York City. With two others he accepted an appointment to organize a Government school in Seoul, Korea. Having served two years, he renewed an engagement for three years more. On this renewal he returned home and m. May Belle Hanna, of New York City, Sept. 18, 1888. In a few weeks they started for Korea. Completing his three years' term of service, he re-engaged with increased compensation, but embarrassed by some official interferences he soon sought release from his engagement. They returned, via India and Europe, in the spring

of 1892. For the year following they resided
with Mr. and Mrs. Rogers at Zanesville, and
taught in the Putnam Military Academy, which
Mr. and Mrs. Rogers had established. But they
were not content, and both felt that their work
was in Korea. There was no Cong. Mission in
Korea, and having formed pleasant acquaintances among the Methodist missionaries, they accepted service under the Methodist board, and in
the autumn of 1893 went on their way. Their
work thus far has been delightful. He preaches
with facility in the Korean language. In a volume,
"Geography and Gazetteer of the World," he
has given to Koreans, in their language, a condensed
history of the civilized nations. Will send a copy
of this vol. to the Dart. Library. Children: (1)
Helen, b. March 17, 1891; (2) Madelina, b. June
1, 1894, both in Seoul, Korea.

V. ARCHER BUTLER is now a senior in Marietta College, Ohio.

VI. ANNE WHEELOCK has been, the past year,
in Mr. Moody's School for Ladies, East Northfield, Mass., and expects to return this autumn
(1894).

Our class-mate has had eight grandchildren, five
of whom are living as above.

HUTCHINSON, JOHN, *,

WEST RANDOLPH, VT.

1 —— Randolph, Vt., March 27, 1830. His father was James Hutchinson, of West Randolph; his mother, before marriage, Sophia Brown.

2 —— West Randolph Acad., under F. U. Powers, A. M., and passed his Freshman year in the Vermont University at Burlington, Vt.

3 —— Lydia A. Fowler, Oct. 1, 1857, at New London, Ct., her native place being Lansingburg, N. Y.

4 —— I. MARY ESTELLE, b. Jan. 5, 1860, in Minneapolis, Minn.

II. A dau. b. 1867, in Leghorn, Italy.

He commenced studying law, Aug. 15, 1853, under the instruction of Hon. Wm. H. Seward, in Auburn, N. Y. In March, 1854, went to Madison, Wis., and finished his law course in the office of Orton, Atwood & Orton. Was admitted to the bar, June 20, 1854. Began practice in Lawrence, Kansas Territory, Sept. of the same year, and in March, 1855, was elected a member of the first Kansas Legislature, in which he declared himself in favor of making Kansas a free state, and for this was violently assailed by pro-slavery members, and after a few days expelled.

Before leaving, he made a speech which was published in the Kansas papers, vindicating his right to a seat, and totally protesting against such unlawful and outrageous proceedings as were being inaugurated in the Territory. He stood armed in the midst of the members who were brandishing revolvers and making threats, believing that he was advocating the cause of liberty and defending the Constitution of his country. In 1855 he was one of the first to move in the formation of a state government, and after a constitution had been adopted, was elected a member of the Legislature and made Speaker of the same. In the fall and winter of 1855-6, he was sent by the Executive Committee of Kansas to the New England States for the purpose of advocating, before their Legislatures the admission of Kansas into the Union. Addressed the legislative bodies of Maine, Vermont and New York, and spoke for three months in New England and New York. In the autumn of 1856 he stumped portions of Iowa, Illinois, Indiana and Ohio, in favor of John C. Fremont, making, in all, sixty-three speeches. During his residence in Kansas he was twice arrested for treason, and when Lawrence was sacked in 1856, his office was pillaged, his college autograph book stolen, and his diploma cut into pieces. He remained in Lawrence till Dec., 1858, when, on account of ill-health, he left Kansas and located in Minnesota, opening a law office at Minneapolis, and there continuing for two years. When President Lincoln was elected (his first term), by Mr. Seward's invitation he went to Washington and was appointed Secretary of Dacotah Territory, March 27, 1861. Soon after this the Governor of the Territory resigned, and till the end of his term, in 1865, Mr. Hutchinson was acting Governor.

The territorial difficulties which led to the resignation of the Governor, brought him into close personal relations with the President, and he was accordingly appointed U. S. Consul to Leghorn, Italy, early in 1865, though his successor to the Secretaryship of Dakota was not confirmed by the Senate till "Jan. 10, 1866." He resided in Italy, with his family, four years, or till 1869; "and they "were happy years." He reported to us from Leghorn, May 24, 1869, and again from Chicago, Ill., June 18, 1878, when he was of the firm "Hutchin-"son & Hinds" (Theodore F. Hinds, Esq.), attorneys-at-law, 79 Dearborn St.

He was, in Chicago, an exemplary member of Trinity Episcopal Church, and prominent in the Lakeside Masonic Lodge.

His death was caused by an obscure complicated disease of the liver, which baffled all the efforts of his physicians, and occurred at his residence, 3143 Indiana ave., at one o'clock in the morning of Dec. 12, 1887, at the age of 57 years and 8 months.

The Chicago "Inter Ocean" of Dec., 1887, in noticing his death, adds to the above statements, that, while a student, "he contracted a life-long "friendship" with the Hon. Wm. H. Seward; that he was sent to the Eastern States to advocate the claims of Kansas "before Congress," as well as the State Legislatures; and that he "made speeches "through the Northern States during both the "Presidential campaigns of 1856 and of 1860."

The following supplementary account is from the pen of J. F. Nichols, Esq., who, for more than

twenty years, was on terms of the closest intimacy
with Mr. Hutchinson.

"Since 1870 he has been a prominent member
"of the Chicago Bar. As a man of sound
"judgment, and a successful advocate, he won
"the respect and esteem of all his judicial
"associates. As a citizen, he was representa-
"tive of all that constitutes the highest qual-
"ities of American citizenship. * * As a
"friend, he was kind and genial, beloved by all
"who intimately knew him. His life was of the
"utmost purity. No word ever escaped his lips
"that could cause a blush upon the cheek of purest
"innocence. In his family, he was a model hus-
"band and father. The failing health of his elder
"daughter—(I) the dear Estelle—in the spring of
"1884, induced the mother and two daughters to
"go to Europe, where Estelle died in Paris, in
"May, 1885, at the age of 25 years. She was
"richly gifted and accomplished in a wide range of
"scholarly attainments. A brief two and a half
"years later, and the father followed the be-
"loved child. During this time, his perturbed
"spirit sometimes questioned as to the verities of
"the future life. But it would seem that all these
"questionings were solved in the vision of glory in
"which his spirit took its flight; his last words
"being, as his look seemed to penetrate within the
"veil, 'And this is death; this is Heaven; I see
" 'God; I see Jesus; I see Estelle. Heaven!
" 'Heaven! Heaven!!' and he was no more with us.
" 'So He giveth His beloved sleep.' He lies by the

"side of his cherished Estelle, in the beautiful
"Oakwood Cemetery of this city."
(The above bears date, Chicago, Jan. 29, 1888.)

ISHAM, JAMES WILLARD, *, N. G.,
NEW ALSTEAD, N. H.

1 —— New Alstead, March 12, 1825. His parents were Dea. James Fuller, and Harriet (Wood) Isham. His pedigree: James W.[6], James F.[5], Joshua[4], Timothy[3], Isaac[2], ——[1]. Name of his immigrant ancestor not known; came from England and settled in Barnstable, Mass., having three sons, Isaac[2], John and Joseph.

2 —— Meriden, N. H., under C. S. Richards, A. M.

3 —— Mrs. Henrietta E. Potter, at New Orleans, La., April 10, 1854. She was a native of London, England, the dau. of William Gardner, and Lucy Ann (Wills) Evans. Was a widow at her second marriage, having m., first, Lyman Potter, Esq., a lawyer in New Orleans.

4 —— I. ALMA, b. Jan. 14, 1855, in New Orleans.

After leaving college, at the end of our first year, he was principal of a public school in the Fourth District in New Orleans; also teacher of vocal music. He there d. of yellow fever, Aug. 4, 1855, after a short illness of three days, aged 30 years and 5 months.

It was a source of grief to his friends, in 1864,

that his remains were still there, and not where he
so often expressed a wish that his body should lie,
beside his brother's, in the little quiet burying
ground of his native place. Mrs. Isham, in Jan.,
1864, was a teacher in Brooklyn, N. Y., 143
Columbia St.; and Alma, described as a frail, delicate child, yet best suited in health by the climate
of New Hampshire, was passing most of her time
with her grandfather in New (East) Alstead.

Mrs. Isham also reported from East Alstead, as
her home, under date of Aug. 16, 1878. She says:
"Many thanks for your kind remembrances of my
"husband; also for the interest expressed for
"Alma." She was m. to J. Thompson Hirst, of
Titusville Penn., Sept. 4, 1877, and there still resides with her mother; where also her father's
brother, J. Henry Isham, was then established as a
jeweler; now of Duluth, Minn.

Though our class-mate was with us but a single
year, yet his pale countenance, earnest expression
and genial manners, can never be forgotten by our
Freshman band. The Secretary, on spending a
few weeks at East Alstead, in 1889, found that all
living traces of the Isham family had disappeared
from that place.

KENDALL, JOHN, *,

WASHINGTON, D. C.

1 —— Frankfort, Ky., April 17, 1832, his father being the Hon. Amos Kendall (D. C., 1811), who was U. S. Postmaster-General 1835-40, and resided many years in Washington, D. C. His grandparents were Dea. Zebedee and Molly (Dakin) Kendall, of Dunstable, Mass. His mother was his father's second wife—Jane, the dau. of Hon. Alexander Kyle, of Kentucky.

2 —— Washington, under Mr. Joseph Perry (D. C., 1811).

3 —— Elizabeth Lawrence Green, of Groton, Mass., Oct. 5, 1854.

He resided at Washington in the position of Telegraph Superintendent; and there d., of typhoid fever, Dec. 7, 1861, in his 30th year.

From his earliest youth he had been habituated to the best society of our country, as found in Washington; and, from his father's political associations, was early brought in contact with public men and affairs.

When he entered college, and all through his course, as will be recollected, he was noted for his quiet reserve, not growing out of the natural diffidence and inexperience which affect most young men, but from a kind of exclusiveness peculiar to himself, and induced by his habits and education, which led him to make but few friends and not to care for many. His mind was acute and refined; he learned quickly and expressed his acquirements gracefully and pointedly. Had he been poor, or subject to the incentives and spurs by which many young men are stimulated, who have only themselves to depend upon for success, he would have stood high and made his mark.

He excelled in conversational powers, and had the ability of making himself very agreeable, and of adapting himself skillfully to all whom he desired to please or influence. During his Junior winter he went to the southwest to look after some property and lands owned by his father in Arkansas. He assumed in the matter an important responsibility, and showed in his management fine business talent and executive ability. This would seem to have directed his attention to a business, rather than a professional life, and soon after graduating he embarked upon the telegraph business, as his life pursuit. Spent some time in the south and west, but afterwards had his headquarters in New York City, being engaged as superintendent of the lines between Washington and New York, and, probably, between Washington and Boston. The position was an important one. He received a large salary, was very successful in his management, and was looked upon with respect, as well fitted for his position. Afterwards took up his residence in Washington, as above stated. He devoted himself to his business, and was personally engaged in many experiments, tending to enlarge the science of telegraphing, and develop that great channel of enterprise. Had he lived he would, no doubt, have become eventually, one of the leading telegraph men in the country. For considerable time before his death he was in poor health, with symptoms of pulmonary disease, and was evidently fearing a fatal result.

It is said on the records that the above is substantially from the pen of an intimate friend; that friend, we may now add, is our class-mate, Washburn.

KENDRICK, CALEB CHANDLER, *, N. G., BEDFORD, N. H.

1 —— Nashua, N. H., March 14, 1832. His father's name was Caleb Kendrick; his mother's, Sally Chandler, she being the dau. of Thomas and Susannah Chandler, of Bedford.

2 —— Francestown, N. H.; two terms at Pembroke, N. H., and the remainder under the instruction of Mr. Charles Tenney (D. C., 1835), at Gilmanton, N. H.

His "own mother" dying April 21, 1832, and his father the 18th of September following, he was thus left an orphan at the very beginning of life. His last winter was spent in the law office of Samuel H. and B. F. Ayer, Esqs., at Manchester, N. H. During the last vacation of his college course, he died, May 26, 1853, after a short illness, at the homestead of his great-grandfather Chandler, in Bedford, which had been the home of his childhood and youth, after the first year of his infancy. His demise was a severe stroke to his parents (by adoption), and all his other relatives, who justly thought that "his mental faculties, su-"perior scholarship and acquired attainments, "coupled with correct deportment and an amiable "disposition, were sufficient sureties that he would "make at least a respected and useful man in the "world."

His mortal remains are now reposing beside those of his father and mother at Nashua. Their lot is in the Nashua cemetery, enclosed with a substantial iron fence.

The following resolutions were passed by his class, and a copy sent to his afflicted friends:

"*Resolved*, That whereas death has again come "among us to snatch from our midst the form of "one whom we sincerely loved, we are led to make "this expression of our heart-felt sympathy with "his bereaved relatives, and particularly her whom "he delighted to call by the endearing name of " 'mother,' and to whom he was ardently attached.

"*Resolved*, That though we are deprived of a "respected and noble-minded companion, learning "of a faithful follower, and society of a benefactor, "we are aware that no other love is worthy to be "compared with that of a mother, who is bereaved "of an affectionate son. We feel that there is

" 'No mind that's honest,
" 'But in it shares some woe, though the main
            part,
" 'Pertains to her alone.'

"*Resolved*, That while we most deeply lament "our irreparable loss, by which is taken from the

"world, one whose diligence, genius and integrity,
"we thought would have honored his friends, his
"college and his country, and that while we feel
"the entire inefficiency of human consolation in the
"case of such a dispensation of Providence, we yet
"hope it may prove an alleviating thought, that we
"are able with one mind to bear affectionate testi-
"mony to his many excellent and attractive quali-
"ties—as those for a long time intimately associated
"with him, by a similarity of pursuits and a union
"of sentiments—as those who have uniformly re-
"spected his strength of mind and correctness of
"judgment—and as those who have experienced
"the influence of his manly and ingenuous dis-
"position.

"*Resolved*, That it becomes us to pause in the
"midst of our career, and first learn so to cultivate
"within us those kindly affections and golden prin-
"ciples, that we, also, may live in peace with all the
"world, possess its esteem and die lamented and
"beloved.

"*Resolved*, That as a public testimonial of re-
"spect for the memory of the deceased, and a
"badge of mourning, each member of the class
"wear crape on the left arm for thirty days."

LAMSON, JOHN AUGUSTUS,

TOPSFIELD, MASS.

1 —— Topsfield, March 3, 1831. His father, John Lamson, was the sixth generation, residing in the same homestead. His mother, nee Priscilla Averill (born in Topsfield), was the eighth generation from Governor Thomas and Dorothy Dudley, the seventh from Ann Dudley and Governor Simon Bradstreet.

2 —— Phillips Academy, Andover, Mass.

3 —— Mary Elizabeth Whitcher, Oct. 18, 1876. She was b. in Milton, Mass., Nov. 14, 1849, dau. of the late Hon. Joseph Batchelder Whitcher and nee Barbara Ann Horton.

He began the study of medicine with the late Charles Haddock, M. D., of Beverly, Mass., then entered the Boylston and Tremont Medical Schools, Boston. He grad. March 12, 1856, from the medical department of Harvard University, being one of six who were honored with the privilege of reading their Theses at the Medical Commencement.

Immediately on receiving his medical degree, he was appointed one of the physicians of the "Boston "Dispensary," which office he held for three years. In 1861 he was appointed Examiner for Volunteers by Surgeon-Gen. Dale.

In 1862 he was appointed surgeon of the 42d Regiment, Mass. Volunteers, and went into camp, but resigned his commission before the regiment left for the seat of war on account of impaired

John A. Lamson

health from the exposure of camp life. (All the officers and three companies of this regiment were captured on arriving at Galveston, Texas, and the surgeon who was Dr. Lamson's successor was held in close confinement till released by death). He was immediately re-appointed by Surgeon-Gen. Dale as Examiner for Volunteers, being approved by Gov. Andrew. In 1863 he was appointed Assistant Examining Surgeon under the "Con-"scription Act." This office he held until the end of the "draft." During the war he examined, of volunteers, conscripts and substitutes, more than 12,000 men.

In Sept., 1863, he was appointed the physician, chief in charge, of the "Discharged Soldiers' "Home," from which he resigned four years later, much to the regret of the trustees of the "Home."

He was a member of the Boston School Board ten years, ending 1871; was the chairman of many important committees, among which were those of text books and salaries.

He was elected a member of the State Legislature in 1871; re-elected to the session of 1872, representing the wealthiest ward of the city. 1873 he spent traveling in Europe, visiting many of the hospitals in London, Dublin, Vienna, Paris and Berlin; then extended his trip to Constantinople and the East.

In 1880 he was appointed Chief Medical Examiner of the "Equitable Life Assurance Society" for Boston and Eastern Massachusetts. He has the appointment of all the examiners in the various towns. This society does the largest business of any insurance company in the world, the new business last year exceeding $200,000,000. He retired from general practice in 1893, the "Equitable" furnishing him all the work he desires. Formerly he resided at the West End, but, driven out by the advance of business, last year removed to the Back Bay, the best residential part of the city, his present home and office being at No. 35 Fairfield street.

As our class-mate, for a period of 37 years, until 1893, was in the continuous and successful practice of his profession in Boston, the Secretary suggested that he furnish us some account of the advance in medicine and surgery during these years.

He has sent us an able, though as he claims, "a hastily prepared" paper. We only regret the necessity of abridging it to some extent.

The medical graduate of thirty-eight years ago has great reason to be thankful that his professional life has covered that most interesting period of progress, during which medicine has been passing from the period of theorizing and dogmatism to a rational scientific basis of well ascertained facts. *   *   In the preceding periods advances had been made slowly and at long intervals. Exceptional men had discovered and pointed out the paths which led to true knowledge, but their teachings often had little influence among the mass of their unenlightened contemporaries. Medicine could not develop without a sound basis of anatomy and physiology to rest upon, nor could it advance except in company with the related sciences of chemistry and physics. The unaided senses had to be supplemented by those instruments of precision, the microscope, opthalmoscope, stethoscope, laryngoscope and clinical thermometer. *   * Perhaps there is no department in which, to the popular eye, such rapid advancement has been made as in surgery. The

discovery of the anaesthetic use of ether in 1846, only ten
years before the beginning of the period which we are
considering, gave an immense impetus to the practice
of surgery. Unlike many preceding discoveries, its value
was at once recognized and put to practical use. The
surgeon could now do his work leisurely and unhindered
by the struggles of the patient. Thus more delicate and
complicated operations now came within reach. There
still remained, however, the dread of the tedious and
frequently fatal results of local inflammation or general blood
poisoning to deter the most skillful operator. The discovery
by Lister of the relation of putrefactive organisms to these in-
flammatory processes and the means of their prevention by the
use of antiseptics has given even a greater impetus to surgery
than the discovery of ether. The most daring operations may
now be undertaken with relative safety, provided the patient is
not too much exhausted by disease. To expose the brain, and
the peritoneal cavity, to remove internal and deep-seated
growths or diseased organs is now a common occurrence. But
this power to operate with impunity carries an increased responsibility, and demands mature judgment. There is often a
great temptation to the young surgeon to seek a rapid fame by
doing the most radical operations; and, undoubtedly, important organs, as the ovaries, have too frequently been removed
for slight disease when more faithful and prolonged medical
treatment would have made such mutilation unnecessary. The
more experienced surgeons are now protesting against too
radical and premature operations. * * In comparison
with the well-known progress of surgery it is a common opinion
that the treatment of strictly medical diseases has not made an
equal advance. One reason for this opinion is that the results
of surgery are plainly visible as the operations are done publicly, while medical treatment is more quietly carried on and the
results are concealed from view. In a sense, surgery is largely
a question of mechanics. In doubtful cases, also, an "explor-
"atory incision" can often be made without harm, and the disease exposed to sight and touch. Disorders of function, on the
other hand, are much more complicated, and we can only infer

the nature of the disease from its secondary effects. The greatest progress has been made in discovering the causes of disease, especially of the infectious diseases caused by micro-organisms, such as cholera, typhoid fever, diphtheria, pneumonia and consumption. This knowledge has been of value chiefly in enabling us to prevent the occurrence of these diseases, a much more important matter even than the cure of the disease when established. But an exact understanding of the cause of disease is sure to lead to the discovery of means for its cure, and such discoveries are now only a question of time. In the treatment of many other diseases there has been important, if not very striking, progress. The first steps were discarding the old fashioned blood-letting, and other heroic and meddlesome forms of treatment. We now know the natural history of most diseases when let alone, and that many of them end spontaneously after running a definite, limited course.

The use of the microscope has been of the greatest assistance in studying the course of disease.   *   *   It reveals the evidence of tuberculosis, while all other signs of pulmonary disease are still doubtful. The opthalmoscope, invented by Helmholtz in 1852 has now placed the diagnosis and treatment of visual disorders on a basis of mathematical accuracy. The laryngoscope, introduced in 1857, has made plain the diseases of the organs of speech and their treatment. The perfection of methods of auscultation and percussion has made possible the great modern advances in the diagnosis and progression of diseases of the heart and lungs. And so the story could be continued.

The medical man now uses as many tools as the mechanic, but instead of being labor-saving devices they impose more labor upon him, while the patient reaps the benefit of the more thorough examination. The work of the physician demands patience, industry, accuracy, and, above all, good judgment. Medicine still offers an almost limitless field for research and discovery. The large number of well equipped hospitals and laboratories, with skilled observers, ever ready instantly to confirm or to compute alleged discoveries, make it certain that the progress of the future will be even more rapid

and comprehensive than the progress of the past. * *
Such is a very brief and imperfect outline of the condition and
progress of medicine during the generation now drawing to a
close.

LOVERING, JOHN DUDLEY, *,
CHESTER, N. H.

1 —— Raymond, N. H., March 8, 1827. His
father's name was Gilman [3] Lovering (Theophilus [2],
John Prescott [1]). His mother's name, before marriage, was Sally Stevens.

2 —— Kingston, N. H., under E. G. Dalton,
and at South Berwick, Me., under Aurin M. Payson (D. C., 1840).

3 —— Sarah Hidden Burnham Cogswell, of
Essex, Mass., April 9, 1866, at Manchester, N. H.,
by the Rev. C. W. Wallace, D. D. She was b. at
Hampstead, N. H., the dau. of Humphrey Choate,
and Sally Hidden (Burnham) Cogswell.

After graduating, he had charge, for several
terms, of the Kingston Acad., and in the spring of
1855 visited the West, traveling through Illinois,
Missouri and Kansas Territory. Finally settled in
the town of Bethel, Ill., and commenced the study
of medicine in the office of J. R. Askew, M. D., of
that place. In the fall of 1856 attended his first
course of lectures at the Rush Medical College,
Chicago, Ill.; and in 1857 entered into partnership,
with his instructor, in the practice of medicine
at Bethel.

Being desirous of extending his travels in the

South before a final settlement, he left Illinois in the spring of 1858, passed through Tennessee, Mississippi, Alabama and Georgia, and again entered upon the business of teaching at Eufaula, Ala. Continued in the South as a teacher till 1860, when he returned North. The Secretary had a delightful meeting with him at Chicago, in the fall of that year. They visited together the shore of the lake, when lashed by a furious northeast gale; a most sublime spectacle.

He afterwards attended a second course of lectures at the Albany Medical School, N. Y., and took his degree of M. D. Prevented from returning South, according to previous design, by the rebellion, in the spring of 1861, and finding an eligible location for a physician in the town of Essex, Mass., he there entered immediately upon the practice of his profession, and continued, "with "a good degree of success," for nearly twenty years, till 1880. Thence to 1883, he was reported "in poor health at Manchester, N. H.;" but afterwards resumed practice at Newton Highlands, Mass., till his decease, March 18, 1891, of phthisis, aged 64 years. He left a pleasant home in Newton, and at his funeral—which the Secretary, being Providentially in Boston on that day, took occasion to attend—very commendatory testimonials were given to his worth as a citizen, a physician, a Christian and a husband, by both his pastors, from the Essex and Newton Highlands Congregational churches.

The notice below was in the "Boston Journal"

CALIFORNIA

Frank McDuffee.

of March 19, and first attracted the Secretary's attention:

"Dr. John D. Lovering died, at his residence, in "Newton Highlands, Wednesday, March 18, after "a short illness, though he had been failing in "health for the past year.   *   *   He settled at "Newton Highlands in 1883, where he has since "resided, engaging in a quiet practice, yet winning "esteem and confidence, universally, as a careful "and wise physician, and a most worthy citizen. "A widow survives him, and a twin brother and "sister, residing in the West. The funeral will "take place from his late residence, on Friday, at "3 o'clock, and the burial will be at Essex, Mass."

McDUFFEE, FRANKLIN, *,
ROCHESTER, N. H.

1 —— Dover, N. H., August 27, 1832. His parents were John and Joanna (Hanson) Mc-Duffee, the family being traced to Fyfe McDuff, of Scotland, A. D. 834; his immediate pedigree,— Franklin[5], John[4], John[3], Daniel[2], John[1]; John[1] having been at the Siege of Londonderry.

2 —— The Rochester schools, and Gilmanton (N. H.) Acad., with Charles Tenney.

3 —— Mary Fannie Hayes, of Rochester, Dec. 4, 1861, by Rev. E. H. Richardson (D. C., 1850). She was b. in Milton, N. H., March 26, 1840, being the dau. of John and Sarah (Wingate) Hayes.

4 —— I. JOHN EDGAR, b. Sept. 8, 1863.

II. WILLIS, b. Mar. 15, 1868, in Rochester.

He entered upon the duties of cashier of the new Rochester Bank, Sept. 5, 1854, previously to which time he was in the law office of Hon. Daniel M. Christie at Dover.

Besides his business as cashier, he had a good deal of outside employment, administering upon estates, serving as director in an insurance company, etc. Was Town Superintending School Committee, First Selectman, Town Treasurer, President of the District Senatorial Convention, and for two years (1861 and 1862) Representative from Rochester in the State Legislature. He was a correspondent of the local newspapers; also for the "Boston Journal" and "Evening Traveller." In 1857 he took a pedestrian tour to Hanover and the White Mountains, 225 miles in about ten days. It was on this trip that he lost his way, and night overtook him—a night peculiar to that mountainous region. He was inhumanly denied a shelter from dwellings that he passed, and, as the result of cold and exposure during the whole night, was in feeble health for a long time, and was troubled with impaired hearing through life. For this reason, on leave of absence from business, he took a voyage to London, England, by sailing vessel, in 1858, in company with his brother, J. Randolph McDuffee, who went away the picture of health, but returned feeling poorly, and died of consumption, in May of the following year. Himself was somewhat recruited on returning, after three month's absence, but came very near taking passage upon the ill-fated "Austria" from South Hampton, hundreds of whose passengers were lost by the burning of that steamer. Providentially delayed, he sailed three days later from the same port, arriving in safety.

He was afterwards cashier and treasurer, both of the Norway Plains Savings Bank, and the Rochester National Bank, for some fourteen years, until his death, which occurred Nov. 11, 1880, at the age of 48. About the year 1870 he joined the Cong. Church of Rochester, and two years afterwards was chosen deacon. Though so modest and retiring in his nature, he was looked upon as "the "great power," morally and religiously, among the laymen of the town.

"His untiring efforts for the church, and, best of "all, his sympathies for the poor of earth, won him "true and steadfast friends. Many a five-dollar "note found its way into some needy pocket, the "grateful recipient not knowing, though perhaps "mistrusting sometimes, the generous hand that "gave it. He displayed little fondness for society, "and was not so easy of approach as some less "agreeable to meet. His intimate associates were "few, but to those he became strongly attached. "Flattery was foreign to his nature, but he was "ready to commend a good deed, and assist those "who needed assistance. He was one of the very "best and most entertaining speakers in Strafford "county, whether as a lecturer or in a social meet- "ing. As a writer he wielded a graceful and "truthful pen; his sketches of town history, pub-

"lished in the 'Courier' several years ago, being "models of simplicity, conciseness and fact."

(From the pen, probably, of Class-mate Hayward.)

His "Report of Committee on Uniformity of "Work," presented at the annual meeting of the Grand Masonic Lodge of N. H., June 8, 1864, was published in pamphlet form.

Address, as "Orator of the Day," at a Citizens' Celebration, Rochester, July 4, 1864; published in "Rochester Weekly Courier" of the 8th.

"Sketches of Town History of Rochester, N. H.," in the "Courier," the series having reached the 45th number in 1878. In consideration of these, he was elected a corresponding member of the Maine Historical Society. He was also a member of the N. H. Historical Society, and was invited by the same to publish, in a volume of their transactions, so much of his town history as had then been written.

"Olden Times in Rochester," an address before the "Rochester Social Library Co.," in the Cong. meeting-house, April 4, 1867; published in the "Courier."

Address on Decoration Day, 1870, published, four columns, in the "Rochester Courier and Ad-"vertiser" of June 6.

He also delivered the "Address of Welcome" at the "Twelfth Annual Convention of the Y. M. C. "A's and Evan. Churches of N. H.," at Rochester, Oct. 23–26, 1879.

His great literary work was posthumous; being

"The History of the Town of Rochester, N. H.;"
2 vols., and 32 full-page illustrations, edited and
completed by Rev. S. Hayward (see his sketch)
and published by "the author's family," as per
their prospective circular of Mar. 10, 1893.

This work is highly commended for its contents,
and for the pains-taking and accuracy with which
it is written.

Our class-mate "was a son of Rochester, and as
"such was keenly alive to the best interests of his
"native town; and, though his large heart reached
"farther out in God's universe, yet this was where
"it centred."

Mr. McDuffee was a member of the State Con-
stitutional Convention in 1876, and took some part,
but not conspicuously, in its discussions.

He also patented a new "time lock," in 1875;
but abandoned the manufacture.

I. J. EDGAR graduated at the Rochester High
School in 1879. From childhood he has shown
unmistakable evidence of a natural love and gift
for music; early began the study of the pianoforte,
and has been under the instruction of the best
musical teachers. His compositions for piano
number about twenty pieces; and in vocal music
he has written twelve songs, besides many part
songs, hymns, etc., all of which are characterized by
serious thought, a thorough conception of the subject in hand, and a happy adaptation of music to
words. He traveled extensively throughout Europe, one season, for the purpose of hearing great
artists and famous organs and organists. As a

performer he is refined, and his touch is delicate and pleasing. Is music teacher, organist and musical director in Rochester.

II. WILLIS, grad. at Dartmouth in 1890; is now editor and propriétor of the "Rochester Courier," with W. W. Lougee (D. C., 1888). They printed the catalogue of Dartmouth for 1893.

MOORE, HENRY WOODBURY,

GILLISONVILLE, S. C.

1 —— Rock Spring, Beaufort District, S. C., Sept. 24, 1832. His pedigree is Henry W.[5], John [4], Nathaniel [3], William [2], John [1]; his family belonging to the noble Scotch-Irish race who migrated from Scotland to Northern Ireland in the days of the Covenanters, and thence to this country, in great numbers, about the year 1719 and onwards.

His father, John [4], was b. in Peterborough, N. H., Jan. 20, 1804; emigrated to South Carolina when a young man in mercantile connection with his uncle, John Ferguson, and there d. May 15, 1871, aged 67 years and 4 months. His mother, before marriage, was Sabrina Beard.

2 —— Gillisonville, under Messrs. Currell and Fickling.

3 —— Martha Elizabeth Rowell, of Beaufort District, by the Rev. Moses Boynton, Jan. 30, 1865. She was b. at Hilton Head, S. C., Feb. 24, 1844, the dau. of Wm. Washington Rowell and nee Clementine Craddock.

Mr. and Mrs. Rowell d. when their two children, Martha E. and William, were quite young. Mr. Peter Craddock raised them.

4 —— I. HARRY CRADDOCK, b. June 20, 1866, in Beaufort District; d. July 25, 1867, at Hendersonville, S. C., aged one year and one month.

II. ANNE SABRINA, b. Dec. 20, 1867.

III. WILLIAM WOODBURY, b. Dec. 30, 1868.

IV. JAMES BEARD, b. Aug. 17, 1870.

V. HENRY AUGUSTUS, b. Jan. 18, 1873, at Gillisonville, and there d. of pneumonia, June 5, 1873, aged 5 months.

VI. GEORGE EDWARD HASKELL, b. April 23, 1874, at Gillisonville.

VII. JOSEPH HENRY, b. Jan. 23, 1876, at Gillisonville.

VIII. KATE DUBOIS, b. Feb. 14, 1878.

IX. FRANKLIN MCDUFFEE, b. Dec. 12, 1879; weight at birth, eleven pounds; named after his father's beloved class-mate, McDuffee, beside whom that father sat in college. He d. at Hendersonville, Oct. 5, 1882, in his third year, of inflammation of the brain, after a few days' illness. "His "sweet temper and affectionate disposition had en-"deared him to all. We have found it hard to for-"get the selfishness of our human nature, and say, "sincerely, 'Thy will, O God, be done.' "

X. JANE, b. Jan. 12, 1882.

XI. LOIS, b. Nov. 6, 1884.

XII. ARTHUR RUNNELS, b. Dec. 31, 1885; named after President Arthur and the Class Secretary.

XIII. IDA ANDERSON, b. Aug. 31, 1888. The above were all b. in Hendersonville, except as otherwise noted.

He studied medicine with Dr. Thomas H. Gregorie, at Gillisonville, from the time of graduating till Nov., 1854, and during the spring and summer of 1855. Attended two courses of lectures at the South Carolina Medical College, Charlestown, S. C., the intervening and succeeding winters, finally graduating in the spring of 1856. Repaired to New York City for hospital advantages and clinical instruction in April of the same year; spent the summer there, and returning, opened an office in Gillisonville, where he continued in the practice of medicine till April, 1858. Then removing to the Southwest, he finally established himself at Houston, Texas; but was seized by the fever in Sept. and returned to South Carolina in Nov. of the same year. Resumed practice in Beaufort District.

At the commencement of the civil war, believing in the right of secession, and having voted for the ordinance, he joined the Beaufort District Troop, a cavalry company, for service in Virginia. Subsequently Dr. Moore received the appointment of assistant surgeon in the Confederate service; followed the fortunes of his regiment (2d S. C. Cav.) through the campaigns of 1862 and '63 in Virginia, Maryland and Pennsylvania; and, attached to Gen. Bragg's army, saw the fall of Fort Fisher, fought at North River, and had some severe skirmishing near Goldsboro, N. C. Before the disbandment of Bragg's forces he was taken sick, and, after a three week's confinement, he and his nurse turned their horses homeward, thankful that they had seen the end. He assures us that during all this time he cherished no bitterness towards his brethren on the other side, and that on all occasions, he extended his sympathy and medical assistance, as a surgeon, with equal cordiality, toward the sick and fallen soldiers of the Union, as of the Confederate army. After the war, he followed hunting for several months, with his brothers, in the swamps of the Savannah river, marketing their game at the city of Savannah, Ga.

During the reconstruction troubles in South Carolina, he was obliged to "refugee" with his family in Georgia, and he gives a racy description of his experience as "Principal of Morven Acad." for nine months, among the pine barrens of Brooks Co., Ga., in 1876–7.

Since then he has been a practicing physician, teacher and farmer, near the village of Hendersonville, Colleton District, his old time sports being relished, now and then, as keenly as ever, and the rod and line being frequently taken to go angling with his boys.

He united with the Presbyterian Church at McPhersonville, Beaufort Co., Nov. 1, 1875; but, there being no church of that order near his home, he has associated with the Methodist Episcopal Church of Hendersonville, and conducted a Bible class in their Sunday School on the Sabbath days. His medical practice is useful, but not lucrative, in the intervals of teaching.

He has also served as private tutor to his children, who have made fair advancement in their studies; while his farm, about one mile distant from the village, has continued to improve under the labor of himself and sons, till in 1892 it attained the profitable yield of three bales of cotton, from ten acres, 175 bushels of corn, and 100 bushels of sweet potatoes, with several varieties of choice fruit and well-fatted fowl.

For about a month (Jan. and Feb., 1884) the Class Secretary was permitted to enjoy the genial hospitality of his Hendersonville home. They were weeks of rare pleasure; and a delightful visit was also enjoyed with his two brothers, John and James, at or near his father's old homestead in Gillisonville, where he was engaged as a teacher during part of the same winter.

Our class-mate is a superior letter writer, and has favored the Secretary with a far greater number of epistles than any other member of the class.

Has always taken a prominent part in educational affairs. For several years has served as Chairman of the Board of Trustees of Hendersonville Graded School.

II. ANNE S., grad. at the Ladies' Sem. in Due West, S. C., in June, 1890; was engaged as a teacher in Hampton Co., and was m. to James F. Jackson, Sept. 22, 1892. They now reside in Charleston. Child (1) Frances McCauly Jackson, b. June, 1893.

III. WILLIAM W. and Loulie Peeples were m. Nov. 6, 1890, in Barnwell Village, where they now

PROF. N. J. MORRISON, D. D.

live. He is doing well as a business man. His first dau. d. at birth; second is named Catharine, 6 months old (Aug., 1894).

MORRISON, NATHAN JACKSON,
FRANKLIN, N. H.

1 ——— Franklin, Nov. 25, 1828. His father was Nathan Smith[5] Morrison, of Franklin, formerly Sanbornton, N. H., (Bradbury[4], David[3], John[2], David[1]), though of this immigrant ancestor there is a little doubt; is supposed to have been among the Scotch-Irish who landed at Boston in 1718, and was afterwards at Haverhill, Mass. His mother, before marriage, was Susannah[7] Chase (Jonathan[6], William[5], William[4], Jonathan[3], Thomas[2], Aquilla[1]), also one of the old and highly respected families of Sanbornton. Aquilla[1] landed at Newburyport, Mass., in 1630. William[5] removed from Stratham, N. H., to Sanbornton, about 1777, and was there first deacon of the Baptist Church.

2 ——— Sanbornton, under S. G. Taylor (D. C., 1847), and D. Putnam (D. C., 1851); at Meriden, N. H., under Mr. Baldwin, and at New Hampton, N. H., under Mr. Aaron W. Chaffin.

3 ——— Miranda Capen Dimond, from the residence of the bride's mother, in Brooklyn, N. Y., Dr. R. S. Storrs, Jr., officiating, July 8, 1863. She was the dau. of Isaac Marquand and Sarah (Capen) Dimond, and was b. at the house of her

grandmother, Mrs. Leonard Woods, in Enfield, Mass., Aug. 23, 1841.

This grandmother was Miranda Colton, dau. of Dea. Rueben Colton, of Enfield; m., first, Theophilus Capen, Jr., who was a graduate of Harvard College, and an eloquent lawyer, first in Salisbury, Vt., lastly in Gainesville, N. Y., where he d. Sept., 1824, aged 34. His widow returned to Enfield; there m., second, Hon. Leonard Woods, as before hinted, and d. April 28, 1860, aged 65. Of her four daughters, Rachel was, first, the wife of Dr. Gray, of Springfield, Mass., who was killed in the Norwalk bridge disaster, April, 1852, and m., second, Charles Merriam, the eminent publisher of Springfield; Sarah, Mrs. Morrison's mother, b. June 8, 1818, in Salisbury, Vt., was one of the earliest graduates of Oberlin (Ohio) College; wrote a good deal for the periodical press—also a book entitled, "Home Whispers to Husbands and Wives"—and has always been noted for her ardent and active philanthrophy. She m., first, Isaac M. Dimond; b. Feb. 24, 1804, in Fairfield, Conn.; prepared for Yale College, but became a silversmith and merchant in New York City, and d. in Brooklyn Dec. 16, 1862. She m., second, Hon. Douglas Putnam, of Marietta, O., where she now resides. Her children, besides Mrs. Morrison, were Mary Bates (Dimond), now of Marietta, a writer of prose and poetry; Sarah Capen and James Crocker, both d. young, and Henry Cipperly, who was educated at Marietta College, was a well read physician, but is now a manufacturer of agricultural implements with his father-in-law, Gen. A. S. Bushnell, in Springfield, Ohio.

4 —— I. SARAH DIMOND, b. Oct. 12, 1865.

II. THEODORE HARLAN, b. Oct. 15, 1869.

III. DOUGLAS PUTNAM, b. Sept. 29, 1872; all in Olivet, Mich.

Sept. 4, 1853, he commenced a select school of 12 weeks in Acworth, N. H., and Jan. 2, 1854, left New Hampshire for Oberlin, Ohio, for the purpose of studying theology. Remained there two years, teaching two or three hours a day, during term time; also in the long winter vacations, first as private tutor in the family of Col. W. H. H. Taylor, son-in-law of the first President Harrison, and living in the original "log cabin" of 1840 celebrity, at North Bend, and next as Principal of a new High School in one of the suburbs of Cincinnati. Was tutor in the languages of the preparatory department, Oberlin, one year, from Aug., 1855, and another year, retaining the tutorship, he resumed theological studies, which were finally completed in Aug., 1857. Was examined for licensure in the Christian ministry, by the Cleveland Conference of Cong. Churches, at Wellington, Ohio, Oct. 20, 1857. Nov. 14, commenced labor at Rochester, Mich., and was ordained pastor of the Cong. Church in that place, Feb. 11, 1858, Rev. H. D. Kitchel, D. D., of Detroit, preaching the sermon. Closed his labors at Rochester, Oct. 16, 1859, having received the appointment of Professor of Ancient Languages in the new college at Olivet, Mich., where also he was pastor of the Cong.

Church for three years, from Nov., 1860, with designations in the catalogue for 1863-4 of "Pro-"fessor of Greek and Mental Philosophy," also "Librarian."

At the annual commencement of Olivet College, July, 1865, he was duly installed President of that institution; labored successfully for its advancement, and resigned his office in 1872. At the late celebration (June 20, 1894) of the Semi-Centennial of Olivet College and Colony, Mr. Morrison was publicly credited with being "the second founder "of Olivet."

Supplied the Cong. Church at Mattoon, Ill., during which time he was maturing the plan of the future Drury College, at Springfield, Mo., which he took charge of at the organization in Sept., 1873. He did a large amount of very hard work in and for this institution, which in its first five years had made such progress as has rarely been reached by colleges of the West in that early period. He drew its charter, wrote out its courses of study, selected nearly all its instructors and officers, pro-- cured by personal solicitation most of its funds (nearly $400,000 in all), planned its buildings, and gathered a library of 19,000 vols.

This college occupies a strategic point, 240 miles southwest of St. Louis, in the march of New England civilization and culture toward the southwest, in a growing town of 25,000 people; and through that our class-mate did a most important work in laying the foundations for Christian education in that portion of our country. The catalogue for Drury College for 1882–83 presented a summary of 286 students, 49 of whom were in the college department. He was providentially led to resign his position December 31, 1887, and was immediately invited by Hon. John Eaton (D. C., 1854), then President at Marietta, Ohio, to a professorship in that college. He has held the department of Philosophy, i. e., "Psychology, Logic "and Ethics," also the "History of Philosophy" and "Christian Apologetics," which position he still retains (1894), besides preaching to feeble home missionary churches in the vicinity of Marietta.

He received the honorary degree "S. T. D." or D. D. from Dart. College in 1868—the first of the class thus honored by our Alma Mater, and that of "LL. D." from the State University of Missouri in 1884.

Took a tour in Europe the same year, in company with Charles Merriam, Esq. (see above). They left this country June 24, 1868, and returned Nov. 21, having traveled through England, Ireland, Scotland, France, Switzerland, Germany (down the Rhine), Prussia, Austria (Vienna to Venice) and Italy.

He was President of the "Missouri State Teach-"ers' Association" in 1880.

Has published (1) a "Memorial Address," on "Olivet College and its History," June 28, 1866.

(2) "The Christian College," an address delivered on the first anniversary of Drury College, at Springfield, Mo., June 25, 1874; pamphlet 19 pp.

(3) An essay read before the Springfield Asso-

ciation, at Lebanon, Mo., Sept. 22, 1877, on the "Relation of Drury College to the Cong. Churches "of Southwestern Missouri;" "Springfield Patriot "and Advertiser," 3 1-2 columns.

(4) "Decay of the People's Sense of Duty;" a Baccalaureate Sermon at Drury College, June 16, 1878, from Eccl. 12:13 and Roman 3:17; pamphlet, 22 pp.

(5) "Young Men;" Baccalaureate at Drury, 1882 (1st John 2:14); "Springfield Weekly "Patriot" of July 13.

Dr. Morrison has been a frequent contributor to the local press of Marietta, and has written a book, "Fourteen Years in Drury College," which is now about ready for publication.

The great sorrow of his life was the death of his dau., (I) SARAH D., April 13, 1891, aged 25 years and 6 months. Her illness was most painful. The best medical skill in Cleveland was called into requisition, and she lingered from Sept., 1890, till she fell "asleep in Jesus," "the light, joy and bless-"ing of the household." A touching "Memorial" of her life, character and aims, with added tributes from various friends, was prepared by her mother; pp. 22. She was educated at Drury College, Mrs. Stearns' School in Amherst, Mass., and at Oberlin College. Early developed an unusually earnest and symmetrical Christian character; offered her-self to the A. B. C. F. M. for missionary work, with the Micronesian field in view, and was only prevented from entering it by her failing health. But she kept up an active sympathy and helpfulness in religious work and organized a society of "King's Daughters," while lying on her bed of pain. She had begun writing for the press, a few of her productions being published.

II. THEODORE II., studied at the Betts Acad., Stamford, Ct., and at Drury and Marietta Colleges, graduating from the latter in 1892. Is now in the law department of the Northwestern University, Masonic Temple, Chicago, Ill.

III. DOUGLAS P., was a student at Betts Acad.; grad. from Marietta College in 1893, and is now studying electrical engineering in the Armour Institute, Chicago.

He has proved a good student, and an earnest Christian.

MORSE, CHARLES OSGOOD, *,
HANOVER, N. II.

1 —— Newburyport, Mass., Sept. 4, 1824, being the son of Peter and Mary (Tewksbury) Morse. His father was b. Jan., 1777, and d. Nov. 20, 1841. His mother, b. Aug. 3, 1784, after the death of her husband, removed, with her son, from Newburyport to South Hampton, N. II., and d. July 9, 1860, in her 76th year.

2 —— Newburyport High School under Messrs. David P. Page and Roger S. Howard (D. C., 1829), and at the Barnard School, South Hampton, under Mr. Ezra W. Gale (D. C., 1843). He had been a student at Dartmouth a few years pre-

viously, and joined our class about the middle of our course.

3 —— Belinda Merrill, at her residence in South Hampton, Jan. 1, 1851 (Dec. 31, 1850).

He was the only one of our number who had a wife while in college. She was the dau. of William and Susan (Jewell) Merrill, the father living and dying at South Hampton. Her grandfathers were Parker Merrill and Jacob Jewell.

4 —— I. CHARLES AUSTIN, b. Dec. 2, 1861, in Newburyport.

He read law three years at Newburyport, immediately after graduating, with Eben. F. Stone, Esq., and was admitted to the Essex bar in Sept., 1856. Resided and practiced law in Newburyport, firm of "Johnson & Morse," with cases in the Police, Superior, Supreme and U. S. District Courts (see Mass. reports).

Prior to 1864, had been three years in the Common Council of the city, and two years its President, officiating also, politically, as Secretary of the Mass. Democratic State Committee. In 1871, Mr: Morse was still an attorney and counsellor-at-law, 25 State St., Newburyport, but in May, 1879, removed to Boston, Mass., opening an office, first in Exchange Place, and afterwards on School St. He was a close student of political matters, and was quite prominently identified with the Democratic party of the state for many years. He wrote for the press, more or less, all his life; was a great reader and much interested in astronomy in his later years.

One of the most genial class letters the Secretary has ever received was from Bro. Morse, in 1878; he says: "Should think it was time for "another 'Memorial,' though I have nothing to add "to my life-work. Fear I am like the servant who "had his one talent in a napkin. Have got that— "held my own—that is all! Thank God for so "much! * * Well, my dear R., we cannot all "or always be handsome; but while one is rich, and "another eminent, you and I will strive to be "good." It is with a feeling of sadness that we must add, he was not permitted to see this second class "Memorial," as he so evidently desired to do.

He d. at his home, 33 West Cottage St., Dorchester, Mass., Aug. 28, 1892, in his 68th year, after a lingering and painful illness of about eight months.

He had not been really well for several years. Was a most patient sufferer in his last sickness, thinking much more of the comfort of those about him than of his own troubles. The last few weeks of his life he was totally blind, which was a very severe trial; but he maintained a steady cheerfulness through all, and his attending friends are unable to recall a complaining word. He seemed especially grateful for what was done for him, and had his reason (except for brief moments) to the last. On the Saturday afternoon preceding his death, early Sunday morning, he desired his son to read to him from Goldsmith's "Deserted Village," commencing,

"His house was known to all the vagrant train," etc.

His end was very peaceful and his last words, "I am happy."

His funeral services in Boston, were conducted by the pastor of the Arlington St. (Unitarian) Church, with a brief service, attended by Rev. Albert W. Hitchcock at Newburyport, where he was buried in the family lot in Oak Hill Cemetery.

Notices of his death and funeral appeared in the Boston "Herald" and "Transcript" of Sept. 1. Besides alluding to other facts of his life, already brought out in this sketch, the "Herald" adds: "Of a quiet and unassuming nature, he was also a "man of the most generous instincts and his many "sterling qualities will be long remembered by his "friends."

His son, (I) CHARLES A. MORSE, grad. from the Brown High School in Newburyport, at about the age of 16, and had the honor of being the valedictorian in a class of some 40 graduates.

For the last fourteen years he has been in the East India line of trade (coffees, spices, gums, etc.) in Boston; address "30 Central street."

His mother resides with him, in very good health, with the mutual hope that they two may be together, in God's good providence, for many years to come.

MORSE, JOHN HERRICK, *,

BROOKFIELD, VT.

1 —— Brookfield, May 20, 1826, and was the son of Elijah and Olive (Herrick) Morse.

2 —— Wesleyan Seminary, Springfield, Vt., and at the Green Mountain Liberal Institute, South Woodstock, Vt.

3 —— Mrs. Delana Porter, of Bridgewater, South Dakota, Jan., 1890. "She was of suitable "age, a widow of rare gentleness and general ex-"cellence, and made his last years very happy."

Our record of Mr. Morse for the "Memorial" of 1864 was quite scanty; to the effect that after graduating he taught for some time in Wisconsin; next resided in Illinois, and was then living at Deerfield, Steele Co., Minnesota, engaged in teaching and farming. Was said to be leading a very secluded life on his farm, entirely alone, though still finding companionship in his books.

His brother, Mr. D. A. Morse, of Brookfield, Vt., and his sister, Mrs. Sarah M. Arnold, of North Randolph, have since supplemented this report, as follows: After graduating, in 1853, he spent considerable time in his native town teaching, before going West; finally located in Deerfield, Minn., there remained several years on a farm; did some public business; practiced surveying, and was justice of the peace. His postoffice address in 1878 was "Medford, Steele Co., Minn." (his home probably remaining the same).

"Some years later, he had a run of lung fever,

"from which he never wholly recovered, leaving his
"lungs in a bad state."

In 1889, "he sold his farm, and soon after came
"East to visit his relatives and friends."

On returning West, "he took up his residence
"at Bridgewater, S. D., the previous home of his
"wife. He had not been able, for many years, to
"do much work, his lungs and his heart being a
"great affliction to him, though confined to his bed
"in his last illness only a short time. He thought
"he might rally till the day before he died. He
"said, 'Jesus was the Corner Stone.' "

He expired Jan 23, 1893, at Bridgewater, aged
66 years and 8 months.

His sister remarks that when he was a young
lad "and commenced studying arithmetic he would
"come home from school and tell how and why his
"examples were done," with remarkable facility.

This is confirmed by our remembrance of him in
the class-room, that he excelled as a mathematician
rather than a linguist.

OAKES, VALENTINE B., *,

SANGERVILLE, ME.

1 —— Sangerville, Dec. 4, 1828. His parents
were Col. William and Mary (Weymouth) Oakes;
his father passing from Sangerville to his final
home in 1873, at the age of 78, and his mother in
1887, aged 89 years. His sister, Mrs. Mary E. O.
Ripley, our correspondent, after the lapse of years,

says: "Nothing more was ever heard of my dear
"brother."   His personal record, below, must therefore remain substantially as it was in the first
"Memorial."

2 —— Foxcroft (Me.) Acad. Took the first of
his collegiate course at Waterville College, Maine,
and came to Dartmouth our Senior year, in the
spring of 1853.

He taught the Acad. at Warren, Me., one year,
1854; studied law with his brother, A. P. Oakes,
Esq., at Waldoboro, Me., 1855, and practiced his
profession, three years (1856–8), at Damariscotta,
Me. Removed thence to Minnesota, and spent the
most of three years in "exploring," eighteen months
of which were passed in the Red river country, and
the then Dakota Territory.

Enlisted in Minn., Dec. 23, 1861, as a private in
the regular army (not the volunteer service), company B, 12th Infantry, 1st Brigade; afterwards
Syke's Division, Army of the Potomac.

Was promoted to the office of sergeant, but was
killed, as is supposed, June 27, 1862, during Mc-
Clellan's retreat before Richmond, Va.

A letter to his sister from a comrade (Edgar A.
Watson), dated at Cedar Point, July 5, 1862, says:
"Your letter came for your brother by to-day's
"mail, but he was not here to receive it. On Fri-
"day of last week, June 27, we were called up in
"line of battle to receive the enemy. They came
"on, and we fought about two hours, when the
"enemy made a desperate charge on our right
"flank, driving us back and killing a great many.

"The men went in every direction. Your brother,
"when last seen, was across the Chickahominy,
"with a few others. The rebel cavalry were then
"charging in that direction, but your brother said
"he 'would die before he would give up,' and it is
"supposed that he was either killed or taken pris-
"oner. He has not been seen or heard from since."

His friends have never received further information from Mr. Watson, or from other sources.

His well remembered spirit and energy, and his
known courage on the field of battle lead us to
conclude that he there found a patriot's grave.

"Dulce et decorum est pro patria mori."

PALMER, WILLIAM STRATTON,
ORFORDVILLE, N. H.

1 —— Orfordville, Aug. 6, 1827; the son of
Stephen West and Nancy (Stratton) Palmer.
Stephen West Palmer came with his father to
Orford, in his boyhood, from Warren, Ct., late
in the eighteenth century. His grandfather was a
physician, and came to Warren from Scotland, Ct.

2 —— Thetford (Vt.) Acad., under Principal
Hiram Orcutt.

3 —— Fannie Parish Walbridge, Feb. 5, 1855,
at Brookfield, Vt., the place of her early residence;
being the youngest dau. of Williams Walbridge,
who came to Brookfield from Stafford, Ct.

He taught at Kingston, R. I., for two years,
after graduating, and then accepted the office of

REV. WILLIAM STRATTON PALMER, D.D.

Principal of Berwick Acad., at South Berwick, Me., which he held till the spring of 1856. From that summer till Jan., 1859, was Principal of the Central High School in Cleveland, Ohio, his daily routine being to give instruction in Latin and Greek, and several of his pupils. afterwards graduating at Dart. and Western Reserve Colleges. Leaving Cleveland, he studied Hebrew at Orfordville, chiefly without a teacher, till Sept., 1859. He was approbated to preach in May, 1859, by the Orange Association assembled at Dr. Lord's in Hanover; and supplied the pulpit more or less at Littleton, N. H., the following summer. From Sept., 1859, till Aug., 1861, he attended the lectures of Profs. Park, Shedd and Phelps, at the Andover Theological Seminary, preaching most of the Sabbaths in various pulpits. Finally settled under peculiarly favorable circumstances, at Wells River, Vt., being ordained and installed over the Cong. Church in that village, Feb. 19, 1862. Here he continued for twelve and a half years, seeing the small church of 1862 become one of the strongest in the State, and specially remarkable for the energetic and devout business and professional men in its membership; while the tone of society in the village and vicinity was happily transformed.

Among the pleasing incidents of this pastorate was the celebration of his "tin wedding," Feb. 5, 1865, when Bro. Burton tied the knot anew and his parishioners crowded the parsonage, bringing quantities of tinware, and other expressions of their good will to the total value of some $200.

Though his salary had from time to time been increased to $1,200, and use of parsonage, yet he felt it his duty, in 1874, disregarding proffered fields in other directions, to accept the call of the Second Cong. Church in Norwich, Ct., where he was installed in Sept., class-mate Hulbert preaching the sermon.

Here his labors were also blessed by the accession of 107 during the first four years, to the membership of the church, and were continued successfully for fifteen years, when, owing to his failing health, suddenly, and greatly to the regret of his congregation, he resigned, Sept. 15, 1889, to take effect Oct. 1.

He then spent nearly one year in a European tour, hardly again expecting to be of effective service; but, on returning to this country, consented, doubtfully, to supply the pulpit of the late Dr. Post, in St. Louis, Mo., for two or three months, if able. His health improved under "the inspiration "of ministering to so intelligent a church," and he remained six months with the unanimous desire that he still prolong his term of service.

For that work he deemed his health too imperfect; but the following June he delivered the annual address to the Y. M. C. A. of Marietta College in Ohio. The next twelve months, having taken up his residence in Norwich Town, he preached in several pulpits—longest in Dr. Merriman's Central Church, Worcester, Mass. July and Aug., 1892, he supplied the Plymouth Church of Minneapolis, Minn., which numbers over 1000 members, and is said to have 100 college graduates in its congregation. The next summer he was invited to render a similar service to the same church, and also invited to take charge of the Pilgrim Church in St. Louis, upon Dr. Stimson's resignation, till a permanent pastor could be secured.

Though greatly improved in health, he deemed it unsafe to undertake the work of a large parish, and while retaining his residence in Norwich Town, in November, 1892, he accepted the pastoral care of the church in the neighboring historic town of Lebanon, Ct., the home of the Trumbulls, and the birthplace of Connecticut's war Governor, Buckingham. That pastorate he still holds, and has seen his labors crowned with a gratifying degree of success. Meanwhile, to a degree quite beyond all expectation of his friends, he has regained his former health and vigor.

Though our class-mate declined giving publicity to his Thanksgiving sermon in 1864, when urged to do so by his Wells River people, yet (1) The Funeral Sermon of Conductor Fisher was published by the Boston, Concord & Montreal Railroad; and (2) articles in the National S. S. Teacher of 1889, on "Aim in Teaching" and "Personal Responsi-"bility for the Conversion of Sinners," were republished in other journals, one of them in London, England.

There were also published (3) his "Address at "the Convention of Y. M. C. A's.," in St. Johnsbury, Vt., 1870, in the Proceedings of that Convention; 5 1-2 pp.

(4) Articles in the "National S. S. Teacher," Chicago, Jan., 1871, and afterwards on "Jesus, the "Christ, a Theme of Study."

(5) "A Centennial Review" of his church in Norwich, by request, 1876.

(6) A "Memorial of Rev. Silas McKeen, D. D.," of Bradford, Vt., in the July number of the Cong. Quarterly, 1878.

(7) A paper upon "Church Work not Directly "Religious," read at the annual meeting of the Connecticut General Conference at Bridgeport, in 1884, published in the Minutes of that body.

(8) "Review of Fifteen Years' Pastorate in "Norwich," published by the church.

(9) Frequent writings for newspapers, etc.

Bro. Palmer served on the Examining Committee of our Alma Mater in Nov., 1864, and upon the Examining Committee of Andover Theological Seminary in 1881. He was a member of the National Congregational Councils, in Boston, in 1865, and in New Haven in 1874; in both cases as a delegate of the Orange County Conference. He preached the anniversary sermon before the graduating class of Tilden Seminary, West Lebanon, N. H., in 1869, and delivered the annual address in the same institution in 1873.

At the Dartmouth Commencement in 1880, the Trustees honored him with the degree of Doctor of Divinity.

Dr. Palmer's duties as Chairman of a Board of Education in Norwich prevented his meeting with us at our 30th class anniversary meeting in 1883;

Isaac A. Parker.

but he favored us with his presence at the 40th, in 1893, though then in much less perfectly restored health than he enjoys at present.

PARKER, ISAAC AUGUSTUS,

WOODSTOCK, VT.

1 —— South Woodstock, Dec. 31, 1825. He was the son of Isaac and Lucia (Wood) Parker; (Isaac A.[4], Isaac[3], Eleazer[2], Zechariah[1]), his mother's family being from Middleboro, Mass., of strictly Puritan descent. His great-grandfather, Zechariah Parker, lived in Mansfield, Ct.

2 —— Ludlow, Vt., under W. B. Bunnell, and at South Woodstock under John Ward.

3 —— Sarah Ann Labaree, of Hartland, Vt., Feb. 18, 1856, at Glover, Vt., by the Rev. George Severance.

Her parents were William and Parthena (Whitmore) Labaree, and she was b. Jan. 8, 1827, in Weathersfield, Vt.; being a great-granddaughter of Peter Labaree, of Charlestown, N. H., who was there taken captive by the Indians, and conveyed to Canada in Aug., 1754. The Labaree family is of Huguenot descent. She was graduated at Thetford (Vt.) Acad., under Hiram Orcutt, as Principal, in 1853; and d. at Galesburg, Ill., June 16, 1889, aged 62 years and 5 months. At her funeral "Dr. Tomlinson spoke touchingly of the quiet, "simple goodness of this noble woman, and re-

"minded the mourning friends that there were two
"sides to the picture of death, the earthward and
"the heavenward."

"President White remarked upon the deep spirit-
"uality of the departed; a spirituality so full, so
"strong, so impressive as to make the invisible
"world stand forth as the real world, the eternal
"life as the actual." Students, alumni and friends,
in large numbers, revealed, by their presence and
demeanor, the deep regard in which Mrs. Parker
was held by all.

4 —— I. IZAH TENNEY, b. Jan. 24, 1857, at
Glover, Vt.

II. WILLIAM AUGUSTUS, b. June 25,
1860, in Galesburg, Ill.

He was Principal of the Orleans Liberal Institute at Glover, Vt., from Sept., 1853, to Nov.,
1858. Was appointed Professor of Ancient Languages (afterwards Williamson Prof. of Greek) in
the Lombard University at Galesburg, Ill., in the
autumn of 1858, and commenced his labors in the
December following, which have continued till the
present, a period of nearly 36 years. This is one
of the longest continuous terms of service in the
same locality, field and department, without interruption, to be noticed in our brotherhood as a
class. Nothing but Allen's and Lamson's medical
careers are, thus far, found to rival it.

Prof. Parker remarked in 1864 that he had been
employed, since graduating, "in institutions of
"learning poorly provided with funds and impos-
"ing the most arduous labors on teachers," and that

he had devoted all his time and energies to this field of labor.

He certainly now merits the commendation due to those who "endure unto the end." He has nobly sustained himself; and has been nobly sustained. He is still able to do his work in the University without difficulty, and has the satisfaction of knowing that the Institution in which he has labored so long is better endowed than formerly—and hence able to do more efficient work—and that its future prospects are bright.

In order to make his beloved daughter as comfortable as possible in her California home, he built a house for her at Banning; and observing that fruit-raising was profitable, he bought ten acres of land and planted it with trees. He says (Oct., 1891), "In the four long summer vacations which I spent "in California, my life was very diverse from what "it was in Illinois, Surroundings, employments "and climate were so different, that I seem to have "been leading a dual life for the last four years. "The little community in which we resided was "very near an Indian reservation, and we saw "nearly as many Indians and Mexicans as people of "our own race. I made pleasant acquaintances "there, and had some dear friends. The people were "very kind to my daughter. I have learned espec-"ially to respect and esteem a few Indians with "whom I became acquainted."

His address before the Glover Library Association in 1855 was published in pamphlet form, by request of the Association.

More recently, his address at a convention of teachers. Also, several articles in newspapers.

He was presented with the honorary degree of "Doctor of Philosophy" from Buchtel College, Akron, Ohio, June, 1892.

I. Izah T., never attended the public schools, but received instruction at home in her earlier years, and at the age of eight could decline a Greek noun or conjugate a Latin verb. Grad. from the Lombard University, June, 1876, in the classical course, and for nine years taught acceptably in the public schools of Galesburg, and in the preparatory department of the College, till declining health compelled her to give up her arduous duties in the schoolroom. For two years prior to 1887 she showed indications of pulmonary disease, but made a brave fight for life, from first to last, and in Dec. of that year repaired to the Pacific slope, hoping that the balmy climate of Southern California might restore her failing health. This was ever afterwards her earthly home, residing at Banning, San Bernardino County, where her kind disposition made her many friends. Her skill, as an artist, was quite superior, as her sketches and paintings attest. She was an earnest worker, and a most estimable woman, whose early death her many friends will greatly deplore.

She d. of consumption at Banning, Sept. 10, 1891, aged 34 years, 7 months and 17 days. She was buried in Galesburg beside her dear mother, at Hope Cemetery, amid such expressions of sympathy and such a wealth of floral tributes as we have rarely seen described.

II. WILLIAM A., grad. from Lombard University in 1880; chose the vocation of a civil engineer. Has done engineering work in Illinois, Indiana, Iowa, Wisconsin and Texas, mostly in constructing railroads and railroad bridges. Was employed two or three years in Chicago, Ill. Just at present (April, 1894), has charge of the construction of water works in Rushville, Ill.

PARSONS, CHASE PRESCOTT, *,
GILMANTON, N. H.

1 —— Gilmanton, Nov. 10, 1832. His earliest ancestor in this country was probably Josiah Parsons, of Cape Ann, Mass., and he was the son of Josiah, Esq., and Judith (Badger) Parsons, of Gilmanton, his father being principal of the Gilmanton Acad., for many years; b. Sept. 26, 1781; d. Dec. 9, 1842, aged 61. His pedigree, though slightly doubtful, is probably as follows: Chase P.^{5}, Josiah ^{4}, Abraham ^{3}, Abraham ^{2}, Josiah ^{1}, as above; Abraham ^{3} marrying Abigail Burleigh, the grandmother of our class-mate.

2 —— Gilmanton Acad., under the Rev. Charles Tenney.

3 —— Hattie A. Howes, at Evansville, Ind., in 1863—a native of Evansville, but the dau. of Massachusetts parents.

4 —— I. KATE EMILY, b. 1864, at Evansville.

II. MARY HOWES, b. at Evansville.

III. Lewis Wheeler, b. April 2, 1870, at Cairo, Ill.

Being disabled by sickness from fulfilling an engagement to the City High School, Cleveland, O., he passed the first year after graduating partly at home, and partly near the sea shore. In Sept., 1854, took charge of the Atkinson (N. H.) Acad., remaining at that post for two and a fourth years. Next became principal of the Gilmanton Acad.—his father's old charge—where he continued till 1858. One year was then passed in the High School at Evansville, Ind., and another year in charge of the classical department of the High School at Xenia, O. Travelled on business connected with the Indiana State Board of Education; and, in 1861, taught a female school at Washington, Ind. Was called from that to the High School in Biddeford, Me., where he remained until the winter of 1862-3, and then accepted an urgent invitation to return to his former position in the Evansville High School.

For a short time, including the year 1870, he was in business at Cairo, Ill., firm of Parsons & Davis, Queen's-ware dealers; but he seems to have gravitated back to his old field at Evansville (for the third time), and to his well-tried vocation of teaching, which he continued till his death, June 13, 1879, of rheumatism of the heart, in the 47th year of his age. His associate teachers in Evansville passed upon him the following eulogy, which afterwards appeared in the "Boston Journal":

"In the death of Prof. Chase P. Parsons, we have

"lost a friend who gave to us in our days of dis-
"tress a genuine, heartfelt sympathy, and in our
"hours of joy, his brightest smiles; a friend who
"never allowed his own personal ills or wrongs to
"be apparent. As a fellow-teacher we would bear
"testimony to the great earnestness and thorough-
"ness of his work, for his high conception of duty,
"made every day of his life as though it were his
"last day. His superior scholarship and ripe judg-
"ment, combined with his constant courtesy, made
"him ever a most valuable assistant in all the diffi-
"culties of the profession. No one can realize the
"cultured manliness of our dead companion as we,
"who have shared the benefits and honors of his
"toil. To the family of Professor Parsons we
"would say that he has left a heritage of noble
"memories and Christian virtues, which, while it
"deepens the intensity of your grief, will in the
"years to come be a most precious legacy."

The Rev. Mr. Adams, his pastor, and pastor of
the Walnut St. Church, Evansville, preached a
sermon at his funeral, liberal extracts from which
have gone upon our class records. "With what
"concientious fidelity he did his work many of you
"can witness; never sparing himself; and so loyal
"to duty that he constantly sought to inspire others
"with his lofty ideals. With such intensity did he
"strive to do this that he sometimes seemed severe
"when he was only trying to lead others to be true
"to God and to duty. * * He was conscien-
"tious in a profession where it often goes un-
"noticed and unrewarded; yes, when it often

"meets nothing but unkind criticism, and even sees
"unfaithfulness winning the prize. But it did not
"matter. When duty called it was not for him to
"falter. * * Rarely is it given to friends to
"watch so long the certain coming of death, while
"the one who is called, with unclouded mind,
"watches with them. And so in the midst of great
"suffering, he patiently, calmly awaited the great
"change. The everlasting arms were underneath
"him, and the word of his God, so often tested be-
"fore, did not fail him. What a commentary is
"this—such a life and such a death—upon the
"Gospel, where 'life and immortality are brought
" 'to light.' And now when his work seemed only
"half done, he has fallen. His family needed him—
"God only knows how much. This Church sorely
"needed him. He was needed everywhere where
"*men* are needed, and never more than now."

PERRIN, DANIEL, *,

NORTHMORELAND, PA.

1 —— Northmoreland, Wyoming Co., Pa., Dec.
23, 1822, being the son of Calvin Perrin.

2 —— Wesleyan Academy, North Wilbraham,
Mass.; at the West Killingly (Ct.) Acad., under
George Canning Williams (D. C., 1844), and at
Hanover, N. H., from Jan. 1, 1849, by private
study, without an instructor.

3 —— Emily M. Handall, of Killingly, Ct., (one
of his pupils), Jan. 29, 1854. It was to this mar-

riage that allusion was made in the introduction to our former "Memorial," where it is said that "one "of our *shortest* men, in obedience to the ruling "maxim of his life, 'aim high,' selected the *tallest* "among his students, who he thought had other "qualifications equal to her stature, wooed, and, al- "most contrary to his expectations, won!"

4 —— I. Julia, b. June 22, 1856, at Paw Paw, Ill.

II. Frank Judson, b. April 11, 1858, at Paw Paw.

III. George, b. March 23, 1861, at Wilson's Grove, Ia.

IV. Celia, b. Aug. 26, 1863, at Wilson's Grove.

V. Charles, b. 1866.

VI. John, b. 1868, and four others, one son and three daughters; it being stated, on good authority, that the whole number of our classmate's children was ten, five sons and five daus. The names of the four youngest, and the recent records of the family have failed to reach us.

In August, 1853, he commenced labor in the West Killingly Acad., Ct., and continued successfully for nearly two years. In May, 1855, he removed to the West, and leaving his family at Norwalk, O., spent the summer in exploring as far as Iowa. In Sept., located at Paw Paw Grove, Lee Co., Ill., where he remained as teacher of an acad., till March, 1859, and then settled, upon his own farm, at Wilson's Grove, Fayette Co., Iowa. He there divided his attention between teaching and farming, with something attempted at writing and lecturing. Held the offices of Town Clerk, Justice of the Peace, and member of the County Board of Supervisors. The pastor of the West Killingly Cong. Church remarked that he was a highly esteemed teacher in that place, and that they scarcely ever had a better principal in their school. Through his whole experience as a teacher, about 2000 pupils were under his care.

His poem, "The Students' Revery," pronounced at our commencement July 27, 1853, was published in the "Dartmouth" for July, 1868.

His voice had failed (Feb. 24, 1872), so that he was obliged to give up teaching. Was then owning and carrying on a good farm of 210 acres at Wilson's Grove, and writing often for the county papers. He sent us the pictures of his four boys. A letter from his second son to Class-mate Hayward, under date of Sept. 15, 1883, at Danielsonville, Ct. (where he was attending school), informed us that our class-mate, finding the climate of Iowa too cold for his diseased throat, resolved, in 1874, to try Texas. The farm at Wilson's Grove was sold in March, and the family sent to live with his brother, Mr. Ezra Perrin, while he went to Texas, "prospecting." After three weeks, he bought 477 acres of land, twenty-five miles north of San Antonio, and wrote for his family to come on. The land was unimproved, and they lived in a tent, until a house could be built, which he did himself, drawing the lumber from San Antonio. Two of his boys were now old enough to

take hold of the work, and twenty acres were
ready to plant in Feb., 1875, which amount was increased from year to year, till now (1883) they
planted 60 acres, corn, cotton and oats being the
principal crops, and the rest of the land being used
as pasture.

He adds: "Concerning my father's death, dur-
"ing the winter of 1879, he had not seemed very
"strong; but had kept along with his work every
"day. His appetite was poor, and he was rather
"thin in flesh, but was never troubled with any
"cough, unless he took cold. About three weeks
"before his death he came in from the field where
"he had been ploughing, and after feeding the
"horses I noticed him lying down on some husks,
"in one corner of the crib. After perhaps half an
"hour, he went into the house and retired early.
"The next day he did not go out to work, but re-
"mained in the house, writing or reading, and so
"continued for two or three days, lying down oc-
"casionally, but eating almost nothing. As his
"strength failed from lack of food, he was more
"confined to the bed, until he grew so weak that
"he was unable to rise at all, and so his life went
"quietly out without a struggle. The doctor pro-
"nounced it liver trouble. He had full control of
"his mind to the last, and sent for such men as he
"wanted to see about settling his business affairs."

Mr. Perrin's death occurred early in 1880, at the
age of 57 years and about 2 months. In June,
1878, his wife had left Texas to visit her old home
in Connecticut, returning in October. His oldest

son, (II) Frank J., also came North in August, 1879, for the purpose of attending school in Danielsonville, and was there when his father died. He returned home in August, 1881, and the next older son, (III) George, repaired to the same place (see above) in December following.

The two oldest girls, (I) Julia, and (IV) Celia, were m. in Texas, and settled within a few miles of their parents' home.

The P. O. address of Mrs. Perrin, in 1883, was "Leon Springs, Texas."

PERRIN, HENRY MARTYN,

Berlin, Vt.

1 —— Berlin, June 23, 1829, and labored with his parents on the home farm until after he was 18 years of age.

2 —— Thetford, Vt., under Hiram Orcutt, entering Dartmouth our Sophomore year.

3 —— Mary Achley, from the house of her father, in Ovid, Mich., May 1, 1862; her parents were farmers.

4 —— I. Lucy, b. Aug. 25, 1863.

II. Ella Luella, b. Aug. 7, 1866, both at St. John's, Mich.

He remained at home during the fall of 1853, and the winter following went to Albany, N. Y., for the finishing of his law studies, which he commenced the winter before. Was admitted to the Bar of New York, at Albany, the next spring

(1854), and removed immediately to Terre Haute, Ind., where he was again admitted to the Bar, and continued sometime in practice. Moved by a "spirit of emigration," he travelled over the Northwest quite extensively, and was variously employed in professional and manual labor, with residence mostly at Detroit, Mich., until 1857. He then settled at St. John's, Mich.; was re-admitted to the Bar—neither certificates of previous admissions, nor diplomas, being in his possession—and has there continued till the present time (1894), in the practice of his profession.

He was honored, prior to 1864, with the office of Judge of Probate.

He received the honorary degree of "Master of "Arts," from Olivet College, Mich., at the annual commencement, July, 1865; and his first degree from our Alma Mater, in 1870.

Was elected to the Michigan State Senate in 1864; and was reported at our class meeting in 1873, as being an active member and supporter of the Cong. Church at St. John's, contributing from $300 to $500 a year for the support of its ministry and other ordinary expenses. When, in 1869, by vote of the class, we made a contribution to aid our class-mate, Young, in his astronomical researches at Dartmouth (he being Professor there at the time), Mr. Perrin contributed nearly one-half, or $100 out of the $215 which were raised. His law firm, "Perrins & Baldwin," was constituted May 1, 1867, and still exists; being one of the oldest law firms in the State.

He has also been engaged in agricultural pursuits, to some extent, working a marsh farm in the vicinity of St. John's.

Our class-mate, though leading a roving life the first few years after leaving College, yet, since 1857, has been one of the most stationary and perseveringly successful of our membership, remaining for 37 years in one locality, profession and line of usefulness. Pecuniarily, he seems to have been one of our most highly prospered men; and that he is inclined to use his money for others' benefit, we have just given evidence.

Both Mrs. Perrin and himself were badly injured by a distressing railroad accident in New York, in 1889 (of which below); but could report themselves Jan., 1893, as "nearly recovered, and still "spared to each other. No additional honors or "emoluments; but very grateful for an apparent "competence. Would really be delighted to meet "the rear guard once more before we cross the "river. But God only knows. Let us trust."

Our brother says, respecting a blank page of manuscript, which we hoped he would fill: "Do "what you please with page 340, only save my life! "As the politicians would say, 'I am in the hands " 'of my friends.' Call on me for the sinews of "war when wanted."

While in College, we always accorded to Bro. Perrin a wonderful spirit of independence (and we really admired it!) even to the time and manner of his taking his diploma.

We make the same concession to him now. We

let him have his own way of doing things, and accept the very unassuming style in which he disposes of himself and of his ancestry; though still unhappily in the dark as to how "Little Perrin," (Daniel), and "Big" or "Tall Perrin," (Henry M.), may possibly have been related!

The elder of his two daughters, (I) LUCY, was m. to Dr. Henry Palmer, Sept. 26, 1887, and resides in St. John's, Mich. They have one child, (1) Ruth E. Palmer, b. Jan. 18, 1889.

His younger, (II) ELLA L., was instantly killed in a railroad wreck, Aug. 10, 1889, aged 23 years and 3 days. She had been with her parents to the old home in Vermont to attend a family centennial, and returning by a route on the south side of Lake Ontario, when opposite Rochester, N. Y., their train ran into another, their car being "telescoped," and this beloved daughter, with two other persons, meeting sudden death.

Our earnest, united sympathies go out to Mr. and Mrs. Perrin for their irreparable loss; but we, all of us, only "a little longer wait."

PUTNAM, ALFRED PORTER, N. G.,

NORTH DANVERS, MASS.

1 —— North Danvers, Jan. 10, 1827; the son of Elias and Eunice (Ross) Putnam; his father being a shoe manufacturer, and prominent office-holder in Essex County, and his mother a native of

Ipswich, Mass. Of their eleven children (five sons) four have deceased, Emily, Elias Endicott, Israel Alden and Louisa Jane. Israel Alden grad. at the Harvard Divinity School, 1848, and d. Oct. 31, of the same year, and another living, is Judge Arthur A. Putnam, of Uxbridge, Mass. Both of these brothers were, for a time, students at Dartmouth. The pedigree of the family is Alfred P.[8], Elias [7], Israel [6], Edmund [5], John [4], John [3], Nathaniel [2], John [1]; the last named being the progenitor of nearly all the Putnams in America, who came hither with his wife, Priscilla, and three sons, from Buckinghamshire, Eng., and settled, in 1634 in Salem Village, now Danvers, Mass. Edmund [5] was deacon of the old Salem Village church for 23 years, but afterwards became one of the pioneer Universalists of that region. He was also captain of an Alarm List Company, in March, 1775, and commanded one of the eight Danvers companies that marched to the Lexington battle, April 19, 1775.

Israel [6] m. Anna Endicott, a lineal descendant of the old Puritan Governor, John; was a highly respected, intelligent farmer, and published several pamphlet discourses of his own, in advocacy of the Universalist faith.

2 —— Literary Gymnasium, Pembroke, N. H., 1844-5; Andover (Mass.), Springfield (Vt.), and Thetford (Vt.) Academies, 1847-9, having been employed as bookkeeper for Allen & Minot, Boston, Mass., 1846-7, and for a brief time subsequently..

3 —— Louise Proctor, Preston, Jan. 10, 1856. She was of an old Danvers family, and there b. Jan. 4, 1828; the dau. of Samuel and Lydia Waters (Proctor) Preston; her father, Samuel, being the son of Capt. Levi Preston, and descended from Roger Preston, emigrant from England. She was a woman of superior character, possessing a high order of mind, a heart devoted to labors of usefulness, and a deep, beautiful and consistent spirit of piety. She greatly endeared herself to the church in Roxbury and d. of consumption, June 12, 1860, aged 32 years and 5 months, lamented by a wide circle of relatives and friends. He was m., second, to Eliza King Buttrick, at Cambridge, Mass., by Rev. A. P. Peabody, D. D., and Rev. R. C. Waterston, Dec. 27, 1865. She was b. Jan. 14, 1833, in Cambridge; the dau. of Ephraim [6], and Mary (King) Buttrick, (Samuel [5], Samuel [4], Jonathan [3], Samuel [2], William [1]); her immigrant ancestor arriving from England in 1635, and settling in Concord, Mass. Among his descendants was Maj. John Buttrick, who gave the memorable first command to "fire" in the Revolutionary War, at the Concord fight. Her father was long a prominent lawyer at the Middlesex Bar, and d. Jan. 13, 1874, aged 80.

4 —— I. Endicott Greenwood (2d wife), b. March 8, 1867, in Cambridge.

II. Alfred Whitwell, b. Jan. 23, 1870, in Brooklyn, N. Y.

III. Helen Langley, b. Jan. 18, 1872, in Brooklyn.

IV. RALPH BUTTRICK, b. May 13, 1873, in Brooklyn.

V. MARGARET ROSS, b. July 2, 1876, in Quincy, Mass.

He remained in our class one year, then went to Brown University, R. I., where he grad. in 1852. Taught a high school at Wenham, Mass., for six months, and then entered the Divinity School at Cambridge, Mass., graduating July 17, 1855, and, the winter previously, receiving a license to preach from the Boston Association of Ministers. Having accepted a call from the Mt. Pleasant Cong. (Unitarian) Society at Roxbury, Mass., he formally assumed the duties of the pastorship, Dec. 19, 1855. But the sicknesses and sorrows of his first few years in the ministry made it desirable that he should seek a change of scene, and May 28, 1862, he embarked, with his Cambridge class-mate, Rev. Frederick Frothingham, upon an extended tour abroad, the itinerary of which we quote from the former edition of our "Memorial": "A hasty trip" (from Liverpool) "through Ireland and Scotland," "and thence to London, by Edinburgh, York and "Cambridge. From Cologne, ascended the Rhine. "A month's tramp among the mountains of Swit- "zerland, and from Geneva to Paris, where re- "mained for several weeks. Thence over Mt. "Cenis, through Turin, Genoa, and along the "Italian shore to Naples, where embarked for the "East, arriving at Alexandria, Egypt, November "14. Making up their Nile party at Cairo, "they ascended the river as far as the second

"cataract, occupying sixty-five days, with a suc-
"cessful and delightful trip, seeing Memphis, the
"pyramids, Thebes, Abu Sambul, etc. A desert
"tour from Cairo to Jerusalem, nearly on the main
"track of the Israelites, ascending Mt. Sinai, turn-
"ing aside to visit Mt. Hor and Petra, and ap-
"proaching Jerusalem, by way of Hebron. Mr.
"Putnam was sick of rheumatic fever at Jerus-
"alem, while his companions made the more
"northern tour, being only able, after five or six
"weeks' confinement, to visit places of interest im-
"mediately around the Holy City. The homeward
"route embraced Smyrna, Ephesus, the classic
" 'Isles of Greece,' Constantinople, a gaze upon the
"Euxine, delightful days at Athens, a 'Month of
" 'Rome, exceedingly instructive and full of the
" 'rarest enjoyment,' Vienna, Munich, Prague,
"Berlin, and other German cities, a brief revisit
"of Paris and London, and finally embarkation
"upon the 'Arabia' at Liverpool for Boston, where
"arrived Sept. 16, 1863."

His labors in Roxbury were closed the last Sabbath of June, 1864, having received a unanimous
call to settle over the First Unitarian Society in
Brooklyn, N. Y.—formerly Dr. F. A. Farley's—
where installed Sept. 28, Dr. E. S. Gannett, of
Boston, preaching the sermon. With this wealthy
and influential society he continued to labor for
more than 22 years, or till the spring of 1887;
establishing the Third Unitarian Church in the
city, building chapels for his own Sunday School
and a Mission School, which he had founded for

the poor, and engaging in other beneficent labors. Was also one of the founders, and one of the Board of the "Brooklyn Union for Christian Work," 1866, and onwards.

He has since resided in Concord, Mass., with frequent visits to Danvers, his native town, as President of the "Danvers Historical Society." Is also a member of the (1) "Long Island," (2) "New "England Historical and Genealogical," (3) "Brooklyn, New England," and (4) the "Concord "Antiquarian" Societies; the American Historical Association, the Victoria Institute, London; and is one of the "Sons of the American Revolution." Prior to 1864 he had delivered various courses of lectures, and prepared articles for papers and magazines, chiefly on his foreign travels. Had also published one sermon (1) in pamphlet form, occasioned by the death of Rev. George Bradford, of Watertown, Mass., 1859. His numerous book and pamphlet publications, after going to Brooklyn (and subsequently), may be catalogued as follows —mostly sermons and discourses, and nearly in chronological order:

(2) "A Happy New Year;" 1865.

(3) "Edward Everett;" 1865.

(4) "The Life to Come;" 1865.

(5) "The Freedom and Largeness of the Chris-"tian Faith;" 1868.

(6) "Unitarianism in Brooklyn;" Historical; 1869.

(7) "The Unitarian Denomination, Past and "Present;" 1870.

(8) "Tribute to the Memory of Mrs. Elizabeth "F. Andree;" 1872.

(9) "Brooklyn Pillars;" 1873.

(10) "Singers and Songs of the Liberal Faith;" 600 hymns and poems, from seventy writers; 500 pp.; growing out of a course of lectures in Brooklyn, first published in 1875.

(11) "Life through Christ;" 1876.

(12) "Christianity, the Law of the Land;" 1876.

(13) "The Memory of Mrs. Elizabeth Frothing- "ham;" 1876.

(14) "Funeral Sermon on George Francis "Thayer;" Dec. 31, 1878, and New Years' Sermon, Jan. 5, 1879; Matt. 24:44.

(15) "Report of the Executive Committee of "the Brooklyn Theatre Fire Relief Association;" presented by himself as Secretary; March 25, 1879.

(16) "A Discourse on William Lloyd Garrison, "and the anti-Slavery Movement;" June 1, 1879; Isaiah 58:6-8.

(17) "Celebration of the 100th Anniversary of "the Birthday of William Ellery Channing, in "Brooklyn, April 6 and 7, 1880;" edited; pp. 205; bound.

(18) "The Whole Family of God;" a memorial discourse; 1884.

(19) "Memorial of Mrs. Martha E. Low;" with a brief sketch of her son, Ethelbert M. Low; 1884; pp. 30.

(20) "Memorial of Mr. Ephraim Buttrick and "Mrs. Mary Buttrick;" pp. 17.

(21) "A Unitarian Oberlin;" or the story of Jasper L. Douthit, of Shelbyville, Ill.; 1888; 72 pp; book.

(22) "The Love that is unto Life;" sermon before the Maine Unitarian Conference, at Kennebunk, June 12, 1888.

(23) "Memorial Sermon on Rev. Charles H. "Wheeler, pastor of the Unitarian Church at Win- "chendon, Mass.," Aug. 5, 1888.

(24) "Sketches of Hon. Elias Putnam, Gen. "Grenville, M. Dodge, A. A. Low and others," in the "History of Essex Co., Mass.;" 1888.

(25) "Biographical Sketch of Gen. Israel Put- "nam," in "History of the Putnam Family;" 1892.

(26) "Wenham Lake and the Ice Trade," in three numbers of "Ice and Refrigeration;" an illustrated monthly; New York and Chicago; 1892.

(27) "Memorial Sermon on Abiel A. Low," at Brooklyn, N. Y., Jan. 15, 1893; 20 pp.

(28) "Rebecca Nurse and her Friends;" an address delivered in Danvers, Mass., July 29, 1892, at the dedication of a tablet in honor of her "Forty "Friends;" 1894; 38 pp.

(29) "Old Anti-Slavery Days;" proceedings of a commemorative meeting, held by the "Danvers "Historical Society," April 26, 1893; bound, pp. 180; introductory chapter (27 pp.), compilation and numerous biographical sketches by our class-mate.

Besides these, more than sixty extended articles of local history in the "Danvers Mirror;" most of them entitled "Danvers at Home and Abroad" were prepared, chiefly as vacation pastime. Also his annual reports as Chairman of the Executive Committee of the "Long Island Historical Society" for the years 1877-81.

Among his magazine contributions, in the "Unitarian Review," were a series of articles: "Liberal "Protestants in France;" a sketch of Helen Maria Williams, author of the hymn, "While Thee I Seek, "Protecting Power," "The Missionary Spirit," and "A Visit at Harworth, the home of Charlotte "Bronte."

Also several articles in the "Unitarian Monthly "Magazine," "Putnam's Monthly" (Salem, Mass.), "Harper's Weekly," etc.

Among his lectures are "Gen. Moses Porter" (now developed into an extended biography for publication), "The Land of the Pharaohs and the "Pyramids," "Famous Places on the French "Riviera," "The Old Guard," and "Personal Rec-"ollections of Notables at Home and Abroad."

Since coming to Concord he has preached in thirty or forty towns and cities and lectured before various Institutions, including courses at Tufts College, and at the Meadville (Pa.) Theological School on "Modern Archæological Discoveries, as "illustrating the Truth of the Bible History," and on "Hymns and Hymn Books."

He was elected President of the "Unitarian "Sunday School Society" in 1863, and was honored with the degree of D. D. from Brown University, in 1871.

A sketch of Dr. Putnam's Life and Character as a Clergyman, up to that date, appeared in the

"New York Sunday Times" of Jan. 1, 1865, and another sketch in the "Essex Co. History," (1888) highly commends the courage and patriotic sentiments of his address in London, Eng., July 4, 1862, in response to the toast, "The Constitution "of the United States."

Sketches appeared also in Patten's "Lives of the "Clergy of New York and Brooklyn," 1874, and in the "Encyclopædia of Contemporary Biography "of New York," 1878, and in other publications.

He visited Europe a second time, sailing from New York on his birthday, Jan. 10, 1883, and returning July 4. This tour included the winter months along the French Riviera (Cannes, Nice, Mentone, etc.), sojourns in Paris, London and other cities, and in the lake country of the great English poets. His addresses to English Unitarians, on this trip, are favorably noticed in the Essex County History. The tour itself was through the generous kindness of his Brooklyn Parish, they continuing his salary, paying for the pulpit supply, and adding $1,500 for his expenses abroad. "Was-"there ever such a church and people?"

Of his five children, (I) ENDICOTT GREENWOOD, is in business in New York; (II) ALFRED WHITWELL, is a law student in the Boston University; (III) HELEN LANGLEY, a graduate of Smith College (1893), is teacher of English Literature in the State Normal School at New Haven, Conn.; (IV) RALPH BUTTRICK, has just graduated (1894) at Amherst College; and (V) MARGARET ROSS, is a member of the High School, Concord, Mass.

CALIFORNIA

ANDREW REED, ESQ.

REED, ANDREW,

REEDSVILLE, PA.

1 —— Kishacoquillas Valley, near Reedsville, Mifflin Co., Pa., Feb. 14, 1832. His father's name was Abner Reed, who was b. at Reedsville, where his father, James Reed, first located. He and his half brother, William Brown, were the earliest white settlers in the Kishacoquillas Valley.

2 —— Academia, Pa., under David Wilson and David Laughlin, joining our class, in company with Hollenbush, near the middle of Sophomore year.

After graduating, he studied law at Easton, Pa., with Judge Washington M'Certny, who there had a small Law School; and a short time with E. L. Benedict, Esq., at Lewistown, Pa. He was admitted to the Bar at Lewistown in August, 1855; since which time he has practiced law in that place (Mifflin Co.), and also in the adjoining counties, for the very extended period of thirty-nine years; thus proving, among the men of our class so far sketched, *the most permanent*, or the longest stationed in the same locality and the same profession.

He was early honored with the office of District Attorney for Mifflin County.

Travelled through the West in the summer of 1863, passing some time at St. Louis, Mo., extending his trip into Mexico—where he spent some weeks and visited a brother, who was mining in that country—and remaining two weeks in San Francisco.

"June 24, 1878," he sends his regrets for not being able, contrary to previous expectation, to attend our 25th anniversary, and his kind regards to the brothers in attendance. He had been, at that date, for some time, Pres. of the National Bank of Lewistown, in connection with his law practice.

He had also sojourned one year, temporarily, in the city of Philadelphia, as a member of the Convention for revising the State Constitution.

In April, 1884, the Secretary was privileged to enjoy a visit at his home in the valley of the "blue "Juniata." Found him standing high as a lawyer and a citizen in Lewiston and vicinity; a man of influence, foremost in every good enterprise, and reputed wealthy; as the permanence of his life-work might well suggest, since it is only the "rolling stone" that "gathers no moss." The favor of his company back to Harrisburg, the splendid entertainment there, and a visit to the State Capitol, under his intelligent escort, can never be forgotten.

In Dec., 1892, he was "pursuing the same line-"of duty;" but had met with a great misfortune in the recent death of Mr. N. C. Wilson, who had been in his office since 1884, and "whose loss, on "account of his great fidelity and long connection "with me, has greatly increased my care."

Mr. Reed was reported by class-mate Young—in letter to our 40th anniversary meeting, June 19, 1893—as at that time seriously out of health, on account of which he was abroad for rest and treatment, having sailed two weeks previously.

Our brother explains the matter more fully in his own letter of Oct. 5, 1894, verifying the statement that he has led quite "a varied life for some "time back."

It seems that Mr. Wilson's death threw a large increase of business on to his hands which he (Mr. Wilson) had previously attended to, to his entire satisfaction. In the midst of this he was prostrated by a severe attack of the grip; and thus was induced the permanent ill-health for which his Philadelphia physician finally advised the ocean voyage. He was accompanied by a brother and a nephew (who has since been in his office); the trip across the Atlantic proving very beneficial to his health, and being passed without sea-sickness. Landed at Antwerp, Belgium; spent some days visiting the celebrated cathedral and art gallery of that city, and greatly admired the paintings of Rubens. Going thence to Brussels; the chief attractions there seen were the famous lace factories. Considerable time was next spent in Paris, and then in London, which he very much enjoyed. Visited Westminster Abbey and heartily agreed with Irving's description of the same; also the House of Commons while in session, and had the pleasure of seeing Gladstone. Finally he went to Liverpool and embarked in the "Umbria" for New York. Landing there a little after dark, he came over to Philadelphia the same night, and, walking down Market street, accidently slipped, broke his knee cap, was taken to a hospital and was there confined for about five months. Since then his health has been better, in many respects, than ever before, and his powers of locomotion are fully restored. This improvement he attributes largely to the *entire rest* from care and business enjoyed in the hospital, *following* the tour abroad.

He is now back at his old post, and living in his own house on the square, in the central part of Lewistown, adjoining the Court House.

This "varied" experience affords forcible evidence of our Heavenly Father's merciful designs;
"From seeming evil still educing good."

REMICK, CHARLES FREDERICK,
Brownington, Vt.

1 —— Brownington, Nov. 11, 1829. He was the son of Paige and Laura (Ward) Remick, and his grandfather was Edward Remick; but his father had removed from Brownington to Barnston, C. E., while we were in College. The Secretary visited our class-mate at this Canada home, soon after our graduation. His father d. Jan. 1, 1882, and his mother shortly after.

2 —— Brownington, under William Scales.

3 —— Harriet Anna Harrington, at Boston, Mass., Aug., 1858, by Rev. Nehemiah Adams, D. D. She was then a resident of Boston, the dau. of Samuel N., and Hannah (Lovejoy) Harrington; but b. in Norway, Me., May 4, 1833, when her parents were away from their home, which was then at Lowell, Mass. She d. in 1883, aged 50,

after being an invalid for years. Bereft of all but his youngest child, he afterwards "sought to bury "sad recollections by a new venture," and was m., second, to a Bohemian girl of 26 years—name not reported.

4 —— I. CHARLES EDWARD, b. July 11, 1859, and d. at Putney, Vt., March 17, 1860, of diphtheria, aged 8 months and 6 days.

II. ABRAHAM LINCOLN, b. March 4, 1861 (President Lincoln's inauguration day); and d. Oct. 3, 1861, of dysentery, aged 7 months.

III. HATTIE GRACE, b. July 24, 1862; d. Oct. 6, 1863, of debility, resulting from dysentery, aged 1 year, 2 months and 12 days. Thus "thrice "did the doating hearts of the parents bemoan the "loss of their only child."

IV. MABEL HORTENSE, b. Jan. 13, 1868.

V. CHARLES FREDERICK, JR., b. April 5, 1872.

VI. CHARLTON PAIGE, b. Mar. 5, 1874. The names of his second wife's children have not been furnished; only the general report (in his very cordial letter of Nov. 30, 1892) of "eleven "children in rapid succession, eight of them twins, "four of whom are still living, all babes or nearly "so." (We have repeatedly solicited this interesting family record, and waited for it in vain, till the latest possible moment).

He taught in an acad. for six months, after graduation, at Barnston, C. E., the residence of his parents. Next became "Advocate's Clerk" by indenture with John S. Sanborn, M. P., (D. C., 1842), at Sherbrooke, C. E., in the meantime writing for a livelihood in the office of the Prothonotary, and Clerk of the Court of Queen's Bench; holding also the office of Deputy Prothonotary and Magistrate's Clerk, and a portion of the time being Secretary of the Board of School Directors for the town of Sherbrooke. Leaving Canada, in Aug., 1855, he went to Boston, Mass., and entered the office of Beard & Nickerson, attorneys, No. 9 State St.; studied also with Gen. B. F. Butler, at Lowell, Mass. In Dec. was admitted to the Bar of Suffolk Co., on examination by Josiah G. Abbott, Judge of the Superior Court of Boston.

Going immediately West, he attended the U. S. land sales, which opened at Decorah, Northern Iowa, Dec. 25, 1855. Lingered at these sales about three months, speculating in real estate, and acquiring control of title to about 5000 acres of land. In March, 1856, in company with an acquaintance, started a new settlement on the then frontier in Howard Co., Iowa, where he remained until fall. Then, from mere curiosity, set out on a tour of speech-making, advocating the election of Col. Fremont to the Presidency.

During this tour he came upon the village of McGregor, Iowa, on the Mississippi river, where he spent the winter, entered upon the practice of his profession, and was still residing in 1863.

From March, 1864, till his next report in 1878, he was a practicing lawyer in Chicago, Ill., office at 208 La Salle St.

Several of his addresses, political, anniversary,

and connected with the legal profession, have been
in print; but all in his possession, as well as all his
books and papers, were destroyed in the great
Chicago fire of 1871, so that no exact list can be
given.

"Accept for yourself (the Secretary), and for
"all of our dear class, yet left on this side, my
"most sincere regards."

He wrote again from "Bird Island, Minn.,
"November 30, 1892" (as above noted), having
left Chicago the August previously, proposing
to remain in this new home, indefinitely, or
"until some other change overtakes me;" for,
in business, his history seems to have been
alike changeful, as in his domestic relations.
In 1885, he embarked with others in a wholesale
business in Chicago; but after four years of disap-
pointment, "to save the wreck from the dishonesty
"and bad management of associates," he was forced
to get out of it, with a loss of not less than $75,000,
all of which fell upon him, and he paid it; but at a
terrible sacrifice of real estate in and near Chicago.
He had previously owned 200 acres within ten
miles of the Court House, besides a large amount
of improved estate inside of the city proper. He
was forced to trade 100 acres of his land near Chicago, with ex-Gov. Marshall of St. Paul, Minn., for
farms, stock, town lots, etc., at Bird Island, at the
inventory price of $44,000, he (Gov. M.) paying
$20,000 in cash at Chicago. "I was thus com-
"pelled to come and see to it" (this property),
"where I now am, working incessantly."

Few of our number have been so bitterly bereaved as Mr. Remick. Besides the previous losses of his little ones, the three years, from 1880-83, seem to have witnessed the accumulation of his sorrows. In 1880, his then oldest boy, (V.) CHARLES "FREDDIE" met a tragic death by being run over in Chicago by a street car, almost before his own eyes.

Both his "dear parents" passed away, near together, early in 1882, as above stated.

In 1883, his dau., (IV.) MABEL H., 15 years old, suddenly d., after only three days' sickness of scarlet fever; which stroke was followed a short time later by his first wife's death.

May it be his happiness to experience that "whom the Lord loveth, He chasteneth."

ROBINSON, LEVI,

NEWPORT, ME.

1 —— Vassalboro, Me., March 13, 1827. His parents were Charles and Elizabeth or Betsey (Pease) Robinson of Vassalboro. His pedigree is Levi [5], Charles [4], Joseph [3], Benjamin [2], Levi [1]. "The "experience of his earlier life very strikingly proves "the adage that 'man proposes, but God disposes.' "When 14 years of age his father had made ar- "rangements to apprentice him to a tailor; but "about that time the tailor's shop was consumed by "fire, and the to-be-master left the state. Soon "after, he had engaged to take a voyage with a

"sea-faring cousin, but met with a severe accident
"by scalding, a few days before he was to set sail,
"and was thus prevented. His cousin's ship sailed,
"but neither ship nor crew have since been heard
"from."

2 —— Waterville, Me., under James H. Hanson;
and having passed the first three years of his course
at Waterville College, joined the Senior class at
Dartmouth in 1853.

3 —— Lydia Ann Curtis, July 26, 1857, by Rev.
C. B. Dunn, at Dexter, Me. She was a former
pupil of Mr. Robinson's, and the dau. of Caleb B.
Curtis, Esq., of Dexter, and nee Lydia H. Swanton; b. at Dexter, Sept. 15, 1832.

4 —— I. Mary Elizabeth, b. Feb. 4, 1860.

II. Amos Dean, b. Jan. 10, 1861.

III. Charles Edwin, b. May 23, 1863.

IV. Frank Bernard, b. June 10, 1865.

V. Lavinia Curtis, b. Nov. 20, 1870.

VI. Lydia Ann, b. June 15, 1873, all
probably in Iowa City, Ia.

After graduating, he fulfilled an engagement for
one year in the Central High School at Cleveland,
Ohio, and then (July, 1854) entered the law office
of Foote & Palmer in that city. He proceeded
thence to the Albany (N. Y.) Law School, Sept.,
1854, and there continued until the last of March,
1855, having been admitted to the Bar at Albany,
Dec. 14, previously, on examination in the Supreme
Court, before Judges Wright, Harris and Watson.
In May, 1855, he opened a law office with a fellow
student, at Iowa City, Ia., firm of "Plaisted &

"Robinson." The next month, his partner having deserted him to settle in Maine, he continued the business alone, and in Aug., 1856, was elected prosecuting attorney for Johnson Co., which office he held till Jan. 1, 1858.

Oct. 5, 1856, he was admitted to practice in the U. S. Courts.

In 1861 formed a business connection with Lemuel B. Patterson, Esq.—"Robinson & Patter-"son"—and after the Internal Revenue Law went into operation, held the position of Deputy Collector of the Second Division, Fourth District of Iowa; also Assessor of U. S. Revenue, 1864-69.

In 1869 he was again County and also City Attorney. He was run by the Republicans for County Judge in 1859, and beaten by the old Democratic incumbent; but after his connection with the Revenue ceased, 10 years later, he eschewed politics except to do his duty as a voter.

Our brother caps the climax for permanence, his record surpassing that of any other member of the class, thus far noted, for continued or uninterrupted labor in the same locality and line of professional pursuit, amounting in duration to 40 years, next May. Meanwhile, the snug little place of some 20 odd acres, in the suburbs and overlooking Iowa City—which in 1864 he made "the source of some "income and much pleasure," as gratifying his rural and agricultural tastes—had become, in 1879, large enough to furnish healthful exercise for the leisure time of himself and boys, and inure the latter to industrious habits. The same, in 1882, had developed into a suburban farm of 76 acres, and, as a matter of recreation, his attention had been turned to the raising of Jersey stock, with a herd of more than sixty head, superintending the business himself; but last year (1893) he was designing to close up that enterprise and return to his residence nearer the heart of the city, for greater quiet in declining years. As another side issue, in 1866 he helped to organize a woolen factory company, which flourished till about 1873.

In 1870 he was elected a member of the Executive Committee of the Iowa State University; and the catalogue of that Institution for 1879–80 represents him as still holding the same office; being also one of the "Board of Regents," while his two oldest sons were in the Senior and Sophomore Classes.

In 1870 Mr. Robinson also became an active member of the First Methodist Episcopal Church in Iowa City; and in 1879, a Trustee of the Church, and the Superintendent of its Sunday School, conceded to be the largest and best Sunday School in the city. In this latter position he was taking a laudable satisfaction as one "of the highest char-"acter, second only in importance to that of the "ministry."

Mr. and Mrs. Robinson have been highly blessed in their children. In 1879 he was permitted to say that three of them were members of the same church with himself, and that all of them were spared to their parents; of studious habits, and in the enjoyment of good health.

"We thank our most merciful Father, who has "so kindly guarded our fold, and signally favored "us."

Alas! that in 1893, they were obliged to record an exception to this family prosperity (as below); though they could still say, "All our other "children are yet living and in them we have great "comfort, as all have consecrated themselves to "their Saviour."

I. Mary E. took a partial course in the Iowa State University, and was m. to Hon. C. I. Crawford, Attorney-General of South Dakota, in 1893, residing at Pierre. They have one son and one dau.

II. Amos D. grad. at the University in 1880; was residing (1893) at Rathdrum, Idaho, as a civil engineer. Besides three years spent on railroad work in Kentucky, he had been largely engaged in government land surveys in Wyoming and Idaho. Was m. and had three children.

III. Charles E. grad. at the University in 1882, and would have graduated from the dental department of the same Institution, the March following his death, which occurred Feb., 1889, in his 26th year, of consumption, which had developed from the previous August. Having been betrothed to a most estimable young lady of Iowa City, he was united to her in marriage, but a short time before his departure.

IV. Frank B. is now a practicing Attorney in Sioux City, Ia., firm of "Blood & Robinson;" is m. and was the father of one child (1) Levi, Jr., named after his grandfather.

Moses Runnels.

The two youngest daughters are "still the light "of our home" (1893).

V. LAVINIA C. is a teacher in Iowa City.

VI. LYDIA A. is in the Sophomore Class of the University.

RUNNELS, MOSES THURSTON,
JAFFREY, N. H.

1 —— Cambridge, Vt., Jan. 23, 1830; was the son of Moses Thurston[4], (Stephen[3], Ebenezer[2], Samuel[1]), the last named being of Scotch descent, via Nova Scotia, at Bradford, Mass., in 1702. His grandfather, Stephen[3], was at the battle of Bunker Hill, from Haverhill, Mass., and his great-grand-father, Moses Thurston, d. very suddenly at Hollis, N. H., April 6, 1800, in his 80th year, while fer-vently engaged in prayer at a Conference meeting. His father, a leading business man in Cambridge, Vt., d. of consumption, Oct. 5, 1831, aged 41 years and 7 months, professing religion in the fellowship of the Cong. Church on his death-bed, and com-mending his only infant child to that Saviour whom he trusted. The mother of Moses T. Runnels, Jr., was nee Caroline Stearns; in the seventh genera-tion from Isaac Stearns, who came in the same ship with Gov. Winthrop and Sir Richard Saltonstall and settled at Watertown, Mass., in 1630; b. Nov. 25, 1797, in Waltham, Mass., and d. at the home of her son in Sanbornton, N. H., April 6, 1876, in her 79th year.

2 —— New Ipswich, N. H., and Jaffrey; under Edward A. Lawrence (D. C., 1843), David C. Chamberlain, and Henry T. Niles (D. C., 1847).

3 —— Fanny Maria, only dau. of Hosea S. Baker, Esq., of Haverhill, N. H., by Bro. Emerson, July 9, 1861. Her mother was nee Fanny Huntington, of the Connecticut family, and her father a lineal descendant of Capt. John Lovewell, of Pequawket fame, at Fryeburgh, Me., in 1725, whose only dau. m. Joseph Baker, his progenitor.

4 —— I. CAROLINE STEARNS, b. May 16, 1862, in Orford, N. H.

II. FANNY HUNTINGTON, b. Dec. 5, 1863, in Orford.

III. MARY AINSWORTH, b. July 22; d. Sept. 24, 1865, aged 2 months, in Orford.

IV. KATHERINE BAKER, b. Dec. 7, 1868, in Sanbornton, N. H.

V. MOSES THURSTON, b. June 13, 1870, in Sanbornton, and there d. suddenly of brain disease, Oct. 24, 1871, aged 1 year and 4 months.

He studied theology, three years, at East Windsor Hill, Ct., under Drs. Bennett Tyler (former President at Dartmouth), William Thompson, and Edward A. Lawrence (D. C., 1834); being there the room-mate and associate of Bro. Burton (two years), and spending three long vacations as "Student Sunday School Missionary," in Oxford County, Canada West. Was ordained as an Evangelist, by his home church at Jaffrey, Aug. 13, 1856, our teacher, Prof. Noyes, of Dartmouth, preaching the sermon. Had previously been approbated to preach by the Berkshire North Association at Dalton, Mass., May 5, 1856, on examination of ex-President Heman Humphrey, D. D.

For three years in the service of the "American "S. S. Union," Philadelphia, Pa., as follows: In Wisconsin as collecting agent, fall of 1856; in Western Texas, as S. S. Missionary, from Dec., 1856, till July, 1857; in Kansas Territory, same capacity, one year (except winter months of 1857-8, while supplying pulpit at Jaffrey), and one year at Boston, Mass., 11 Cornhill, as Superintendent of S. S. Missionaries, and General Agent of the Society.

Returned to Illinois, in the fall of 1859, and passed the following winter teaching at Durham, Hancock Co., at the same time preaching in that and neighboring towns. Having visited Kansas for the third time, also Northern Iowa, he made the trip from Chicago to Montreal by water, in company with his beloved mother, in Sept., 1860; and on the last Sabbath of the same month, commenced labors at Orford, N. H., as stated supply of the West Cong. Church.

His pastorates in Cong. Churches of New Hampshire may thus be tabulated:

(1) Orford West, 5 years (exactly) till October, 1865.

(2) Sanbornton, 21 years (exactly), till Oct., 1886.

(3) East Jaffrey, three years, till 1889.

(4) Charlestown, two years, till Nov., 1891.

(5) Croydon, Goshen and Unity (itinerant

Home Missionary service), one year, till Nov., 1892.

(6) Croydon, two years, till Nov., 1894; and still continues.

He now attends four services each Sabbath (involving 14 miles' travel) with less fatigue than two services, in his early ministry—*Laus Deo.* His present home is in Newport, N. H.

He rode several thousand miles on horseback during two years' missionary labor on the frontier. Was commissioned "Captain's Clerk," U. S. N., on board the "San Jacinto," East Gulf Squadron, on a vacation of three months, from April, 1864, receiving nearly $100 prize money above his salary, and being under Captain, late Rear Admiral, Theodore P. Greene, yet as his "mess-mate" and companion.

Took another vacation tour of four months, Jan. to May, 1884, to South Carolina, Florida and East Tennessee; also several other shorter excursions.

Attended Mr. Webster's funeral at Marshfield, Mass., in Oct., 1852, with Class-mate Crosby, they two being appointed delegates from the Senior Class.

Visited the tomb of the great statesman a second time with his son-in-law, Mr. Poole, Oct., 1893.

Was on the Examining Committee of Dartmouth College in Nov., 1863, and a delegate to the Cong. National Councils, of 1865, in Boston, and of 1874 in New Haven, Ct.; the latter in company with Bros. Burton and Palmer.

Was resident member of the N. H. Historical

Society for several years, from 1869, and a Trustee of the Gilmanton (N. H.) Academy.

His first newspaper article was in a Boston daily, of 1852, entitled "An Abducted Oration of Daniel "Webster's;" has since been a frequent correspondent of the local presses in or near every place where he has lived or labored, besides contributing a few articles to magazines. Several of his reports were published by the "American S. S. Union," in the "S. S. Journal" and "New York Observer," and he corresponded from the West in 1856-58 with the Keene (N. H.) "Sentinel," and "N. H. "Congregational Journal," and was its first Boston correspondent in 1859, of the Philadelphia "Sunday "School Times."

He published, while in College, as Chairman of the Executive Com. of the "United Fraternity," (1) A catalogue of their library, 1852.

(2) "A Memorial of Mrs. E. C. K. Garvey;" funeral sermon preached at Topeka, Kansas, Aug. 2, 1858; 32 pp.

(3) "A Memorial of the Class of 1853, Dart. "College;" 1864; 59 pp.

(4) "A Discussion with the Editor of the 'La- " 'conia Democrat,' " suggested by his sermon on Daniel 12:11-12; 1870; 14 pp.

(5) "Walking with God and its Results;" funeral sermon of Dea. James B. Abbott, M. D., Sanbornton, July 8, 1870; 12 pp.

(6) "Centennial Proceedings of the Cong. "Church in Sanbornton" (edited with introduction and appendixes); 1872.

(7) "A Genealogy of Runnels and Reynolds "Families in America;" 1873; 370 pp.

(8) Sermon preached in Hill, N. H., at the funeral of Mrs. Ednah Shaw; 1873; 11 pp.

(9) "A Memorial of Miss Martha A. Piper," of Claremont, N. H. (a Sanbornton parishioner), with compilation; 1875; 66 pp.

(10) "A History of Sanbornton, N. H.," in 2 vols.; vol. I., "Annals;" vol. II., "Genealogies;" with 75 illustrations, including maps; edition 1500 copies; 1881-82; total pp., 1662.

(11) The present (second) "Class Memorial" or "Biographical Sketches" of the Class of 1853, Dartmouth College.

I. CAROLINE S. was educated at the Gilmanton Acad., and the N. H. Conference Seminary, Tilton; was a successful school teacher for several years; was m. by her father to Fred D. Jardine, of Charlestown, N. H., at Newport, May 10, 1893; is an active church worker.

II. FANNY H. attended the same schools with her sister; also studied music in Boston, Mass.; was teacher of music at the Parksburg (Pa.) Acad., 1883-84, and in other places; was m. to Allan A Paul Poole, of Boston, by her father, at the Newport home, Dec. 25, 1891.. He is a native of St. Johnswood, London, Eng., and a nephew of Paul Poole, Royal Academician and Historical Painter. Upwards of 100 of her poems have been "accepted" by various newspapers and magazines, and her name appears in "The New Hampshire "Poets," a book compiled by Bela Chapin, of

Claremont, as also, with sketch, in the "Magazine "of Poetry," Buffalo, N. Y. Children, (1) Fanny Ethel (Poole), b. Sept. 30, 1892; (2) Robert Runnels, b. Dec. 10, 1893.

IV. KATHERINE B. was educated at the Cushing Acad., Ashburnham, Mass.; is now at home with her parents, in Newport.

SARGENT, DAVID JAMES BOYD, *,
TAMWORTH, N. H.

1 —— Tamworth, Feb. 8, 1829; being the son of Joel Sargent of that town.

2 —— The Free Will Baptist Seminary, New Hampton, N. H., and at Whitestown, N. Y., with private teachers.

Immediately after graduation, he became connected with the Seminary at North Scituate, R. I., as teacher, under the Rev. H. Quimby. He held this position one year and a half, and while there was consecrated to the work of the ministry in the Free Will Baptist denomination; and, the church in that place being destitute of a pastor, he supplied the pulpit a portion of the time, winning for himself many warm friends.

After his retirement from Scituate, he was associate teacher in the Literary Institution at New Hampton, N. H., and by his urbanity, devotedness and sympathy gained the love and attention of the students, and the respect and confidence of his associates. He continued to discharge his duties here with ability and fidelity between one and two years, when his health failed and he journeyed to the West.

He was acting professor in the College at Hillsdale, Mich., from Dec., 1856, till March, 1857, and then spent a few months at Oberlin, Ohio.

On his return to New England, he received a call to the pastorate of the church in Olneyville, R. I., which he accepted, Aug., 1857, at a salary of $1000 per annum.

After three months' successful labor, his health again failed him, and he was advised to a Southern tour. He went as far as Philadelphia. Here, being carefully examined by skillful physicians, he was advised by them to return to his friends. Previously to his starting for the South, he had requested a release from his pastoral relation, but his people declined. He therefore returned to them from Philadelphia, but "his pale face, trembling "limbs and hollow cough gave plain indications "that consumption was doing its slow, but sure "work."

After nearly another month spent among his beloved people, he came to Tamworth, to be in the family of his sister, then living, and under the care of her husband, Dr. Huntress. He reached their house in Dec., 1857. His disease was pulmonary consumption, and on Sabbath eve., May 9, 1858, he died, aged 29 years, and 3 months. The religious services of his funeral were attended at the Cong. House of Worship, in Tamworth, and a discourse was delivered by Rev. John Runnells, of Tamworth Iron Works (of his own denomination), from 1st Corinthians 13:12. His remains were interred in the Central burying ground, within a few rods of the former residence of his parents, and their remains, with his, and those of a brother and five sisters, compose one of the largest family groups in the oldest cemetery of Tamworth.

Mr. Sargent was held in high esteem for the virtues of his character, for his talents and his scholarship.

He was eloquent and popular as a preacher, and gave promise of taking a high position among the lights of his denomination. His manner in the pulpit was without much passion or gesture, and yet it was natural, dignified and impressive. As a pastor, he was highly esteemed and successful. His people would never consent to his dismission, and he died their pastor. He did not relinquish all hopes of recovery until within about a month of his decease. Then his face was set towards the Heavenly Jerusalem. "If it were the will of the "Lord," he remarked, "that I should live a while "longer, to preach Christ and care for my Church, "I should be glad, but for nothing else." At another time he remarked, "I have no ecstacies, no "visions, but I have tranquillity."

His early fondness for books, and his struggles for an education were somewhat remarkable. At five years of age he had read the New Testament through by course.

The circumstances of his father prevented his receiving aid in the prosecution of his studies, but he learned to endure hardness as a good soldier, to rely on himself, and to encounter and surmount obstacles. With great energy and self-denial—known to but few of his fellow students—did he hold on his way through College. Touching statements might be made in regard to weary journeyings, performed on foot, and other economical expedients designed to suit his outgoes to his limited income—expedients, involving sometimes, perhaps, too great a degree of hardship, yet ever illustrating his singleness of purpose.

Obituary notices appeared in the "Morning Star," Dover, N. H., March 2, 1859, from Rev. John Runnells and others, from which extracts, above; as also from the letters of Rev. S. H. Riddel, Tamworth, and his brother, Rev. W. A. Sargent, Houlton, Me.

SESSIONS, GILMAN LYMAN,
WEST WOODSTOCK, CT.

1 —— Woodstock, Feb. 8, 1829, being the son of Lyman Sessions.

After graduating from Dartmouth, he taught for one year in the city of Washington, D. C., and then quietly settled down to the mastering of his profession, the law, studying with Gov. Daniel S. Dickinson, of Binghampton, N. Y.; where also he has since been practicing, as far as health would admit. In 1860, had succeeded in attaining a desirable position at the Bar, when his health, "for

"some time before treacherous, entirely deserted
"him," and for two or three years he was "leading
"quite an idle, bohemian life, sometimes dabbling a
"little in the courts, sometimes shut up in his room,
"sometimes languidly floating about the world in
"pursuit of strength."

During the spring of 1864 he was again completely prostrated in health, for months unable to
walk, and for many weeks a close prisoner in his
room. The latter part of the summer was able to
be removed to his old home in Woodstock, Ct.,
having turned over his office and library to a
brother lawyer. Was still remaining at Woodstock, Dec. 28, of that year.

May 4, 1869, he was again at his home in Binghampton, where, with better health, he was "prac-
"ticing his profession, pleasantly and successfully."

In his class letter, 1878, from Binghampton,
"Law office, 48 Court St.," he says: "I have but
"little of a personal nature to report. Am living
"on through the successive years in this beautiful
"city, attending to the duties of my profession in
"such a way, that while it confines me rather
"closely, it does not quite enslave me. My posi-
"tion in it is such that it commands all the busi-
"ness I am able or care to do. I have never writ-
"ten an autobiography of myself, and therefore I
"cannot send you one. I will say, however, that
"long ago I came to the conclusion that a pleasant
"private life was more independent and desirable
"than a public or official one; and I have kept my-
"self steadily aloof from all offices, cliques and fac-

"tions—rejecting office whenever proffered—and "have thus far succeeded in keeping out of the "penitentiary and the inebriate asylum! There "is a Mrs. Sessions, an agreeable lady of twelve "years of matrimonial experience, and also a baby "boy, to both of whom I shall be most happy to in- "troduce you, if you will favor us with a visit. We "have a pleasant home of our own in a very pleas- "ant neighborhood of a most pleasant city, where "we live in a pleasant sort of way, and are always "glad to see our friends. My own life is, of course, "a somewhat busy one, but I find, or take more or "less time for literature, books, flowers and society. "Mrs. Sessions always enjoys seeing the old time "friends of her husband; and should you, or any of "my class-mates, in your vacation ramblings, be "able to come and see us, I trust to convince you "that the friendships of old Dartmouth days, though "allowed to slumber, do not die out of heart and "memory."

He was still "pursuing the even tenor of his "way" at Binghampton, June 13, 1893, thus prov- ing himself one of the most *permanent* men of the Class, probably *the* longest fixed, professionally, in one locality, if we reckon in his law-student life at the same place.

"With me," he says, "it has been constant work "—often interrupted by ill-health—with little in- "terest in political campaigns, or trials for heresy, "and with no curiosity about college regattas or "base ball games. A quiet life in my profession, "and a pleasant life at home, is about what there is

"of it. Our home remains the same as of old. It
"still possesses the wife and mother and 'the boy,'
"with books and flowers and such accessories.
"Said boy is now passed his fifteenth year, and is
"struggling with the difficulties of Latin and
"Geometry and all that they imply."

He again proffers his liberal hospitality, and
speaks very tenderly of Class-mate Burton, with
whom he once enjoyed a fishing excursion to the
Goose Pond region!

While living in Charlestown, N. H., the Secretary heard directly from Bro. Sessions through the
Rev. Thos. D. Howard, an associate clergyman of
that place, who, on visiting his friends in Binghampton, took occasion to inquire particularly after
Mr. Sessions, and call upon him. Mr. Howard reports his standing there as high in the estimation
of his fellow citizens, both professionally and socially. Our class-mate will be recalled as one of
the most brilliant composition writers of our number, a supposed admirer and imitator of Thomas
Carlyle, though abhorring statistics, as his Class
record shows. At least one beautiful effusion of
his pen has been given to the world, being "A
"Memorial Tribute to Hon. Orlow W. Chapman,
"late Solicitor-General of the United States," pronounced before the Supreme Court at Binghampton, Feb. 25, 1890.

STANTON, HENRY ELIJAH, *,

MANCHESTER, N. H.

1 —— Brookfield, N. H., July 23, 1831. His parents were Dea. Charles F. and Betsey (Cook) Stanton, of Brookfield. His brother, Benjamin F. Stanton, was a printer; came to Lake Village, N. H. (now Lakeport, in the city of Laconia), about 1866, and started a newspaper, the "Lake Village "Times," with which our Class Secretary was considerably identified for several years. He took in a partner, Col. Martin H. Haynes, afterwards M. C., firm of "Stanton & Haynes." He possessed like talents and genial qualities of mind and heart with his brother Henry; also the same feeble constitution. After making his paper a complete success, he returned to Manchester and there, as it is reported, died.

2 —— High School in Manchester, from 1846 till 1850.

Our class-mate's health continuing poor after leaving college, his physicians and friends advised him to spend the winter at the South.

In the winter of 1854-5 he taught at Portsmouth, Va.; there also delivered a course of lectures, which were highly spoken of by the papers of the day.

The next season he assumed the position of "Professor of Languages and Mathematics," in the Leavenworth Collegiate Institute, at Petersburg, Va., where he labored for about one year with good success.

He d. at Petersburg, Feb. 22, 1856, of typhoid fever and congestion of the brain, aged 24 years and 7 months.

Of his life previously to entering College, his pastor bears the following testimony:

"Henry I have known well from a boy of 12 "years till his death, and never knew aught against "him. I may confidently say, though not openly a "professor of religion, he was no skeptic—indulged "in no secret infidelity, as many of our young men, "who are taught in our high schools and colleges "do, in these days."

A friend of his in Virginia, who had a favorable opportunity for forming an estimate of his character, in writing to his deeply afflicted mother, says: "I have seldom met with a young man so "pure, so gifted, so highly cultivated, possessing "so little of earth's alloy, and so much that was "truly lovely and attractive. Notwithstanding his "shyness, he was so prepossessing that he excited "the interest of a number of visitors" (i. e., to the Public Library, of which the writer was Librarian), "yet he made but few intimate acquaintances."

The writer of the above was with him in his last illness, and during the sad night of his death, and says he was calm, prayerful and resigned; repeating several verses of poetry and one stanza frequently, from Longfellow's Psalm of Life:

> "Life is real! life is earnest!
> "And the grave is not its goal;
> "Dust·thou art, to dust returnest,
> "Was not spoken of the soul."

The following resolutions were passed by the faculty and students of the Leavenworth Collegiate Institute, and published in the "Petersburg Intelli-"gencer":

"*Resolved*, That, we bow with profound grief be-"neath the afflicting stroke which has suddenly "laid low in death our much esteemed fellow Pro-"fessor, and our zealous, devoted and revered "teacher; and that while we cannot fathom the "solemn event, we would 'be still,' hear the voice "of God, and receive the lesson which it contains.

"*Resolved*, That, to a richly endowed and culti-"vated mind were united in him a delicate and re-"fined taste, a uniformly kind, considerate and gen-"erous heart, and a life of unsullied and irreproach-"able purity; and that in all the relations which he "sustained we knew him only as a gentleman of "modest, but undoubted and excellent worth."

Mr. Stanton wrote considerably for the newspapers, and, during the years 1851-3, was a frequent contributor to the "Manchester American." He left more than 500 manuscript papers; and one of his last, written a short time before his death, and seemingly prophetic of that event, was an Introduction to a Lecture upon Edgar Allan Poe.

His mortal remains were brought from Virginia, and his dust now lies in the beautiful cemetery at Manchester.

STATHAM, FRANCIS CUMMINS,

GREENSBORO, GA.

1 —— Greensboro, Oct. 29, 1829. His father's name was M. Walker Statham; or, as we may infer, more correctly, from his cousin's statement, "Mr. Emory Statham." He was named after Francis Cummins, D. D., an itinerant Presbyterian clergyman of great power in the Carolinas and Georgia, 1780-1832.

2 —— Greensboro Male Acad. in part, and privately in part.

He entered Princeton (N. J.) Theological Seminary in 1853, and graduated in 1856. The writer visited him there, in April of his last year, and found him standing well as a student.

Was ordained at Rome, Ga., in the fall of the same year, and spent the next eighteen months in Home Missionary service, visiting all the most important places in Georgia and Florida; six months of that time in charge of the Presbyterian Church at Bellevue, Ga., and six months at Ocala, Fla., in the same capacity.

In the summer of 1858 he removed to New York City, and resided in the General Theological Sem. until he was ordained Deacon in the Protestant Episcopal Church, Nov., 1859.

Had charge of a parish on Long Island about two years, until April 1, 1862, but resumed his residence in New York City the May following, and was there living in March, 1864, with location at 223 West 20th street. He had assisted the

Rector of St. Luke's Church, Brooklyn, N. Y., for three months; the Rector of St. Bartholomew's, N. Y., for the same length of time; the Rector of Calvary Church, N. Y., for about six weeks, daily; the Clergy of Trinity Church for some nine months, and at the date last given was assisting the Rector of St. Peter's Church, West 20th street, N. Y.

In the discharge of his professional duties while in Georgia and Florida, he travelled over 4,000 miles on horseback. Was engaged with others in several literary enterprises—especially in those departments requiring the use of the modern languages—the chief of which was connected with church hymnody, involving six months' labor in 1863, in company with the Rev. John Freeman Young, of Trinity Church.

No further tidings from Mr. Statham for more than thirty years, or since last seen by the Secre-. tary in New York City, July, 1864.

A letter to him, dated Jan. 10, 1893, and sent to Greensboro, Ga., with special request that it be "forwarded" to his present address, was, in April following, remanded to the writer from the "Dead "Letter Office."

His cousin, Mrs. P. S. Dudley, of Grenada, Miss., under date of April 29, 1894, confesses to a total ignorance of his whereabouts for many years, though thinking that from his "large connection" formerly, in Greensboro, some information might be obtained; but C. C. Norton, of Greensboro (May 25, 1894), says: "Nobody here knows the

"address of the Rev. F. C. Statham. He has not
"been heard of in twenty years. The last intelli-
"gence was that he went to Europe."

STATHAM, WALTER SCOTT, *, N. G.,
AUGUSTA, GA.

1 —— Danburg, Wilkes Co., Ga., July, 1832,
being the second son of Dr. Augustin Davis and
Lucy Bullock (Tate) Statham. His mother's family were from Virginia. His parents removed to
Yalabusha Co., Miss., in 1842, with a family of six
children, their two oldest having died before they
left Georgia. On his father's maternal side he was
related to Jefferson Davis; on the paternal side to
Hon. L. Q. C. Lamar. Dr. Statham (his father)
had d. two weeks previously to his own death,
July 14, 1862. Walter S. Statham was an own
cousin of our class-mate last sketched. While in
College he seems to have been again residing, temporarily at least, in Georgia.

2 —— Augusta, Ga. (probably).

3 —— Annie V. Elliotte, of Grenada, Miss.,
June, 1858; she being the dau. of Dr. Elliott, of
Alabama, and her mother, a sister of the gallant
Lieutenant, I. N. Brown, of the U. S. Navy, afterwards a Commodore in the Confederate service,
and commander of the well remembered "Arkansas"
of Mississippi river and Vicksburg fame.

She was an Episcopalian, though her mother
(still living) and her sisters are all Presbyterians.

Her step-father was brother-in-law to ex-Gov. Foote, of Mississippi. She died "broken-hearted, "and was laid beside her husband, six years after "his death," in 1868.

4 —— I. ELLIOTTE WINTER, b. March, 1860, in Grenada; d. July, 1861, aged one year and four months, in Yalabusha Co., at his grandmother's country home. His devoted father was allowed only the privilege of seeing him die and be laid to rest, ere the duties of the field demanded his return to his regiment.

Having commenced the study of Law immediately on leaving our class, Mr. Statham entered into practice as the partner of Gen. E. L. Acee, in Grenada, Miss., in 1855.

Mr. Acee was previously from South Carolina, and a General of the militia in that state, in former years. He continued in this partnership till his marriage in 1858, and then practiced alone till he joined the Southern Army near the commencement of the Civil War. He was first enlisted as Captain (by election) of Co. G.—the Grenada Rifle Co.—and the first to leave Grenada in 1861. They rendezvoused at Corinth, Miss., where he was elected Colonel of the 15th Miss. regiment, and finally succeeded Gen. Zollicoffer, as acting Brigadier-General after the battle of Shiloh. In command of a brigade, he was sent to hold Vicksburg, Miss., in July, 1862, where he died of hæmaturia, and malarial fever, on the 30th of that month, aged 30 years. . His remains were brought for interment to Grenada, to rest in the I. O. O. F.

cemetery, beside those of his father and his little son. Indeed, the news of his father's death, so recently coming upon him, when "worn out from ex-"posure," produced a shock to which he soon yielded. His death left only a sister and brother as survivors of the once numerous family. His photograph was received through a friend who was visiting N. H. in 1878, and inserted in the class album.

It may be remembered that our class-mate had a brother, Lafayette S. Statham, who was with him at Hanover for some time, also that this brother became warmly attached to one of the brightest of the Hanover boys, Byron J. Dudley, who went back with him to the South. This now only surviving sister had married Mr. Dudley, June 18, 1857; and the same summer our class-mate revisited Hanover in company with Mr. and Mrs. Dudley.

Mr. Dudley d. Feb. 15, 1867, leaving a little son of four weeks, (1) Byron Statham Dudley.. Mrs. Dudley's last and youngest brother also d. at Grenada, Aug. 10, 1883, leaving her and her son "to struggle on alone through many disappoint-"ments and vicissitudes."

She again visited Hanover in 1871, when her boy was 4 years old.

Has been for many years, and is still, a teacher at Grenada. Speaks of her son as a noble and good young man, an elder in the Presbyterian Church, much loved and respected; taking first honors in the Dental Department of Vanderbilt

University, Nashville, Tenn., in Feb. last, and hoping to graduate from the same in Feb. 1895.

She speaks very tenderly of our class-mate. Hopes he was a Christian, though he was not a member of any church. Their parents were of the Baptist persuasion.

"I certainly appreciate the honor of knowing "that my dear brother's memory is still cherished "by the survivors of his class.   *   *   With sin-"cere good wishes for the welfare of those who "still linger 'on this side of the river,' I am "earnestly and respectfully your friend, Mrs. P. S. "Dudley, nee P. T. Statham."

STEWART, LEVI MERRICK,

CORINNA, ME.

1 —— Corinna, Dec. 10, 1827; the son of David and Eliza (Merrick) Stewart; "of Scotch descent— "family tradition says from Charles II. and Nell "Gwynn."

2 —— Hartland, Me., principally; also, one term each, at Cornith and Bloomfield, Me. He entered Dartmouth College one year in advance, at the beginning of his Class Sophomore year. Went his Junior year to Waterville College, Me., and returned his Senior year to Dartmouth, in company with M. D. Brown, Oakes and Robinson.

After graduating, he taught the Searsport (Me.) Union School; read Law with his brother, David D. Stewart, Esq., at St. Albans, Me., and took his degree at the Harvard Law School, in Cambridge, Mass. Was admitted to the Bar, in Maine, in September. Settled in practice at Minneapolis, Minn., Oct. 29, 1856, and there continues to the present time.

We have previously alluded to the "sticking "qualities" of Bros. Allen, Chase, Lamson, Parker, H. M. Perrin, Reed, Robinson and Sessions, to which list M. D. Brown should probably be added, to be hereafter supplemented by the names of Strow and Waterhouse. And now comes Bro. Stewart to claim, next to Robinson, the honor of the longest period of continued employment in the same place; as he commenced in Minneapolis less than a year and a half later than Robinson in Iowa City.

In his letter of Jan. 20, 1893—the first he had ever written to any of his class-mates—he directs the Secretary 'simply to say of himself that he is 'still in the practice of the Law at Minneapolis.'

With all respect to our brother's modesty, we must beg the privilege of indulging in a few notices which have already been made public. The "New York Tribune Monthly" for June, 1892, is a pamphlet of 93 pp.; giving a list of American Millionaires, and the lines of business in which their fortunes were made. The name of L. M. Stewart is given among them—and 43 others in Minneapolis—with the added statement, "Law "practice for many years, and investments."

We also feel at liberty to subjoin the following extracts from a leading Minneapolis newspaper:

"One of the unique features of Minneapolis'
"business centre, is the green grass plat, grove and
"cottages which constitute 'Elder Stewart's Corner,'
"on Fourth street and Hennepin avenue. This
"cheerful spot is in pleasing contrast with the sur-
"rounding monotony of business blocks, and af-
"fords a visual relief to all who view it. It is a
"living oasis in the midst of a dead expanse of
"brick and stone. Levi M. Stewart, better known
"as 'the Elder,' who owns and occupies this prop-
"erty, is one of this city's best known citizens, hav-
"ing been with it almost from its beginning. The
"increase in the city's population has been about
"an hundred fold since Elder Stewart arrived here.
"He is one of the many men from Maine who have
"made this place their home and have formed one
"of the most sterling elements of the community.
"Tradition says that his birthplace was a farm in
"Penobscot County, and that the date of his ar-
"rival there is entirely unknown; but the Elder
"seems to have served an injunction on Father
"Time, so that his years are usually discounted
"about thirty per cent."

Allusions are next made to his education at
Dartmouth and the Cambridge Law School, as
above, and it adds: "He never did a stroke of
"business before coming here" (we might take ex-
ceptions to this statement, in view of his well-
remembered diligence in 'working his way' through
the Academy and College). "He is a great col-
"lector of law and other literature, and now
"possesses at his commodious offices, in the Kasota

"block, the finest law library in the West. For
"many years Elder Stewart has been one of the
"hardest workers in his profession. It is said that
"he has averaged during that time more than
"eighteen hours of labor, daily. It is consequently
"not surprising that he has accumulated a fortune,
"popularly estimated at from $8,000,000 to $10,-
"000,000, having invested his earnings largely in
"Minneapolis real estate. In everything he is
"guided by the wise and conservative counsel of
"his 'wife,' whom nobody ever saw, but whom he
"claims to consult on all subjects of importance.
"With all his assiduous toil, he believes in inno-
"cent amusement, and is one of the best patrons of
"every good show that appears. 'Joshua Whit-
" 'comb' is said to be one of his favorite plays, and
"he has probably witnessed it as many as forty
"times. He expects to go to the World's Fair,
"and will doubtless 'do' it with a thoroughness
"equalled by very few persons. He enjoys a good
"story, and don't believe in worrying about any-
"thing. For physical exercise he acts as his 'wife's
" 'hired man,' labors in the early morning hours,
"and keeps the oasis in apple pie order. People
"who don't know him sometimes sympathize with
"the 'hired man.' In religion he is a 'Home
" 'Baptist,' and the only members of his denomina-
"tion are himself and wife, so that it is one of the
"most harmonious religious sects ever known.
"The 'Home Baptist' pulpit is located in a tree by
"the cottage where he lives. His active exercise
"and tranquil spirit render him impervious to the

"assaults of Jack Frost so he finds no occasion for
"the use of an overcoat. While Elder Stewart
"practices careful economy in all business trans-
"actions, he has a warm heart for suffering human-
"ity, and many are the generous deeds which
"should be credited to him, but which are known
"to but few aside from the immediate beneficiaries.
"To his kindness the Northwestern Hospital is in-
"debted for its present site. His gifts in various
"ways probably mount into hundreds of thousands
"of dollars in aggregate. The needs of helpless
"women and children appeal especially to his sym-
"pathy. His charitable deeds are performed in an
"unostentatious manner that avoids publicity.
"Though he talks much about his 'wife', he never
"talks about himself. While ever ready to listen
"to appeals for worthy aid, he is keen to detect
"fraud and deception. His handwriting is done
"with microscopic exactness, and the same char-
"acteristic is noted in all his business affairs.
"While he might readily make a $10,000 gift to a
"deserving cause, he would spend a thousand dol-
"lars to fight the man who wanted to cheat him
"out of a cent."

Then follows an account of the celebrated law
case in which the title to a part of the grounds he
now occupies was stoutly contested by David M.
Cochran, of Springfield, Ohio. The action for
ejectment was commenced in April, 1867, and was
first decided against the defendant by the District
Court, in January, 1870. Mr. Stewart appealed to
the Supreme Court, and after long delays the

former decision has been totally reversed, Aug. 24, 1893; the plaintiff being ordered to pay the defendant $969, which he did, together with the defendant's costs sustained.

Through much of this case Mr. Stewart was his own attorney. The contest was an unusual one. Both plaintiff and defendant claimed title to the premises under the same mortgage, but under separate foreclosures thereof. The final decision was that Stewart is the legal owner of the premises in dispute, that the plaintiff never had any title or claim to any part thereof, and that Stewart's title to the premises, under the mortgage and foreclosure of the same, was good and valid.

"The property, being located in the heart of the "city, great values were involved in the contest for "its title. The result leaves the site of the 'Home " 'Baptist' pulpit in the undisturbed possession of "its long-time occupant and owner, who has often "declined to allow any further encroachment of "business improvements upon its park-like beauties. "Elder Stewart and his estimable 'wife' have "doubtless many years of quiet enjoyment before "them, in their humble cottage among the trees of "the 'Oasis'" (generally known as "Zion's Hill").

Mr. Stewart has never held, never tried for, and never wanted any office, civil, clerical or political.

A discerning lady of our acquaintance has decided that there can be no other Mrs. Stewart but the guardian spirit who is continually suggesting to him words of sympathy, and practical wisdom, and acts of kindness and beneficence.

STROW, JOHN DE WAYNE,

WEATHERSFIELD, VT.

1 —— Weathersfield, April 11, 1831. His parents were Reuben and Elizabeth M. Strow; the former of English, the latter of Scotch descent. His sister, now deceased, was Mrs. Dr. L. J. Graves, late of Claremont, N. H., whose two daus. (his nieces), Mrs. P. P. Colburn, of Claremont, and Miss Mary E. Graves, who is at the head of the Arcadia Seminary at Wolfeville, Nova Scotia, are now his only surviving relatives in the East.

2 —— Springfield, Vt., and Thetford, Vt.

3 —— Maria B. Fox of Schoharie Co., N. Y., at Fort Dodge, Ia., by Rev. E. L. Dodden, Dec. 31, 1856. She was b. April 17, 1833, in Sharon, N. Y.; her father being Dr. George F. Fox, and her mother nee Catherine Shafer, of German descent.

4 —— I. ANNA, b. Sept. 10, 1861, in Fort Dodge, Ia.

II. EDWIN JAMES, b. Jan. 17, 1865, in Des Moines, Ia.

III. CLARENCE DE WAYNE, b. June 14, 1868, at Fort Dodge.

IV. JOHN LELAND, b. Jan. 3, 1871, at Fort Dodge.

Leaving Dartmouth in 1852, he first went to New York City and entered into real estate business with his brother, James R. Strow, and at the same time commenced reading Law. Was there admitted to the Bar in 1854. In August, 1855, he removed to Fort Dodge, Ia., and has since resided there continuously (with the brief exception below noted), till the present time (1894), principally engaged in dealing in real estate. He is thus to be reckoned among the most permanent men of our class in his life-work, rivalling in adhesiveness, Robinson and Stewart, who commenced in their respective cities the same and the following years, though without a temporary residence elsewhere.

Mr. Strow was at Des Moines, Ia., from the spring of 1863 to the fall of 1865, acting as chief clerk in the office of the Provost Marshal, at a salary of $1,200 per annum, and some perquisites. He was at that time the possessor of some 1000 acres of choice bottom lands on the Iowa river.

In the fall of 1865, after his "temporary resi-"dence" at Des Moines, he returned to Fort Dodge.

In his letter for one of our class meetings (probably 1878), he says: "While circumstances "will prevent my being with you in person, I shall "be with you in spirit. I have nothing to report "as to my career since leaving College that would "be interesting. Have had no particularly good "or bad fortune, and no reason to complain of my "lot, having slid through life, so far, rather smooth-"ly. I notice with pleasure the eminence attained "by some of our class who have earned a world-"wide reputation in science."

Still at Fort Dodge, Feb. 10, 1893, he adds: "I "have passed along quietly, having attained no "exalted position nor met with any adverses or "misfortunes; and think I have enough, with "economy and good management, to carry me "through the short balance of my life."

The blessing of Heaven has indeed rested upon our brother in his family relations. What a contrast with the experience of some of us who used to sit so near to him in the halls of old Dartmouth!

In 1878, he could say he had lost no children, and had but very little sickness in his family. And again, at last reported date, as above, his four children were all living, though away from home. "So, Mrs. Strow and I are alone, the same as when "we commenced life. My health is good and I am "strong and vigorous for a man of my age." (The youngest son has since returned to the home circle, as below).

I. Anna resides in Des Moines; was m. Nov. 5, 1890, to J. H. Woods of that city. Child (1) Helen (Woods) b. Aug. 5, 1893.

II. Edwin J. is at Council Bluffs, Ia., employed in running a cigar and news-stand in Grand Hotel.

III. Clarence D. is in Chicago, Ill., in real estate and loan business, at 69 Dearborn street.

IV. John L., previously at Eagle Grove, Ia., is now at Fort Dodge, in the jewelry business, residing with his parents.

THOMPSON, WILLIAM CHARLES,

WORCESTER, MASS.

1 —— Plymouth, N. H., Sept. 25, 1832. He was the son of William Coombs Thompson, Esq. (D. C., 1820), a lawyer, for many years in Plymouth; his pedigree was William C.[4], William C.[3], Thomas W.[2], Thomas[1]; the last named having migrated from Scotland directly to this country. His grandparents were Hon. Thomas W. Thompson, of Concord, N. H., and Elizabeth (Porter) Thompson, of Salisbury, N. H. His mother's maiden name was Martha Higginson Leverett, dau. of Mr. John Leverett, of Windsor, Vt. He was the older brother of Gen. John Leverett Thompson, of Chicago, Ill., who was a student at Dartmouth soon after our graduation, and commenced his military career as Captain of one of the four New Hampshire companies in the Rhode Island Cavalry, 1862, receiving the degree of LL. B. from Harvard, in 1858, and the honorary degree of A. M. from Dartmouth, in 1867, and also from Williams in 1875.

2 —— Kimball Union Acad., Meriden, N. H., under C. S. Richards.

He studied Law for the first year after graduating with Hon. Dwight Foster, at Worcester, Mass., and two years at the Law School, in Cambridge, Mass. Was admitted to the Bar in Worcester in 1856 and commenced the practice of Law in Oct. of the same year, in St. Paul, Minn., where he continued till June, 1862.

His health failing, he then returned to Worcester, and the same year went to New York City, and was re-admitted to the Bar with the intention of practicing there. But his health continued to fail, and having been attacked with hemorrhage of the lungs, in March, 1863, he went to Nassau, New Providence, to obtain a warmer climate. Soon after arriving there, he was appointed United States Vice Consul, and acted in that capacity till the close of the war in 1865, when he returned to this country.

It proved a matter of regret to his friends that the improvement of his health experienced on the island was only temporary.

He resided at Worcester and Somerville, Mass., from 1866 to 1877. His health was then so far renewed that in May, of the latter year, he took up his residence in Pepperell, Mass., where he has remained till the present year, 1894. He boarded at first with Dr. Howe, where first seen by the Secretary (after our several pleasant vacation visits in Worcester, 1854-6), in 1884. He was then employing himself in reading solid, never light, literature, reviewing his law studies and writing letters.

His health has continued to improve since residing in Pepperell. The Secretary has visited him repeatedly, and always with satisfaction. Oct. 24, 1887, he was occupying a very pleasant home and private boarding place at C. H. Peck's, one and a half miles from Pepperell Centre, where he probably is at present.

We well recall Mr. Thompson as one of the most

brilliant recitation scholars in our class, especially the first year, in Prof. Sanborn's department, and we have not forgotten his generous nature and genial qualities of mind and heart.

We have often, in these later years, almost envied our brother, the life of dignified ease and freedom from care, as well as of literary leisure and independence, which he is permitted to lead.

In appearance he has grown old but slightly. Would be pleased to receive letters from any of his class-mates.

His last report of himself (Nov. 1, 1894) is that 'his health has not been sufficiently good of late 'years to admit of the practice of his profession, 'and he has lived in quiet and retirement, mostly 'occupied in the study of Law and working at his 'trade as a carpenter.'

THOMPSON, WILLIAM SMITH,
WILMOT, N. H.

1 —— Wilmot, Aug. 22, 1828. His father was Samuel [3] Thompson (William [2], Moses [1]); his mother, Anna True Smith, the dau. of Dea. William True Smith. His parents were natives of Deerfield, N H., father b. June 5, 1800; mother b. Dec. 5, 1803. They were m. in Deerfield, by their pastor, Rev. Nathaniel Wells, Oct. 17, 1827, and immediately moved to the home in Wilmot, where they spent the remainder of their lives in diligent and successful farming employments. His mother

d. Feb. 12, 1862; his father d. Aug. 11, 1866.

2 —— Meriden, N. H., under Rev. C. S. Richards.

3 —— Harriet Tibbetts, of Reading, Mass., Nov. 30, 1860, by Dr. William Barrows. She was the dau. of Enos and Cynthia (Parker) Tibbetts; b. in Reading, May 31, 1833. Her father was b. in Rochester, N. H., Aug. 12, 1795, and d. April 17, 1865; her mother was b. in Reading, Mass., July 6, 1804, and d. Sept. 1, 1875. Their married life was spent in Reading, Mass., at the farm home to which they first moved.

4 —— I. HARRIET ANNA, b. Jan. 28, 1862, in Alna, Me.

II. WILLIAM HENRY, b. May 17, 1869, in Acton, Me.

He reported of these children in their early years that they were "active, mirthful and giving prom-"ise, with favorable opportunities, of becoming "average scholars."

The first fall and winter after graduating he taught at Northwood, N. H., and the spring ensuing at Salisbury, N. H. Studied for the ministry at the Andover Theological Seminary, entering in 1854, and graduating in 1857. Was licensed to preach the gospel by the Andover Association, at Andover, Mass., Feb. 10, 1857, and ordained as an Evangelist, at Solon, Me., Oct. 17, 1860. He had remained at Andover as a resident licentiate, for a few months, after taking his degree, preaching in the meantime as opportunity offered, and five or six Sabbaths at Stoddard, N. H. Engaged for one year as minister at Enfield, N. H., after which he spent a few months in New York City and Brooklyn, attending lectures at the Union Theol. Sem., and taking lessons in elocution. Subsequently he preached three months at Guilford, Vt., and elsewhere, till Feb., 1860, when he engaged for one year in supply of the churches at Solon and at Bingham, Me.

In March, 1861, Mr. Thompson took up his residence at Alna, Me., Lincoln Co., near the coast, where in 1863, with encouraging prospects of usefulness, he was the acting pastor of two churches, the Cong. Church in Alna, and the 1st Cong. Church in New Castle. His labors in this field were closed Sept. 15, 1866, after which he again resided at Andover, Mass., during a portion of 1867, and supplied pulpits in different places—one or more Sabbaths in each of the New England States. He was stated supply of the Cong. Church in Loudon, N. H., for one year, from Sept., 1867; and Jan. 1, 1869, entered upon his longest and very successful pastorate of sixteen years and two months over the Cong. Church of Acton, Me. In 1885 he commenced a seven years' pastorate with the Cong. Church in Newington, N. H., which closed June 1, 1892. In October following, largely on account of his son's health, he entered upon his "seventh field of labor—an agricultural one," removing his family to Hampton Falls, N. H.— yet within three miles of the heart of Exeter Village, which is his post-office address—and here holding himself in readiness for occasional pulpit supplies. Our brother wrote for the "Congregational "Journal," Concord, N. H., while a member of the Seminary, and afterwards; and furnished frequent articles for the Portland "Christian Mirror" during his residence in Maine.

An article published in the Christian Mirror, "Shall we Help," presenting the duty of the weaker churches, when home missionary funds are low, received favorable comment. Several articles were published earlier under the title "Winter Repose," showing the tendency of many of the weaker churches to be without earnest action in the winter season. The papers have not been perserved and the titles of other articles are forgotten.

I. HARRIET A. was m. to John Franklin Turner, of West Lebanon, N. H. Their present residence is in Reading, Mass. The couple were joined in marriage at Newington, March 18, 1886, by the bride's father. Mr. Turner is head clerk in auditor's room of the Boston & Maine railroad. They have three healthy and bright children: (1) William Franklin (Turner), b. in Newington, May 6, 1887; (2) Edward Harrison, b. in Medford, Mass., April 19, 1889; (3) Anna Rebecca, b. Nov. 6, 1892, in Reading, Mass. They usually, as a family, pass several weeks with their grandparents each summer.

II. WILLIAM H. was an invalid with five years of constant illness, "having had a wide experience "in physical suffering." He had begun to gain slowly in strength, and had continued to improve after his father's last removal to a home of their own. so that in Feb., 1893, he was attempting a little light work about the buildings, and riding considerably as a book agent. Nov. 1, 1894, he has worked vigorously on the farm for about eighteen months, conducting the farm business with marked ability and success. He has worked beyond his strength, and is at present suffering from what the doctor calls a severe attack of bronchitis.

THOMSON, HOMER ALEXANDER, * N. G.

PERKINSVILLE, VT.

1 —— Perkinsville (Weathersfield township), Feb. 22, 1827. He was one of the seven children of Menzies A. and Huldah (Selden) Thomson; all but three of whom were deceased in 1879.

2 —— Wesleyan Seminary, Springfield, Vt., and Thetford Acad., Thetford, Vt., spending his first two years of college life with us at Dartmouth.

He entered Brown University, Junior year, and was there graduated in 1853. Commenced the study of Law, and afterwards, during one session, was Principal of an Academy in New Jersey. In the winter of 1854, he took up his residence in New York City, and there continued nearly three years. Leaving the study of Law, he adopted teaching as his profession, and from 1857 till 1864 had charge of the Classical department in Flushing Institute, Flushing, Long Island, N. Y. Was also

Professor of Ancient Languages in the Flushing Female College, a portion of the time.

"He steadfastly remained a very faithful and "conscientious instructor in Ancient Languages at "the Flushing Institute, in all 22 years," till his death, Dec. 17, 1878, of complicated kidney disease, in his 52d year.

"He was a thorough classical scholar, and so "much the master of Latin and Greek as to be "able to compose in those languages. In litera- "ture he was a wide reader, being well informed "on various subjects. In the history of his coun- "try, and on all important legislative or political "questions, he was so versed that it is doubtful if "he had an equal in the community where he lived. "He was an ardent lover of music and a proficient "in song, having in charge, for many years, the "music of St. George's Church. Hundreds of "pupils from every part of the country have stud- "ied under him. He was a man of retiring dis- "position, tender-hearted, and a devout Christian. "His life knew no guile. In his sickness, which- "was not long, but very painful, he bore all his suf- "fering patiently. He was forewarned that death "was probable, and he said, 'I am not afraid.' "His two sisters, from Springfield, Vt., hastened "to be at his bedside, but arrived too late. They "are to return with his remains, to be buried at "Perkinsville, beside those of his mother, whom he "tenderly loved and regularly visited in her widow- "hood, each year, until her death, two years ago. "The students of the Institute have procured a

"beautiful floral tribute, and are to attend his fun-
"eral services in a body. His only surviving
"brother resides in Iowa."

(The above sketch is from the "Flushing Daily
"Times" of Dec. 17, 1878, the day of his death).

His sister, Miss H. E. Thomson, of Chester
Centre, Ia., under date of Nov. 5, 1894, has aided
in the completion of this record.

UPHAM, NATHANIEL LORD,

Concord, N. H.

1 —— Concord, April 28, 1833. His father was
Hon. Nathaniel Gookin Upham (D. C., 1820), of
Concord; his grandparents, Hon. Nathaniel and
Judith (Cogswell) Upham, of Rochester, N. H.
The earliest known ancestor of the family was
Hugo de Upham, A. D., 1208. All the Uphams
in America are said to be descended from Thomas,
the first born in this country, the son of John
Upham, who migrated hither with the Hull, Mass.,
colony, and finally settled in Malden, Mass. His
mother was nee Betsey Watts Lord, a supposed
relative of President Nathan Lord, D. D. She
died when he was very young; consecrating this
infant son of hers to the work of the Gospel ministry.

2 —— At Concord (probably). Part of his
College course was pursued at Bowdoin College,
Maine, coming to Dartmouth our Second year.

3 —— Anna Howell Janeway, at Kingston, N. J., June 5, 1861. She was the youngest dau. of the Rev. John L. Janeway, D. D., Secretary of the Presbyterian Board of Domestic Missions.

4 —— I. BESSIE LORD, b. May 6, 1862, at Philadelphia, Pa.; d. May 20, 1862, aged 2 weeks.

II. ANNA JANEWAY, b. April 3, 1863, at Trenton, N. J.

III. NATHANIEL JANEWAY, b. Aug. 28, 1865, at Reaville, N. J.

IV. LILLIAN HOWELL, b. Sept. 2, 1867, at Reaville.

V. T. FRANCIS JANEWAY, b. Sept. 30, 1869, at Reaville.

VI. JOHN HOWELL JANEWAY, b. Aug. 12, 1871, at Trenton.

VII. ABBY HOWELL JANEWAY, b. June 8, 1876, at Merchantville, N. J.

He was Secretary of the Commission on Claims, between the United States and Great Britain, at London, Eng., from the time of graduating till 1855.

Having returned to this country, he studied Divinity at the Andover (Mass.) Theological Seminary, and graduated in 1858. Was stated supply of the Cong. Church, Manchester, Vt., from Sept., 1858, and ordained its pastor, Mar. 10, 1859. Dismissed Oct. 30, 1861.

He afterwards resided at Trenton, N. J., and supplied the pulpit of Rev. Dr. Janeway, at Flemington, N. J., for one year, till Nov., 1863, expecting to settle as Junior Pastor. But at that time he accepted an urgent request to become Chaplain of the 35th New Jersey regiment, then operating in Mississippi, and in March, 1864, reported himself at Jackson, Miss., having participated in Gen. Sherman's recent expedition from Vicksburg. He afterwards continued with Gen. Sherman till he reached Atlanta, Ga., and there received a severe sunstroke, on account of which he came home on furlough, after being in the army several months. Returning directly to Savannah, Ga., from New York, he met his regiment 20 miles from Savannah, preached Christmas and New Year's sermons to his soldiers and proceeded on Gen. Sherman's march till they reached Beaufort, S. C.

Having received a call from the church in Reaville, N. J., he left the army, finally, in Feb., 1865.

He labored at Reaville among a generous people, who were accustomed to give him donations, above his salary, in amount, from $200 to $300 per annum. He was also engaged in the cause of education, holding county meetings, etc. Closing his labors there, sometime prior to 1876, he took another pastorate over the Presbyterian Church at Merchantville, N. J., four miles from Philadelphia, where he was instrumental in building a meeting-house, and also built a dwelling for himself. Since 1884 he has been "Secretary of the Presbyterian "Ministers' Fund," and also (since 1892) Secretary of the "Philadelphia Tract and Mission Society," having under him four missionaries and between 700 and 800 voluntary Christian helpers. His residence in Philadelphia is at No. 1800 Park Ave.

The heading of his letter (June 19, 1893) represents him as the President of a very important and honorable organization, "The Christian Arbitra-"tion and Peace Society," founded in 1886; an "International Association to promote harmony." Twelve Vice Presidents and twelve of an Executive Council are associated with him, the former, men of distinguished names all over the world; the latter, men of eminence in the vicinity of Philadelphia; Central office, 310 Chestnut street, Philadelphia; other offices in New York City and various European cities. Cable address, "Arbitrate, "Philadelphia, Pa."

Mr. Upham published, while in England (1853-5), a report on his commission, his father being at the head of the same, under appointment from President Franklin Pierce. He was also said, at our class meeting in 1873, to be publishing a Polyglott Bible in Philadelphia.

His two oldest sons, (III) NATHANIEL J., and (V) T. FRANCIS J., were in business at Duluth, Minn. (1893); one the President, and the other the Secretary of the "Duluth Loan, Deposit and Trust "Company," capital (paid in) $150,000; resources vs. liabilities, for Nov. 30, 1892, balancing at $192,868.

His daughter, (IV) LILLIAN H. was m. Dec. 4, 1890, to Samuel Griffith McConaughy, Secretary of the Y. M. C. A., Duluth, Minn., formerly of Philadelphia, Pa., and Worcester, Mass.; children, (1) Samuel Griffith, Jr. (McConaughy), b. Aug. 22, 1891; (2) Dwight Dunn, b. Jan. 21, 1893.

Our Class-mate's youngest son, (VI.) John H. J., was on his second year (1893), as a student in medicine at the "University of Philadelphia."

WALKER, WILLIAM, * n. g.
Barnstead, N. H.

1 —— Barnstead, Jan. 4, 1828. His grandfather was William Walker, of Portsmouth, N. H.; his father, Joseph A., was b. in Portsmouth, but removed (with William, his father) to Barnstead when quite young. His mother's name, before marriage, was Abigail Murrey, of New Market, N. H.—where born.

2 —— Gilmanton Acad., N. H., under Rev. Charles Tenney, afterwards of Biddeford, Me., and entered Bowdoin College in 1849, but shortly after transferred his connection to Dartmouth.

3 —— Augusta Webster, only dau. of Hon· Samuel Webster, of Barnstead, Sept. 14, 1854. Her mother was Lois (Smith) Webster. Both her parents were b. in East Kingston, N. H. She was still residing at North Barnstead in 1879, having the care of her aged mother. "Accept thanks for "the kind interest you manifest in both myself and "him whose name is so dear—whose memory is so "fresh to me."

A predisposition to pulmonary complaints induced him to abandon his collegiate studies and enter on a medical course. He attended one term of lectures at Hanover; studied nearly one year with Dr. J. A. Bussell, Winchendon, Mass.; also with Dr. A. G. Weeks (D. C., 1844), of Barnstead; finally receiving his medical degree at Philadelphia, in the spring of 1853.

He began practice under the happiest auspices in his native town, as the successor of Dr. Weeks, deceased; but in two years after the death of his instructor and predecessor, he himself died, July 14, 1855, at the residence of his father, whither he had gone in rapidly declining health for a few days' stay. His age was 27 years and 6 months.

Rev. Enos George preached his funeral sermon, and his remains were laid in the cemetery near his own home in North Barnstead, where his widow was still living in 1864.

"He had some trials, as most young physicians "do, but these he met cheerfully, and ever brought "to his home a large share of happiness."

Soon after his decease an obituary notice appeared in the "Congregational Journal," from which the following extracts:

"In the death of this young man the promised. "fruit of a useful and beautiful life has been "blighted, and a large circle of friends mourn his "early departure. But their loss is his gain, for "he 'knew whom he had believed.' At the age of "fifteen he became savingly interested in religious "things, the result of which was a determination to "unite himself with the people of God, which he "did by a public profession of faith in Christ, at the "Cong. Church in North Barnstead, in July, 1843. " * * After his marriage, with health much

"improved, by exercise in the open air, required by
"his business, a life of usefulness and professional
"success seemed opening upon him. But that life
"was destined to be short. In March, 1855, a
"severe cold, followed by an attack of measles,
"threw him upon a sick bed and superinduced a
"rapid decline. Much was hoped from the genial
"influences of warm weather, but he and his friends
"hoped against hope. Although he was able again
"in the early summer to ride out, his strength
"gradually failed, and he died as above intimated.
"Life seemed desirable to him, for he had every-
"thing to make life pleasant. But 'there is a bet-
" 'ter world,' he said, and he looked towards it with
"an unfaltering trust in Jesus Christ, the only true
" 'way' thither. 'Blessed are the dead which die
" 'in the Lord, from henceforth.' "

WARREN, JOSEPH, N. G.

COLUMBIA, N. Y.

1 —— Columbia, Herkimer Co., N. Y., July 13,
1830; son of Peter Horton and Emeline (Morgan)
Warren. His father came from Fishkill, Duchess
Co., N. Y., in 1805, while yet a boy, to Columbia.
His mother was a daughter of James Morgan, a
descendant of James Morgan, one of the first settlers at New London, Conn.

2 —— The Clinton Liberal Institute, Clinton,
Oneida Co., N. Y., Rev. T. J. Sawyer, Principal.

Leaving Dartmouth at the close of Sophomore year, he entered Yale at the same grade, and there graduated in July, 1853.

Most of the autumn following he spent in travelling, and in Jan., 1854, entered the Mohawk Valley Bank, in the village of Mohawk, N. Y., as a clerk.

In 1856 he went to Oswego, N. Y., and engaged with a friend in starting a bank at that place, where he remained until March, 1863. Was then obliged to give up business on account of ill-health.

In April, 1864, he was at his home near Mohawk, Herkimer Co., with improved health, and a prospect of being enabled by another year of out-door life, to report himself off the sick list.

Later, in 1864, he engaged in the business of tanning with his father at Columbia, and continued to reside there until 1870, when he took up his residence in Boston, Mass. His experience and acquaintance with the leather trade naturally brought him to this city when looking for business.

He sends from Boston (P. O. Box 3481), June 6, 1883, "a hearty greeting and best wishes to the "Class." Had previously arranged to attend his Class meeting at New Haven, Ct., on the 26th, otherwise would have been with us at Hanover. He was then engaged in the leather trade, in which continued till about 1888.

"March 27, 1893," still in Boston, same P. O. Box as ten years before: "Although the last two "years of my College course were passed at Yale, "I have many pleasant memories of the time spent "at Dartmouth. 'I am at present doing the work "of an expert accountant and auditor."

Mr. Warren's location in Boston (Nov. 9, 1894) is at the Exchange Building, 53 State St., continuing the business of accountant and auditor, and he would be pleased to greet any of his class-mates (the "Old Guard of '53") who may visit Boston.

WASHBURN, JOHN SETH, *,
Ludlow, Vt.

1 —— Ludlow, July 13, 1832. His paternal pedigree is John S.[8], Reuben[7], Asa[6], Seth[5], Joseph[4], Joseph[3], John[2], John[1]. John[1] Washburn was the first Secretary of the Governor and company of the Massachusetts Bay, in England, before their removal to this country, and finally settled in Mass. Col. Seth[5] Washburn was prominent in military and civil affairs during the revolution, and afterwards. Our Class-mate's grandparents were Asa[6] and Sarah (Upham) Washburn, of Leicester, Mass., where his father was born—the Hon. Reuben[7] Washburn, of Ludlow (D. C., 1808), d. 1860, aged 78. His mother was nee Hannah Blaney Thacher, and his maternal pedigree is Hannah B.[8], Thomas Cushing[7], Peter[6], Oxenbridge[5], Oxenbridge[4], Peter[3], Thomas[2], Peter[1]. Peter[1] Thacher was matriculated in Queen's College, Oxford, Eng., May 3, 1603; was Rector of St. Edmund's, Salisbury, and there d. in 1640. Thomas[2] Thacher, his youngest son, who

came to this country when fifteen years old, was first pastor of the Old South Church, Boston, Mass., having been educated here under the tuition of Rev. C. Chauncey, afterwards President of Harvard College. Peter[3] Thacher graduated, H. C., 1676, and was pastor of the church in Milton, Mass. Oxenbridge[4] Thacher was grad., H. C., 1698, and Oxenbridge[5], H. C., 1738, was a noted lawyer, who is alluded to by Bancroft as "The Silver-tongued Thacher." His son, Peter[6] Thacher, D. D. (H. C., 1760), was pastor of the Brattle St. Church, Boston; and Mr. Washburn's grandfather—of the next generation—Rev. Thomas C.[7] Thacher (H. C., 1790), was pastor in Lynn, Mass.

2 —— Black River Acad., Ludlow, Vt., and lastly under the Rev. Claudius B. Smith. He had passed his previous boyhood in Ludlow; entered Dartmouth at the age of 17, and taught school winters during his College course, as did the majority of his class-mates.

3 —— Mary L. Richardson, in New York City, by the Rev. Roswell D. Hitchcock, D. D., Nov. 25, 1862. She was then of New York, but a native of Vermont, and d. of consumption, March 20, 1869. He was m., second, to Georgiana Thacher Cooper, in New York, Nov. 15, 1869. She was the dau. of David M. and Georgiana P. Cooper.

4 —— I. Georgiana Cooper (2d wife), b. July 12, 1872.

II. Mabel Thacher, b. Aug. 18, 1874.

III. Florence Blaney, b. Sept. 21, 1876; d. April 23, 1879, aged 2 years and 7 months.

Immediately after graduating he became associate Principal of the Black River Acad., Ludlow, with Rev. Mark H. Cummings.

The winter following he commenced the study of Law with his brother, Hon. Peter T. Washburn (D. C., 1835; Gov. Vt. 1869–70), at Woodstock, Vt., and continued one year. He was then appointed Assistant Clerk in the Vermont House of Representatives for one term. Early in the spring of 1855, he entered the Cambridge (Mass.) Law School; and finally, having been admitted to the Windsor Co. Bar, he commenced the practice of his profession, at Rutland, Vt., Feb., 1856. He passed one year with fair success in business, and also in the diligent reading of legal text books, with a sprinkling of politics, speaking some, and writing for a political paper with which connected. In Feb., 1857, he removed to New York City, according to original intention. In May following entered into partnership with H. E. Smith, Esq. (brother of President Asa D. Smith). Dec., 1858, they dissolved, Mr. Washburn retaining the business situation. In May, 1859, he formed another partnership with J. P. Sullivan, Esq., firm of "Washburn & Sullivan," which continued for two years. Was subsequently alone till Jan., 1863, when he formed with David D. Ranlett, Esq., the firm of "Washburn & Ranlett," 132 Nassau St., which connection was retained for several years. After going to New York he attended closely to professional business, and avoided politics as seriously detrimental to a lawyer's success. His business was increasingly good and profitable. "Prac-"tice general; U. S. Courts, Patent and some Ad-"mirality; also considerable Equity and Counsel."

In his letter of June 20, 1878 (from his law office, 132 Nassau St.), Mr. Washburn says: "I "have your invitation to attend meeting of our "Class, on the 25th anniversary of our graduation, "at the ensuing commencement. I regret that my "professional engagements will prevent my doing "so. But I send to you and to all my class-mates, "who are present, my earnest regards and good "wishes. As we get older and, necessarily, more "engrossed by business and the occupations, duties "and ties of life, I think our College associations "become more distinct and pleasant to look back "upon in the distance. I shall be greatly pleased "if measures can be taken to obtain, and inform us "of, each other's condition, and of the events of "our lives, during the past twenty-five years."

Thus by anticipation did our honored class-mate most happily express the object and design of the present Memorial.

We regret to add that in less than one and a half years from the date of his letter, Nov., 1879, he was obliged by ill-health to give up the practice of the profession which he loved, and in which he so highly excelled. He, however, continued to reside in New York until the following May (1880), when he removed to Georgetown, D. C., and there remained till his death, Oct. 18, 1880, aged 48 years and 3 months. The cause of his death was general paralysis. (Mrs. Washburn's letter, April 5, 1881.)

He was buried at Greenwood, Brooklyn, N. Y., where he owned a lot.

The following notice is taken substantially from "The Dartmouth," of Nov. 26, 1880:

"Mr. Washburn was a member of the Union "League Club, and of the Historical, Scientific and "Bar Associations of New York; also an active "member of the Dartmouth Alumni Association. "He was energetic, persevering, and interested in "whatever he undertook; never letting pleasure "interfere with duty. Of a sanguine temperament, "always looking on the bright side of life, he had "an intense love for his work. He was uniformly "cheerful, generous, and unselfish; and entered "with zest into the pastimes of his leisure hours. "During his summer vacations his greatest enjoy-"ment was trout fishing; he would explore the "brooks among his native hills, day after day, ever "rewarded, not only with a basket of fish, but with "healthful fatigue, and renewed strength for "another year's work."

His widow, now the wife of Prof. C. H. Coyle, resides in New York City.

His two daughters reside with their mother, (I) GEORGIA C. being a student in the Art League, and (II) MABEL T. devoting herself to the study of Dramatic art.

His brother, Hon. Peter Thacher Washburn, Governor of Vermont, d. in 1870, aged 55.

His oldest sister, Sarah Elizabeth, b. in Cavendish, Vt., Oct. 13, 1820, was m. to Daniel A. Heald—of late years President of the Home Insurance Co.—Aug. 31, 1843; and d. greatly lamented, at West Orange, N. J., April, 1894, in her 74th year. She was an early contributor in prose and verse to the "Knickerbocker Magazine," and has since published a number of useful and popular books for children. She was also deeply interested in the Orange Memorial Hospital, and edited the "Hospital Messenger" nine years, till the time of her death.

His sister, Miss Hannah M. Washburn, the only surviving member of the family, still resides at the paternal homestead in Ludlow.

WATERHOUSE, SYLVESTER, N. G.,
BARRINGTON, N. H.

1 —— Barrington, Sept. 15, 1830, being the youngest of the six children of Samuel H., and Dolla (Kingman) Waterhouse. His pedigree is Sylvester[7], Samuel H.[6], Benjamin[5], Timothy[4], John[3], Timothy[2], Richard[1]. Richard[1] Waterhouse, tanner, came from England, 1678; married Sarah, dau. of Dr. Renald Fernald, and owned and occupied Pierce's Island, near Portsmouth, N. H., in 1688. His third son, Timothy[2], located, as tanner and shoemaker, at or near Freeman's Point, soon after 1700; whose son, John[3], was first settler in Barrington, having m. Alice Babb. Tim-

PROF. SYLVESTER WATERHOUSE.

othy[4] m. Mary Tibbetts, and his son, Benjamin[5], was the father of five children, among them Samuel H.[6], our class-mate's father; b. March 20, 1788; d. Oct. 30, 1855, aged 67 years and 7 months. Another branch of the Waterhouse family was Dr. Benjamin[4], for 30 years Professor in Harvard University, and the father of vaccination in this country. He was the cousin of Sylvester's great-grandfather—the youngest of the eleven sons of Timothy[3] (brother of John[3]) who settled in Rhode Island. Dolla Kingman (b. Jan. 20, 1790; d. Aug. 3, 1867), was the dau. of John Kingman (b. Dec. 23, 1747; d. Nov. 14, 1807), he being the oldest son of William Kingman, who d. May 17, 1775, aged 55, having m. Elizabeth Webster, of Rye, N. H., of the same family from which the Hon. Daniel Webster was descended. Samuel H. Waterhouse and Dolla Kingman were m. Jan. 25, 1815. Their four oldest children were daughters, and the three oldest were married; the two youngest were sons, Albert K. and Sylvester, our class-mate, as above.

2 —— Exeter (N. H.) Phillips Acad., under the late Chancellor Hoyt, of Washington University, St. Louis, Mo.

Coming to Dartmouth in March, 1851, he completed with us the Sophomore year, and then rejoined his Eexter Class-mates at Harvard Univ., where graduated in 1853.

This Memorial being in part a second edition of the first (printed in 1864), we reproduce the following incident of his student life. "His Harvard

"class-mates, as a mark of esteem, had presented
"him, at graduation, with an elegant and service-
"able artificial leg. This had been kept a pro-
"found secret from his parents, they supposing that
"his bodily misfortune could never thus be rem-
"edied. He purposed, therefore, on returning
"home, to surprise his friends by a brief and pleas-
"ant deception, playing upon them 'Franklin's
" 'trick.' Completely disguised with false hair and
"the habiliments of a poor traveller, weary and
"footsore, he knocked at the door of his father's
"house, on a dark and stormy night, begging a
"shelter from the inclement weather. Having en-
"joyed their proffered hospitality, he pretended in
"the morning to take his leave, and gave his
"mother, as in payment for his lodging, an elegant
"miniature of himself. Glancing at it without
"recognizing whose it was, and thinking he had
"given that because he had nothing else to give,
"she burst into tears and said, 'what if my son were
" 'reduced to such a condition!' Meanwhile he
"had left the house, but his mother sent for him,
"made him take back the miniature, and pressed
"him to stay and enjoy still further their hospital-
"ities. Reluctantly (?) he consented; but soon there
"was a scene of wild joy and laughter, when he
"revealed himself, his mother still weeping, but
"now for joy. At this stage his father unexpect-
"ly came in with the utmost astonishment, and
"passed into the room from which his son had
"come out, after putting off the disguise, to see
"*what had become of the other man!*"

The autumn after his graduation, he entered the
Cambridge Law School, went through the full
course and received the degree of LL. B.   In 1856
was appointed "Professor of the Latin Language
"and Literature," in Antioch College, Ohio, and
one year later accepted the position which he has
continued to hold to the present time—a period of
more than 37 years—in the "Washington Univer-
"sity," St. Louis, Mo., as "Collier Professor of
"Greek."

Prior to 1864 he had published articles of sterling merit in the "Missouri Democrat" and other
papers, sketches of character, and political papers,
the longest series of the latter being entitled
"Reflections on the Southern Rebellion."   All his
articles in behalf of the Union would make several
volumes; and some of them were widely copied.
He also published a "Eulogy on the late Chancel-
"lor Joseph Gibson Hoyt," of Washington University, delivered at the Hall of the University Jan.
20, 1863.

Since then Prof. Waterhouse has proved himself
the most prolific writer of our Class, and many of
his pamphlets and other treatises have attained an
immense circulation, as will be noticed below.
Among these were:

(1) "The Resources of Missouri," 64 pp., 1869;
more than five-hundred thousand copies of which
were circulated in various forms, and one article
exceeding a million copies.

(2) "The Natural Adaptation of St. Louis to
"Iron Manufactures;" 31 pp., 1869.

(3) "Advantages of Educated Labor in Mis-
"souri;" a lecture delivered at the University Apr.
21, 1872; printed in pamphlet form, 10,000 copies,
and in various newspapers.

On other industrial topics were:

(4) "The Construction of the St. Louis Bridge."

(5) "The Extension of Our Trade with Brazil."

(6) "The Erection of Union Stock Yards in St.
"Louis."

(7) "The Removal of the National Capital"
(first article ever written on that subject).

(8) "The Establishment in St. Louis of Smelt-
"ing Works for Rocky Mountain Ores."

(9) "The Adoption of the Barge System on the
"Mississippi and its Affluents."

(10) "The Expansion of the Grain Trade; and
"the Movement of our Cereals by way of the
"Mississippi."

(11) "Give us an Unobstructed Mississippi;"
being a Memorial to Congress, with an appendix,
respecting the commercial interests of the Mississippi Valley, 39 pp. He was appointed to prepare this by a convention at St. Paul, Minn., Oct.
11, 1877; a large pamphlet edition was first published; it was then copied by hundreds of newspapers in the bordering states.

(12) "The Merits of the Texas & Pacific Rail-
"road" (previously), 1875; 7 pp.

Scharf's History of St. Louis also adds the following—in a list of his principal writings—"besides
"hundreds of contributions to the press."

(13) "The Protectorate of the Holy Places."

(14) "The Commercial Suggestions of the Paris
"Exposition."

(15) "Papers on Jute in the U. S. Agricultural
"Reports."

(16) "Sketch of Jeremiah Kingman, in Cun-
"ningham's History of Phillips Exeter Academy."

(17) "Sketch of St. Louis in the U. S. Census
Reports" (1880).

(18) "The Early Annals of St. Louis" (in the
same History—Scharf's).

(19) "Address before the First National Convention of American Cattlemen," at St. Louis,
Nov. 18, 1884; pamphlet; 8 pp.

(20 and 21) "Two Addresses on the Nicaragua
"Canal;" printed in pamphlet form and copied by
one or more papers in several different States;
translated into German (as many others of his
writings have been); called forth favorable testimonials from ex-Senator Miller, President, and Mr.
Chable, Secretary of the Canal Company.

We also notice the following supplementary
pamphlets, 1891-3:

(22) "New St. Louis, Its Causes, Needs and
"Duties."

(23) "Speech at the Second Trustees' (Shaw)
"Banquet."

(24) "American Commerce in 1900."

(25) "Sketches of Mr. and Mrs. Stephen
"Ridgely."

(26) "The Mississippi and its Affluents."

(27) "Our Northern Forests and the Missis-
"sippi."

(28) "The Nicaragua Canal; Government Con-
"trol;" and, in addition to these, many able articles
in recent numbers of the "Age of Steel."

A more complete list of Prof. Waterhouse's publications has very recently come to hand. Probably as many more as are numbered above, might
be added; for all the titles of which we have not
space. We also learn that the "Protectorate of
"the Holy Places" (No. 13 above) was first written
at Harvard, in 1854, as a series of articles on the
Cause of the Crimean War. Some of this recent
list are:

"The Statesmanship of Washington;" 1861.

"Lectures on Grecian Literature and Art;"
1863.

"The Financial Value of Ideas;" 1867.

"Speech at New England Banquet;" pamphlet;
1869.

"Lectures on Personal Travels in Japan;" 1874.

"Letters to President Grant and Gov. Critten-
"den, on the proposed 'International Exhibition;'"
1881.

"An Address to the National Cotton Planters'
"Convention at Vicksburg, Miss.;" proceedings;
1883.

"The Industrial Revival of Mexico;" translated
into Spanish; 1884.

"A Trip to Puget Sound;" 1891.

"A Letter to the State Commissioners of the
"Columbian Exposition on the Industrial Value of
"New Hampshire Scenery;" Oct. 21, 1892.

"Pamphlet on Ramie;" Jan., 1894; and "An

"Address on the Nicaragua Canal, before the
"Trans-Mississippi Commercial Congress, St.
"Louis;" Nov., 1894.

Our class-mate has been entirely disinterested in
his numerous and popular writings. "The Re-
"sources," etc. (1, above) cost him 12 months of
hard work and more than $2000, without a dime of
assistance. "The Natural Adaptation of St. Louis
"to Iron Manufacturers" cost him about five months
of work and $400, not a dollar of which amount
was ever, directly or indirectly, repaid to him.

He was one of the Examination Committee at
our Alma Mater, July, 1864, in company with
Emerson.

In 1871 was appointed, by Gov. B. Gratz Brown,
one of the managers of the "Bureau of Geology
"and Mines," of the State of Missouri.

Resigned his place as Secretary of the St. Louis
Board of Trade, May 24, 1872, in view of his proposed absence for a tour round the world; receiving also from said Board an elegant gold watch
and chain; also from several members of the
Faculty of the University another new cane and a
flattering written testimonial in their behalf, from
W. G. Eliot, President of the Board of Directors,
and Chancellor of the University, dated June 7,
1872.

His appointment, in the spring of 1878, was
from President Hayes, as one of the U. S. Commissioners to the French Exposition (jointly also
as Commissioner from the city of St. Louis), on
account of which he was unable to attend our 25th

anniversary—being about to sail for Europe June 19. He was absent just two months, visiting various places in Scotland and England; proceeding from Brussels and Amsterdam up the Rhine; over the St. Gothard Pass to Upper Italy, and back through Switzerland again to Paris, for his Exposition duties. His health, though feeble, was improved by this trip.

"It has now been my good fortune to make a "tour around the world and a second visit to Eu-"rope. Notwithstanding the infirmity of lameness "I am never so happy as when I am travelling." (Letter of Jan. 1, 1879).

In a St. Louis paper, which came to hand Jan., 1884, we read: "Prof. Waterhouse has received an "invitation from the National Cotton Planters' As-"sociation to deliver an address before that body, "which will convene at Vicksburg, Miss., Nov. 21, "(1883). He has also received a commission from "Gov. Crittenden to act as a delegate to this Con-"vention. The Professor has always taken great "interest in developing the agricultural resources "of the country, and we are sure that should he "accept the invitation, he would render valuable "assistance to this Convention."

Our class-mate's biographical sketch from the "History of St. Louis City and County" was beautifully republished in a five-page pamphlet by Louis H. Everts & Co., Philadelphia, 1883.

We are especially referred to a fine sketch of Prof. Waterhouse, by Dr. Morgan, sent, as supposed, to the Secretary, in 1893 (but not received);

also to a shorter sketch of him in the recently published volume, entitled "New Hampshire Men."

The loss of his right leg, by an accident in 1840, changed his whole course from a mechanical to a literary life. He was also thrown from a carriage in 1867, receiving a severe spinal injury, since which he has never been free from bodily pain. "Under conditions so unfavorable to literary effort, "most men would have abstained from all avoidable "labor, but the restless energy of Prof. Waterhouse "would not allow him to be idle, and the accidents "which have restricted his physical activity and "subjected him to constant and cureless suffering, "have not prevented his leading a life of public "usefulness."

He received an LL. D., by favor of the Missouri University in 1883, and a Ph. D., in 1884, from our own Dartmouth.

Just as the printers are at this stage of the sketch (Nov. 28), we hasten to add to the list of his writings, "A series of twenty-four articles on "the Early History and Social Customs of St. "Louis" (unpublished), 1892.

Also—at the latest possible date—we notice his appointment "by the Mayor of St. Louis, as a "Delegate to the Trans-Mississippi Commercial "Congress," now being "held in St. Louis, Nov. "26–30, 1894."

WHITCOMB, GEORGE PARKS,

Stow, Mass.

1 —— Stow, Dec. 2, 1827. His parents' names were Jeremiah and Salome (Braley) Whitcomb; his supposed pedigree, George P.[4], Jeremiah[3], Oliver[2], Simeon[1]; a more remote descendant perhaps of Simon Whitcomb, "who, in 1628, with Sir "Henry Roswell, et al., received a patent from the "King (of England) for a tract of land extending "from three miles N. to three miles S. of Charles "river."

2 —— New Ipswich, N. H., under Edward A. Lawrence, A. M. (D. C., 1843).

3 —— Abbie Theresa Hodgkins, of Davenport, Ia., by the Rev. G. F. Magoon (then of Lyons, Ia.), June 3, 1863. She was formerly of Maine, near Bangor; b. May 19, 1841, at Passadumkeag, Me.; the dau. of Elijah B., and Mary A. (Morrill) Hodgkins, whose second husband was Asa Page Kelley, of Conway, N. H., late of Chicago, Ill.

4 —— I. Mary Morrill, b. June 17, 1864; d. in Chicago, Ill., Sept. 26, 1868, aged 4 years and 3 months, in consequence of her clothes taking fire while standing on the grate, to reach an ornament on the mantel.

II. Fannie Hodgkins, b. Nov. 5, 1865; d. at Ontario, Cal., May 26, 1894, of heart disease.

III. Jessie, b. March 28, 1868.

IV. Adele, b. April 11, 1870; children all b. in Davenport.

He studied Law with the Hon. Henry Hoge-

George P. Whitcomb, Esq.

CALIFORNIA

boom at Albany and Hudson, N. Y., and was admitted to the Bar in the Court of Appeals, at Albany, Feb. 6, 1855. Commenced practice in Davenport, Ia., Dec., 1855, and, aside from two visits to New England, in July and Aug., 1859, and in Jan. and Feb., 1863, he was quietly engaged in the practice of his profession there, for nearly 14 years, roaming but little and adhering closely to his business. He had in 1864 a very pleasant residence three miles from the city, overlooking Rock Island, Ill., and the Mississippi below, with a large garden well furnished with fruit and ornamental trees, affording manual exercise before and after business hours. He was also City Attorney in Davenport, and held the offices of County Supervisor and School Superintendent for Scott County, and President of the Davenport City School Board.

This continued until the fall of 1869, when he entered upon the practice of Law in Chicago, Ill.— 80 Dearborn St.—and in Oct., 1870, moved his family to that city.

One of the most fraternal of the letters received on occasion of our 25th anniversary, was from Mr. Whitcomb. "I had hoped till now (June 18, 1878) "that possibly I might appear in person, and on the "call of the roll once more answer 'Present.' * * "Twenty-five years ago; it seems a long time since "the charter of our freedom, from our College ties, "was 'signed, sealed and delivered;' and yet, disre- "garding the lapse of time, as we look back to our "daily routine of College life, and go over again in "memory the living past, how vivid and recent it

"all appears! Of my 'history,' or my 'family,' or
" 'myself,' I know of nothing of interest since my
"last report that is worthy of mention. My good
"wife and my three darling girls and myself all en-
"joy excellent health and live quietly and peace-
"ably with all mankind. As my motto in business
"is 'Owe no man anything,' riches don't trouble
"me, nor poverty greatly annoy. My whole time
"is given to the practice of my profession, which
"hitherto has furnished me a competent support,
"and perhaps as much satisfaction as any other
"business employment in which I might have en-
"gaged. * * Should business, or pleasure, or
"chance ever bring you to or near Chicago, please
"bear in mind that my office is 41 Clark St., my
"residence at 64 24th St.; that my latch string will
"be out, and that instead of one you knew 25
"years ago, there are now five who will cordially
"welcome you and entertain you as well as we
"know how to do. And now, wishing all those of
"you, who may be present at the 25th anniversary
"meeting, a glorious time; and all, both present
"and absent, good health and a long and happy
"life, I bid you, each and everyone, 'socially' and
" 'fraternally,' farewell."

He also sent two dozen of his card pictures to be
distributed among the class-mates at this meeting.

He was still at 41 Clark St., June 28, 1883, expecting to sail, the 30th, from New York, for a
tour of two months in Europe. His trip was
greatly enjoyed. "Saw a little of Ireland and
"Scotland, visiting Glasgow, Edinburgh, the Lakes,

"Walter Scott's old home, Sterling, etc. Spent
"some two weeks in London, about the same time
"in Paris, and three weeks at Vichy, a noted sum-
"mer resort some 300 miles south of Paris. The
"ocean voyage, going, was all that could be wished.
"The return passage was somewhat rough, as we
"were in the 'tail end of a hurricane' for several
"days, and were eleven days from Liverpool to
"New York. But I was glad to get home, for I
"nowhere saw a better land than our own America."

His last report is from 167 Dearborn St., Chicago, Nov. 18, 1892; "Thank Providence, that I
"still live and plod on, as ever, hoping, but not
"achieving—a sort of tread-mill life, seeking in the
"main to do good rather than evil, yet with credit-
"balance I fear so small as to be not worthy of
"mention when the books are finally closed."

We thank our brother for these sound and can-
did suggestions, indicating the ground we ought
all of us to occupy.

II. FANNIE H., having graduated at the Chicago High School, finished her course of education at the Ladies' Seminary, in Rockford, Ill.
She had been afflicted for about seven years with a
valvular disease of the heart, and had spent the
winters, except 1892-3, with her mother, and some
times her younger sister, in California, Texas,
Mexico, or on the Gulf Coast, between Mobile and
New Orleans. Jan. 15, 1894, the dear girl, with
her sister Jessie, again went South, visiting San
Antonio, Los Angeles, San Francisco and Ontario,
where, from the flowers, the perfumes, the joys and

sorrows of life, she was called to her heavenly home, at the age of twenty-eight.

III. JESSIE was also educated at the Chicago High School, with two years at the Mount Holyoke Seminary, Mass. Was spending the winter, 1893-4, with her sister in California, and is now with her parents at home in Chicago.

IV. ADELE has grad. after a four years' course at Vassar College, N. Y. (1893), and since has been taking a special course at the Chicago Univ. in statistical and political economy.

— — —

WIGHT, JOHN FLETCHER,

SHELBY COUNTY, KY.

1 —— Frankfort, Ky., April 20, 1832, being the son of James Wight.

2 —— The County Schools, with one year in the Preparatory Department of Shelby College, which he entered two years previously to his joining us at Dartmouth, Junior year.

3 —— Martha J. Oglesby, of Panola County, Miss., Dec. 20, 1859.

4 —— I. MARTHA DUKE, b. Oct. 7, 1860.

II. JOHN FLETCHER, JR., b. Feb. 27, 1862.

III. SARAH BELLE, b. Mar. 9, 1864.

IV. JAMES ALBERT, b. April 30, 1866.

V. MARY JOSEPHINE, b. April 21, 1868.

VI. WILLIAM A., b. May 28, 1872. Children were all born in Shelby County, Ky.

He entered the Law School at Louisville, Ky.;

but his health failing, he was obliged to return to his home in Shelby County (Poplar Ridge), where most of his time was passed until 1891, as a farmer, upon the paternal homestead, near Todd's Point, Ky.

In August, 1869, he was elected a member of the Kentucky Legislature, for two years. The Class Secretary, having occasion to make a brief visit at Frankfort, in Dec., 1887, found on inquiry, that Mr. Wight was well known and favorably regarded at the Capital of his State.

It was rumored at our class meeting, in 1878, that 'he had become a Methodist preacher in the 'Church South.' In his letter of June 25, 1893, though refuting this rumor, he adds: "While I "never attempted to preach, I am now very sorry "that I didn't; as I am fully persuaded that this "was my proper calling, and the one in which I "should have been the most useful and happy."

It seems that in 1891 he sold the "old Kentucky "home," and went, with Mrs. Wight, to Santa Barbara, Cal., where all her immediate relatives were living. His intention was to settle in that vicinity, but he found farm property so high that he returned to Kentucky and bought another farm near Shelbyville, where he has since been striving to make a new home. His original purchase was 255 acres, including all the old improvements— much out of repair—with a delightful situation and rich soil. Seventy-six acres have since been sold off, with a view to building everything new. Here, or in better quarters later on, he would be glad to entertain his old class-mates, or any members of their families. His P. O. address is "Wightwood, "Ky."

Our brother has not forgotten how to wield the pen of a forcible and augumentative writer, as in our Dartmouth days. One of the ablest political tracts we have ever read is "An Open Letter to "Democrats upon our Tariff and Silver Policy, by "a Kentucky Democrat and farmer;" published at Shelbyville, Ky., April, 1892. Mr. Wight has also been highly blessed in his family, as he thankfully acknowledges, and to a degree that very few of our number, from a human stand-point, can claim.

His children, in 1893, were all living, though "truly scattered abroad." The oldest, (I) MARTHA D., had been for several years a teacher in Santa Barbara, Cal.

II. JOHN F., JR., graduated, both in Literature and Law, at Bloomington, Ill., where he now lives, and is in partnership with Mr. Ewing, U. S. Minister to Belgium, and a former partner of Vice-President Stevenson.

III. SARAH B. was teaching music in Santa Paula, Cal., having spent two years with her grandmother in Cal., with whom also she passed several years of her early childhood; though then (July, 1893), expected at her parents' home in a few weeks.

IV. JAMES A. was a graduate of the Central University, Richmond, Ky., and is now at Chicago, Ill., engaged in business.

V. MARY J. graduated from the New England

Conservatory of Music, at Boston, Mass., in 1892, and continued her studies there through the next year. She stands high and is universally popular in musical circles. Had declined an offer to serve as musician for the summer in one of the White Mountain (N. H.) hotels, and was visiting Nantucket, Mass., prior to her return home.

VI. WILLIAM A. was for a time with his brother Albert in Chicago, but latterly in business at Denver, Colo.

All our class-mate's children 'are regular grad-'uates, except the youngest, Willie, whom he could 'not make stick, though one of the brightest of the 'family group.'

WILMOT, LUCIUS WILLIAM PERRY, N. G.

THETFORD, VT.

1 —— Thetford, Feb. 4, 1826. His father was Willard W. Wilmot, of Thetford; his grandfather, Timothy David Wilmot, who m. Polly Copp, dau. of Solomon, one of the first settlers of Sanbornton, N. H.

2 —— Thetford Acad., under the tuition of Hiram Orcutt, A. M.

3 —— Helen Ware, of Fairlee, Vt., at Thetford, by Rev. J. Marsh, Aug. 29, 1855.

Leaving College at the close of the fall term, 1849, he taught the following winter in Thetford; engaged in manual labor, the summer of 1850; taught the next winter in Fairlee, and in April,

1851, removed to California. After spending four years in the gold mines of Nevada City and vicinity, he returned to Vermont in August, 1855.

Having continued in Vermont upwards of two years, chiefly at manual labor, he went to Illinois in Jan., 1858, and taught nearly one year in the Public School at Dwight, Livingston Co. He then returned to New England on account of the ill-health of Mrs. Wilmot, and during the same winter taught the school at North Thetford, Vt.

Spent the following summer on a farm in Fairlee, and again removed to Illinois in Nov., 1859.

Was engaged in teaching, first at Preemption, Mercer Co.; and next, having removed to Southern Illinois in Sept., 1860, as Principal of the Public Schools at Du Quoin, Perry County, for one year.

A similar position for the same length of time at Virden, Macoupin Co. He spent the summer of 1862 on a visit to the East; resumed labors in Sept., at Sandwich, De Kalb Co., Ill., as Principal of the Public Schools, and finally returned to Dwight in the same position as at Sandwich.

In Nov., 1863, he was President of the Livingston County Teachers' Institute.

Repeated attempts have been made to learn of Mr. Wilmot's history, since 1863, but all thus far in vain. It might be well nigh impossible to record all his movements if as numerous during the last 30 as during the first 10 years of our post-graduate course.

A letter addressed to him from Newport, N. H., Feb. 22, 1893, was sent to Dwight, Ill.; "for-

"warded" to Aurora, Ill., and returned to the Secretary, in April following, from the "Dead Letter "Office," Washington, D. C.

WOOD, EDWARD JESUP, *,

MARIANNA, FLA.

1 —— Marianna, Aug. 2, 1834. He was the son of Elizur Wood, of Westport, Ct. His paternal grandparents were Elizur, Sen., and Eleanor (Jesup) Wood. His great-grandfather was the Rev. Samuel Wood, a native of Boxford, Mass., a graduate of Harvard, and a Chaplain in the Revolutionary War. He was stationed at Fort Washington, N. Y., and when that was captured in 1776, was taken prisoner and shut up on board a prison ship, where he perished as did hundreds of other patriots, whose bones were gathered in 1808, and placed in a receptacle at the Brooklyn navy yard. The wife of Rev. Samuel Wood was Miss Ripley, a great-granddaughter of Gov. William Bradford, of the Plymouth Colony. Our class-mate's pedigree is thus established, as Edward J.[4], Elizur[3], Elizur[2], Samuel[1], and back through his great-grandmother to the renowned Gov. Bradford. His father, Elizur[3], was born in New York City; early removed to Florida, and there m. Mary Elizabeth Gautier, Oct. 3, 1832; who (after her husband's death in New York City, Aug. 24, 1840), m., second, Mr. Corliss, of Marianna, Fla.; m., third,

Mr. Walker, a wealthy planter near Madison, Ga.; then moved to Chattanooga, Tenn., where she died, March 17, 1892, in her 74th year, and was buried under the shadow of Lookout Mountain. She was b. June 15, 1818, the dau. of Peter William Gautier and nee Lucy Chilton Walley, of Georgia—our class-mate's maternal grandparents. His father (E. J. Wood's great-grandfather) lived in Normandy, was an Episcopal clergyman of high repute, but was obliged by religious persecution to flee to Bristol, Eng., where, a few months after his arrival, his son, Peter William, the grandfather, was born, May 1, ·1771. The latter came to this country when quite young and settled in Wilmington, N. C.; became a Methodist minister of great oratorical distinction, and d. June 12, 1842, aged 71 years.

2 —— South Woodstock, Ct., under the tutorage of James Willis Patterson (D. C., 1848, afterwards Prof. at Dartmouth, M. C., and N. H. Superintendent of Public Instruction).

3 —— Jane Augusta Williams, at Syracuse, N. Y., Oct. 25, 1859. She was the dau. of Coddington Billings Williams, Esq., and was b. Oct. 25, 1835, in Syracuse. Her mother was Sarah Smith of Groton, Ct., her father was b. in Stonington, Ct.; came to Syracuse at an early day, and was one of its pioneer business men, being engaged extensively in the salt industry. She d. April 14, 1892, at Syracuse, aged fifty-six and a half years; and was buried in the Oakwood cemetery.

4 —— I. MARIE GAUTIER, b. May 18, 1861.

II. FREDERICK WILLIAMS, b. Jan. 10; d. Feb. 17, 1867, aged 1 month and 7 days.

III. CLARENCE WILLIAMS, b. July 20, 1868. Children all born in Goshen, Ind.

In September, 1853, having chosen the employment of Civil Engineer—he went to Toledo, Ohio, in service of the Michigan Southern and Northern Indiana Railroad Co., then constructing an "Air "Line" from Toledo to Goshen, Ind., 120 miles.

After some months in preliminary surveys, he was stationed at Goshen in charge of 15 miles of the road, as Assistant Engineer, where he remained till its completion; in the fall of 1857. Made speeches for "Freedom and Fremont" in 1856, in that and the adjoining counties "with all the ardor "of a neophyte in politics."

In 1857 he entered the law office of Hon. Joseph H. Mather, at Goshen, and remained associated with him—lastly in practice—till Mr. M.'s death, in the spring of 1859, when he opened an office with Hon. E. N. Metcalf, Judge of the Common Pleas Court, and continued in this connection till he entered the army service, in 1861.

In the fall of 1859, he was elected County Surveyor for Elkhart Co.; but not wishing to relinquish the practice of Law, he performed the duties of his office by deputy.

On the 25th of Nov., 1861, Mr. Wood received a commission as Captain, having previously raised a company for the 48th Indiana Infantry Volunteers, then rendezvousing at Goshen. The regiment left camp early in Feb., 1862, and was stationed at Paducah, Ky., till the latter part of April, on port and garrison duty, during which time Capt. Wood was Provost Marshal of the city. The regiment was present during the siege, and at the evacuation of Corinth, Miss., by the rebels, under Beauregard. Its mettle was first tested Sept. 19, 1862, on the comparatively unknown, but bloody field of Iuka, when a single brigade withstood the attack of Price's whole army for more than three hours, forcing them to withdraw under cover of night. It lost 40 killed and heavily in wounded, among the latter Col. John B. Sanborn (a Dartmouth student in 1852), afterwards Brigadier-General at Lexington, Missouri.

The 48th also participated in the hard-fought battle of Corinth, Oct. 3 and 4, 1862; and a vacancy occurring, Capt. Wood received a commission as Major, Oct. 20, 1862. In November his regiment formed a part of the expedition under Gen. Grant, which started for the rear of Vicksburg, Miss., by land; but Van Dorn's successful raid on Holly Springs caused the expedition to be abandoned at Grenada, Miss. Concentrating near Memphis, Tenn., he was afterwards assigned to the 17th Army Corps, under Maj.-Gen. McPherson, and embarking March 1, 1863, from Memphis, shared in the Yazoo Pass expedition, finally made the march from Milliken's Bend, La., above Vicksburg, to a point opposite Grand Gulf below, crossed the river and was in all but one of the battles of that brief, but glorious campaign, which terminated in the close investment and subsequent fall of Vicksburg. In April, 1863, the Lieut.-Colonel having resigned from the effects of a wound, Major Wood was appointed to the vacancy; and in July, 1863, Col. Sanborn being obliged by his impaired health to leave the Southern climate, also resigned, after which time he was in command of the regiment.

In September, 1863, as a part of Gen. John E. Smith's division he was ordered up the river from Vicksburg to Helena, Ark., to support Gen. Steele's advance on Little Rock. Subsequently, as a part of Gen. Sherman's 15th Army Corps, he marched across the country to re-enforce our beleaguered army at Chattanooga, Tenn., arriving in time to assist in driving the enemy from his strong positions.

"The Indiana 48th, by a singular Providence, "has never known defeat. 'Iuka,' 'Corinth,' 'Ray-" 'mond,' 'Jackson,' 'Champion Hills,' 'Vicksburg,' "and 'Chattanooga' are words that may well stir "an honest pride in the breast of everyone of my "brave boys; and when the halo of glory that sur-"rounds the battlefield shall have been mellowed "by time, our childrens' children, regarding these "names as a part of the nation's successful strug-"gle for existence, will not be ashamed to know "that we were there. * * The gallant few who "are left—only 200 fit for duty—are ready to re-"enlist as veteran volunteers."

These eloquent words (from Col. Wood's letter, Bridgeport, Ala., Dec. 17, 1863), forcibly remind us of our class-mate's brilliant translations from the 9th Book of Livy, our Freshman year. Though among the youngest, he was one of the best translators in the class.

He continued in the service, and was mustered out but little before the close of the war.

H. D. Wilson, Esq., of Goshen, Ind:, under date of Nov. 14, 1878, summarily confirms the above record by saying: "He served with credit in the "48th Regiment, Indiana Volunteers, and was "brevetted Colonel."

Was residing at Goshen in 1868. Was elected Clerk of Circuit and Common Pleas Courts, and held the office four years.

As an attorney he practiced but little; yet was well regarded as a generous, courteous and honorable man among his legal friends. He held from the Governor of Indiana the appointment of Judge of Common Pleas for the 17th Judicial District, composed of the four largest counties in the north part of the state. After serving thus on the bench for two years (1870–72), the appointment was confirmed by a unanimous nomination at the mass-Republican Judicial Convention at South Bend, June 12, 1872. He humorously reports himself, in letter of Aug. 5, 1872, as being a "white-headed "portly, bald old man."

Less than a year later, April 9, 1873, his lamented death occurred at Jackson, Mich., in his 39th year.

It will be recalled that Wood and Proctor, of the Class of '51, were very intimate friends in College. The latter is now the Hon. Redfield Proctor, ex-Secretary of War and U. S. Senator from

Vermont. This friendship continued in after life, and Mr. Proctor once visited our class-mate at his home in Goshen.

His widow returned to Syracuse and there lived till her demise.

I. MARIE G., received her education at the the Misses Mackies' School, at Newburg on the Hudson. She kept their family home with her brother, till the spring of 1894. Her present position is that of clerk in E. B. McClelland's Art-Jewelry store, Syracuse.

III. CLARENCE W. was educated in the schools of Syracuse, but started to earn his own living at the age of fifteen in the First National Bank of Syracuse. Later, for several years, he was in the office of the Syracuse Glass Works, where he gained a thorough knowledge of the business. At 23 (1891) he commenced doing business for himself, the firm name being "The Wood Glass Co.," jobbers in glass, located on North Salina street, Syracuse. He was m. in Syracuse Sept. 27, 1894, to Harriet Belle, dau. of William E. and Ellen B. Hopkins.

YOUNG, CHARLES AUGUSTUS,
Hanover, N. H.

1 —— Hanover, Dec. 15, 1834. His parents were Ira and Eliza Minot (Adams) Young; the former (D. C., 1828) being Professor of Nat. Philosophy and Astronomy, and our esteemed instructor in Dart. College. Pedigree, on his father's side, is Charles A.[7], Ira[6], Samuel[5], David[4], David[3], Joseph[2], Sir John[1]; though there may be a missing link between the two last. Sir John[1] emigrated from England, first to Bermuda, thence to Salem, Mass., having, with five others, received a grant of land, including Salem and Boston, dated "March, 1627." His wife was Elizabeth Sleeper. Joseph[2] was one of the original settlers of Kingston, N. H. David[3] b. Jan. 9, 1710, in Kingston, was killed by Indians in Nova Scotia while in the service of the British Government, erecting mills; was present at the taking of Louisburg. David[4] was b. July 13, 1746; lived in Hopkinton, N. H.; there Dea. of the church. Samuel[5], b. March 4, 1775; m. Rebecca Burnham, of Royalton, Vt.; settled in Lebanon, N. H.; was a joiner and builder, designing and constructing many public buildings in New Hampshire and Vermont (1800 and onwards), and d. in Lebanon about 1845. One of his sons, Ammi B., was the architect of the Vermont State House, at Montpelier, and of the Boston Custom House; and was the first supervising architect of the U. S. Treasury Department. His son, Prof. Ira Young, was b. in Lebanon, May 23,

PROF. CHARLES A. YOUNG.

1801; d. at Hanover, Sept. 13, 1858, aged 57 years and 4 months. Our class-mate's mother was born Feb. 9, 1810, being the dau. of Ebenezer Adams, Prof. of Mathematics and Nat. Philosophy in our Alma Mater, 1810-33. Prof. Adams' father was Dea. Ephraim Adams, of New Ipswich, N. H., a man of local note in Revolutionary times, whose wife was Rebecca Locke. Our class-mate's grandmother was Beulah (Minot) Adams from Billerica, Mass.

2 —— Hanover, mostly under his father, and at the Academy, under the instruction of Asa Weeks (D. C., 1846) and others.

3 —— Augusta S. Mixer, of Concord, N. H., Aug. 26, 1857. She was the dau. of Charles H. and Eliza Jane (Morrill) Mixer, of Saco, Me.; there b. May 27, 1835. Her mother was the dau. of Hon. Samuel Morrill, M. D., of Concord.

4 —— I. CLARA ELIZA, b. Sept. 7, 1858, in Hudson, Ohio.

II. CHARLES IRA, b. April 14, 1862, in Hudson.

III. FREDERIC ALBERT, b. March 23, 1864, in Hudson.

He was absent with his father in Europe at the time of our graduation. Returning in Sept., 1853, he became assistant teacher in Phillips Academy, Andover, Mass., and held the position two years. In 1855 he entered the Theological Seminary with the ministry in view, but only completed the first year of the course; also the last four months taking charge of the classical instruction of the Academy, with Prof. Packard, in the absence of Dr. Taylor.

In July, 1856, he received the appointment of Professor of Mathematics and Nat. Philosophy in the Western Reserve College, Hudson, O., and entered upon his duties there in Jan., 1857, having spent the autumn before at Hanover, in preparatory study.

During the winter of 1858-9, was temporarily an assistant of Capt. (afterwards General) Meade in the U. S. Lake Survey, occupied mainly at Hudson, in effecting telegraphic connections.

Having previously drilled a company of students at Hudson for eight months, he offered his services to Gov. Tod, and in June, 1862, was elected and commissioned Captain and mustered in with his men, as Co. B., 85th Ohio V. I. Assigned to State service, he was occupied at Camp Chase (near Columbus) till August 26, guarding rebel prisoners. Was then detailed as an escort to about 1200, who were paroled and sent to Vicksburg, Miss., for exchange. A long and very unpleasant trip, running the gauntlet of guerillas, though under a flag of truce; but arriving safely back at camp, Oct. 1, with loss, during the service, of only two men.

Oct. 5 he was mustered out and returned to peaceful duties at Hudson.

Was appointed lecturer on Natural Philosophy in the "Lake Erie Female Seminary," May, 1863, and in August of the same year received, but declined, appointment to the Professorship of Mathematics at Dartmouth College.

While at Hudson he was a member of the standing committee of the College Church, ranking ecclesiastically, as Elder.

He was again upon the Lake Survey, summer vacation of 1864, among other duties, measuring a base line on Chambers' Island, Green Bay (also in 1865).

Was elected to the position formerly held by his father at Dartmouth in 1864; began work Feb., 1865, and removed his family in August following.

In 1869 was engaged by the Nautical Almanac office to take observations on the sun's eclipse, Aug. 7, stationed at Burlington, Iowa.

He was next appointed on the Government expedition for observing the total eclipse of the sun Dec. 22, 1870, sailing for Liverpool Nov. 3, and being stationed at Jerez, Spain. March 10, 1871, he delivered a lecture at Hanover on this expedition and was noticed in the "Dartmouth" as having purchased, during his absence, $3000 worth of apparatus for the department of Natural Philosophy, and as being authorized by the trustees of the College to order a new telescope for the Observatory at an expense not exceeding $2,500. He had good success in observing the solar eclipses, and discovered, in 1869, the so-called "1474" bright line in the spectrum of the corona, which settled the question whether the corona was of solar or terrestrial origin. In 1871 he also discovered the stratum close to the sun's surface which gives a spectrum of bright lines, and is known as the "Reversing Layer," though the term is of doubtful

propriety. Richard A. Proctor refers to this in an
article in "St. Paul's Magazine" (republished in
the "Eclectic" for July, 1871), entitled "The Sun's
"Atmosphere at length Discovered."

In July and August, 1872, he was six weeks at
the summit of the Union Pacific R. R., Sherman
Station, with the large telescope of. the Observatory, making spectroscopic and other observations.
Expenses of the party paid by a special appropria-
tion, through the Coast Survey.

In July, 1874, he sailed for China from San
Francisco, Cal., as a member of the party sent out
by Government to observe the "Transit of Venus,"
at Pekin. Was associated with Prof. Watson, of
Ann Arbor, Mich. Observations on the whole
successful, though somewhat troubled by clouds.
Returned in Feb., 1875.

Winter of 1873-4 he delivered a course of. Lectures at the "Peabody Institute," Baltimore, Md.
Winter of 1875-6 gave a course of "Lowell Lec-
"tures" at Boston, Mass., and a second course in
the spring of 1886. Autumns of 1873 and 1875
gave courses of Lectures on Astronomy at Williams College.

For the last twenty-five years he has given reg-
ular courses of lectures, annual or biennial, at Mt.
Holyoke College, Mass., and nearly as long at
Bradford Academy, Mass.; also for a shorter time
at Wheaton Seminary, Mass., at Miss Porter's
School, Farmington, Ct., and at Wilson College,
Chambersburg, Pa.; with occasional courses at Ab-
bot Academy, Mass., at St. Paul's School, Con-

cord, N. H., and at some other institutions of similar grade. Besides these, has delivered a large number of popular lectures on various astronomical subjects in our cities.

He accepted a call to the Professorship of Astronomy in the College of New Jersey, in March, 1877, and removed to Princeton, with his family, the following August. Occupies a house built for him by the College, in connection with the Observatory. He took a party to Denver, Col., to observe the eclipse of July 29, 1878—funds furnished by friends of the College; favorable observations, but no new discoveries. This expedition only prevented his being at our 25th anniversary meeting. Also, in 1887, he headed a Princeton expedition which went to Russia to observe the total solar eclipse of August 19. The station was near the city of Rschew, about a 100 miles east of Moscow. A rain-storm prevented all observation.

Our brother was early chosen a delegate to the New School General Assembly at Pittsburg, Pa., in 1860, and the success of his career as a scientist has since brought him many additional honors. The University of Pennsylvania conferred on him the honorary degree of Ph. D. in 1870. Hamilton College, N. Y., also bestowed the degree of Ph. D. in 1871, and the Wesleyan University, Conn., that of LL.D. in 1876. In 1887 Columbia College, N. Y., gave him the same degree, and in 1894 another LL.D. came to him from "Adelbert College," Ohio, or rather from the "Western Reserve University," of which Adelbert is one of the component institu-

tions. Prof. Young is "Associate Fellow of the Am.
"Academy of Arts and Sciences," Boston, Mass.;
Fellow of the "American Philosophical Society,"
Philadelphia, Pa.; Fellow of the "National Acad.
"of Sciences;" and "Foreign Associate" of the
"Royal (British) Astronomical Society," and of a
number of other more or less important scientific
organizations.

He was also "honored with the Janssen medal
"from the French Academy of Science in 1891, on
"account of his scientific discoveries."

Among his numerous publications we notice:

(1) "A Paper on Printing Chromograph;"
Silliman's Journal, 1869.

(2) An article on his Observations of the Sun's
Eclipse from Burlington, Ia., in the "Dartmouth,"
for Sept., 1869.

(3) Two letters addressed to Prof. Henry Mor-
ton, and published by him in the "N. Y. Tribune,"
Oct. 3, 1870, under the heading, "Photographing
"Sun Flames without an Eclipse." Prof. Morgan
adds that "the discoveries announced by Prof.
"Young are of the highest scientific value."

(4) Report of observations in a "Letter from
"Spain," in the "Dartmouth" for Feb., 1871.

(5) "A Bit of Foreign Correspondence," in
"Dartmouth" of March, 1871.

(6) Reprint of his article "On the Solar Corona"
("Am. Journal of Science and Arts," Vol. 1, May,
1871); soon after appeared in a pamphlet form.

(7) His lecture delivered at New Haven, Ct.,
Jan., 1872, on the Sun and the Solar Protuber-

ancies; reprinted and enlarged in a pamphlet of 55 pp. under the title of "The Sun and the Phenomena of its Atmosphere." Very favorably noticed in the "N. Y. Independent."

(8) Several articles upon "Solar Spectroscopy" in Journal of the "Franklin Institute" and the "Am. "Journal of Science and Art," 1869-70.

(9) Numerous papers in Scientific Journals; and Lecture on the Sun, published by "Chatfield & "Co." in their Scientific series, 1872.

(10) "Annual Address" as Vice President of the "Am. Association for the Advancement of "Science," at the Buffalo (N. Y.) meeting, 1876; published in proceedings of that year.

(11) Report of Expedition to Denver, Col., 1878, under the head of "Familiar Science;" in "Boston Journal of Chemistry," for Oct. 1878. (This "Journal" had elsewhere paid him a high compliment).

(12) Address on "Pending Problems in Astron-"omy," at the Philadelphia meeting of "Am. Asso-"ciation for the Advancement of Science," Sept. 5, 1884, as the retiring President of said association; published in "Science" for Sept., 1884; also in seperate pamphlet form; 27 pp.

(13) "God's Glory in the Heavens;" article in the "S. S. Times," Aug. 16, 1884. Same republished in pamphlet form, 1894, 20 pp.

(14) An admirable practical article of his, on "Courage for the Duties of Life," appears in "Portraits and Principles," 1894.

His more important writings, however, have been

published in periodicals purely scientific, and have not come to our notice.

IIis only books, so far, are:

(15) "The Sun;" 12 mo.; 331 pp.; 3d edition, 1887; translated into French, German and Italian; and (16) A series of text books on Astronomy; the first "General Astronomy" for Colleges, having appeared in 1889, and the two others, "Elements "of Astronomy" for High Schools, and "Lessons in "Astronomy" for Lower Schools in 1890 and 1891. They have been very successful. Over 40,000 copies having been sold already.

Besides his "serious writing," alluded to above, he has published some twenty or more popular articles in the "North American Review," "Forum," "Princeton Review," "Scribner's" (one article), "Popular Science Monthly," "Presbyterian Review," etc., also many newspaper articles (mostly editorial) in the "New York Times," "Independent" (science notes) and others.

Prof. Young was likewise a collaborator on the "Century Dictionary" to the extent of several. hundred dollars. The published articles which we have numbered above, except the two last, are not regarded as his most important. There are at least 132 in all, varying in length from one to forty pages each, about fifty of which may be regarded as of permanent scientific value.

We cannot forbear subjoining the following critique on his principal work, from the "New York Independent":

"Prof, C. A. Young's book on "The Sun" (Vol.

"XXXIV. in Appleton's International Scientific
"Series) is a model treatise. The author has
"adapted himself to his readers, and while he
"keeps out of technical ruts he writes in unpro-
"fessional, intelligible English, with enough ful-
"ness and accuracy to satisfy the requirements of
"the large class of readers not engaged in scien-
"tific pursuits, but competent to understand the
"principles involved and the conclusions reached.
"The subject is itself extremely interesting, and
"gains rather than loses interest in Professor
"Young's hands. · At the present rate of advance
"in scientific discovery, it is not altogether easy to
"complete a volume before some portions of it have
"already been left behind. For anything in ad-
"vance of this volume, however, the reader will
"have to consult the scientific journals of the last
"six months. As to dogmatic opinion, Professor
"Young has the merit of marking the line between
"conjecture and discovery. He reviews the solar
"astronomy and methods of observation and
"measurement, gives full accounts of the spectro-
"scope and how it is used, discusses the solar
"spots, the chromosphere, the protuberancies, the
"corona, the solar light and heat, how they are
"maintained, and their permanence, reaching the
"general conclusion (cautiously expressed) that
"our present knowledge indicates a past duration
"of about fifteen million years for the solar system,
"and an equal future duration—thirty millions of
"years to cover the entire solar history. He by no
"means commits himself, however, to the opinion

"that the system will ever fail, but expressly states
"that we do not know what reserve forces there are
"in nature for the restoration of decayed systems,
"and that the limits of conjectural possibility are
"too vast to allow a dogmatic conclusion.   *   *
"We may add that while the author does not an-
"nounce religious opinions in his pages, there are
"no implications, either in the work itself, nor in its
"methods which are unfriendly to faith.   On the
"contrary, the devout spirit is left in full possession
"of its freedom, as when alone in the presence of
"nature herself."

In October, 1892, he writes that 'his College
'work, with the big classes, gives him all he can
'well take care of.'

That year there were 225 Juniors, whom 'he
'handles in two divisions. Writes an article, now
'and then, for some astronomical journal, and makes
'occasional spectroscopic observations, besides more
'or less of popular lecturing; but feels that he is
'growing old in many ways, and that two or three
'hours' work with a class tires him much more than.
'formerly.'

Ill-health alone prevented our class-mate from
joining us at the 40th anniversary; but his condition has since greatly improved, and in Dec., 1893.
having returned from his Hanover vacation in September, he is able to report himself 'quite well
'again, though not so vigorous as he used to be.'
A similarly favorable report for himself and Mrs.
Young, Oct. 24, 1894.   Next to Hulbert, Palmer.
Strow and Robinson, he has been permitted to en-

joy the longest period of uninterrupted conjugal felicity.

I. CLARA E. was m. to Prof. Hiram A. Hitchcock, of the Dartmouth Thayer School, Hanover, N. H., June 26, 1888, at the Marquand Chapel, Princeton. Child (1) Charles Young (Hitchcock) b. May 7, 1891, at Hanover.

II. CHARLES IRA, grad. at Princeton, 1883, is an electrician, connected with the Westinghouse Electric Co., Pittsburg, Pa. Is partially crippled in consequence of a severe accident by electricity, which occurred at Pittsburg in Feb., 1888, succeeded by paralysis at New Orleans, La., two months later; but he is so far restored as to write readily with his left hand and to perform his required office work. Before this accident he was a highly accomplished musician and organist, and is a musical composer to the present.

III. FREDERIC A. was also graduated at Princeton, and took his degree of "C. E." (Civil Engineer) with the J. C. Green School of Science, Class of 1886. He is now assistant on the U. S. Coast and Geodetic Survey.

CALIPO

IN THE COLLEGE PARK.

SHATTUCK OBSERVATORY.

IN THE MUSEUM.

GENERAL HISTORY

CLASS OF 1853,

DARTMOUTH COLLEGE.

This Class was entered in the autumn of 1849, with 36 members, according to the official catalogue of 1849-50. This catalogue was "printed at the Dartmouth Press," Sept., 1849, but its artistic qualities were not satisfactory, the names of the large Sophomore Class being unduly crowded together on one of its pages, with other typographical blemishes. "The "Students," therefore, published another catalogue, a few weeks later, printed by "J. C. Kneeland's Steam Press, Troy, "N. Y." On this second catalogue the name of W. S. Statham was added to our list, making our total enumeration for the Freshman Fall term, 37. Several additions were made in the spring of 1850, and the catalogue for our Sophomore year, 1850-51, presented the new names of Allen, Blood, Burnet, Emerson, Fairbanks, Goodwin, Hutchinson, Moore, Palmer, Parsons, H. M. Perrin, Sargent, Stanton, Stewart, Upham and Walker (16 in all); while Putnam and Wilmot had fallen out, leaving our Sophomore sum total 51, the highest we ever attained at one time, by the catalogues; though to this number should also be added the name of Waterhouse, who, being with us only the Sophomore Spring and Summer terms, does not appear on a catalogue; making our true Sophomore enumeration, 52.

As "Junior Sophisters" we received for accessions, Farnsworth, Hollenbush, C. O. Morse, Reed, F. C. Statham and Wight (six); but had lost, in the meantime, the following nine: Allen, Babcock, Dearborn, Goodwin, W. S. Statham, Stewart, Walker, Warren and Waterhouse, leaving our catalogue number for 1851-52, 49.

For some reason, the next catalogue, 1852-53, presented a different heading for the Classes, "Senior Class," instead of "Senior Sophisters," etc., in which we were numbered 45; no additions having been made, but the four following having dropped out: Blood, Isham, Strow and Thomson.

Between the issuing of this catalogue and the first official list of the "graduating Class," in the spring of 1853, M. D. Brown, Oakes and Robinson had been given to us from the East, and Dickson from the West; while Stewart also had been "restored" to us from his native Maine, so that this graduating list numbered 50. During our last vacation, however, Kendrick was called from earth, and H. M. Perrin did not see fit to take his degree till after our commencement, so that the second list of graduates, in July, 1853, was given as only 48; though our actual number of graduates has usually been reckoned as 49, and the number as given in the "Dartmouth Gen-"eral Catalogue" for 1880 (Kendrick being "A. B. post obit.") is 50. Thus, adding to the "old guard of forty-niners," 37 in number, who first entered the Class, the 17 accessions of the second year, the six of the third year, and the five of the fourth and then diminishing the sum by one (as one of the Class, Stewart, acceded to us twice), and we find 64 as our full complement, whose sketches are given in the foregoing "Memorial."

Of the original 37, however, ten fell out by death or removal, leaving only 27 who both began and completed the full collegiate course together.

At this stage it may be interesting to note the names of our honored instructors. The following is a complete list of the "Academical Faculty," as it appeared in our first catalogue, with the date of each death, in parenthesis, after the several names:

REV. NATHAN LORD, D. D.,

[Died Sept. 9, 1870, aged 78]

PRESIDENT.

REV. ROSWELL SHURTLEFF, D. D.

[Died Feb. 4, 1861, aged 87]

PROFESSOR EMERITUS OF MORAL PHILOSOPHY AND POLITICAL ECONOMY.

Rev. DANIEL JAMES NOYES, A. M.,

(in Students' Catalogue),

[Died Dec. 22, 1885, aged 73]

PHILLIPS PROFESSOR OF THEOLOGY.

Rev. CHARLES BRICKETT HADDOCK, D. D.,

[Died Jan. 15, 1861, aged 64]

PROFESSOR OF INTELLECTUAL PHILOSOPHY AND POLITICAL ECONOMY.

ALPHEUS CROSBY, A. M.,

[Died April 17, 1874, aged 63] .

PROFESSOR EMERITUS OF THE GREEK LANGUAGE AND LITERATURE.

IRA YOUNG, A. M.,

[Died Sept. 13, 1858, aged 57]

APPLETON PROFESSOR OF NATURAL PHILOSOPHY AND PROFESSOR OF ASTRONOMY.

OLIVER PAYSON HUBBARD, M. D.,

HALL PROFESSOR OF MINERALOGY AND GEOLOGY, AND PROFESSOR OF CHEMISTRY
AND PHARMACY.

SAMUEL GILMAN BROWN, A. M.,

[Died Nov. 4, 1885, aged 72]

EVANS PROFESSOR OF ORATORY AND BELLES-LETTRES.

EDWIN DAVID SANBORN, A. M.,

[Died Dec. 20, 1885, aged 77]

PROFESSOR OF THE LATIN LANGUAGE AND LITERATURE.

STEPHEN CHASE, A. M.,

[Died Jan. 9, 1851, aged 37]

PROFESSOR OF MATHEMATICS.

JOHN NEWTON PUTNAM, A. M.,

[Died Oct. 22, 1863, aged 40]

PROFESSOR OF THE GREEK LANGUAGE AND LITERATURE.

Under all the above we came directly, with the exception of
Dr. Shurtleff, Professor Haddock (though he conducted our

Chapel devotions several times during our first term), and Professor Crosby (though his admirable Greek grammar was our vade mecum through the entire classical course).

Our additional instructors, as found in the subsequent catalogues, were:

JOHN SMITH WOODMAN, A. M.,

[Died May 9, 1871, aged 51]

PROFESSOR OF MATHEMATICS.

Rev. CLEMENT LONG, D. D.,

[Died Oct. 14, 1861, aged 54]

INSTRUCTOR IN INTELLECTUAL PHILOSOPHY AND POLITICAL ECONOMY.

We must, however, add to the above, from the "Medical "Faculty," the name of

EDMUND RANDOLPH PEASLEE, M. D.,

[Died Jan. 21, 1878, aged 63]

PROFESSOR OF ANATOMY AND PHYSIOLOGY, AND (MEDICAL) LIBRARIAN,

in view of his excellent physiological lectures to our Class, early in the course; repeating also the names of the "College Librarians," Professor Charles B. Haddock, the first two years, and Professor Oliver P. Hubbard the last two years of our connection, as students, with the College. By the catalogue list of the "Corporation" the well remembered fact is suggested that the urbane Daniel Blaisdell, Esq., was College Treasurer through all our course; while "Their Excellencies." Samuel Dinsmoor, LL. D., "ex-officio," of Keene; and Noah Martin, M. D., "ex-officio." of Dover, were Governors of the State of New Hampshire during our College life; the former, the first three years, and the latter, the last year. We would also add the name of Rev. John Richards, D. D., our respected College pastor.

All the above. including the whole company of our beloved teachers (with the single exception of Professor Hubbard) have now gone to their long home; and three, it will be observed,—having lived beyond the "three score years and ten"—passed away the same year, viz : Professors Brown, Noyes and Sanborn, all within two months of each other, and the two last "divided" in their deaths, only by a single week.

As a Class, the men of '53 were modest and retiring, and through their whole student life commendably harmonious among themselves.

As Freshmen, with a Sophomore Class of nearly twice our size, we made no pretensions at coping with them in foot ball and other athletic games; though in the traditional "rushes" down the Chapel steps (as the Classes were formerly arranged) we were quite successful in keeping back the whole College, when our own "Big Chase" had once braced himself. While during our Sophomore year, with such powerful men as Chase and Stewart, we were regarded as no mean antagonists by those who came after us. Our Class prayer meetings were held on Wednesday noons for half an hour before dinner; also for an hour on Sabbath mornings from the ringing of the first bell. At our Class business meetings Chase was usually elected President. For the drawing up of resolutions at the deaths of our deceased members, Goodwin and Kendrick, McDuffee was the chief appointee. Crosby and Runnels were chosen by the students to attend, as delegates of our Class, the funeral of Dartmouth's greatest son, Daniel Webster, in Oct., 1852.

Though the two literary societies, the "Social Friends" and the "United Fraternity," took each an equal number from our original membership, yet as the result of changes the "Socials" had a majority of nine at the beginning of our Senior year; the whole number 45 being divided, Socials 27, and Fraters 18.

Emerson was first President of the Socials, and Chase of the Fraters (these officers being always chosen from the Senior Class) ; Hayward and Farnsworth were their Librarians, respectively. Emerson was also first President of the Theological Society, Senior year ; and Runnels the second (spring term). Chase was President of the "Handel Society" and Director of the College Music during the entire Senior year, and for some time before. Young was first President of the Society of Inquiry (missionary) ; and Howard of the "Dartmouth Temper-

"ance Society." Among the secret orders Senior fall term, seven of our number were members of the "Psi Upsilon" Society; seven of the "Kappa Kappa Kappa" Society, and nine of the "Alpha Delta Phi" Society.

At our Commencement in 1853 Chase and Crosby were the Marshals. "Class Day" exercises were not inaugurated at Dartmouth till the next year.

The occasion was rendered unusually attractive by the announcement that "On Wednesday afternoon (July 27) the "usual anniversary of the Literary Societies will give place to a "Eulogy on Daniel Webster by Hon. Rufus Choate of Boston." This had been preceded, on Wednesday forenoon, by the address of Hon. Ogden Hoffman, of New York City, before the Phi Beta Kappa Society; and on Tuesday evening, July 26, Rev. R. S. Storrs, Jr., of Brooklyn, N. Y., had addressed the Theological Society. The Germania Serenade Band, of Boston, furnished our music, giving their concert on Wednesday evening.

We will here reproduce our "Order of Exercises" for Commencement day as nearly as may be in its original four page form :

ORDER OF EXERCISES.

JULY 28, 1853.

PRAYER.

MUSIC.

The speakers were selected and arranged without reference to
scholarship.

---

1. The Problem of Liberty.
   WILLIAM STRATTON PALMER,
   Orfordville.

2. The Influence of Great Men.
   ALPHEUS BENNING CROSBY,
   Hanover.

3. The British Colonies in America.
   ISAAC AUGUSTUS PARKER,
   Woodstock, Vt.

4. The Passions a Criterion of Mental Power.
   NATHAN JACKSON MORRISON,
   Franklin.

5. The Test of an Original Mind its Awakening Power.
   JOHN FLETCHER WIGHT,
   Shelby, Ky.

MUSIC.

——

6.   The Mormons—their Origin and Destiny.

CHASE PRESCOTT PARSONS,
Gilmanton.

7.   Suffering, a Necessity of Greatness.

DAVID JAMES BOYD SARGENT,
Tamworth.

8.   Want—a Stimulus to Effort.

GEORGE WILLIAM CAHOON,
Lyndon, Vt.

9.   The true Relations of England and America, friendly,
    not hostile.

CLARENCE LINDEN BURNET,
Ticonderoga, N. Y.

——

MUSIC.

——

10.   The Power of Mystery.

JOHN HUTCHINSON,
West Randolph, Vt.

11.   Improvements in the Practical Arts as affecting the
     Stability of our Institutions.

ALFRED OSGOOD BLAISDELL,
Hanover.

12. California and Australia in their Relation to General
Civilization.

JOHN HERRICK MORSE,
Brookfield, Vt.

13. A Poem. The Student's Revery.

DANIEL PERRIN.
Northmoreland, Pa.

MUSIC.

14. Wellington—and his Place in History.

JONATHAN BREWER FARNSWORTH,
Woodstock, Vt.

15. The Struggle of Hungary against Mahomet.

JOHN KENDALL,
Washington, D. C.

16. The Quakers as Legislators.

ANDREW REED.
Reedsville, Pa.

17. The Relation of Words and Things.

MOSES THURSTON RUNNELLS,
Jaffrey.

MUSIC.

18. The Contest between Naturalism and Supernaturalism.

HORATIO NELSON BURTON.
Washington, Vt.

19. The Retributions of Providence in French History.
		Francis Cummins Statham.
			Greensboro', Ga.

20. The World of the Enthusiast and the Satirist compared.
		Gilman L. Sessions.
			West Woodstock, Ct.

21. A Poem.	Youth in Age.
		Silvanus Hayward,
			Gilsum.

—

MUSIC.

—

DEGREES CONFERRED.

—

MUSIC.

—

PRAYER.

The following are the principal variations of this order from the original assignment, the May previously, when it was said "The speakers, to whom the following subjects were assigned, "were drawn by lot from the Class."

There were 23 names in this assignment, six of which fell out, including Kendrick's, occasioned by his death.   Of the 17 remaining, the subject of No. 5 was changed from "The "present questions of Science," on the original assignment ; of No. 6, from "Depreciation of the precious Metals ;" of No. 10, from "Cultivation of a taste for Art among a People ;" and of No. 13, from "The Wit of different Nations."   Thus only 13 of the 23 first drawn spoke on the themes originally assigned them ; while Nos. 2, 3, 4 and 12 of the final order were added by a second drawing, to take the place (partially) of the six who, for various causes, had fallen out, or were excused from speaking.   The whole number of speakers was therefore 21, two less than at first drawn.

It is remembered that Mr. Choate, who listened to the speaking at our Commencement, expressed himself as well pleased with the general character of our efforts, and that he especially commended the address of Mr. Wight.

Our post-graduate history, as a Class, may be briefly given ; being almost wholly confined to the records and suggestions of the "Class Book"—a large, ledger-like volume, eleven inches by sixteen in size, and containing 477 blank pages, which was purchased the last weeks of our course, and consigned to Bro. Blaisdell, as the first elected "Class Secretary."

He entered our names and the few items of our history which we gave him at graduating ; and he had good reason to complain of us for not co-operating with him in the giving of subsequent information, as at first agreed upon.

His records of our three years' meeting afford six pages of racy and readable composition. The first session was an informal gathering on Tuesday at 11 a. m., July 29, 1856, at Crosby's office ; the second at 8 o'clock, Wednesday morning. The third session was at Frary's Hotel, with a supper, at 10 o'clock "Thursday evening, after the Levee."

The fortunes of each member, during the three years were related at this session, by those present, of themselves, and, so far as known, of those absent. Twelve members were in attendance (according to the table herewith appended) ; and, as at nearly all our other meetings, all left their autographs in the "Big Book." It was voted to try and procure "lithographic "likenesses" of all who were willing to invest in the same. Bro. Upham was chosen a "central committee" to carry out this action'; but, we believe, it never materialized.

The first session of our "Ten Years' Meeting" was also informal, at the house of Prof. Dixi Crosby, M. D., July 22, 1868, on invitation from our brother, Dr. Crosby, directly after the address of Ralph Waldo Emerson. Eight present, as per table. Two hours spent in giving and receiving information about the members of the Class. Our Secretary being absent, Runnels was chosen Secretary, pro tem., and, at our adjourned meeting next day, "in southwest corner of the vestry "soon after the opening of Commencement exercises," he was chosen to act as Secretary in the place of Blaisdell—not yet appearing—and Bro. Young was sent to find the "Class Book," at the office of Daniel Blaisdell, Esq. It was also voted to empower the Secretary to gain new information respecting each member of the Class, and to print the details in a cheap pamphlet form for distribution. using the funds now assessed ($1 upon each member), together with what may afterwards be added. Our final adjournment was from the Commencement dinner-table, to the Centennial celebration of the College, in 1869.

The first "Class Memorial" was accordingly published in the spring of 1864. The total expense of publishing, with other Class expenses till March, 1865, was $60.76. Total amount received from the Class assessments, and sale of Memorials, $88.65. The balance of $27.89 was afterwards (in 1869) voted to the Secretary for his services.

The largest Class meeting we ever held was July 21, 1869, in connection with the College Centennial.

A special circular-invitation (No. 1) to this meeting had been issued by the Secretary, April 15. We met, by invitation of

Professor and Mrs. C. A. Young, at their house—the then second residence north of Wentworth Hall—at 6 o'clock p. m.

After supper we organized for business—Bro. Chase being called to the chair—and continued our session till midnight. Eighteen members were present, as per schedule. The history of the Class, since publication of "Memorial," was read from the records, supplemented by verbal statements from those present.

The most important votes at this meeting were, on motion of Crosby, that we now levy a tax of $2, upon each member, to meet Class expenses; that a complete list of the P. O. addresses of our class-mates be made by the Secretary, and sent, at an early date, to each member; also that a "Class Album" be purchased by the Secretary, and that the present "photo- "graph representations" of the class-mates be solicited. It was also voted—in view of the proposed effort on the part of the Alumni to raise $200,000 for the College—that the Secretary be requested, by circular and letters, to solicit benefactions from all members of the Class, "the smallest sums being "equally acceptable with the largest, and that from the money "thus raised Prof. Young be authorized to draw, with the con- "sent of the Trustees and Faculty, whatever he desires for "special, scientific work in his department."

Voted our thanks to Bro. Young and Mrs. Young for their kind entertainment.

Adjourned—after an informal meeting at the Commencement dinner—till our next "10 years' meeting" in 1873.

In accordance with the above votes, a circular (No. 2) was issued in Aug., 1869, with register and P. O. addresses of the eighteen members present at the class-meeting, of the thirty-three living members not present; and of the nearest friends of the thirteen deceased members; giving also, some account of the Class meeting, and of the proposals made for the collection and interchange of photographs.

At nearly the same date a circular appeal (No. 3) was issued, inviting responses to the College and Class funds. The moneys received by the Secretary were collected from twelve living members. and in behalf of three others deceased, amounting in all to $215, which was made over to our class-mate, Professor Young, as per previous vote.

No additional sums ever passed through the Secretary's hands; though it is known that other sums were paid by members of our Class to the general alumni fund, and that one of our number, at least, presented to the same the gift of $1000.

The Album was also procured, and is now in the Secretary's possession, to be hereafter disposed of, with the Record Book, by vote of the Class. The photographs of 40 of our members, and of one wife and four children (D. Perrin's), are now in the Album.

The 20 years' Class meeting was held on the evening of June 25, 1873, also at the house of Prof. Young, in Hanover, eight being present. Voted that a new circular be issued by the Secretary, consisting of a catalogue of the living members with their present residences; and with "designations" for those deceased, for those present at this meeting and for those whose pictures are now in the Class Album.

Voted that our thanks be again extended to Prof. and Mrs. Young for their generous hospitality.

The circular catalogue (Class document No. 4) was prepared according to the above vote, and printed in the "Dartmouth "Anvil" for Dec. 4, 1873.

The adjustment of accounts at the 20 years' meeting—covering the expenses of Centennial year, and subsequently—is as follows:

Raised by the Class in 1869, $34.00
Expense of Centennial meeting, including Class tents, $10.80
Circulars, album, etc., afterwards, 17.10

$27.90

leaving a balance of $6.10 in the treasury. At the 20 years' meeting $7.00 more were added to this sum. The expenses of that meeting and of subsequent publication were $7.50, leaving a final balance of $5.60, which in 1878, on motion of Cahoon, was voted to the Secretary for his services.

The 25th anniversary meeting was held by previous arrangement in one of the rooms of the Dartmouth Hotel, at 4.30

p. m., June 26, 1878.   Bro. Chase was elected chairman. Eleven members present, who responded for themselves; letters also being read from several absent brothers, and the stock of information about other absent ones, in the Class book and in the possession of those present, being levied.

We took tea together, as a Class, in the hotel dining-room, at the usual hour, after which we resumed the meeting at our room.   Were favored with a brief original poem, prepared for the occasion by Brother Hayward, and herewith appended. Chose the President and Secretary as a committee to call upon the widow of our late Brother Crosby and express our sympathies, as a Class, at our common loss (which they did, accordingly, on the following day).   Voted that the Secretary be requested to prepare another "Memorial" of the Class.   Adjourned at 12 o'clock a. m. to meet at our 30th anniversary commencement.

[Poem by Rev. Silvanus Hayward.]

QUARTER CENTURY.

Class Meeting, June 26, 1878.

Stay, Clotho, stay thy fervid wheel!
  Let Lachesis cease twining!
The quarter skein upon her reel,
  Our threads of life combining;—

Threads, tinged by Life's "dissolving views"
  In shades of countless number;
Some decked with Joy's celestial dews,
  Some smirched with Sorrow's umber.

We come from out the dusty maze,
  Where weaponed warriors glisten,
Into each other's eyes to gaze,
  Each other's accents listen.

Nor absent those whom duties hold
  To-day from our collection,
Nor those whose dust 'neath grassy mold
  Awaits the resurrection.

We feel the presence of our dead;
  There are no vacant places;
Though Atropos has cut their thread,
  We see the vanished faces.

For bonds which classmates here assume,
　Nor Time nor Death can sever;
The shuttle flies in Friendship's loom
　Forever and forever.

On Time's tempestuous, trackless sea,
　A momentary meeting,
Then gliding to the far To Be,
　"Hail and farewell," our greeting.

O Heavenly Pilot, do thou guide
　To that fair port of entry
Beyond this billowy, treacherous tide,
　Guarded by angel sentry.

Who next of our departing band,
　The crown immortal winning,
Shall pass within that veil-ed land?—
　Clotho, resume thy spinning!

In pursuance of the above vote for a "Memorial," the Secretary issued a two-page circular (No. 5) Aug. 1, 1878; giving some account of the meeting and a list of those present; proposing also to issue the said Memorial in case the requisite information should be promptly sent in.　He suggested that we make the records more full, than heretofore, in the ancestral and genealogical history of our wives and of ourselves; that the full names of our parents and children, with birth and death dates, be repeated, to avoid errors; and that lists of all books, treatises and addresses published (titles and dates), with public offices held, inventions patented, scientific or other discoveries made, and works of general utility, either accomplished or in progress, since 1863, be added.　It was also distinctly stated, in this circular, that the "Memorial" would not be printed unless the responses should warrant the Secretary in so doing—that "the full tale of the 'bricks' must not be expect-"ed unless the 'straw' and other material be forthcoming."　It may as well here be said that the responses to that circular did not warrant the immediate preparation of the "Memorial," and that it is only at the present time, that, with such material as has been furnished and procured from all sources, the vote of the Class in 1878 is being carried out.

Our thirtieth anniversary meeting was held Wednesday eve.,
June 27, 1883, being called at the Dartmouth Hotel, where ·
most of us took supper together, at 6 o'clock, and immediately adjourned, on special invitation from Mrs. Young
and Mrs. Proctor (the mother and sister of our class-mate), to
their parlor, at the old Prof. Adams homestead, where we sub-
scribed our names, eight in number, (see table). The place of
our meeting was kindly committed to our disposal for the night,
though Fairbanks' duties as trustee, required his absence a portion of the evening, and Carter was obliged to retire at an
earlier hour, on account of ill-health. But the rest of us
"remained and chatted of affairs, personal or general, till the
" 'small hours;' noticably Chase and Hayward, who took the
"cars north and south at 2 and 3 of the clock, June 28, and
"Runnels who kept possession of the same parlor (there being
" 'no room in the inn') till the early birds of Hanover began
"their carols, as of old." (Class records).

"In connection with the Commencement of June 28, 1888,
"Fairbanks and Hayward were the only members of the Class
"who put in an appearance, and consequently our 35th anni-
"versary meeting was not held in due form. The Secretary
"being upon the sick list, was unable to go to Hanover; but the
" 'Big Book' was sent by express from East Jaffrey, and re-
"turned thither by Hayward before the end of the week."
(Class records, July 12, 1888).

The following is Class circular invitation (No. 6) to the
Fortieth Anniversary, Banquet and Reunion, at "The
"Wheelock," dining-room No. 3, Wednesday, June 28, 1893,
at 9 o'clock p. m. : most of the invitations to Class meetings,
except this and that for 1869, being issued upon postal cards :

You are earnestly invited to be present on this occasion. Out
of the sixty-four (64) who were members of this Class, thirty-
seven (37) are now supposed to be living. The Class Secretary has had new or special returns from twenty-six (26) of
this number; as also from our beloved BURTON, who has fallen
by the way, or rather gone to his high reward, since this last
series of letters to the Class was commenced.

His letters to two others, Wilmot, and F. C. Statham, have
been returned from the Dead Letter Office; leaving only eight
(8), from whom he has failed to receive recent information.

The records of each class-mate, with full obituaries of the departed, have been entered in the "Big Book," with an index to the pages where each is mentioned, so that their histories can be readily traced. The major part of those who expressed an opinion upon the subject, have desired that the Class should have a reunion and supper at the "Wheelock," not unlike those provided for other Classes; and the expenses, to be met by those "present," at so much per sitting, will not be unreasonably high.

"Come one, Come all," brothers of '53! and let us, in God's good Providence, enjoy one more social gathering, as in the olden time!

Cordially and respectfully yours,
MOSES T. RUNNELS, Class Sec.

Newport, N. H., June 16, 1893.

In response to the above, nine, whose autographs are given on page 173 of the record book, met as proposed. In the larger adjoining room was the much larger ten years' meeting of the Class of '83; but notwithstanding their uproariousness, we, the men of '53, pursued the even tenor of our way in dignified silence, and outlasted them by several hours.

Each man was invited to make remarks upon his own history and life work as now viewed, and taken as a whole, beginning with Chase, our President. The addresses of Carter and Hayward were closed with original poems, which are here given:

[Poem by Rev. Nathan F. Carter.]

DARTMOUTH COLLEGE, 1853-1893.

Since from Old Dartmouth's classic halls,
  In untried armor for the strife,
  We sought the tented fields of life,
Responsive to the world's clear calls,

The golden sands of forty years
  Have rounded out their silent flow!
  To-day we see their after-glow,
Or shadows of their hopes and fears!

From scattered homes and varied cares,
  We come to scan in fond review,
  Times once so fresh with morning dew,
But now beyond our wisest prayers!

No longer novices in thought,
  No longer novices in deed ;
  Life has to-day its ripening creed,
The glory patient hands have wrought!

But eyes a growing dimness know,
  Our ears, perchance, a muffling wear,
  Our foreheads deepening seams of care,
Our locks the touch of winter's snow!

Not quite so strong our willing hands
  To bear the burdens of the day ;
  We sooner weary in the way
O'er rugged rocks and drifting sands.

However strong and tense the will
  To lay broad plans, and do high deeds
  Of valor, face to face with needs
That bode the great world only ill ;—

However great the burning zeal
  To wield in hand an Aaron's rod,
  And make our work the work of God,
For God's high glory, human weal ;—

We cannot do as once we did ;
  We cannot bear the constant strain ;
  Our energies begin to wane,
And buoyant dreams of youth forbid!

But still our hearts may be as young,
  As ever in the days of old,
  To climb the sunset heights as bold,
As glad to hear day's vespers sung !

As true and loyal to the right,
  As firmly set against the wrong,
  As brave to suffer and grow strong,
As brave to dare Faith's holy fight !

So let us clasp our hands in love,
  In glad response, heart touching heart,
  As brothers act a brother's part,
As ever sainted ones above !

Nor in the mornward flow of thought,
  To youthful visions so remote,
  In passing would we fail to note
The shadowed changes time has wrought!

How many from our ranks we miss,
　So full of life in those young days!
　They faltered in Toil's weary ways,
And left the world their good-night kiss!

So lately one of sober mien,
　A valiant soldier of the Cross!
　To-day we sadly mourn his loss,
And leave him in his tent of green!

And facing now Life's western sun,
　And waiting Eden's fairer lands,
　Till called to fold our weary hands,
And know our earthly work is done,

While passing down the sunset slope,
　With hands clasped in the hands of God,
　In paths the Master's feet have trod,
Led by the light of heavenly hope,—

May life grow sweet as June's red morn,
　With perfume of our Christian deeds,
　Give blessed worth to sects and creeds,
And golden grow as shocks of corn!

So through the mercy of our Lord,
　As pilgrims, fall we one by one,
　May it be ours, with work well done,
Gladly to go to Heaven's reward!

[Poem by Rev. Silvanus Hayward.]

CLASS OF '53, JUNE 28, 1893.

In youthful years, when Life before us lay
　Fair as mirage upon Sahara's sands,
With gilded domes, bright as celestial day,
　And countless treasures waiting for our hands,

Where palm trees twined with gorgeous passion flowers,
　And flaming cacti in rough armor clad,
And sleepy cerei decked the fairy bowers,
　And bright-winged warblers made the listener glad;

'Twas here we wandered, here we dreamed of Fame,
  Here swarmed those visions through our busy brain,
Here kindled first the Muse's holy flame,
  Here drank deep draughts of sparkling Hippocrene.

Hence parting from each brother's lingering hand,
  Our mother's blessing crowned the closing day;
Like scattering rain-drops sprinkled o'er the land,
  Through the wide world each took his lonely way.

Now, from the devious ways of busy life,
  Once more we gather at our mother's feet,
From thronging cares, and toil, and bitter strife,
  Seeking refreshment in this dear retreat.

But where are those at whose revered feet
  We sat as learners in those days of yore?
The cultured Brown with eloquence replete?
  Precisest Putnam rich in Grecian lore?

That prince of teachers, philosophic Young?
  The genial Sanborn, and exacting Chase?
Noyes the pure-hearted, and keen-thinking Long?—
  Translated, vanished,—others fill their place.

Gone too their head, who as a master came,
  A teacher rare, with eloquence endowed,
With heart of molten gold, and royal name,
  With facile power to quell the surging crowd.

When youthful heads had caught some foolish flame,
  His lifted hand awed to a sudden hush;
When summoned culprits to his presence came,
  His quiet keeness made the boldest blush.

Intensely loyal to God's written word
  Small heed to Science by his heart was given;
In eager longing for his lingering Lord
  His soul lay open to the smiles of heaven.

Nor should we wonder if his dazzled eyes,
  Filled with the luster of his Lord's own light,
Saw the discoveries which the world surprise
  As fancied phantoms of mephitic night.

Who has forgotten that Commencement scene,
  When waiting calmly for the "parting sigh,"
Our loving steps turned from the College green,
  To pass once more beneath our master's eye?

His windowed glance a benediction seemed,
  A patriarch's blessing on his children shed ;
A glimpse of glory from the heavens gleamed,
  A shining aureole round the saintly head.

Save Hubbard, quiet chemist, none remains
  Of all our teachers in those halcyon days ;
But Dartmouth still her vigorous youth retains ;
  Still Wisdom's irridescent fountain plays.

Round all these scenes what myriad memories twine !
  Historic echoes haunt this classic plain,
Since clasping hands around yon blasted pine
  Three swarthy friends first sang the immortal strain.

What grand orations, poems manifold,
  Have here resounded on Commencement days !
Invited guests here poured their thoughts of gold,
  And crowned their temples with collegiate bays !

Here sparkled Holmes, and Saxe keen maxims gave ;
  Here eager fledglings up Parnassus soared ;
Here Webster thundered, and beside his grave
  The wizard Choate his matchless periods poured.

Here many others flashed the glowing light
  First kindled at this altar's living flame,
And home returning, conquerors in the fight,
  Have hither brought the laurels of their fame.

Learning and genius here maintain their ground,
  Still clear and bright Castalian waters flow,
Here fervid eloquence and thought profound
  Still touch the heart with Faith's eternal glow.

No "vox clamantis in deserto" calls,
  But many hither wend their willing way
To gather knowledge in these ancient halls,
  And dream of greatness in some distant day.

Slow swung the years when first with eager eyes
  . We launched our boats upon the world's wide sea ;
Now Time's pale pendulum with swift Fate flies
  Sweeping us onward as the shadows flee.

Full forty years have winged their circling flight,
  Loved comrades falling by the weary road,
While we still linger 'neath the waning light,
  And wait the lifting of Life's heavy load.

Again we part, and to our scattered homes
  Our slower steps with feebler pace retreat ;
With thinner ranks our fifth decennial comes ;—
  Alas ! how few and feeble tottering forms shall meet !

And one by one, as swift years glide away,
  Shall slip lamented to the silent tomb !
Till happily reaching his centennial day,
  The last survivor shall in sadness come,

And lingering lonely mid the strangers here,
  Shall call the death roll, as he sits apart,
While o'er each name shall fall the tender tear,
  And precious memories swell his longing heart !

And he shall sleep ; but like the changeless sea,
  Fresh youthful tides shall swiftly onward press,
And through the golden ages yet to be,
  Old Dartmouth still her springing sons shall bless.

After these addresses, which had succeeded the banquet, the letters of other class-mates were listened to and talked over, and finally, at the hour of 4 a. m., Thursday, June 29, our 40th anniversary reunion was adjourned for five years ; and, by the light of the approaching day and the music of the morning birds we repaired to our several lodgings. On the afternoon of Wednesday, June 28, a photographic group picture of eight of us was taken, at the rooms of Mr. Langill, the present Hanver artist. The picture herewith appears. Much to t he regret of us all, and of other class-mates, as we have since learned. our President, Mr. Chase, was not with us at that sitting, as he came from Lyndon on the evening train, only to be present at the banquet and reunion.

One of the most pleasing incidents of the following day was the call of several of us in company upon Mrs. H. A. Hitchcock, the daughter of Bro. Young, and upon Master Charles A. Young Hitchcock, his only grandchild. The menu cards, several of which were sent as souvenirs to absent members, constitute Class document No. 7.

Circular No. 8, being the final proposal for the present work, and as indicating, in some measuré, its aim and purpose, is here given in full :

To the Surviving Members of the Class of 1853, Dartmouth

College, and the Friends of Deceased Classmates:

The time has now providentially arrived when your Secretary can see his way clear to attempt the publication of another Class Memorial.

He proposes to do so (D. V.), within a few months.

He will embody, in condensed form, all the information, statistical, genealogical, and biographical, which the "Class "Book" contains.

The design is, to make it, as one of you has earnestly desired, "a book of Class biography, as complete as it can be "made, going into genealogical, and other particulars, as far as "possible," the whole to be issued in a neat and substantial form. Will each of the Class, therefore communicate to the Secretary, IMMEDIATELY, all "*vital statistics*" and "*changes*" *down to the present time*; as it is desirable to have the Class History extend to the *latest possible date*, while yet, we cannot *wait* for additional information beyond a very few weeks.

Wanted, especially, *full names* of wives and children—where they have not previously been furnished,—with the *dates* of marriages, births and deaths. Also brief notices of the schooling, residences and employments of children,—as many of them are, by this time, settled in life; and the *names*, at least, of all *grandchildren*. The *pedigrees* of yourselves and wives are also desired (briefly indicated), as was requested in a Class circular, some years ago.

Let the wives and children of *deceased* class-mates consider themselves included in this invitation.

We wish to make the forthcoming Class History a worthy connecting link between the past and future generations in the families of each and all the members of the Class.

Respectfully yours,

MOSES T. RUNNELS,

Sec'y of the Class of '53.

Newport, N. H., March 20, 1894.

Circular No. 9 was issued Nov., 1894, inviting members of the Class to furnish their pictures, in one form or another, for this "Memorial." We may judge of the responses to this last document by the appearance of the present volume; and with this announcement, and a fervent "God bless you," to all who are interested in its perusal, we may well bring our General Class History to a close.

TABULAR SCHEDULE OF THE MEMBERS OF THE CLASS PRESENT AT THE SEVERAL MEETINGS.

	'56	'63	'69	'73	'78	'83	'88	'93	Totals
Allen, . . .					x				1
Blaisdell, . .	x								1
Burton, . . .			x						1
Cahoon, . .	x		x		x				3
Carter, . . .	x		x	x	x	x		x	6
Chase, . . .			x		x	x		x	4
Crosby, . .	x	x	x	x					4
Dickson, . .			x						1
Emerson, . .		x		x	x	x		x	5
Fairbanks, . .		x	x	x	x	x	x	x	7
Farnsworth, .			x						1
Hayward, . .			x	x	x	x	x	x	6
Hollenbush, .	x								1
Howard, . .		x							1
Hulbert, . .			x			x			2
McDuffee. .	x		x		x				3
Morrison, . .				x					1
Palmer, . .	x	x	x					x	4
Parker, . .	x				x			x	3
Perrin, H. M.			x						1
Reed, . . .			x						1
Robinson, .			x						1
Runnels, . .	x	x	x	x	x	x		x	7
Sargent, . .	x								1
Thompson, W. S.		x			x	x			3
Upham, . .	x		x					x	3
Young, . . .	x	x	x	x					4
Totals, . .	12	8	18	8	11	8	2	9	

SUMMARY

—OF—

THE CHIEF OCCUPATIONS

OF THE CLASS.

BANKING—McDuffee, 1.

BUSINESS—Blood, Fairbanks, Strow, Warren, 4.

CIVIL ENGINEERING—Blaisdell, 1.

EDITORSHIP—Chase, 1.

FARMING—J. H. Morse, D. Perrin, Wight, 3.

LAW—M. D. Brown, Burnet, Cahoon, Farnsworth, Howard, Hutchinson, C. O. Morse, Oakes, H. M. Perrin, Reed, Remick, Robinson, Sessions, W. S. Statham, Stewart, W. C. Thompson, Washburn, Whitcomb, Wight, Wood, 20.

MEDICINE—Allen, Crosby, Hollenbush, Lamson, Lovering, Moore, Walker, 7.

TEACHING—Babcock, J. C. Brown, Fairbanks, Isham, Morrison, J. H. Morse, Parker, Parsons, D. Perrin, Stanton, Thomson, Waterhouse, Wilmot, Young, 14.

TELEGRAPHY—Kendall, 1.

THEOLOGY—Burton, Carter, Dickson, Emerson, Fairbanks, Hayward, Hulbert, Morrison, Palmer, Putnam, Runnels, Sargent, F. C. Statham, W. S. Thompson, Upham, 15.

The two following have been Presidents of Colleges: Hulbert, Morrison.

The eleven following have been Professors in Colleges: Babcock, Crosby, Fairbanks, Hayward, Morrison, Parker, Sargent, Stanton, Thomson, Waterhouse, Young.

DENOMINATIONAL PREFERENCES

SO FAR AS INDICATED (INCIDENTALLY) IN THE
PRECEDING SKETCHES.

Baptist	3
Congregational	21
Episcopalian	3
Methodist	1
Presbyterian	5
Swedenborgian	1
Unitarian	3
Not indicated in the sketches	27
Total	64

VITAL STATISTICS.

MARRIAGES AND DEATHS IN THE ORDER OF THEIR
OCCURRENCE.

MARRIAGES.

*Morse, C. O.	Jan. 1, 1851
*Howard	Aug. 3, 1853
Hayward	{ Nov. 23, 1853
	{ Dec. 17, 1891
*Perrin, D.	Jan. 29, 1854
*Isham	Apr. 10, 1854
Hulbert	Aug. 28, 1854
*Walker	Sept. 14, 1854
*Kendall	Oct. 5, 1854
Palmer	Feb. 5, 1855
Wilmot	Aug. 29, 1855
Putnam	{ Jan. 10, 1856
	{ Dec. 27, 1865
*Cahoon	{ Jan. 23, 1865
	{ Sept. 9, 1869
	{ —— 1882 (?)
Parker	Feb. 18, 1856
Strow.	Dec. 21, 1856

Robinson	July 26, 1857
Young	Aug. 26, 1857
*Hutchinson	Oct. 1, 1857
Brown, M. D.	Oct. 8, 1857
Dickson	{ Apr. 7, 1858 { Sept. 30, 1863
*Burton	May 18, 1858
*Statham, W. S.	June, 1858
Remick	{ August, 1858
*Blood	Mar. 31, 1859
Emerson	{ June 2, 1859 { Nov. 25, 1863 { Aug. 19, 1873
Farnsworth	June 23, 1859
*Wood	Oct. 25, 1859
Wight	Dec. 20, 1859
Carter	{ Mar. 12, 1860 { Oct. 12, 1892
Thompson, W. S.	Nov. 30, 1860
Blaisdell	Dec. 31, 1860
Upham	June 5, 1861
Runnels	July 9, 1861
*Babcock	July 30, 1861
*McDuffee	Dec. 4, 1861
Fairbanks	{ Apr. 30, 1862 { May 5, 1874
Perrin, H. M.	May 1, 1862
*Crosby	July 26, 1862
*Washburn	{ Nov. 25, 1862 { Nov. 15, 1869
Whitcomb	June 3, 1863
Morrison	July 8, 1863
*Parsons	1863
Chase	June 15, 1864
Moore	Jan. 30, 1865
*Lovering	Apr. 9, 1866
Sessions	1866
*Burnet	July 1, 1875
Lamson	Oct. 18, 1876
*Morse, J. H.	Jan.. 1890

Total, 48 ; deceased, 20.

It thus appears that just three-fourths of our number, or 48, were enabled or disposed to enter into the matrimonial state ; while the other fourth, or 16, were not.

The coincidence is also manifest that our first Morse was the first of the Class to be married, and our second Morse the last.

DEATHS.

Goodwin - - - - -	Oct. 28, 1850
Dearborn - - - - -	Dec. 30, 1851
Kendrick - - - - -	May 26, 1853
Walker - - - - -	July 14, 1855
Isham - - - - - -	Aug. 4, 1855
Stanton - - - - -	Feb. 22, 1856
Sargent - - - - -	May 9, 1858
Hollenbush - - - -	Aug. 6, 1861
Kendall - - - - -	Dec. 7, 1861
Oakes - - - - -	June 27, 1862
Statham, W. S. - - - -	July 30, 1862
Howard - - - - -	Jan. 6, 1864
Blood - - - - -	June 16, 1867
Wood - - - - -	Apr. 9, 1873
Crosby - - - - -	Aug. 9, 1877
Thomson - - - - -	Dec. 17, 1878
Parsons - - - - -	June 13, 1879
Perrin, D. - - - -	Feb., 1880
Washburn - - - - -	Oct. 18, 1880
McDuffee - - - -	Nov. 11, 1880
Brown, J. C. - - - -	Aug. 18, 1881
Babcock - - - - - -	Nov. 7, 1881
Burnet - - - - -	May 5, 1883
Hutchinson - - - -	Dec. 12, 1887
Lovering - - - - -	Mar. 18, 1891
Cahoon - - - - -	July 13, 1891
Morse, C. O. - - - -	Aug. 28, 1892
Morse, J. H. - - - -	Jan. 23, 1893
Burton - - - - -	Mar. 5, 1893

Total 29 ; leaving 35, or three more than half our membership, who are supposed, at this writing, to be alive. The three earliest deaths were of undergraduates. 1880 seems to have been the most fatal year. Three of the above met their deaths in consequence of their connection with the late civil war. The mortality of the class seems also to have prevailed most largely in sections ; say, as we sat, from Blood to Dearborn, and from Goodwin to McDuffee. Eighteen out of the first half of the Class have been called away ; only eleven out of the second half. Our two Morses, in the dates of their deaths, are again brought together.

ROLL OF HONOR.

The following members of the Class served in some capacity, and for longer or shorter periods, in the defence of their country during the civil war, 1861-65 :

*Blood (N. G.),	Lamson,
*Burnet,	*Oakes,
Chase,	Runnels,
*Crosby,	Upham.
*Hollenbush,	*Wood,
Young.	

Total, 11 ; deceased, 6.

The two following were also enlisted upon the other side, in behalf of the Southern Confederacy :

Moore,	Statham.

The grim fact confronts us that in all probability two members of the Class, Wood and Statham, who both hailed from the South, and were intimate friends in College, were personally arrayed against each other in the military operations around Corinth, Miss., being officers in the two opposing forces there engaged.

RESIDENCES

AND PRESENT

POST OFFICE ADDRESSES

Of the 64 members of the Class of 1853, the 29 deceased, at the times of their deaths, and the 35 survivors, at last accounts, were finding their homes in the different states, as follows :

In New Hampshire	10
In Massachusetts	8
In New York	7
In Illinois	6
In Vermont	5
In Minnesota	4
In Pennsylvania	3
In Maine, Ohio, Indiana, Missouri and Iowa, 2 each	10
In Rhode Island, Connecticut, New Jersey, Virginia, South Carolina, Mississippi, Louisiana, Texas, Kentucky, Michigan and District of Columbia, one each	11
Total	64

POST OFFICE ADDRESSES, 1894.

Justin Allen, M. D., Topsfield, Mass.

Alfred O. Blaisdell, A. M., 268 Clermont Ave., Brooklyn, N. Y.

Moses D. Brown, Esq., 69 Dearborn St., Chicago, Ill.

Rev. Nathan F. Carter, 51 Rumford St., Concord, N. H.

Charles M. Chase, Esq., Lyndon, Vt.

Rev. James M. Dickson, D. D., 53 Vermont Ave., Brooklyn, N. Y.

Rev. John D. Emerson, Peru, Vt., and 155 Hill St., Biddeford, Me.

Rev. Henry Fairbanks, Ph. D., St. Johnsbury, Vt.

Jonathan Farnsworth, Esq., Windsor, Vt.

Rev. Silvanus Hayward, Globe Village, Mass.

Rev. Calvin B. Hulbert, D. D., Adams Mills, Ohio.

John A. Lamson, M. D., 35 Fairfield St., Boston, Mass.

Henry W. Moore, M. D., Hendersonville, S. C.

Prof. Nathan J. Morrison, D. D., 514 Fifth St., Marietta, Ohio.

Rev. William S. Palmer, D. D., Norwichtown, Conn.

Prof. Isaac A. Parker, Ph. D., Galesburg, Ill.

Hon. Henry M. Perrin, St. John's, Mich.

Rev. Alfred P. Putnam, D. D., Concord, Mass.

Andrew Reed, Esq., Lewistown, Penn.

Charles F. Remick, Esq., Bird Island, Minn.

Levi Robinson, Esq., 14 1-2 Clinton St., Iowa City, Ia.

Rev. Moses T. Runnels, 52 South Main St., Newport, N. H.

Gilman L. Sessions, Esq., Binghampton, N. Y.

Rev. Francis C. Statham, unknown.

Levi M. Stewart, Esq., 412 Hennepin Ave., Minneapolis, Minn.

John De W. Strow, Esq., Fort Dodge, Ia.

William C. Thompson, Esq., Pepperell, Mass.

Rev. William S. Thompson, Exeter, N. H., (Hampton Falls).

Rev. Nathaniel L. Upham, 1800 Park Ave., Philadelphia, Penn.

Joseph Warren, Esq., Exchange Bldg, 53 State St., Boston, Mass.

Prof. Sylvester Waterhouse, Ph. D., LL. D., 1704 Washington Ave., St. Louis, Mo.

Geo. P. Whitcomb, Esq., 64 Twenty-fourth St., Chicago, Ill.

John F. Wight, Esq., Shelbyville, Ky.

Lucius W. P. Wilmot, Esq., unknown.

Prof. Charles A. Young, Ph. D., LL. D., Princeton, N. J.

Total 35.

SUPPLEMENTAL.

LEVI ROBINSON.

(Pages 168 to 171.)

As brother Robinson was absent from home on a journey, when the first draft of his sketch was sent him, he was not able to return it till after a second "copy" had been furnished the printers, and it had finally gone to the press. We, therefore, add the items—in part of sad intelligence—with which he designed to supplement his record as it now stands. First the fact is stated that his law firm, "Robinson & Patterson," office St. James' Hotel Block, was still in continuance (Oct., 1894) as the oldest in the State of Iowa, covering a period of more than 33 years.

Still our brother is now 'gradually closing out 'his law business with a view to retiring from the 'practice altogether and of enjoying what ease and 'comfort may be in store for him; firmly resting on 'the promises of Him who doeth all things well, 'and has said "I will never leave thee nor forsake 'thee." ' He retains his official connection with the First Methodist Episcopal Church, being chairman of its board of trustees; and is also one of the trustees of the Y. M. C. A., a flourishing branch connected with the Iowa State University, serving as treasurer of the Building Association, which has erected a building costing over $33,000.

The following are the additional items respecting his children and grandchildren:

His oldest, I. MARY E., after leaving the University, was grad. with high honors, from the National School of Oratory in Philadelphia, 1882; was m. to Hon. Coe I. Crawford, Oct. 2, 1884; but her death, by consumption, occurred at Pierre, S. D., July 20, 1894, at the age of 34 and a half years. Her remains were brought to Iowa City for interment, amid the tenderest expressions of sympathy and respect. Her children were (1) Miriam (Crawford), b. July 8, 1886; (2) Irving Robinson, b. May 7, 1892.

II. AMOS D., was m. June 2, 1883, to Maude H. Smith, of Cheyenne, Wyoming, formerly of New York. His present residence is at Spokane, Washington. Children: (1) Levi Swan, b. Aug. 8, 1885; (2) Maudean, b. Sept. 2, 1887; (3) Carroll Burton, b. Jan. 6, 1891; (4) Jeannette Curtis, b. Dec. 3, 1893.

III. CHARLES E. d. Feb. 24, 1888. He was m. to Miss Hattie C. Cochran.

IV. FRANK B., grad. from the State Univ. Classical Department, and from the Law School connected therewith; is now alone in law business, at Sioux City, has an additional son (if we read the record correctly) (2) Wilbur Hudson.

V. LAVINIA C. is still teaching in Iowa City; and

VI. LYDIA A. is in the Junior Class of the State University.

"The enclosed will show you how we have been "bereaved by the loss of our eldest, who now sleeps

"beside her earlier-called brother, C. E., in our
"Iowa City cemetery. At rest! At rest! Sin-
"cerely yours, in sorrow and yet in hope,

"LEVI ROBINSON."

JOHN F. WIGHT.

(Pages 236 to 239.)

Brother Wight's "return" was also received after
the original "sketch" had gone to press.

We, therefore, subjoin his interesting ancestral
record, to "1 ——," page 236.

His father, James Wight, was born in Ormiston,
Scotland, in 1792, and was the son of James and
Jane (McConochie) Wight; she—our class-mate's
grandmother—being a sister of Lord Meadowbank.
The family came to America about 1797, bought a
farm and settled in Virginia, at the mouth of Black
Creek, on the Potomac river. His grandfather
there died, and some years afterwards his grandmother and family removed to Kentucky. His
father, James Wight, Jr., was a soldier in the war
of 1812, and m. Sarah Ratcliffe (his mother), who
was b. on the peninsular of Virginia, near Richmond, in 1793. Her father's name was Francis
Ratcliffe, who was for five years a soldier under
Washington, in the Revolutionary War; and her
mother—J. F. Wight's maternal grandmother—
was Sarah Bridges of an old, honorable and patriotic family in the same locality.

We are now also enabled to give the full maiden name of Mrs. Wight ("3 ——," page 236) as Martha Jane Oglesby, the dau. of Albert and Belle (Abernathy) Oglesby, of Surrey Co., North Carolina, who was there b. Feb. 29, 1842. In the autumn of 1852, her parents removed to Panola County, Miss., where she was married; and "thence "they moved, in 1870, to Santa Barbara, Cal., "where their bodies now sleep upon the sounding "shore of the great Pacific."

We also correct the children's birth records, giving the full name of VI. WILLIAM AUGUSTUS. They were all b., as stated on page 236, except I. MARTHA DUKE, who was b. in Oldham County, Kentucky, and IV. JAMES ALBERT, who was b. in Panola County, Miss.

Page 237, line 2, read "Elm Tree Place" as our class-mate's seat in Shelby County, instead of "Poplar Ridge."

His present P. O. address (page 238, line 2) is "Shelbyville, Ky.," instead of "Wightwood."

Mr. Wight adds that the "Open Letter" (page 238) 'was written with the view of influencing the "action of his party in framing the present tariff 'bill;' the writer holding 'that as there could be no 'tariff which did not protect the labor and capital 'involved in the production of the thing to which 'it was applied, it ought to have application to 'everything produced in this country; and, as nearly 'as might be, in proportion to the cost of its pro- 'duction.'

No changes in the record of his children are

noted (page 238-9) except that III. SARAH B. is now (1894) with her parents at Wightwood; that IV. JAMES A. has now returned to Shelbyville, Ky., a bright energetic and faithful young man; that V. MARY J.'s health being impaired by excessive application to the study and practice of music, at the Conservatory, she spent the last year in Santa Barbara, Cal., only teaching a small private class, and devoting herself to the recovery of her strength. This year she is teaching music in Coate's College, Terre Haute, Ind.; and that VI. WILLIAM A. is now 'in the law office of 'George Hyde, Esq., a prosperous attorney in New 'York City, and bids fair to make a man of himself.'

ADDITIONS.

The two leading poets of our Class, being both New Hampshire men, are well represented in "The Poets of New Hamp-"shire," Claremont, 1883 ; each by four pieces ; Carter occupying three and a half pages, and Hayward three pages.

We find at the eleventh hour, that in reporting the publications of Bro. Emerson, we omitted to mention one of his best, and would, therefore, now add, as ("31") on page 57 : His address at the Soldier's Monument, Candia, N. H., Oct. 13, 1893 : also that Bro. Putnam's contribution to Judge Neilson's "Memorial of Rufus Choate" is worthy of special notice, as ("30") on page 156.

In the "Literary Review" of the New York "Home Journal" for Nov. 14, 1894, appears the following announcement—which may be added to her record on page 177 : "A volume of "verses by F. H. Runnells Poole, an occasional contributor to "the Home Journal, will be published in February by. the "Putnam's."

As these last pages are being made up we are pained to announce the death of Professor Hiram A. Hitchcock (referred to on page 259), which occurred at Hanover, Jan. 17, 1895, of pneumonia.   His age was about thirty-eight.

The "Concord Evening Monitor" of Jan. 19, says of him : "Besides being one of the most valuable members of Dart-"mouth's faculty, he was one of the most popular of her "younger alumni.   His death, therefore, not only means a sad "loss to his classes in engineering, but to all who claim New "Hampshire's old College as their Alma Mater."

A Rambling History.

We borrow this title, and are kindly permitted to appropriate the information contained under it, from ex-Gov. B. F. Prescott's admirable "History "of the Classes of 1856."

We propose to close our volume therewith, as Gov. Prescott closes his; making only such verbal changes as the progress of the years of publication, from 1888 to 1895, may seem to require.

It may be interesting to those who have not been at Hanover since 1853, and to the class-mates who left before that time, to know what has been done since their departure, in and about the College and the village. In a rambling way some information is here given, though not arranged in chronological order, and it must, of necessity, be very incomplete.

Dr. Lord (of blessed memory) continued as President of the College until July 24, 1863, when he read his letter of resignation to the Board of Trustees. His resignation was accepted Sept. 21, 1863. Rev. Asa Dodge Smith, D. D., (Class of 1830), then the pastor of the 14th Street Presbyterian Church, in New York City, was soon after elected President, and was inaugurated Oct. 18, 1863. He occupied the chair thirteen years with great success. His labors were arduous, but the College grew in strength and influence under his administration of its affairs. On account of failing health, he resigned, Dec. 21, 1876, the resignation to take effect March 1, 1877. During his presidency Bissell Hall (the gymnasium) was erected by George H. Bissell (Class of 1845) at a cost of nearly $25,-000. It is located on the corner, south of the campus and facing it. and directly opposite the Gates House, or what is now the new Library building. The Medical College was thoroughly refitted and remodelled inside, with a marked improvement

in its external appearance, by a gift of $10,000 from Hon.
Edwin W. Stoughton, LL. D., of New York City, who also
gave $2,000 additional at the time of his death. The Thayer
School of Civil Engineering was established in 1871, and has
been in successful operation ever since. This associated institution was created by a gift of $70,000, in estimated value,
from Gen. Sylvanus Thayer (Class of 1807). The number of
students in the classes has not been large, though constantly
increasing. Rooms were fitted up on the first floor of Thorn-
ton Hall for recitations in this department, till its separate
building was secured. In 1866, the New Hampshire College of
Agriculture and the Mechanic Arts was located at Hanover by
an act of the Legislature. The amount received from the sale
of government lands allotted to New Hampshire was $80,000;
from the Hon. John Conant of Jaffrey, N. H., $70,000; from
Hon. David Culver and wife of Lyme, N. H., nearly $30,000,
besides many appropriations from the state, nearly every year
after its establishment. A farm of 360 acres was purchased,
lying south of the highway, leading from the village to Hanover Centre, and upon it Conant Hall was erected, a few rods
east of the Gates House; and nearly opposite this building,
east of Reed Hall, and upon the land of Dartmouth College—
where stood what was known to us as the Burke-Haskell
house—Culver Hall was built, which was owned jointly by the
old College and the Agricultural College. In Culver Hall are
located the extensive museum and the chemical laboratory.
Since the removal of the State Agricultural College to Durham,
these two buildings (Conant and Culver) have wholly reverted
to the old institution.

Moor's Charity School building was remodelled and refitted
by contributions given for that purpose, and is now occupied
by the Chandler Scientific Department.

Eventually large sums of money will come to the College,
which were made known during the presidency of Dr. Smith,
notably the bequest of Hon. Tappan Wentworth of Lowell,
Mass., when the amount shall reach $500,000. Some years will
pass before the College can use this gift, though it is fast approaching availability; also the bequest of $100,000 of Hon.

ROLLINS CHAPEL.

Richard Fletcher (Class of 1806), which comes to the College by installments, as certain beneficiaries cease to use the income.

Pres. Smith secured also many scholarships, which have proved of great aid to poor young men. Much else was done, such as the consolidation of the College and Society Libraries, and the appointment of a permanent librarian by the trustees of the College; the change of the astronomical instruments to those of greater power and of modern construction; the increase of apparatus in the professorships of chemistry and physics; the introduction of steam and furnace heating in some of the halls—and many other improvements.

After the resignation of President Smith, the trustees elected as his successor, Rev. Samuel Colcord Bartlett. D. D. (Class of 1836), then of Chicago, Ill. Dr. Bartlett was inaugurated on Wednesday, the 27th of June, 1877. His administration of 15 years was eminently successful, and the College, during that period, made constant progress and permanent growth. He was indefatigable in his efforts to increase the capacity of the College for its great work, and to keep it abreast with the foremost institutions of the country. During his administration two important College buildings were erected—Rollins Chapel, and Wilson Hall (the Library). The Chapel was erected and completely finished and furnished by Hon Edwin Ashton Rollins (Class of 1851) at a cost of $33,000—a memorial to his father, mother and wife. It is located on the lot north of the College yard and Wentworth Hall. It is constructed of granite in irregular courses, with red sand-stone trimmings. It is pronounced by all one of the most unique and attractive College buildings in the country. Besides its massiveness and beauty of finish, it has elegant memorial windows to all the ex-Presidents of the College—gifts from families and friends. In it is also a fine organ, costing $2,500, the generous gift of Harold C. Bullard (Class of 1884), of New York City. Wilson Hall is constructed of brick, with red sand-stone trimmings. It stands upon the former site of the Gates House, and is one of the finest library buildings connected with our New England Colleges. It is named in honor of George Francis Wilson, of Providence, R. I., who gave $50,000 to the

College ; and it can be safely said that Dartmouth is indebted to Hon. Halsey J. Boardman (Class of 1858), of Boston, Mass., for this munificent bequest. When he was asked by the donor where he could give $50,000 to good advantage. our Alma Mater was recommended. The consolidated libraries, numbering nearly 66,000 volumes, are now conveniently arranged in this fire-proof structure, which is of elegant design and rich finish. The art treasures are also here, besides reading and reference rooms, and the President's office. This hall cost about $65,000. The trustees added $15,000 in order that a building should be constructed to meet the present wants and future requirements of the College. The corner stones of both these attractive structures were laid with appropriate ceremony at commencement in 1884, and both were completed and ready for occupancy, and dedicated at commencement in 1885. In addition to the above named buildings, liberal gifts in money came into the College treasury during President Bartlett's occupancy of the chair. From Benjamin Pierce Cheney, of Boston, Mass., $50,000 ; Henry Winkley, Philadelphia, Penn., $60,000 ; Mrs. Valeria G. Stone, Malden, Mass., $35.000 ; Julius Hallgarten, New York City, $50,000 ; Henry Bond. Boston, Mass., $23,000 ; Hon. Joel Parker (Class of 1811), Cambridge, Mass., $70,000—on which has been established a professorship of Law and Political Science, as the amount realized from his bequest was not sufficient to establish a law school, and was less than Judge Parker calculated when he made his will ; the state of New Hampshire, $10,000 ; Hon. George G. Fogg (Class of 1839), of Concord, N. H., $5,000 ; Hon. Micajah C. Burleigh. of Somersworth, N. H., $6,000 ; Hon. Levi P. Morton, of New York City, purchased for $7,250, and presented to the College. the house on the corner adjoining the residence of Dr. Lord (the old "Nunnery" and (site of Lang Hall) ; and many other donations of $1,000 each and more, were received for different purposes, besides many scholarships. The whole amount thus received has been about $450,000, and none of it has been tied up or surrounded with conditions. President Bartlett, besides his other great work in the management and government of the College. personally

WILSON HALL.

raised much money for many purposes, from which the institution has derived permanent benefit. The following professorships were endowed during the first eleven years of his incumbency: The *Daniel Webster* professorship of Latin; *Stone* professorship of Intellectual and Moral Philosophy; *Cheney* professorship of Mathematics; *Winkley* professorship of Anglo Saxon and English, and the *Parker* professorship of Law. The residence of Prof. Noyes was purchased for the President's house for $9,500. The residence of Prof. Sanborn was also purchased and is owned by the College. The Gates House was removed to a lot nearly opposite the South Hotel, and refitted for the occupancy of students, and the South Hotel itself was repaired and is now used as a boarding house for students. The first floor of Reed Hall is now wholly occupied by the Professor of Physics, and the second story finished into students' rooms.

The College Church has undergone repairs, particularly in the arrangement of the galleries. The walks and street crossings about the village and College grounds have been concreted, adding much to the comfort and convenience of the students and all others.

The tract of land northeast of the College, which in our day was an uneven and unattractive place, is now one of the most picturesque and attractive parks in the state. The great variety of trees, foreign and native, the gift of Hon. Joel Parker, and set out about the time of our leaving College, have now become large and beautiful, and are delightful to look upon. Drives have been constructed, walks made, rustic bridges erected, and seats placed at attractive points, largely by the students under surveys and plans of the professors in the engineering departments. It is now a pleasure-resort for the students and the great number of visitors to the College and town.

A tower has been erected near the "Old Pine" by several successive classes at their graduation, presenting an odd appearance, but affording a fine place from which to look at the beautiful scenery in all directions. The College buildings have been repaired and painted, and some of them heated by steam, or furnaces, and lighted by gas. The curriculum has been expanded, new professorships have been established, and ample means provided for the illustration of the branches taught. Practical physics and chemistry have been introduced, and every student now goes through a course of experimental chemistry.

The professors are critical, and labor for a high standard of scholarship among the pupils, and they keep the College abreast with similar institutions in the country, and send out as well equipped men yearly as can be found anywhere. The Chandler Scientific Department, which was in its infancy in our day, has constantly grown, and graduates yearly a goodly number of men who take high rank wherever they go.

The original gift of $50,000 has now reached, by accumulations and gifts, fully $150,000. Our teacher, Professor John S. Woodman, and his wife, gave $20,000 each, and Francis B. Hayes, of Boston, for many years a visitor, gave $10,000. The residence of Dr. Dixi Crosby has been purchased with the money of this department. Permanent prizes have been established in many of the departments of study.

Two magazines are now published by the students, both well and ably edited. "The Dartmouth" starts out with "No 1 of "Vol. XVI," this Sept. 21, 1894, and "The Dartmouth Literary "Monthly" was upon its second year in 1888. The village has also improved in its appearance, and increased in size, by the erection of costly dwellings, new Episcopal and Catholic Churches, and new and attractive stores upon the site of the "Tontine;" the Dartmouth National Bank and the Dartmouth Savings Bank are in successful operation. Gas has been introduced for the streets and buildings. A large and attractive school edifice for the village has been erected; and on the corner where Profs. Haddock and Brown used to reside, is now an elegant structure, which, for a while, was the residence of Adna P. Balch, but is now used in part as a store, and by the students. The Alpha Delta Phi, and Kappa Kappa Kappa societies have erected buildings for their accommodation, while the other secret societies have convenient and well arranged halls for their meetings.

CULVER HALL.

THAYER SCHOOL BUILDING.

A modern hotel, "the Wheelock," with convenient appointments, has been erected on the site of the old Dartmouth Hotel. In passing, it may be said that important additions have been made in the museum. A large collection of the papers of Eleazar Wheelock, and other documents connected with the early history of the College, has also been made. A collection of rare and valuable coins has been begun, which it is hoped will be steadily enlarged by contributions.

Thus far, with slight modifications and abridgements, have we followed "the Rambling History" of Gov. Prescott. We are sure that in no other way could a clear idea of the improvements in and about our Alma Mater have been conveyed to us in so short a space. But he has also conferred upon us the greater additional favor of supplementing his previous account with the following summary in his own handwriting, of more recent changes from 1888 to the present time. Being an honored Trustee of the College, as well as the Secretary and Historian of his own Class of 1856, there certainly could be no other one better qualified to supply for us this additional information. He says, under date of April 19, 1894:

"The following items may indicate the progress of the College—all being in addition to what I published—though not "given in chronological order: (1) The N. H. College of "Agriculture and Mechanic Arts was separated from Dartmouth, and is now at Durham. Dartmouth comes by purchase, and otherwise, into possession of Culver and Conant "Halls, the Experiment Station building, and 25 acres of land. "The Thayer School now occupies the last named building. "(2) The Chandler School has been more closely united with "Dartmouth (see last catalogue). (3) The Tappan Wentworth estate in Lowell has just about reached $500.000 by

"appraisal.   (4) Dr. Ralph Butterfield (1839) lately gave
"from $150,000 to $200,000 to the College (see catalogue).
"(5) An abundant supply of water has been secured (1893)
"for College and village.   (6) Electricity (generated in Leb-
"anon) for College and village was introduced in 1893.   Heat-
"ing of buildings improved, and many conveniences added.
"(7) Bartlett Hall (Y. M. C. A.) has been erected and furn-
"ished at a cost of about $16,000.   (8) Library increased to
"75,000 volumes.   (9) 'The Wheelock,' a spacious and ele-
"gant hotel, has been erected on the old Dartmouth Hotel site.
"(10) Tower, near the 'Old Pine,' completed (1893).   (11)
"The Mary Hitchcock Hospital, one of the finest in the coun-
"try, erected at great cost, by Hiram Hitchcock, Esq., her
"husband.   It is not under the management of trustees of the
"College, but of a separate board (1893).   (12) A superior
"athletic field has been constructed (1893) near the College.
"(13) Fence around the common has been removed.   (14)
"President Bartlett retired from office in 1892, and Prof. John
"K. Lord was acting President, one year.   William J. Tucker,
"D. D. (Class of 1861), was inaugurated June, 1893.   (15)
"Several new professorships were established last year (1893).
"(16) Henry Winkley gave $20,000 by will, making his gift
"$80,000.   The John D. Willard (1819) legacy of $10,000 has
"reached $40,000, and is now used.   Jason Downes (1838)
"gave $10,000.   Mrs. Isaac Spaulding, of Nashua, $10,000;
"besides scholarships and other amounts, given by others.
"(17) The Art gallery is large and rapidly increasing."

Some of the matters alluded to in the above—e. g. regarding
the "Wheelock" and the "Tower"—may seem to have been
anticipated in the previous "Rambling History." Gov. Prescott, in his Class History, did not, of course, refer to those
structures as already completed. For the present work, his
original allusions to tower, contemplated hotel, and some other
things, were modified to suit the present time. In justice to
Gov. Prescott, it should be added that the increase in the Art
gallery, last referred to, has been largely owing to his own intelligent and persevering efforts, especially in procuring, from
various sources, the portraits of distinguished alumni and others.

THE LATEST.

As the latest intelligence pertaining to the present and prospective prosperity of our Alma Mater, we clip the following items from the Manchester "Mirror and Farmer" of Jan. 17, 1895, adding two or three explanatory statements in brackets:

DARTMOUTH BOOMS !

COSTLY NEW BUILDINGS FOR THE

COLLEGE AT HANOVER.

HANOVER, January 14.—The Trustees of Dartmouth College have formally accepted the designs of a New York architect for the new buildings to be erected on the proposed quadrangle north of the campus. For the present, according to the plans, the college church and its chapel will remain. The residences of Rev. S. P. Leeds, D. D., emeritus college chaplain, and Prof. Arthur Sherburne Hardy, and the Rood house, a college domitory [the former young ladies' school, or "nunnery"] will be removed. On Rood house corner [including the former site of Lang Hall] will stand the Alumni Memorial Hall.

Between the church and Memorial Hall [embracing the old Dr. Lord residence], 100 feet back from the street, will be the location of the $250,000 Butterfield Hall,—the archæological museum. Two other domitories are shown on the plans, but will not be erected now.

The specifications for Butterfield Hall are now being prepared. The contract will be let in February, and work on it will begin in April. The Alumni Memorial Hall is the next in order, and will be started in the fall. Within three years the quadrangle will be completed with over $1,000,000 worth of buildings, and will be the finest of its kind in the country.

CORRECTIONS.

Will the owner of this book please correct, with pen, the following typographical errors :—

Page 8, line 16, first word—For "Endora," read "Eudora."

Page 39, line 12, first word—For "Barston," read "Barstow."

Page 50, line 18—For "II." before "Clarence," read "III." Also, line 24—For "III., Margarilla, read ' IV.," Margarella."

Page 67, line 24, last word but one—For "*bear*," read "*wear*."

Page 84, line 12—For "*its*," before "following," read "*the*."

Page 114, line 8—For "Charlestown," read "Charleston."

Page 156, line 11—Erase comma after "Grenville."

Page 174, fifth line from bottom—For "1863" read "1862."

Page 189, line 6—For "Dauburg", read "Danburg."

Page 198, line 1—After "DeWayne" insert "N. G."

Page 244, line 8—For "when", read "where."

Page 254, line 21, last word—For "*Morgan*" read "*Morton*."

Page 287, last line—For Dec. 21, read 31.

INDEX.

This Index contains the names (1) of all members of the class of 1853 wherever referred to ; (2) of their parents, and their earliest and more prominent ancestors, herein recorded ; (3) of their wives, (with parents and ancestors, so far as given) : (4) of their children, and grandchildren ; (5) of their instructors, one or more, both before and after leaving College ; (6) of all under-graduates, officers, and alumni of Dartmouth College referred to in this book. Other names of which mere mention is made are not generally included. The numbers indicate the pages, on each of which are to be found one or more references to the names immediately preceding.

SUMMARIES.

Whole number of references to classmates in this Index, (each page or part-page of the Sketches being reckoned as one) 692.

Whole number of the children of classmates given in the preceding Sketches, 164

<table>
<tr><td>Number of references to the same, in Index,</td><td>295</td></tr>
<tr><td>Number of grand-children in Sketches and Index,</td><td>36</td></tr>
<tr><td>Whole number of names referred to in the Index,</td><td>844</td></tr>
</table>

www.ingramcontent.com/pod-product-compliance
Lightning Source LLC
Chambersburg PA
CBHW021714110726
47902CB00005B/1194